John William Cole

The Life and Theatrical Times of Charles Kean, F.S.A.

John William Cole

The Life and Theatrical Times of Charles Kean, F.S.A.

ISBN/EAN: 9783743393479

Manufactured in Europe, USA, Canada, Australia, Japa

Cover: Foto ©Raphael Reischuk / pixelio.de

Manufactured and distributed by brebook publishing software (www.brebook.com)

John William Cole

The Life and Theatrical Times of Charles Kean, F.S.A.

PREFACE.

Many reasons and suggestions not necessary to enumerate here, have induced me to offer these volumes, which have been long thought of, to the consideration of the public. Years of uninterrupted private friendship, and professional association of the most intimate. nature with the leading personage of the work, have afforded me facilities and information which no one else possesses to the same extent. With these advantages and materials, I shall endeavour to add a faithful and, as I trust, a profitable contribution to the dramatic records of our country.

It is an easier, as well as a less delicate task, to write a memoir of the dead than of the living. Facts may be stated and opinions delivered with more unreserved confidence, and diminished danger of offence or controversy, when they relate to one whose transitory probation has been completed, whose earthly career is finally closed, and to whom may be applied the touching elegy of Shakespeare :—

> " Fear no more the heat of the sun,
> Nor the furious winter's rages ;
> Thou, thy worldly task hast done,
> Home art gone and ta'en thy wages."

In the present instance, we may safely foreshadow the future by the past, and predict with certainty

* Cymbeline.

that the end (far distant may it be) will crown the work, and that " the catastrophe will do no dishonour to the conduct of the piece." *

A biography must be undertaken by one of four persons: by the subject of it himself, by a stranger, an enemy, or a friend.

If a man chronicles his own deeds, although it is quite certain that he knows his motives of action and phases of thought, more minutely than they can be interpreted by another, human weakness interferes with a true delineation. In spite of himself, or his inherent conscientiousness, he will palliate or justify his errors, exaggerate his good intentions, or gloss them over to avoid the charge of egotism. If he descends to " Confessions," he commits moral suicide. The reputation of Rousseau, unenviable as it is, suffered immeasurably from his; and the fame of Lord Byron would have been tarnished for ever, if Moore had not consigned his " private diary " to the flames.

A stranger must acquire his knowledge from desultory sources, when and where he can; from current report, popular fallacies, general conversation, or imperfect documents. He can scarcely be ranked higher than a secondary evidence.

An enemy dips his pen in gall, misrepresents everything, and systematically distorts truth for the express purpose of presenting a repulsive portrait.

An honest friend is most to be depended on. He speaks from his own knowledge, has means at command, and may be expected to use them fairly. In this light I hope to be considered; and if the following pages evince a general disposition to praise rather than

* Junius.

to censure, I have at least chosen the less popular course of the two, and would rather be accused of partiality than malice.

A few passages, scattered here and there, have appeared before. They are my own, and I trust there is no plagiarism in borrowing from myself. I have been most anxious to state facts correctly. The opinions and inferences are merely ventured as the results of a single experience. Let them be taken at their value, and judged according to the weight of argument by which they are supported.

There are those who think that personal memoirs should be withheld altogether during the lifetime of the parties to whom they refer. In answer to this it may be observed, that the motives and actions of public men, in whatever positions they may be placed, are frequently misrepresented or open to erroneous interpretation. Surely, under such circumstances, those who know them best are permitted, if they are not absolutely called upon, to rectify mistakes before they are sanctioned by time, or receive the stamp of current value in the absence of refutatory explanation.

JOHN WILLIAM COLE.

LONDON,

July 25, 1859.

CONTENTS TO VOLUME I.

CHAPTER I.

CHAPTER II.

CHAPTER III.

CHAPTER IV.

CHAPTER V.

CHAPTER VI.

CHAPTER VII.

CHAPTER VIII.

CHAPTER IX.

CHAPTER X.

CHAPTER XIV.

CHAPTER XV.

CHAPTER XVI.

CHAPTER XVII.

CHAPTER XVIII.

CHAPTER XIX.

THE
LIFE AND THEATRICAL TIMES

OF

CHARLES KEAN, F.S.A.

CHAPTER I.

CHARLES JOHN KEAN, the leading object of this work, and the most prominent character in the following pages, was born on the 18th of January, 1811. From about that date, we propose to bring together a few passing records of the art with which his name is so honourably and inseparably associated, and to accompany these details with such reflections as the subject may suggest. Historians and biographers usually preliminarize in a lengthened introduction, in which they

often go back to a remote period, connecting antecedents
with actualities, and tracing effects from causes in a
complicated chain.   The long-winded advocate in
Racine's comedy ("Les Plaideurs") opens his case
" before the commencement of the world ; " whereupon
the dismayed judge directs him at once to " pass on
to the deluge."   We abstain from such remote retrospection for several reasons.   In the first place, because
Horace, an acknowledged preceptor in composition, has
laid down a contrary rule, and recommends plunging at
once " *in medias res ;* "—Secondly, because introductory
chapters are usually passed over by impatient, rapid
readers, who form a strong majority ;—and, Thirdly,
from the impossibility of saying anything new or interesting on matters which have been worn threadbare in
a thousand specific volumes, and a whole library of
detached essays and lectures.

All who have bestowed any attention on theatrical
topics are well aware that the precursors of the Drama
in England (and other countries of modern Europe)
were mysteries and moralities, founded generally on
sacred subjects, and sometimes handled with singular
irreverence :—that in time, these strange conceptions
gave way to interludes and plays of rude construction
and homely incident ; of which " Gammer Gurton's
Needle," by Bishop Still, and " Gorboduc," by Sackville,
Lord Buckhurst, and Thomas Norton, may be named as
amongst the earliest and most remarkable ; that the sun
of Shakespeare rose and expanded to unparalleled perfection under the fostering patronage of Elizabeth and
the first James ; that his contemporaries and immediate
successors were Heywood, Lyly, Marlowe, Ben Jonson,
Marston, Green, Beaumont and Fletcher, Webster, Ford,
Massinger, and others of less note ; that, in 1633, theatres
and plays had become so popular and licentious that they

excited the ire of the puritanical Prynne, who denounced them and their frequenters in a monstrous *helluo librorum*, entitled, " Histriomastix ; or, the Players' Scourge and Actors' Tragedie," a quarto of one thousand and twelve close pages (that nobody ever read through), which took nine years to compile, and seven to print, and cost the author his worldly substance, his ears, and his liberty ; that during the long quarrel between Charles I. and his parliament the theatres were suppressed, and nothing flourished but " civil dudgeon," and cut-and-thrust polemics ; that the actors fought, like loyal subjects, on the king's side ; that some were killed, and others promoted ; that, under the Protectorate, they gained precarious bread by stealth ; that, at the Restoration, they again basked in the rays of royal favour, but that foreign taste and corrupted fashion banished Shakespeare for a while ; that he was re-installed by Betterton, to whom succeeded Booth, who was followed by Quin, who was deposed by Garrick, who substituted nature and passion for frigid declamation, and established what was then called the new school, which would now be considered as stiff, formal, and antiquated as the cumbrous court suits and powdered wigs in which (to use honest *Bottom's* phrase) he discharged the heroes of the tragic drama. There he stands, taken from the life, in Zoffany's painting of the murder scene in " Macbeth " (now in the unrivalled gallery of the Garrick Club), with Mrs. Pritchard by his side, and looks the *beau ideal* of a small state-coachman in full and gorgeous livery on a gala day. The pair are much more suggestive of the butler and housekeeper contriving the death of the intoxicated squire than of a Saxon or Celtic thane and his helpmate of the eleventh century perpetrating the murder of a sleeping king. Prodigious, indeed, must have been the talent that could triumph over the associations which such a grotesque costume inevitably provokes.

The secession of Garrick in 1776 made way for Henderson, who did wonders, in defiance of more physical deficiencies than even those of Le Kain, the great French Roscius. But he was cut off prematurely by an accident, in 1785, before he had completed his thirty-eighth year.* Then the Kemble dynasty reigned for more than a quarter of a century in acknowledged supremacy. George Frederick Cooke came, like a meteor, in 1800, and, as he said himself, " made black Jack tremble in his shoes ; " but irregular habits marred his fortunes and enfeebled his genius. In 1810, he departed for America, whence he returned no more. His death took place at New York, on the 26th of September, 1812. The physician who attended him in his last illness said, that systematic intemperance had destroyed one of the finest constitutions that man could have possessed. Edmund Kean, who partly modelled himself on Cooke, and surpassed his original, erected a monument to his memory when he visited the New World.

When sober and himself, Cooke was not only a great actor but a well-bred gentleman in appearance, manner, and conversation. When drunk, he degenerated into a noisy, brutish bacchanal, fit only to herd with the rout of Comus or Silenus. His style was as opposite to that of Kemble as can possibly be conceived. It was fiery, impulsive energy, opposed to dignified collectedness ; quick, impassioned utterance, instead of regulated intonation ; epigrammatic terseness and pungency, in place of lofty eloquence ; rapid motion and

---

* His wife gave him a wrong medicine by mistake—an embrocation instead of a draught—which killed him. She was never made acquainted with the immediate cause of his death.

gesticulation, rather than studied attitudes, or lengthened pauses. Deficient in artificial refinement, he sought to be natural. In a soliloquy, he was eminently effective. Instead of flourishing about, and crossing the stage backwards and forwards, as many actors do, he concentrated himself, and stood almost motionless, not addressing the audience, or making them a party to his thoughts, but wrapped up in a kind of self-conference, in which the soliloquizer may be said to be communing with his own soul.

Cooke was not gifted with the elegant figure and deportment of John Kemble. His arms were short, and his movements abrupt and angular. His features were powerfully expressive of the darker passions, and he had a strong vein of sarcastic humour. His voice, though somewhat high and sharp in its ordinary tone, possessed great compass, and carried him without failure through the most arduous character; a pre-eminence over his rival in which he absolutely revelled, and never omitted to exercise when he found an opportunity. His best parts were *Iago, Richard the Third, Glenalvon, Shylock, Stukely, Sir Giles Overreach, Kitely, Sir Archy MacSarcasm*, and *Sir Pertinax Mac-Sycophant.* The latter, as a whole, may be considered one of the most complete pictures ever presented on the stage. Those who have seen it (and a few still survive) can never forget the impression it left upon them. Of Cooke's many followers, the late Charles Young was the only one who recalled their prototype in this particular character. All the others were either tame, or outrageously coarse, without humour.* King George III. commanded the "Man of the World" five

---

* Mr. Phelps must be quoted as a living exception. He never could have seen Cooke. We have not witnessed his performance, but have heard it highly extolled by good judges.

times in two seasons, and declared that Cooke's *Sir Pertinax* surpassed all that he recollected of Garrick in his very best assumptions. Cooke's genius confined itself to a narrow range. It was well remarked by a critic of the day, that he did not play many parts to perfection, but that he played those in which he really excelled better than anybody else. That critic had not then seen Edmund Kean, who went beyond Cooke in *Shylock, Richard,* and *Sir Giles Overreach,* not to speak of his *Othello,* in which he stood alone and unapproachable.

We must here request our readers to go back with us for a year or two, behind the commencement of our proposed reminiscences, while we give a short paragraph to the memory of William Thomas Lewis, of whom, we believe, no separate biography has ever been written. He came to London in 1773, and retired on the 29th of May, 1809. The Covent Garden company, being recently burnt out of their own theatre, were then playing at the Haymarket. Lewis took leave in his favourite character of *Michael Perez,* the " Copper Captain." For a long time, during his early progress, he was compelled to toil, with adverse attributes, in tragic parts. In these he acquitted himself respectably ; but in the more congenial line of light comedy, he soon surpassed all competitors. In this walk, Elliston followed Lewis with a voice of greater power and variety, which enabled him to round off a sentiment or wind up a pathetic appeal with superior effect.

Lewis filled the difficult office of acting and stage manager at Covent Garden, for twenty years, with admirable tact and great practical skill. Few, in that invidious post, so thoroughly escaped the ill-will of authors and performers. The former he easily made his friends, for he was the chief support of modern comedies ;

but the complaints of the latter he was sometimes obliged to bear, which he did with most enviable equanimity of temper. His style suffered from the extravagant parts which the authors of the day, and Reynolds in particular, thought proper to write for him in their five-act farces. In these he received great applause; but no judicious observer would place his performance of such ephemeral eccentricities on a level with his *Ranger*, *Mercutio*, or *Benedick*. "I saw him," says Cooke in his Journal (quoted in Dunlap's Memoirs), "in his best style, before he descended to be the genteel buffoon of modern farce, miscalled comedy. For thirty years he was the unrivalled favourite of the laughing Muse, in all that was gay, frolicsome, humorous, whimsical, and, at the same time, elegant." He then adds, " Billy Lewis, as a stage manager, was the model for making every one do his duty by kindness and gentlemanlike treatment."

Lewis had a natural animation, an overflowing exuberance of spirits, which never tired, and of which modern audiences and actors have not the most remote conception. Were he to be suddenly produced now, he would be pronounced insufferably extravagant, and set down as a lunatic escaped from Hanwell or Bedlam. We have seen *light comedians*, as they are called, and call themselves (heaven save the mark!), take more time with a sentence than he usually allowed to a scene. The very sound of his voice at the wing, before he entered, was the signal for mirth and increased pulsation, which flagged no more until the curtain fell. He was never quiet for an instant. His speed anticipated the express train and the electric telegraph. He was here, there, and everywhere, in a twinkling, always doing something; and although it must be admitted that he not unfrequently " o'erstepped the modesty of

nature," yet there was a grace and a charm in his extravagance, and an epidemic infection in his hilarity,
which belonged to himself alone. Long before the
audience had time to think whether he was right or
wrong, or whether they ought to laugh or appear
shocked, he was off to something else, which carried
them along with him in spite of themselves, and
drowned criticism in a tempestuous whirlwind of applause. "Push on, keep moving," was his perpetual
maxim and practice. To be tame or prosy, when by
his side on the stage, was utterly impossible. He was
well versed in every minute point connected with the
mechanism of the dramatic art, and the means of producing the most certain effects. One of his favourite
axioms was, that no change of dress, however characteristic or essential, no excellence in acting, could
restore the good temper of the audience, or revive their
excitement, if either should be interrupted by a long
wait between the acts. Perhaps he learned this during
his early acquaintance with our old friends of the
Dublin gallery, who, in days of yore, never failed to
cry, "Up with the rag!" even before the act-drop,
so classically designated, had time to reach the ground.

Reader, you probably remember, and may have often
seen, the late Richard Jones. He was a lively, agreeable, gentlemanlike, animated actor, but he assured
that he was not William Thomas Lewis, who has never
had a legitimate successor, or an equal in his peculiar
vein—unless, perhaps, we may be induced to consider
Elliston as entitled to the inheritance.

Lewis died within two years after his retirement,
aged sixty-three. Amongst his best characters may be
reckoned, *Belcour*, *Rover*, *Ranger*, *Mercutio*, *Petruchio*,
the *Copper Captain*, *Benedick*, *Millamour*, *Atall*, *Marplot*, *Lackland*, *Vapid*, *Goldfinch*, *Tom Shuffleton*, and

Jeremy Diddler. His son, the late Thomas Lewis, many years lessee of the Liverpool Theatre, bequeathed, in an evil moment, a celebrated full-length portrait of his father, as the *Marquis*, in the " Midnight Hour,"— an admirable likeness and painting,—to the National Gallery. Who has ever seen it there? and in what dark lumber-room or damp cellar is it condemned to rot? Far better would it have been to have left such a memorial to the Garrick Club (the house was once his private residence), where it would have been hung up in light and warmth, equally safe from the rats and the remorseless restorer.

That the stage has declined in modern times, and that the true love for the drama has evaporated, more especially amongst the higher classes, are assertions so often repeated, and so generally believed, that it may appear hopeless to combat them. In support of these assumed facts, a host of causes are duly assigned ; some substantial, others visionary, but all tending to the same effect. Amongst them are prominently set forward,—the degeneracy of living actors ; the incompetence of managers ; the constantly increasing number of theatres ; the annulling of the old law of limitation ; the bad taste of the public, which inclines in other directions ; the spread of education, that mighty leveller, which dispels all mists, opens all eyes, and brings all seeming marvels down to their true standard ; the late dinner hour ; the all-absorbing spirit of speculation ; the decrease of cash ; the increase of outward piety; the income-tax ; the rail-roads, which carry all the world to see everything somewhere else ; the rapid character of the age, which fevers the blood of humanity, and incapacitates everybody from listening patiently to any one given subject for half an hour at a time; the vast multiplication of cheap amusements, in and out of doors ; mechanics' institutes, " *salons musicales,*" clubs and debating societies, casinos, monster concerts, drum polkas, and music for the million; lectures on every conceivable science and invention; mesmerism, table-rapping, spirit-raising, and clairvoyance; phrenology, geology, toxicology, ontology, nosology, and electro-biology.* These, and other objections which baffle enumeration, are brought to bear on the question with the crushing force of a breaching battery or an avalanche. What can be advanced on the other side, in arrest of judgment? It is useless to argue; we must look for facts.

The date of Charles Kean's birth falls within the period which has been called, by a hackneyed and pedantic figure, "the palmy days of the drama." According to the census of 1811, London, in its extended capacity, then contained 1,009,546 inhabitants. There were within this boundary eleven theatres: three with what were considered perpetual patents, Drury Lane and Covent Garden unrestricted as to time, the Haymarket open in the summer only; and eight minors limited to certain periods and performances. In this list, the Italian Opera House is not included, being then, as now, looked upon in the light of an exotic exception. In 1859, the population of this overgrown metropolis approaches two millions and a-half, and has more than doubled within forty-eight years; while, despite the supposed counteracting influences, the number of places in which, under various names, stage representations are given, amount at least to twenty-eight. There are not so many in Paris, although the French capital has long been universally quoted as, beyond all comparison, the most theatrical city in the world. The population, it is true, is little more than half that of London; but mere extent of

---

* The latest of the *Ologies*. What does it mean?

population is no criterion by which to test the love of amusement.   All Paris lives in the theatres.

The London patents, alluded to above, if they still exist, have ceased to possess any value.   They resemble the hereditary championship—a nominal office, of which the duties are in abeyance.   The Lord Chamberlain's annual licence, wherever it extends, has abrogated exclusive privileges, and sanctions dramatic performances generally, without reference to the vexed questions of legitimate and illegitimate, regular and irregular—questions on which much ink and argument have been unprofitably wasted, and which never were, and never could be brought to any conclusive definition.   It may be added, as a corollary, that although adaptations from the French, and melo-dramatic spectacles, have many, followers, the great plays of Shakespeare are more popular, more attractive, and more frequently represented now, than at any former epoch which may be selected for parallel.

From these facts, the following inferences may be mathematically deduced :—

Notwithstanding the despondent prophecies and elegiac lamentations of the elders, who are ever exclaiming that our pure national drama is dying, dead, and buried; who aggrandize the past at the expense of the present, and advocate the inherent decay of every human invention,—the stage is still alive, and flourishing in wholesome vigour.

The taste for the drama has increased rather than declined, and in the right direction, from which it wandered only in the absence of trustworthy guide-posts.

The extinction or deterioration of what were once called the two great national theatres, the double Palladium of dramatic prosperity, has neither extinguished nor deteriorated Shakespeare.

And, finally, there is no lack of brilliant living talent on the stage, although not concentrated, as formerly, in one or two prominent fields of action. The three-deckers may not be as numerous, but the aggregate weight of metal is much greater.

When Liston, during his early apprenticeship at Newcastle-on-Tyne (where he was a great favourite) quarrelled with the manager, Stephen Kemble, and threatened to resign his engagement unless relieved from an inferior part, the burly autocrat told him that he might go as soon as he pleased, for actors were to be found under every hedge. He was wrong.* More than fifty years later, Charles Kemble, in the course of his examination before the Committee of the House of Commons, on the theatrical question, informed that august section of elected legislature, that they might, if they pleased, build theatres at the corner of every street in London, but that actors were beyond the creative powers of Parliament. He was right.

Yet actors (such as they are) have been forthcoming on demand, as fresh merchandise finds its way into the market, according to increased consumption. But the new supply, though abundant in quantity, is not equal in quality to the ancient stock. The living talent, of which we have already spoken, is to be sought for amongst the scattered remains of the " Old Guard," rather than in the ranks of their half-educated recruits. Fifty years ago, an engagement in London amounted to a settlement for life. As soon as a new actor's position was ascertained in one of the national theatres, he left it

---

* A day or two after, while taking a walk in the fields, King Stephen observed his rebellious subject seated in a ditch, carefully watching the opposite hedge. " What are you doing there, Mr. Liston," said he, " when you ought to be at rehearsal ?" " Looking for actors, sir," replied the son of Momus, " but I haven't found any yet."

no more; service became inheritance, as in other communities. To obtain this post, he waited for a vacancy, and then graduated in due course, from Dublin, Edinburgh, Bath, or Liverpool. These were the acknowledged training-houses from whence supplies were regularly drawn for the metropolitan boards. They exist no longer as such. Cheap prices and free trade have brought them down to the level of large minors. Railroads carry all who have cash and curiosity, to see the attractive novelties produced in London, long before they can reach the out-quarters. Our ancestors ventured on long journeys once or twice in a century. Their descendants half live in an express train. The twenty-eight theatres and theatrical saloons of the metropolis are ever in want of hands. They tempt away the rising talent while crude and half-drilled, and, in nine cases out of ten, induct it into a worse school than it has quitted.

The modern disciples of Thespis, it must be admitted, are not as soundly brought up as were their predecessors under the old system, and many of them are ill qualified for a profession which demands high intellect, varied acquirements, polished bearing, and regular gentlemanlike habits. This might be remedied, and the theatre elevated to its proper position, if the authorities could be induced to consider the stage, as in other countries, a portion of the state, and a valuable implement in the hands of government. But this is not within the category of probabilities. For who is there to take such an enlarged view, to break down the barriers of precedent and routine, and to reason prejudice into an experiment which would surely be rejected on proposal as equally unimportant and impracticable?

They take a very different view of these matters in Paris, where the four leading theatres, which are considered national, receive an annual grant of 1,160,000 francs (48,333*l.* 6*s.* 8*d.*), apportioned as follows:—

To the Académie Impériale	620,000 fr.
„ Théatre Français	200,000 „
„ Opéra Comique	240,000 „
„ Odéon	100,000 „

The young actors of the present day are, perhaps, the fastest pupils of a fast age. They are not content to walk before they run: nothing satisfies them but to begin with a gallop. "Vaulting ambition," in their eyes, supersedes the necessity of education—education in general, and theatrical education in particular. Inclination is too often mistaken for genius, while inclination itself is frequently prompted by idleness. Luxurious midshipmen, in the olden times, who disliked the severe discipline of the forecastle and mast-head, were wont to exclaim, "I can't stand this any longer; I'll sail large, and bear up for a marine"—the marine officer's life being considered one of unmingled ease. He kept no watch, superintended the mess, played all day at backgammon, and slept eleven hours on an average. All he had to do was to fight when required, which he did most gallantly.

In the same manner, aspiring youngsters, who groan under the monotonous drudgery of the office or the counter, suddenly behold bright visions of fame and fortune through the certain, immediate, and easy avenue of the stage. Vain is it to reason with man or woman, youth or damsel, when he or she is once imbued with the theatrical mania. Nothing satisfies them but the experiment, which, in a great majority of cases, eventuates in utter failure or hopeless mediocrity. Success and profit will smoothe the roughest road, and lighten the heaviest task ; but obscurity and small pay, joined to hard work, are enough to break the back of Hercules himself. The life of a galley-slave is not enviable, but it may be looked upon as one continued siesta when compared with that of the rank and file, or utility-men of a theatre. How they get through the duties of their position is beyond a miracle. In a pantomime, for instance, they represent, on the average, four characters in the opening, with treble that number in the comic sequel, and a change of dress for each. Young ambitionists of honours histrionic, who are weary of their indentures, and fancy they have souls for poetry, figure to themselves the stage as a haven of refuge and enjoyment, a nice, jolly, easy, idle kind of do-nothing life. Let them begin at the beginning, and enlist as utilitarians for the run of the Christmas spectacle. There is nothing like experience for cooling down enthusiasm. Long before their term of service has expired, they will petition for dismissal, commit some breach of discipline to entail immediate discharge, or use interest for a speedy exchange into the comparative comfort and relaxation of the tread-mill.

Truly there must be a fascination in acting peculiar to itself, and beyond that fabulously attributed to the basilisk or the rattle-snake. As war is called "the needy bankrupt's last resort," so is the stage often considered a certain resource for all who are unfit for anything else, or too lazy to learn the rudiments of a laborious calling. It is the only trade which teaches itself, or comes by inspiration, without apprenticeship. As Pitt was a "heaven-born minister," why not a perfect actor, without practice? "I think I could do it quite as well, if not better!" This is a common delusion of the conceited, untried, theatrical tyro who from pit or gallery listens to the applause which a Kemble or a Kean can only elicit after twenty years of hard service. It is worse than useless to point this out to him. He pages you with ready instances, and tells you of Holland, and Powell, and Mossop, and the elder Sheridan, who became great actors all at once; and of Spranger Barry who stepped from behind a counter on the boards a perfect *Othello, Jaffier*, and *Varanes*, and two years afterwards shook Garrick on his throne. All this, and more to the same effect was once said to an experienced manager, by a shambling, blear-eyed stripling, without a voice, and scarcely five feet one in stature, who panted to come out in Hamlet or Macbeth. It was remarked to him in reply, that Barry was singularly gifted by nature with physical requisites, such as are seldom combined in the same individual, and that without some external advantages, and at least, moderate lungs, the case would be hopeless. "Oh," said he contemptuously, "genius can do without such paltry aids. Le Kain, the great French tragedian, was little and deformed, with a cast in one eye, a defective utterance, and an ugly, inexpressive face. Henderson's voice was thick, he spoke as if his mouth was stuffed with worsted, had flat features and a clumsy figure. Garrick was diminutive and inclined to fat, and Edmund Kean was often husky." Heaven only knows where he had picked up these rebutting facts, for he seemed perfectly uneducated, and rejoiced in a broad, provincial accent, which made the blood curdle.

A manager's correspondence supplies a curious and varied chapter in the history of human character. It includes remonstrances and applications from authors, actors, amateurs, and ambitious aspirants; anonymous counsellors, anxious partisans, secret enemies, petitioners with claims, and pretenders without any; useful and useless hints, friendly and hostile admonitions from well-wishers and evil-wishers; threatenings and denunciations from the discharged, the rebellious, the neglected, the ill-treated, or the incompetent.

The following are genuine specimens, culled from a huge mass, preserved by the parties to whom they were addressed, and submitted to the selection of the writer of these volumes :—

" Sir—i am a yung man is dasiros of actin sheekspeer in yur theter. I hav had a gud eddicashun, and am careless of trubl and ixpinsis—I luk for no remunerashong i am worthy to command, an in the meane time waite yure plaisure. an anser to a B at 3 Boot lane will cunfur obbligashun. i doe not minshun my name till resaiving a favrite anser.

Yours &c.
PATRICK FLYNN."

Here is another, in a different strain, from a fair lady :—

" I have long resolved on a plunge which will determine the colour of my future life. The stage is my passion, and I am well read in the best dramatic authors. I have never acted, but have rehearsed before good judges, who assure me I shall soar above all competition. I wish to know what I am to expect for three performances of *Lady Macbeth*, *Julia* in the ' Hunchback,' and *Ophelia;* the three plays, altered and re-written by myself to suit my own conceptions. I am twenty-three, my figure is *petite*, and has been pronounced faultless. My features are expressive, my eyes and hair of the raven's hue, and my voice melodious. I do not think much of any actress now on the stage ; and have formed ideas of my own, which I shall be happy to communicate on a proper understanding, if this letter leads to what I expect, an interview. The bearer waits for your reply."

On this occasion, managerial curiosity excited a desire to see the correspondent. Time and place being appointed, she came in form, attended by a duenna, and presented to view a little, corpulent, swarthy personage, unquestionably on the shady side of thirty-five, and altogether what the French ungallantly call *laide. a faire peur!* Nothing could exceed her astonishment and indignation when she found her views discouraged, and her improvements on Shakespeare and Sheridan Knowles denied a hearing.

A third letter ran thus :—

" Sir,—I feel very desirous to 'smell the lamps.' I have been flattered by friends that 'my mission' is decidedly to preach Shakespeareanity. I shall esteem it a favour your informing me your terms for a dozen lessons in elocution. This is all I require for my stock-in-trade."

A fourth contained a more formidable announcement :—

" Sir,—I am a riter of tradgedys, and with gode inspirashun, can doe one in a week. I have a large stok reddy. If you will name a time when I can call uppon you the terms will sone bi setled. I was burn (Qy. born ?) a poet."

No. 5, varied again :—

" Sir,—Should there be a vacancy for a junior actor in your theatre, I should be happy to offer myself as a candidate. I am eighteen years of age, and of good, plain English education. I have never figured on the stage, but have a great desire to do so. I can have excellent testimonials, am a great reader, and six feet two in height."

No. 6 resembles the preceding :—

" I hope you will excuse me for the trouble I give you, but I am so terrible stage-struck I cannot help it. A few gentlemen advised me to write to you, to try and get on the stage. I acted but once, that was in the ' Lady of Lyons.' I acted *Claude.* I would rival you, if such a thing could be."

No. 7 is singular and interesting, from a lowly but educated youth, written and spelt correctly, and suggestive of very salutary reflections :—

" Sir,—I hope you will excuse the liberty I have taken in thus writing to you, and which I have no doubt you will when you know the cause that prompts me to do so. I am in my nineteenth year, and finding that Heaven has gifted me with talents for both poetic and dramatic writing, I appeal to your world-famed generosity for support ; being so poor myself that I can hardly furnish paper to write upon. I have been employed for the last two years in the Great Western Railway as engine-cleaner at 1*s.* 6*d.* per day !—upon which small sum I have managed to live honestly ; but now even that has failed me, and as a last resource I look to you for assistance, which, if refused, I know not where to turn my thoughts but to the army.

" I do not write to you, Sir, as a humble petitioner for money, but as one conscious of the powers which Providence has bestowed upon him, and feels it a duty to seek for that aid which would enable him to use them to advantage. I have written a great deal, both poetic and dramatic, and mostly in those hours when I should be resting my body after the toil of the day, but which for want of patronage I have not been able to turn to any good. Therefore if you could give me any berth in the theatre where my services would be worth 12*s.* per week, that I might be enabled to pursue my literary labours, the everlasting prayers and thanks should be due of

"Your very humble and obedient Servant,

* * * * *.

"P.S. I inclose a few of my pieces in their first writing (which I have not been able to finish for want of time), as specimens, leaving to yourself to judge what difference is caused by leisure, place, and position in such kinds of composition. I should be for ever grateful if you would give me an audience. Will call on Monday, 10 A.M.

"*Dec. 21st, 1855.*"

The last epistle we shall quote at present is of a higher order than No. 7, and even more painful in character :—

"I am the son of a clergyman, and lately a member of the University of Cambridge. My father has left me to work my own way in the world,—in fact to live by my wits, and I see nothing before me save the stage or enlistment, as my education fits me for nothing else. I need not say I should prefer the former, and could you give me any employment, however small the emolument, and in the humblest capacity, I should be much obliged. In short, if there be any post in your establishment in which a gentleman, and, if I may so call myself, a scholar, may be of use to you, I shall rejoice to fill it, and do my best to merit your approval."

In every scientific or intellectual profession, the stage alone excepted, some rudimentary acquirement is deemed necessary. There must be instruction, preparatory discipline, examination, a qualifying certificate, a degree, or a diploma. The elements of any single art can only be conquered by a regular course of study, while the art of acting, which combines many in one, is supposed to be attainable at once, by instinct or volition. On what rational principle can an actor be made off-hand more readily than a painter, a sculptor, an architect, an astronomer, a mathematician, an engineer, a medical practitioner, or a lawyer? It has often been thought and urged that schools or colleges might be established for the regular training of dramatic neophytes. Garrick more than once contemplated some institution for this purpose, but gave way before the apparent obstacles. These are numerous, no doubt, but not insurmountable. The most difficult to grapple with is the general apathy on the subject which unfortunately prevails, and is likely to increase.

It can scarcely be disputed, that the stage will continue to exist as long as civilization lasts and human nature retains its present development. Next to the religious principle, a desire to imitate in action is the strongest innate feeling of the human mind. The first indication of reason that a child gives, is to copy something that it has seen or heard. The propensity is universal. Blind fanatics may persuade themselves and endeavour to convince their listeners, that theatres are purely Satanic in origin and influence, and that they will be, or ought to be, abolished. As well might they attempt to alter the system of creation. They would employ their time to more advantage in trying to elevate what they cannot overturn. Why should not the stage be regulated and improved by salutary restrictions and indispensable education? In many countries on the continent the number of physicians, surgeons, and apothecaries is strictly regulated by municipal law, according to the population of the town or district, and the bills of mortality proclaim the advantage of the enactment. If actors were confined within the same limitations, and the exercise of their vocation pronounced unlawful without a certificate, both art and artists would hold their heads higher than they do at present; they would rise in general estimation; the social and political utility of either would be increased, and the stage would then become permanently what Cicero says it was intended for, "*Imitatio vitæ, speculum consuetudinis.*"

The uninitiated in the arcana of theatrical government will scarcely believe in the number of new pieces, of every conceivable form and construction, which are sent in every season for acceptance. Half a dozen per week is a moderate computation for a leading metropolitan theatre. There is a continual glut of dramatic genius in the market, if bulk be taken as a test of merit. Then follows the physical labour of reading them all, either in person or by competent deputy. Many authors are so impatient, that they propose to call the next day for an answer; and some will even wait, or come back the same evening. The manager's most dreaded nightmare is when the applicant proposes to read his own play. It has been said, and loudly echoed (by themselves), that writers of talent and brilliant promise have been crushed or held back by the tyranny of theatrical potentates, who, from utter ignorance and incapacity, from want of common judgment, from pique or undue partiality, or from sheer laziness, are given to discard good plays, and to adopt bad ones; or to reject indiscriminately all the rich prizes that are offered to their acceptance. Such things have happened certainly, but not often. Managers may commit errors, like other people, but it is reasonable to suppose that they study their own interest, and understand something of their own business. If they do not, they suffer in a tender point, in the pocket, and pay dearly for mistakes. A balance on the wrong side of the ledger is a great remover of prejudices.

Garrick was thrifty and acute, generally right in his tactics, cautious, clear, and calculating; but still not infallible. He either would not, or could not see the talent of Mrs. Siddons, and Henderson. This might be jealousy, for he was an incarnation of that weakness; he trembled and fidgetted even if Punch obtained a larger audience than usual. An author himself, he undervalued and feared to accept Goldsmith's " Good-natured Man," while living on the most friendly terms with him ; he played fast and loose with his comedy, tortured him by vexatious delays, winding up with a refusal; drove him to Covent Garden, and lost " She Stoops to Conquer," which met with the greatest success, and still holds its place on the acting list. He was also blind to the merit of Home's " Douglas," which he repudiated, while he accepted subsequently, " Agis," the " Siege of Aquilcia," and the " Fatal Discovery," three very inferior, unattractive, and forgotten productions from the same hand.

When Colman sent in his play of " The Africans " to Covent Garden, it fell to John Kemble to read it, in his capacity of acting-manager. The story is simply this. Three brothers of an African tribe are burnt out of their village by enemies, and fly to the woods with an aged mother. They are reduced to the last extremity of physical suffering, and cast lots that one may be sold to obtain sustenance for their parent. " What is this new thing of Colman's about?" said Harris to his partner and deputy; " Oh," replied Kemble (who had skimmed it carelessly, or perhaps had not quite recovered the preface to the " Iron Chest "), " it will never do. Here are three black men, who sell their mother." " Colman must be mad," rejoined Harris; " return it to him at once."

The play was afterwards produced at the Haymarket, and rather coldly received. Its moderate attraction arose principally from a ridiculous parody on "Will you come to the Bower," introduced by Liston, as *Matthew Mug*, and nightly encored.

Not a great many years since, a·band of authors, who conceived themselves victimized by managerial caprice, formed a confederacy or club, and published at their own expense a series of plays entitled "The Rejected Drama," one or more of which they also contrived to get acted. But the public voice, in both experiments, vindicated the individual judgment. The authors stood condemned on their own evidence. They perpetrated self-immolation, as the Hindoo widows were wont to do at the Suttees, and as Thelwall would have done when tried for high treason in 1794, if he had persisted in pleading his own cause. "I'll make my own defence, I'll be hanged if I don't," whispered he to Erskine, his leading counsel. "You'll be hanged if you do," replied the future Lord Chancellor, calmly, which brought the refractory client to his senses in a twinkling. It is something to save a man from his friends, but it is even better to save him from himself.

What can induce any one to encounter the endless turmoil, the dissatisfaction, the risk, the anxiety, the incessant wear and tear, both mental and physical, which are inseparable from the management of a theatre? It must be one of three controlling impulses which entraps so many into this devouring maelstroom—lofty emulation, an enthusiastic passion for genuine art, or love of power; which last enthrals the human species as rats are subdued and fascinated by prussic acid and oil of rhodium. The arch-enemy of man angles with many baits, but he catches more unwary victims with power than with any other lure in his magazine of temptations.

It has been often said, and truly, that a theatre represents an epitome of a kingdom, a microcosm or miniature of the great globe itself, a condensed edition of humanity, combining within its narrow limits all the complicated machinery, all the mingled passions, propensities, antipathies, conflicting interests and jarring feelings, which are exhibited on a more expanded scale in the political and moral legislation of a mighty empire. Man may be subdivided into distinct classifications, and each may retain its own identical characteristics; but a theatrical community alone embraces man *in extenso*, and calls into operation at once, and in bold relief, every variation of which his subtle components are susceptible. As Shakespeare said, with undeniable truth, " all the world's a stage," so may we transpose his apothegm, with equal fidelity, and say, " the stage reflects a picture of all the world." The philosopher who studies human nature can open few volumes in which he will find such ample information.

A manager of a theatre is a tolerably potent monarch, on a small scale, as far as mere power is concerned; that is, the power to order, direct, and control the internal economy of his little dominion, as swayed by judgment or prejudice. He may do good or evil, justice or injustice, and render those under him happy or miserable, to a considerable extent, according to the bent of his disposition, which may be benevolent or capricious, kind or cruel, mild or vindictive, long-suffering or impatient under contradiction. He is not compelled by the constitution of his kingdom to have either ministry or cabinet council unless he pleases; and can dismiss or rule without them if they interfere with troublesome suggestions, or run counter to his wishes. He can make a law, if one is wanted on an emergency, without waiting for the forms of a debate, or the cavils of opposition. He has only to say, "let this be, *le Roi le vent*," affix his sign manual, send forth the edict, and the Sultan's Firman is not more implicitly acknowledged by his well-disciplined subjects. - Mutiny is almost unknown, as a special article in the Codex Dramaticus provides that disobedience of lawful orders, or misprision of rebellion, is followed by constant discharge, without benefit of remonstrance.

But this exalted position has its " drawbacks," as the valet said of his place, which he would not change with the king, if his master only got drunk six nights in the week, and gave him a single chance. A manager does not of necessity inherit the purse of Fortunatus. His banker's book represents finity. He is often compelled to pause in an important enterprise for want of supplies. He has no power to levy constitutional taxes by Act of Parliament; his state resources are drawn from voluntary contributions alone. If the public and he happen to fall out, and take different views, his royal prerogative dwindles into an empty shadow, enveloped by harassing and unprofitable responsibility. Theodore of Corsica may be quoted as a substantial monarch in comparison.

Talleyrand, the witty and unscrupulous, defined the government of Russia as an absolute despotism, limited by assassination. He might have described a theatre also as an uncontrolled monarchy, not unfrequently bounded by an empty exchequer. In fine, to manage a theatre is to live in a perpetual fever of excitement, to wear out existence in hopes more constantly disappointed than realized, to see the best calculated arrangements shattered by an unforeseen casualty, and to be daily building up the fortunes of others, while you are hourly wasting your own health and store. More than one dramatic potentate has been compelled to take home to himself the powerful description in which Spenser sums up the ills that beset the career of another class of popularity-seekers,—placemen and political dependents :—

> " To lose good days that might be better spent,
> To waste long nights in pensive discontent,
> To speed to-day, to be put back to-morrow,
> To feed on hope, to pine with fear and sorrow,
> To fret the soul with crosses and with cares,
> To eat the heart through comfortless despairs,
> To fawn, to crouch, to wait, to ride, to run,
> To spend, to give, to want, to be undone !"

CHAPTER II.

ABOUT two years before the birth of Charles Kean, both
the great theatres were burnt to the ground within five
months of each other,—Covent-garden on the 19th of
November, 1808; Drury-lane on the 24th of February,
1809. The close proximity of these lamentable events
gave rise to many suspicions of foul play, but nothing
ever transpired beyond surmise. The received opinion
now is, that the first arose from accident, the second
from shameful neglect. Covent Garden sprang again
from its ashes in renovated splendour within twelve
months. Drury Lane, being beset by heavier incum-
brances, remained in abeyance for more than three
years and a-half, until the 12th of December, 1812,
during the greater part of which interval the company
set up their standard at the Lyceum.

It is surprising that theatres are not burnt down
more frequently than they are, considering the increased

danger arising from gas, if not properly tended (when is it so?), the indigenous facility of combustion, and the difficulty of watching the watchmen. A fire in a theatre may be prevented, but is not easily extinguished when once it gains head. The best precautions, next to a general system of carefulness, are, a small portable engine on the stage, with a fifty-foot hose attached, and a good supply of water ready in tanks on the roof. All the mischief is done in the first few minutes, while messengers are despatched for the brigade engines, the alarmed neighbours are shouting " Fire !" and a few are knocking their heads against each other, in a futile search for the plug, which, of course, no one can find at the critical moment. A fire-plug resembles a policeman—always in the way except when it is wanted. Tell-tale clocks are good common-place evidences of the care or neglect of the night guardians ; but if these functionaries are experienced in their business, and " know what belongs to a watch," they can find out ways and means of putting them into such a thorough state of disrepair as would baffle the mechanical skill of Archimedes, or defy Mr. Hobbs, the great American pick-lock, to restore them to serviceable condition.

During the parliamentary session of 1810 and 1811, great efforts were made to obtain a patent for a third winter theatre. The bill to that effect, strongly supported, was thrown out chiefly through the exertions of Mr. Whitbread, who took much interest in the affairs of Drury Lane. His vehement opposition in the House of Commons decided the question in the negative. The promoters of the measure issued prospectuses, and wrote pamphlets containing many proposed reforms and good resolutions. Amongst others, no freedoms of any kind, or orders, even to authors and performers, were to be granted, on the ground that such privileges gave rise to cabals, by introducing partisans for invidious purposes, or were used as matters of unlawful traffic, and often as decoys, to give a factitious appearance of success to a theatre deserted by the paying community. In the list they forgot to enumerate the best of all arguments on their side,—an *orderly* house is constitutionally a dull one. Your sons of freedom form a cold audience. They never applaud heartily, and discourage the lengthened run of a new piece. There they are in their places every night, and want variety. It is a curious fact in physiology that people who never visit a theatre until by some means or other they get on the free list, are seldom absent from it afterwards. They go, not from enthusiasm, but because they have nothing else to do. We think more highly of what we pay for than of that which we can obtain for nothing. Two or three shillings form a serious investment, and those who risk it do so with a full conviction that they will get value received for their money. They expect to be entertained, and the anticipation feeds the result. Their minds are predisposed to admire all they see and hear, rather than to cavil or criticise.

In 1811, Covent Garden had scarcely recovered from the celebrated O. P. riots, which destroyed the first season, and marred the opening of the second. A long and tedious account of these disgraceful proceedings is contained in two octavo volumes, entitled " The Covent Garden Journal," compiled for Stockdale, and published by him in 1810. The facts, on the whole, are correctly, but not impartially, stated, the tone of the work being hostile to the proprietors beyond what they deserved. The public were more in the wrong, and more unreasonable in their demands, than were the managers in their proposed scale of prices, and the reasons assigned for the augmented tariff. Cobbett, the great radical of the day, observed in his "Register," "the demand for old prices was unreasonable, as being a violation of the rights of property, and an attempt to compel people to sell entertainment at the price pointed out by the purchaser." The *Times* newspaper took another view, and said, "Let the company play to empty benches—let the public agree to desert the theatre—and the proprietors must come down." If the O. P. party had pursued this plan, nothing could have been said against them; but they had no right to disturb the quiet spectator, and prevent him from hearing what he had paid his money to hear. Right, however, on such occasions, is the last thing thought of. As *Kate Matchlock* says, in Steele's comedy of the "Funeral," "a war is a war;" so with the majority of playhouse insurgents, a riot is a riot, let the original cause be what it may.

The managers committed a fatal error in the employment of professional pugilists to coerce the refractory pit. This direct attack upon his independence, roused the ire of John Bull beyond fever heat, and induced him to exact severe and humiliating terms before he granted an amnesty to the vanquished authorities. Peace was at length concluded, after sixty-seven nights of unintermitting hostility. The dismissal of Brandon, the box book-keeper, was peremptorily and most unjustly insisted on, as a *sine quâ non*, although the unlucky official had merely obeyed orders, and discharged his duty faithfully to his employers.*

During this sharp rebellion, John Kemble, hitherto the popular idol, and the classic pillar of the stage, was nightly exposed, in his capacity of acting proprietor and manager, to the most scurrilous abuse and outrageous indignity. The conduct of the O. P. faction towards Charles Kemble was, if possible, still worse, as he held

* Brandon was subsequently reinstated.

no post in the obnoxious government, and it was never pretended that he had given them any personal offence. Yet he too was to be insulted, and for no reason on earth but because he was John's brother.

In the course of the dispute, much had been said and written against the increased number of private boxes, insinuating they were likely to be converted into places of assignation and intrigue. Cobbett said on this point, " As to the *private boxes*, considered as a source of *immorality*, I do not think much of that, being of opinion that the quantity of immorality will remain much the same, whether those boxes be public or private."

The year 1811, in which Charles Kean first saw the light, was one prolific in public events of great importance. Three battles were won by the English in Spain,—Barossa, Albucra, and Fuentes D'Onore; General Hill surprised Girard at Arroyo de Molinos, and nearly annihilated his corps; an action was fought between the British sloop, *Little Belt*, and the American frigate, *President*, which led to the subsequent war; more than half-a-million sterling was subscribed in England to relieve the sufferers by the French invasion of Portugal; the Duke of York resumed the office he had so long ably filled, of Commander-in-Chief; the Prince of Wales became Regent of the United Kingdom; and the fortunes of the French Emperor appeared to reach their consummation by the birth of a son. The theatres flourished, notwithstanding the heavy taxes, and the continual drain of the war, which seemed to resemble an interminable Chancery suit, or a never-ending game of chess, to be bequeathed to posterity.

The company at Covent Garden included great names: Mrs. Siddons, Mrs. Jordan, Mrs. C. Kemble, Mrs. H. Johnston, Mrs. Dickens, Mrs. Liston, Mrs. Davenport,

Miss Bolton, Miss S. Booth, Mrs. Gibbs, John and Charles Kemble, Young, Liston, Emery, Fawcett, Farley, Munden, Blanchard, Simmons, and Richard Jones. A wonderful phalanx of talent, such as we are not likely to see collected together again under the free trade system. Yet, "Henry the Fifth," reputed to be one of John Kemble's most successful revivals, attracted but five audiences ; and the far-famed "Julius Cæsar" (in the following year), the renown of which rang through the world, with his own *Brutus*, the *Cassius* of Young, and the *Mark Antony* of Charles Kemble, a cast of the play which has never since been approached, could not command more than eighteen repetitions. Mrs. Siddons, then on the eve of her departure, acted only thirty-three times during the season of 1810–1811. The attractive novelty was, beyond all dispute, the grand melo-dramatic equestrian spectacle of "Timour the Tartar," written expressly for the display of live cavalry, and which, although produced so late as the 29th of April, ran, without intermission or failure, for forty-four nights.

Mrs. Siddons retired formally on the 29th of June, 1812, the night being announced as her benefit. She selected *Lady Macbeth* for her closing performance. Her friends insisted on having the play terminated, when she made her final exit, in the sleeping scene. There were those amongst the audience who disliked this abrupt conclusion, and expressed themselves to that effect; but they were overpowered and silenced. This extravagant compliment was an absurdity imported from enthusiastic Ireland. When Mrs. Siddons died towards the close of a tragedy, it had been for years usual in Dublin to drop the curtain immediately, as she was often so exhausted as to render it expedient to do so. But the case was quite different with regard to "Macbeth." It looked like sacrificing Shakespeare to his representative. Thus, if she had selected the *Lady Constance* for her leave-taking, "King John" must have been cut short with the close of the third act.

After a pause of about twenty minutes, Mrs. Siddons was once more discovered, sitting at a table, simply attired in white. She rose, came forward, and delivered a poetical farewell, written for the occasion by her nephew, Mr. Horace Twiss.

A great actor or actress, after a premeditated and announced retirement, ought never to appear again. The curtain, once fallen, should rise no more. A return resembles a revival of the dead. Such yearnings, if voluntary, are as little entitled to respect as the resumption of imperial power by Maximian after his abdication. Mrs. Siddons was solicited in a very urgent manner to come back to the stage. A regular committee was formed for the purpose, but she had the good taste to resist their importunities. The gentleman who began the attempt greatly suspected that in her heart she wished to form a new engagement. Between the years 1813 and 1819, she acted on nineteen occasions, always without personal profit, and for benevolent purposes. Three of these performances were for the theatrical funds; ten for the advantage of the family of her deceased son, in Edinburgh; two at the express desire of the Princess Charlotte, in 1816; and four for the benefits of Charles Kemble and his wife. Her *real* last appearance occurred at Covent Garden, as *Lady Randolph*, on the 9th of July, 1819.* She was then within a few days of sixty-four, having been born on the 5th of July, 1755.

When Mrs. Siddons closed her regular professional career, in 1812, her powers had in no way declined, but her figure had become corpulent and unwieldy; so much

---

* For the benefit of Mr. and Mrs. C. Kemble.

so, that, latterly, cushions were brought and placed on the stage for her convenience in the dying scene of *Zara* in the "Mourning Bride." When she knelt to the Duke, as *Isabella* in "Measure for Measure," she was unable to rise without assistance.

This great actress, who may almost be said to have been born on the stage, was the eldest of a singularly gifted family. Her father, Roger Kemble, was a provincial manager and actor of good repute. In early youth, she lived for some time in a dependent condition with Lady Mary Greathead, at Guy's Cliff in Warwickshire, from whence, in her nineteenth year, she married for love; the object of her choice being Mr. Siddons, a performer in her father's company, an indifferent actor, but a very handsome man. She herself was in her youth transcendently beautiful, with every physical requisite that could lead to eminence on the stage. Yet her first appearance in London, in 1776, during Garrick's last season, amounted to a failure. She appeared as *Portia* in the "Merchant of Venice," without producing much effect, acted with the retiring Roscius as *Mrs. Strickland* in the "Suspicious Husband," and *Lady Anne* in "Richard the Third," and then subsided into *Venus* in the walking pageant of the "Jubilee." Six years later she returned in the full bloom of womanhood, after mature practice, and took the town by storm as *Isabella*, in Southern's "Fatal Marriage," which character she repeated twenty-five times during the season. Her supremacy was at once acknowledged, and never afterwards disputed. For thirty years she reigned without a rival. All who have written on the subject, and all who remember her personally, have agreed in saying that she far surpassed her ablest predecessors and contemporaries. She was, perhaps, the greatest tragic actress that ever trod the boards of any stage, or adorned the theatre of any country; but it would have been better for her fame if she had never attempted comedy. Nature, which had so bountifully lavished her gifts in other respects, denied the versatility which could command equal admiration in the double worship of the sister Muses.

It was no uncommon occurrence for females to be carried out of the house in fits during some of Mrs. Siddons' impassioned scenes in her early career; and the actors declared that the best comedians, in the richest farces, failed to revive the spirits of the audience to mirth, so totally had she depressed them. Mrs. Clive came up from her retirement to see her act, and exclaimed, with honest enthusiasm, "It is all truth and beauty from beginning to end!" Dr. Johnson paid her several eloquent compliments when she visited him in Bolt Court. After she had retired, he loudly expressed his admiration to Dr. Glover, who was present. "Sir," said he, "she is a prodigiously fine woman!" "Yes, sir," replied Dr. Glover; "but do you not think she is much finer on the stage, when adorned by art?" "Sir," rejoined Dr. Johnson, "on the stage art does not adorn; nature adorns her there, and art glorifies her."

Mrs. Siddons studied laboriously and incessantly. She was never satisfied with her execution of any part, and thought she could improve it to the last. Bishop Horne, in his "Essays and Thoughts on various Subjects," has the following observations with regard to this fact:—"Mrs. Siddons, the famous actress, receiving many invitations to the houses of the great and opulent, excused herself from accepting any of them, because her time was due to the public, that she might prepare herself in the most perfect manner for the duties she had undertaken. When a clergyman is invited to spend his hours at card-playing, or chit-chat meetings, has he not an apology to make of the same kind, but of a more important and interesting nature? And if he be deficient in the duties of *his* profession for want of so exercising himself, will not Mrs. Siddons rise up in judgment against him, and condemn him?" *

It has been recorded that John Kemble wrote out the part of *Hamlet* thirty times, and each time discovered some new and effective reading which had escaped him before. During his last season, he said, " Now that the failure of my physical powers has warned me to retire, I am only beginning thoroughly to understand my art." After Mrs. Siddons had left the stage, a friend, calling on her one morning, found her walking in the garden with a book in her hand. " What are you reading?" inquired the visitor. " You will hardly guess," replied she; " I am looking over *Lady Macbeth*, and am amazed to find some points in the character that never struck me until now."

Such is the true nature of the profession which the enemies of the stage are pleased to call idle, and casual observers, who enjoy the effect without knowing the labour by which it is accomplished, are apt to consider easy. They little know the constant exercise of mind and body it requires. As Cumberland has justly remarked, in his " Observer," " there is no calling or employment in life that can less endure the distractions of intemperance and dissipation." From Dow's History of Hindostan, the above-named writer has copied the following anecdote:—" During these transactions, the gates of Delhi were kept shut. Famine began to rage every day more and more, but the Schah was deaf to the miseries of mankind. The public spirit of Tucki, a famous actor, deserves to be recorded on this occasion. He exhibited a play before Nadir Schah, with which that monarch was so well pleased, that he commanded

* Bishop Horne's Works, vol. i. p. 357.

Tucki to ask, and what he wished should be done for him. Tucki fell on his face, and said, 'O king, command the gates to be opened, that the poor may not perish.' His request was granted; half the city poured into the country, and the place was supplied in a few days with plenty of provisions." Few actors can expect to reach the eminence or good fortune of rescuing a city from starvation, but the humblest can render themselves useful and respectable members of society, and may aspire to catch a few of the reflected rays which the great lights of the profession have cast around the youngest and most complicated of the ornamental arts.

To return to Mrs. Siddons. In her youth she excelled in delineating the tender pathos of *Juliet, Belvidera, Monimia, Desdemona, Mrs. Beverley,* and *Isabella.* In these she drew as many tears as she commanded plaudits. As she became mature and matronly, the grander and more stately heroines identified themselves with her peculiar attributes. Amongst her best characters may be placed foremost, *Lady Macbeth; Zara,* in the " Mourning Bride;" *Margaret of Anjou,* in the " Earl of Warwick;" *Elvira, Constance, Queen Katharine, Volumnia, Hermione,* and *Lady Randolph.* She was not fortunate in original parts. Perhaps the greatest triumph of her genius was the importance and interest with which she contrived to invest the repulsive mistress of *Pizarro,* in Sheridan's inflated paraphrase of Kotzebue's melodrama. James Ballantine, Sir Walter Scott's friend and printer, editor of the *Edinburgh Weekly Journal,* and one of the ablest theatrical critics of his day, in a notice of what was then supposed to be Mrs. Siddons' last appearance in Edinburgh, on the 13th of March, 1812, thus sums up his eulogy—and those who never saw the subject of it may be assured that it is not in the slightest degree exaggerated :—" We have lost, and for ever, an artist, whose performances rendered appropriate praise either difficult or unnecessary, and adequate praise impossible. Future times may wonder at, and perhaps doubt, in their honest love of some contemporary favourite, the magic wonders delivered to them by the present age, of the powers of Siddons; but we can only say, and, we think, truly say, that no sculptor or painter, in the sublimest flights of his fancy, ever embodied—no poet, in the most luxurious indulgence of his imagination, ever described—a creature so formed, so gifted, to agitate, to awe, and to astonish mankind by her professional powers as she whose matchless form, face, voice, and eye are now finally withdrawn from our public admiration." It is truly invigorating to read this manly, fervid tribute to exalted genius, untainted as it is by the leaven of critical restraint or exceptional qualification. And this leads us to say a few words on criticism in the abstract—an art which accompanies the art of acting as an inseparable pendant, freely indulged, as freely abused, and sometimes little understood by many of its practitioners.

No human excellence has ever yet achieved universal suffrage. The most ambitious votary of fame must content himself with a majority. To be without detractors is a certain indication of mediocrity. Homer, Plato, Isocrates, and Aristotle had their Zoilus and Aristarchus; Crebillon, Voltaire, and the wits of the age of Louis XV. had their Fréron ; Addison and Pope their Dennis ; Garrick his Ralph and Kenrick ; Talma, Molè, and La Rive, their Geoffroy ; and Charles Kean his Douglas Jerrold.

> " Ten censure wrong for one who writes amiss ;"

so said or sang the bard of Twickenham, in his celebrated essay. Professed critics will not be disposed to admit the soundness of this dictum. Our modern Zoili are, to the full, as imperative in their decisions, and quite as well convinced of their infallibility, as were the ancient founders of their school. Perhaps the two easiest things in the world are, to give advice and to find fault; and these very faculties may be taken as the leading reason why both propensities are so constantly indulged. The converse of the proposition is equally true. Nothing can be more difficult than to give good advice or to find fault judiciously.

As the drama includes a combination of many arts, to examine and report correctly on the merits of a play or an actor, requires a far wider scope of knowledge, with a greater variety of acquirement, than would suffice to pronounce opinion on any particular poem, painting, or statue. In the vast quantity of theatrical criticism that passes under the public eye, we meet with endless theories, and very often these theories are extravagant and contradictory. The writers name promptly enough what appears to them erroneous, but they are not so ready to point out how error is to be rectified. They see the disease, but are usually unprovided with a cure. Amongst these gentlemen, some are also dramatic writers themselves—a questionable foundation for general impartiality. We should certainly not select them, by choice, on a special jury to try the merits of their brethren whose productions had been chosen by managers in preference to their own.

A novice in writing is apt to imagine that he can master the difficulties of criticism by inspiration. It is enough to be employed, and he becomes at once an *ex officio* oracle. Some are governed by *cliquerie*, private partiality, or personal prejudice. Others are bound together in a solemn league and covenant of dogmatical opinions, drawn within a narrow circle. Any dissenters

from their own code they impale with unsparing severity. Let it not be supposed that these remarks are
intended for sweeping or universal application. We
admit unhesitatingly that there are many honourable,
independent, and accomplished exceptions.

Theatrical notices are, from necessity, often composed
and committed to the press in a few hurried moments
late at night, after the performance is over, when the
writer is fatigued in body and jaded in mind, before he
has allowed himself time to arrange his ideas, or to feel
certain as to his own impressions. This part of the
system was fully discussed in an article headed " London Newspapers and London Theatres," which appeared
in No. 342 of *Chambers' Edinburgh Journal* on the
20th of July, 1850. The author has evidently been behind the scenes, and is well acquainted with theatrical
machinery.

Strange eccentricities are sometimes indulged in by
professional chroniclers, who undertake to instruct the
world on the passing events of the day. Criticisms
have been written beforehand, in anticipation of the
performance of a play duly announced, but suddenly
changed in consequence of the illness of a principal
performer; the writer not intending to be present, but
having made up his mind as to who he should praise
and who condemn. On the following morning the
public have been enlightened with an elaborate disquisition on what never took place. More than once, in
such cases, actions have been brought, and damages
recovered for libel.

Stephen Kemble, during his management of the
theatre at Newcastle-on-Tyne, severely punished a local
journal which had assailed him by this hazardous mode
of vituperation. The same course was adopted with
equal effect by Jackson, of Edinburgh. On Saturday,

the 5th of October, 1805, a revival of Farquhar's comedy of the " Constant Couple " was announced for that evening at Drury Lane, but postponed on account of the illness of Elliston. A Sunday paper, however, contained the following account :—

" Last night, Farquhar's sprightly comedy of the ' Constant Couple ' was most laboriously and successfully murdered at this theatre. Elliston tamed down the gaiety of *Sir Harry Wildair* with a felicity which they who admire such doings can never sufficiently extol. The gay knight was, by the care of his misrepresentative, reduced to a figure of as little fantastic vivacity, as could be shown by *Tom Errand* in *Beau Clincher's* clothes. *Beau Clincher* himself was quite lost in Jack Bannister ; it was Bannister, not the *Clincher* of Farquhar, that the performance suggested to the audience. Miss Mellon was not an unpleasing representative of *Angelica ;* but criticism has not language severe enough to mark, as it deserves, the impertinence of Barrymore's presuming to put himself forward in the part of *Colonel Standard.* We were less offended, although it was impossible to be much pleased, with Dowton's attempt to enact *Alderman Smuggler.* But the acting was altogether very sorry."

The maligned actors brought an action against the authorities of the paper, who compromised, and got off cheaply, by paying 50*l.* to the theatrical fund.

During the summer of 1857, a morning paper published a studied criticism on the first performance of Madame Bosio and Mario, at the Italian Opera House, Lyceum, in " *La Traviata,*" telling how the theatre was crowded from floor to ceiling, how the great singers were applauded, how they were called for at the end of each act, and how they were crowned with acclamations and bouquets at the close. There were also many flourishes on *andante* movements, ascending scales, *fioriture,* and other musical obscurities, known only to the chosen few who are learned in the Eleusinian mysteries of the opera. But the whole was a fiction, for the piece had been unexpectedly withdrawn, and another substituted. On the next day, an editorial apology announced the summary discharge of the inventive reporter. We would suggest to gentlemen of this lively turn of imagination, that if they find it convenient to write their articles beforehand, common prudence might whisper that it is dangerous to commit them to press without being quite sure that the event came off as recorded. The same paper seems to have inherited lineal tendencies to this clairvoyant mode of anticipating what does not happen. In the *Theatrical Inquisitor* for October, 1812 (a periodical in continuation of the *Monthly Mirror*), we find the following extract, headed " Newspaper Criticism," taken from the pages of the identical journal's predecessor.

" Oct. 3d.—We were supremely gratified on Tuesday evening, at Covent Garden Theatre, during the representation of the opera of the " Cabinet," to hear that Mr. Sinclair had attended to our critical advice, and that his adoption of it was eminently serviceable to his professional character. In executing the *polacca*, he very prudently abstained from any wild flourishes, but kept strictly to the law of melody, by which he gained upon the public ear so strongly, and so deservedly, that he was encored three times, by the unanimous desire of the whole audience ; and we trust, after so decided a victory upon the part of true melody over the vagaries of science, that he will never more be fantastical. Unadulterated nature is modest and simple, and, like the pure beauty, is ever most efficient in attraction when she is unbedizened by the frippery of art. A meretricious female resorts to finery in the hope of acquiring a substitute for the lost loveliness of virtue ; but the most cunning labour of her toilette is not propitious to the aims of her desire."

On this foggy jargon the *Inquisitor* comments thus :—

" To this exquisitely-laboured piece of criticism there is but one solitary objection,—the opera of the ' Cabinet ' was indeed underlined at the bottom of the Monday play-bills, for the following night; but in those of Tuesday it was changed to the ' English Fleet,' which

was accordingly represented on the Tuesday evening—
that very evening on which the reporter of the veracious
journal to which we allude heard Mr. Sinclair thrice
encored in the *polacca*. This is exercising the power of
second sight with a vengeance; but we suspect that
most of our readers may be, like the governor of Tilbury
Fort in the 'Critic,' very little disposed to admit the
possibility of seeing things that are invisible :—

> ' The Spanish fleet thou can'st not see, because
> It is not yet in sight.' "

When Bouffé was last in London, in 1851, it so
happened that the writer of these pages had never seen
him. Watching the announcement of one of his most
popular characters, he repaired to the St. James's
theatre, full of expectation. But the great luminary
was suffering a temporary eclipse, and unable to shine.
Instead of flourishing on the boards, he lay writhing in
bed, under the gentle discipline of two physicians.
There was a total change of performance, but, of course,
no Bouffé. The next day, a paper of extensive circula-
tion stated that he had appeared on the previous evening
with unwonted brilliancy, and had sent the audience
home in a state of rapturous delight. Particular points
were noticed with particular praise. The reader was
sorely puzzled, and began to doubt if he had been
there ; long habit having induced him to place implicit
reliance on anything he saw in such responsible columns.
" Can such things be ? " thought he, " and am I only a
myth, a fabulous existence, an embodied chimera, a sort
of physical dream ? "   He was fast lapsing into
Pyrrhonism ; and felt himself in much the same predicament in which he once saw the late heroic Marquis of
Anglesea at his own table, who, during a conversation

on the battle of Waterloo, became so bewildered by the inventions and details of a gasconading amateur, who had not been present in that great field, that he looked down on the cork substitute which supplied the place of the leg he had left there, and rubbed it several times, to be convinced that he was really himself, and not a surreptitious double. More than twenty years before the demise of the late Duke of Cumberland, afterwards King of Hanover, a Bath paper announced his death officially, with a black border and several minute particulars.

Not many months since, a daily paper animadverted most harshly on the singing of an eminent tenor in Haydn's "Creation," at Exeter Hall. He had been announced, but was absent from severe indisposition. Shortly after, a ludicrous incident occurred at Cheltenham. A black man, patronised by a physician of that fashionable resort, undertook to deliver a lecture on the social condition of his class. The room was filled, and the audience expectant, but the lecturer was found to be "Bacchi plenus," as Dr. Pangloss says, and unfit to appear. The money was returned, with the best apology that could be made; but nevertheless, on the following morning, a detailed account of the lecture appeared in a well-circulated paper, which must have considerably astonished any of its readers who had formed a portion of the disappointed assembly.

When newspapers are thus committed, through the carelessness of their subordinates, if the mistake inclines to the side of panegyric, it may be passed over with a smile, although injurious to the credit of the journal in question, and tending to lower the character of criticism in general; but when an opposite course is adopted, when certain individuals are selected for specific censure, and slashed right and left with a mortal tomahawk, the matter becomes too serious for pleasantry, and gives rise to painful reflections.

As a general rule, criticism which inclines to extreme censure rather than to praise, attracts by far the greater share of attention. There is more nerve and more excitement in vituperation than in eulogy. Few like to confess the fact, but there is a latent pleasure in seeing a hole picked in your neighbour's coat, especially if you have any suspicion that the said neighbour sets up for a better or a wiser man than yourself. No one brooks assumed superiority with complaisance, and it is meat and drink to find our betters assailed with ourselves. A tale of scandal is propagated much more quickly than a deed of benevolence. Unpleasant tidings travel fast, and an ill-natured article in a newspaper or magazine is sure to be communicated by some anxious friend whose optics are less on the alert to discover a panegyric. Writers write with a view to being read, consequently they study the prevailing taste, while the actual merits of the subject under discussion may chance to be a secondary point in their consideration; as in selection for public office, fitness or capability are usually the last recommendations which influence the bestowing patron.

Amongst other peculiar features of dramatic criticism, may be remarked a vice of recent growth,—the affectation of interlarding foreign words and idioms to such an extent that the whole composition becomes an ill-assorted hybrid, neither French nor English, but an unnatural jumble of both, in the midst of which the honest vernacular loses all sense of identity, and wonders at its own transformation, and how it has got mixed up in such a fantastical masquerade. Acting a part is now called *interpreting a rôle;* songs are not sung, but *rendered;* a play is no longer simply got up, but *mounted;* the dresses and decorations are mystified into the *mise en scène*, and the whole affair is called the *ensemble*. But these are transparent obscurities compared with the *idiosyncratics*, *æsthetics*, *syncretics*, *synthetics*, *architectonics*, *esoterics*, *idealisms*, *transcendentalisms*, and a legion of other incomprehensible *modernisms*, which, as Junius says of Sir William Draper's figures of speech, "dance through" some of these articles "in all the mazes of metaphorical confusion." A recent author talks of an *æsthetical tea*, at which he assisted in Dresden. We have heard of a dancing and dining tea in London (*Thé dansante*, or *dînante*), and either of these has a strange sound; but an æsthetical tea is quite appalling. These hard compounds, so frequently and unmercifully dragged in, remind us of the poet's lines,—

> " The words themselves are neither rich nor rare,
> The wonder 's how the devil they got there."

The abuse complained of is not confined to dramatic critics, but is, we are sorry to observe, gaining ground with writers in general;—a sad act of injustice to the native, vigorous Saxon, which is thus pushed from its legitimate position to make way for imported intruders with very inferior pretensions. At the present rate, we shall soon cease to have a national tongue. English will disappear into French, and our standard authors of fifty years' antiquity will require the help of a glossary, and be classed, with Greek and Latin, amongst the dead languages.

There seems to have been always a conventional style exclusively appropriated to criticism. Sterne, more than eighty years ago, gives an amusing imitation of the mode in his day, winding up thus:—"Grant me patience! Of all the cants which are canted in this canting world, though the cant of hypocrisy may be the worst, the cant of criticism is the most tormenting."

Excellent rules are laid down by approved authorities for acquiring this difficult art. Those who wish to study it soundly cannot do better than apply themselves to Pope's Essay, or to a very elaborate treatise by Dryden, called the " Grounds of Criticism in Tragedy," prefixed to his alteration of Shakespeare's " Troilus and Cressida," and to be found in the collected edition of his works. There is no occasion to travel back to Aristotle or Quintilian. Others, who may desire to be ingeniously wrong, or simply scurrilous, will find tolerable guides in the pages of Rymer, Gildon, or Dennis, and some recent followers of that school. Goldsmith says that, as regards painting, criticism lies in a very small compass; " all consists in saying the picture would have been better if the painter had taken more pains, and in praising the works of Pietro Perugino." A well-known authority of our own days built his reputation on never committing himself by a decision. He was a patient listener (rare and inestimable gift!), and when his judgment was appealed to, answered, after much deliberation, and with the solemnity of a bench of bishops, " There's a great deal to be said on both sides."

Menage has proposed an easy general rule. One day the Cardinal de Retz requested that he would oblige him with a few lectures on poetry, " for," said he, " such quantities of verses are brought to me, that I ought at least to appear to be somewhat of a judge." " It would," replied Menage, " be difficult to give your eminence many rudiments of criticism without taking up too much of your time; but I would advise you, as a practice, to look over the first page or two, and then exclaim, ' Sad stuff! wretched poetaster! miserable verses!' and, ninety-nine times in 'a hundred, you may be sure you are right."

Edmund Kean was a great favourite with Mrs. Garrick, the widow of his celebrated predecessor. It was usual with the Drury Lane committee, when they wanted a new-comer to make a hit, to bring the venerable old lady out to her private box, and then to prompt her to say that he reminded her of David. She said so, and the saying went the round of the papers accordingly. In the case of Kean she spoke honestly. He *did* remind her of her husband, and was nearer to him by many degrees than any actor she had seen since his death, although both agreed that he could not play *Abel Drugger*.*

Mrs. Garrick frequently visited at Kean's house, in Clarges Street; and one day, making a morning call, she found the tragedian in the drawing-room in a state of unusual excitement. He received his guest rather abruptly, and retired. The old lady's eyes followed him with some astonishment, and turning to Mrs. Kean she said, in her broken English, "What is the matter with your husband? he seems disturbed." "Oh," replied Mrs. Kean, "you mustn't mind him; he has just read a spiteful notice of his *Othello* in one of the newspapers, which has terribly vexed him." "But why should he mind that?" said Mrs. Garrick; "he is above the papers, and can afford to be abused." "Yes," observed Mrs. Kean; "but he says the article is so well written: but for that, he wouldn't care for the abuse." "Then, my dear Mrs. Kean, he should do as David did, and he would be spared this annoyance." "What's that?" exclaimed the anxious wife, with in-

---

* Kean essayed *Abel Drugger* for his first benefit on the 24th of May, 1814, which drew the following laconic note from Mrs. Garrick :— "Dear Sir,—You cannot play *Abel Drugger*.—Yours, Eva Garrick." He replied :—" Dear Madam,—I know it.—Yours, Edmund Kean." But he balanced this inferiority by discovering that David was unable to sing, while he warbled melodiously.

tense eagerness. " Write the articles himself: David always did so."

Assuredly David was a good general, and never exercised his tactics with more skill than in adopting this sound conservative practice.* Those were really the " palmy days of the drama," when journals paid for the advertisements, and shopkeepers for exhibiting the bills. These are well-authenticated facts. In Andrews' " History of British Journalism," published by Bentley, 1858, we find the following paragraph (vol. i. p. 192) with reference to the *Public Advertiser* and the expenses of that paper for one year, as copied from the ledger of Henry Woodfall :—

" The theatres are a great expense to the papers. Amongst the items of payment are—playhouses 100*l.*; Drury Lane advertisements, 64*l.* 8*s.* 6*d.*; Covent Garden, ditto, 66*l.* 11*s.* The papers paid 200*l.* a-year to each theatre for the accounts of new plays, and would reward the messenger with a shilling or half-a-crown who brought them the first copy of a play-bill."

More than once, in conversation with the writer of these volumes, Edmund Kean, when he had been vexed by recent criticisms, complained that the newspapers made sad mistakes as to his conceptions of character, readings, points, and other peculiarities of acting. " These people," said he, " don't understand their business. They give me credit where I make no effort to deserve praise, and pass over passages on which I have bestowed the utmost care and attention.† They think because my style is new, and

---

* Garrick was a shareholder in the *Public Advertiser.* It must be remembered that the newspapers in his time were few in number, while at present their name is legion.

† It was his practice to rehearse scene by scene to his wife, and to repeat a speech twenty times, until both were satisfied that he had hit the true vein.

appears natural, that I never study; and talk about the sudden impulse of genius. With genuine artists there is no such thing as impulsive acting; all is arranged beforehand; else, why should we rehearse? We may act better or worse on a particular night, from particular circumstances, but the conception is the same. I have done all these things a thousand times in country theatres, and perhaps better, before I was recognised as a great actor, and have been loudly applauded; but the sound in those days never reached as far as London."

In 1807 a small volume was published by Leigh Hunt, entitled "Critical Essays on the Performers of the London Theatres," being a *rifaccimento* or enlarged edition of a course of theatrical articles which originally appeared in a weekly paper called *The News*. Many of these are ably written, and the work may be referred to as a fair specimen of this class of composition. Hazlitt's notices, supplied when he was connected with more than one paper, have also re-appeared in a separate volume, which has gone through several editions, under the title of "A View of the English Stage," and have acquired a standard reputation; but they are inferior to Hunt's, both in judgment and impartiality. They abound in smart severities, and epigrammatic *ad captandum* turns; yet the book is valuable as a stage record, as it contains accounts of the first appearances of Miss O'Neill, Miss Foote, Miss Stephens, Kean, and Macready; and also of the last performances of Mrs. Siddons, John Kemble, and John Bannister. In Hazlitt's pages will be found a much greater amount of prejudice than candour, and infinitely more gall than honey. He undervalues Miss O'Neill, billingsgates Conway, absolutely libels Young, and deifies the two or three fortunate exceptions who find favour in his eyes. A few extracts will corroborate this statement more convincingly than a simple assertion :—

"The best thing we remember in Coleridge's tragedy of 'Remorse,' and which gave the greatest satisfaction to the audience, was that part in which Mr. D—— was precipitated into a deep pit, from which, by the elaborate description bestowed on it by the poet, it was plainly 'impossible he should ever rise again.' If Mr. W—— is to be puffed up, and stuck at the head of his profession at this unmerciful rate, it would almost induce us to wish Mr. Coleridge would write another tragedy, to dispose of him in the same way as his predecessor."

Speaking of one of the most elegant and classical actors of the day, recognised by the public as such, he says :—

"Mr. Young ought never to condescend to play comedy, nor aspire to play tragedy. Sentimental pantomime is his *forte*."

"Mr. Young is brought forward as a downright common madman, just broken loose from a mad-house at Richmond, and is going to dash out the brains of his daughter and her infant with a club. The infant is no other than a large wooden doll. It fell on the floor the other evening without receiving any hurt, at which the audience laughed."

"As to Mr. Young's *Iago*, we never saw a gentleman acted finer."

"Mr. Young's *Prospero* was good for nothing, and consequently was indescribably bad. Mr. Emery had nothing of *Caliban* but his gaberdine, which did not become him."

"Mr. C. Kemble seemed to be rehearsing *Don Felix* with an eye to *Macduff*, or some face-making character."

"Mr. Incledon both speaks and sings as if he had a lozenge or a slice of marmalade in his mouth. If he would go to America, and leave his voice behind him, it would be a great benefit—to the parent country."

"Mrs. Dickens never appeared to us anything but an ordinary musical instrument, and at present she is very much out of tune."

"Mr. Jones acts as if he was moved by wires. He is a very lively automaton."

"Mr. Jones is no favourite of ours. He is always the same Mr. Jones, who shows his teeth, and rolls his eyes, and looks like 'a jackdaw just caught in a snare.' "

"Mr. Terry, as *Sir Oliver Surface*, wore a great coat with yellow buttons; Mr. Farley, in *Trip*, had a large bouquet; and why should we refuse to do justice to Mr. Claremont, who was dressed in black?"

"Mr. Conway topped the part of *Comus* with his usual felicity, and seemed almost as if the genius of a maypole had inspired a human form. He is said to make a very handsome *Comus*; so he would make a very handsome *Caliban*, and the common sense of the transformation would be the same."

"Of Mr. Conway's *Romeo* we cannot speak with patience. He bestrides the stage like a Colossus, throws his arms into the air like the sails of a windmill, and his motion is as unwieldy as that of a young elephant. Query: Why does he not marry?"

Now all these flippant, sarcastic nothings are very easily written, very well calculated to lacerate sensitive feelings, and admirably disposed to amuse a breakfast table, or to elicit exclamations of "How good!" "Capital!" "Deuced keen!" &c.; but we ask any unprejudiced reader, are they criticism?

Perhaps the best sentence in Hazlitt's book is this:—

" Mr. Kemble has been compared lately (in the *Times*) to the ruins of a magnificent temple, in which the divinity still resides. This is not the case. The temple is unimpaired, but the divinity is sometimes from home."

One of the most apt remarks, in this line of notice, that we recollect, was made by a critic in a London paper (not Hazlitt) on a new *Richard the Third*, who was too good to be hissed and not good enough to be applauded. The writer said, " We never until now thoroughly understood honest Dogberry's meaning when he uses the phrase, ' most tolerable, and not to be endured.' "

All public characters, in every grade of life, are lawfully open to public animadversion, from the sovereign on the throne and the prime minister, down to the lowest subordinate on the stage, who says "The coach is at the door," or "The dinner is served." " 'Tis the rough brake that virtue must go through," and should be endured by great and small with becoming philosophy. Any thin-skinned patient who writhes under this discipline should get rid as soon as possible, and how he may, of the outer cuticle with which his natural construction has invested him, and encase himself in the hide of a rhinoceros. It is certainly not pleasant to think that the professional reputation which it has taken a quarter of a century to establish may be damaged, if not " snuffed out by an article," and possibly an incompetent or prejudiced one, written hastily, in a quarter of an hour. But the sufferer must console himself by reflecting that mighty names have, ere now, been extinguished by trifling agencies. King Pyrrhus, who shook Rome to her centre, was slain by an old woman who threw a tile on his head from a garret window; Abyssinian Bruce fell down-stairs while hastening to hand an aged lady

into her carriage, pitched on his head, and never spoke
again; Lord Anson, who sailed round the world, caught
his death by tumbling into a brook; and the great Duke
of Marlborough died of sixpence.*

* He walked home from the Rooms at Bath, on a rainy night, rather
than pay sixpence for a chair, got wet, and thus laid the foundation of
the disease which killed him. To make the story more characteristic,
it was said that he borrowed the sixpence from Lord Chesterfield, and
never repaid it.

CHAPTER III.

THE NAME OF KEAN IN ASSOCIATION WITH THE DRAMA—REPUTED GENE-
ALOGY OF EDMUND KEAN—POSITION OF THE FAMILY DURING THE IN-
FANCY OF CHARLES KEAN—FIRST ENGAGEMENT OF EDMUND KEAN IN
LONDON—HIS DEBÛT IN SHYLOCK AT DRURY LANE—TRIUMPHANT SUC-
CESS—GREAT INFLUENCE OF THE NEWSPAPERS—MR. WHITBREAD'S
SPEECH ON THE CLOSE OF THE SEASON.

SIR PHILIP SIDNEY was wont to say that the old ballad
of "Chevy Chase" had that in it which stirred the soul
like the effect of a trumpet. So has the name of KEAN
a thrilling sound in association with the annals of the
stage. The brilliant career of Edmund Kean, the father,
dazzling and eccentric as that of a comet, with its
melancholy close, are still vivid in the remembrance of
his contemporaries, and by them as vividly conveyed to
the present generation. Two years after his decease (in
1835), memoirs of his life, in two volumes, were published by Moxon, without the author's name, but generally reputed to be from the pen of Barry Cornwall.
The materials with which he was supplied were authentic; the facts are correctly stated, and may be fully
depended on. The book is agreeably written, and con-
pression that, as a whole, it is meagre and hurried,
especially towards the close. It has more the appearance of being undertaken as an imposed task, than as a
voluntary labour of love. The general tone is little
calculated to elevate the profession of which it treats, or
to raise the genius of the individual subject above the

failings by which that rare endowment was clouded and prematurely destroyed. History and biography require truth; but truth does not, of necessity, demand that the defective features of any given portrait should be thrust with undue prominence into the foreground. Frailties and weakness ought not to be entirely blotted out from a genuine record; neither should they be coloured up into ludicrous exaggeration. The point of difficulty lies in the discrimination with which such delicate matters are handled. Shakespeare says, with amiable and just philosophy, " The web of our life is of a mingled yarn, good and ill together; our virtues would be proud, if our faults whipped them not; and our crimes would despair, if they were not cherished by our virtues."* It is a common theory that, in sketching the lives of public characters, we have no right to allude to their private transactions; that the veil by which the latter are hidden should never be withdrawn. False premises, and unsound conclusion. How can we pronounce on the true merit of a medal, unless we examine the reverse side as well as the face? Lord Lyttleton, in his history of Henry II., suppressed all mention of certain traditionary incidents in the conduct of Queen Elinor, and some of the fair ornaments of her court. This omission being charged against him, he replied, with courtly gallantry, " I cannot lend myself to the perpetuation of scandal against ladies of high rank so long deceased." Oliver Cromwell, with a total absence of personal vanity, desired his painters on no account to omit the unsightly warts by which his physiognomy was defaced. If a remarkable blemish is either passed over entirely, or distorted, the identity of the picture is lost, and its reflected value, either as an example or a warning, sinks into insignificance.

* " All's Well that Ends Well," Act IV. Sc. iii.

Charles Kean, inheriting the genius and success of his father, but avoiding the fatal improvidence by which both were rendered unavailing, has, while yet within the meridian of life, placed himself at the head of a difficult profession, for which he was not trained or intended; realized a competent independence by his own exertions; established a new epoch in the history of dramatic art, and won an honourable estimation in the eyes of all who are acquainted with him. It is not given to many to achieve such multiplied advantages; nor have they been gained in the present instance without trial, persevering effort, disappointment, and vicissitude. Scenes of exciting interest have been passed through, and many difficulties met and surmounted. The history of a career so active and varied, can scarcely fail to amuse the careless, and instruct the reflecting reader.

Charles Kean is an Irishman, and a native of Waterford; the *urbs intacta*, as it is proudly designated in Hibernian annals. The same place had previously given birth to Dorothea Jordan, and Tyrone Power was born in the county. Edmund Kean, at the time of Charles's birth, formed one of the company attached to the theatre in the above-named city. Of his own parentage and ancestry little is known, and that little is involved in much uncertainty. He was not clearly informed on the subject himself, and gave contradictory accounts whenever it was introduced. A modern historian, of high repute, claims for him a noble, though a left-handed, descent from George Savile, Marquis of Halifax, one of the most honest and least trimming statesmen who lived and flourished in the trimming times of Charles II., James, and William. In the third volume of Macaulay (page 543), the following passage occurs:—"It is, perhaps, not generally known that some adventurers, who, without advantages of fortune or position, made themselves conspicuous by the mere force of ability, inherited the blood of Halifax. He left a natural son, Henry Carey, whose dramas once drew crowded audiences to the theatres, and some of whose gay and spirited verses still live in the memory of hundreds of thousands.[*] From Henry Carey descended that Edmund Kean, who, in our own time, transformed himself so marvellously into *Shylock*, *Iago*, and *Othello*."

This Henry Carey left a son, George Savile Carey, whose daughter, Ann Carey, was the reputed mother of the great tragedian, although he sometimes doubted and questioned the claim, while he supported and allowed her an annuity. It has also been said that Miss Tidswell was his mother, and the Duke of Norfolk, who succeeded to the title in 1786, his father. Being once directly asked the question by the Hon. Douglas Kinnaird, one of the Drury Lane committee, his Grace replied, good-humouredly, " I am not aware of the fact ; but I should be very proud of a son possessed of such talent."

Ovid, writing eighteen hundred years ago, says :—

> " Nam genus et proavos et quæ non fecimus ipsi,
> Vix ea nostra voco."

Birth and ancestry, and what we have not ourselves achieved, we can scarcely call our own. The sentiment contains a just rebuke to empty pride, unsustained by inborn worth ; but as good blood manifests itself in the higher animals, so is it something in man, and not to be under-rated, if, as it ought and often does, it acts as an incentive to virtue, and as a rampart in support of integrity. Nevertheless, everything must have a begin-

---

* Henry Carey, who died by his own hand in 1743, is supposed by many to have been the author and composer of the words and melody of " God save the King ;" but stronger evidence inclines in favour of Dr. John Bull, who was chamber musician to James I., and lived more than a century earlier than Carey. His monument may be seen in Hereford Cathedral.

ning; and there is more satisfaction in winning fame and fortune by personal merit than in being accidentally the "tenth transmitter" of hereditary distinction.

Mary Chambers, the mother of Charles Kean, was also a native of Waterford, closely connected with the highly respectable family of Cuffe, long settled in that part of Ireland. Miss Chambers, with a sister, had, from family embarrassments, been induced to attempt the stage as a means of livelihood, and first became acquainted with her destined husband while both were performing in the Gloucester theatre, under the management of Mr. Beverley. The future Mrs. Kean was at that time acting as an amateur, receiving no pay. After a courtship of a few months, they were married at Stroud, in Gloucestershire, in July, 1808, he being under twenty, and several years junior to his wife. At Swansea, on the 13th of September, 1809, their first child, a boy, who received the name of Howard, was born. For this elder brother, Charles has sometimes been mistaken. He died of water on the brain, at Dorchester, in November, 1813, when he had only entered on his fifth year; but even at that early age remarkable for his beauty and promise of theatrical talent, having occasionally appeared with his father in infantine characters. Kean felt deeply the loss of his eldest-born, nor was his grief of a transient nature; for months later, on the night of his great success in *Shylock*, when rejoicing with his wife over the triumph he had at last accomplished, a sad reminiscence crossed his mind, his spirits fell, and he exclaimed, in a broken tone, "Oh, that Howard was alive now!—but he is better where he is."

When Charles Kean was born, and for more than two years after, the fortunes of his parents were at the lowest possible ebb; they had barely a subsistence for the present, and were almost hopeless of the future. The father, toiling in the endless drudgery of an itinerant life, acted every night in wretched country theatres, in play, interlude, and farce ; not unfrequently *Richard the Third* and *Harlequin* on the same evening ; and, during the day, endeavoured to eke out a scanty and doubtful salary of some five-and-twenty shillings per week, by giving lessons in boxing, fencing, dancing, and riding. Yet ignorance and prejudice have again and again designated the stage as " an idle avocation." Those who think so would do well to test the fact by experiment for a short period, and then reduce the value of their opinions to the most unanswerable of all solutions.

At the time of which we are now writing, none saw in Edmund Kean—the undistinguished and insignificant country actor, whose want of lofty stature was declared even by the few who perceived his ability to be an insurmountable bar—the future prop of Drury Lane, the magnet of unprecedented attraction, the embryo luminary, before whose brightness all rival influences were to turn pale. The genius was, unquestionably, there, where it had ever been, but the long anticipated and anxiously looked for opportunity had not yet arrived. It came at last. Towards the close of 1813, Kean obtained an engagement, on a trifling salary, at Drury Lane, but such was the slender state of his finances, that, when the family removed to the metropolis, they entered in the most legitimate of Thespian conveyances—a waggon.*

* At this period, the new theatre of Drury Lane had not been open more than two years under the Committee of Management, of which Mr. Whitbread was chairman ; but it was already immersed in heavy liabilities, and bankruptcy seemed impending at no great distance. The company was numerous but not effective, neither were the available forces used to the best advantage. Amongst the leaders were many established favourites, including Miss Duncan, Miss Kelly, Mrs. Edwin, Miss Mellon, Mrs. Glover, Miss Smith afterwards Mrs. Bartley, Messrs. Elliston, Dowton, Munden, Rae, J. Bannister, Lovegrove, Irish Johnstone. R. Palmer, Russell, and Wallack. There was much divided talent,

Wednesday, the 26th of January, 1814, proved to be a " *dies albo lapide notata* " in the annals of the drama, and in the life of the actor who, on that evening, established a name which will never be forgotten. At length, after a sickening interval of hope deferred, with an endurance of penury and disappointment, which had nearly crushed his spirit, Edmund Kean found himself in the position for which he had so long ardently sighed. "Let me once get upon the boards of Old Drury, with the footlights before me, and I will show them what I can do." This had been his constant exclamation to his wife for years—and there he stood at last, the cherished hope of his life converted to reality. The audience were at once impressed with his appearance. As if by an intuitive impulse they felt that something out of the ordinary way was about to take place. He was hailed with the encouragement commonly accorded to a stranger, and acknowledged his reception by a bow of unusual grace. " I could scarcely draw my breath," said his friend, Dr. Drury, to him on the following day, "when you entered. But directly you took your position, and leaned upon your cane, I saw that all was right."

Before many words had been spoken, he startled the audience into their first applause by the epigrammatic point with which he replied to *Bassanio*, on the question of *Antonio's* security. A general burst of approbation followed the speech ending with these lines :—

> " Fair sir, you spat on me on Wednesday last ;
> You spurn'd me such a day ; another time
> You call'd me *dog ;* and for these *courtesies*
> I'll lend you thus much monies."

but as a whole, they could not stand in comparison with the great phalanx at Covent Garden. Many new candidates for public favour had been introduced, but none attained permanent reputation in the first class.

By the conclusion of his first scene, all doubts as to success had vanished. He went on winning his way, step by step, through the tremendous display of passion with *Solanio, Salarino,* and *Tubal* in the third act, until he made his final exit in the trial scene, accompanied by repeated peals of acclamation. Such acting had not been witnessed, and such universal applause had not for many previous years resounded through the walls of Drury. The house, at the commencement, was thin, and there was truth in the droll remark of Oxberry, who said,— "How the devil so few of them kicked up such a row was marvellous!" When Kean had finished, two or three second-rate performers volunteered their congratulations. The magnates still kept at a distance, from jealousy or disappointment. Mr. Arnold sent for him to the manager's room, and said, rather formally, "You have exceeded our expectations, sir; the play will be repeated next Wednesday." But the actor felt that he had conquered the public, and he knew that the opinions of the management would rapidly veer round to that point of the compass which looked in the direction of their interest. He hastened to his humble lodging with a lighter heart than he had carried with him when he went to the theatre on that decisive evening. He left home doubtful and anxious; he returned overflowing with brilliant anticipations. "Now, Mary," said he to his wife, "you shall ride in your own carriage, and Charles shall go to Eton." The child was roused from sleep that the promise might be sealed with a kiss.

The scene changed rapidly and effectually. Success, that potent wand of the enchanter at once established the rising tragedian on the pinnacle of fame and the high road to opulence. The doors of the rich and influential were thrown open to him; he might have chosen his own society; his praises filled the columns of the daily papers, and his attraction replenished the long exhausted treasury of the theatre. It was, in fact, the realization of a dream, " and all went merry as a marriage bell." But this complete triumph was not achieved by the unaided force of genius. Time and opportunity will carry great talent over many obstacles; but without an assisting lever the progress may be slow, and with active opposition has sometimes been checked altogether. Those who witnessed the first performances of Edmund Kean in London, were struck at once by the originality of his conceptive power and the force of his execution. They admired with unrestrained enthusiasm, but they were limited in number. A succession of failures had blunted the edge of expectation, and the public held aloof from proffered novelty. They had been too often deceived. Soon after the commencement of the season now in progress, Stephen Kemble had actually been presented in this same part of *Shylock*. It proved, as might be expected, a palpable mistake. Then followed Huddart from Dublin, who was more unfortunate than his immediate predecessor, and the last failure only preceded the coming of Edmund Kean by a single month. The announcement of a first appearance had lost its charm; a new *Hamlet* or *Richard* produced no run on the box-book. The Drury Lane Committee, timid and short-sighted, began to doubt whether Kean's was a genuine success, and even talked of removing his name from the bills. Lord Byron, who was influential in the conclave, had clearer optics, and stepped in to prevent the contemplated suicide. His colleagues, as a body, possessed the average share of intellect by which all managing committees have ever been distinguished, up to the present year of grace inclusive. They could audit accounts according to the most pedantic formula, draw up a report as lucid as a speech from the throne or a ministerial programme, and get into difficulties or accumulate debt with business-like perseverance; but they were bankrupt in resources and expedients down to the fractional minimum of the theatrical exchequer. The practical poet saw the value of the trump card that had turned up, and how it was likely to be thrown away by unskilful playing. "You have got a great genius amongst you," said he, "and you don't know it. But he will fall through, like many others, unless we lift him, and force the town to come and see him. There is enough in Kean to bear out any extent of panegyric, and it will not do to trust an opportunity like this to the mere routine of the ordinary chances. We must go in a body, call upon the proprietors and editors of the leading papers, ask them to attend in person and write the articles themselves."

On this occasion, the pressure from *within*, the no balance at the bankers, seconded a sound argument. The advice was followed; the great guns of all the most influential journals complied, and the result rapidly carried up to an unprecedented figure the attraction of the new candidate. Without this impetus, he might have toiled on for months, wasting his energies on empty benches, and unprofitable applause. But this expedient, so effectual with true genius, would have broken down if applied to mediocrity.

On Edmund Kean's first appearance in *Shylock*, the money paid at the doors amounted only to 164*l*. On his second night, the receipts nearly doubled, and on the 12th of February, within a fortnight after, the house literally overflowed in every quarter to witness his *Richard the Third*. After this, he performed *Hamlet*, *Othello*, and *Iago* alternately, and for his benefit on the 25th of May, *Luke*, in a play entitled "Riches," constructed on Massinger's "City Madam" by Sir James

Bland Burges. His original engagement was speedily cancelled, and a new one entered into more commensurate with the unprecedented attraction. The season closed on the 16th of July, by which time Kean had played sixty-eight nights, the gross receipts of which amounted to 34,642*l.* Before he came out, the average had sunk to 212*l.* per night. During his performances it amounted to 509*l.* This calculation shows that the theatre cleared by his individual services, in less than six months, upwards of 20,000*l.*

On the termination of the season, the unlooked-for novelty of a dividend of five per cent. was announced by Mr. Whitbread, the chairman, at the annual meeting of the proprietors held at the Crown and Anchor. This "agreeable surprise" was received, as might be expected, with reiterated cheers. Mr. Whitbread in the course of his speech, as reported at the time in the papers, included a warm eulogium on Kean. He said, "the extraordinary powers of this eminent actor had, as well might be imagined, drawn forth the criticisms of all theatrical amateurs and judges; and though there might be some few who did not agree with him in regarding Mr. Kean as the most shining actor that had appeared in the theatrical hemisphere for many years, yet he was happy to find that the general opinion concurred with his own in that respect. A combination of all the qualities that were essential to form a complete actor, was found to unite in one man very rarely indeed; and though objections might be set up to the figure of Mr. Kean, as objections had at all times and in all ages of the world been set up to some one or other of the qualities and proportions of every actor, yet, judging of him in all the great attributes of the art, he was one of those prodigies that occur only once or twice in a century. He had the highest respect for the talents, the erudition, the accomplishments of Mr. Kemble, who was another of those rare instances of superior ability in the histrionic profession; and he had no desire, in speaking of Mr. Kean, to deteriorate from the merit of Mr. Kemble; but it was too much the practice of persons, in speaking of an actor, to compare him with another, and those who affected to criticize the talents of Mr. Kean most scrupulously, wished always to put him in comparison with Mr. Garrick. Of that great actor he wished to speak with the most marked respect, but who of all those who compared Kean with Garrick remembered the performances of Garrick in his twenty-fifth year? They remembered him only after long study and experience had improved and matured all the faculties of his youth; and he was ready also to pay the same compliment to Mr. Kemble, that years of application and study, with a cultivated mind and strong judgment, had acquired him the celebrity he possessed. But in judging of Mr. Kean, we must look at him as he is, not the copyist of any other, not the pupil of any school, not a mannerist, but an actor who found all his resources in nature, who delineated his passions only from the expression that the soul gives to the voice and features of a man, not from the images that have before him been represented by others upon the stage. It is from the wonderful truth, energy, and force with which he strikes out and presents to the eye this natural working of the passions of the human frame, that he excites the emotions and engages the sympathy of his spectators and auditors. It is to him that, after one hundred and thirty-five nights of continued loss and disappointment, the subscribers are indebted for the success of the season, and that the public are indebted for the high treat which they received by the variety of characters he had represented."

This was a lofty position for a man to find himself in, who not more than seven months before had been unknown, neglected, and literally "whistled down the wind to prey at fortune." The ball was at his foot, but he kicked it from him, and threw away one of the most golden opportunities ever presented to struggling and successful genius.

CHAPTER IV.

LAST PERFORMANCES OF MRS. JORDAN AT COVENT GARDEN—HER DEATH
AT ST. CLOUD—MISS STEPHENS—MISS O'NEILL—HER SHORT AND BRIL-
LIANT CAREER—RETIREMENT OF JOHN BANNISTER—HIS ADMIRATION
OF KEAN—FIRST APPEARANCE OF JOHN P. HARLEY AT DRURY LANE—
AND OF WILLIAM CHARLES MACREADY AT COVENT GARDEN.

THE same year which gave Edmund Kean to Drury
Lane witnessed the last performance of that incomparable
daughter of Thalia, Mrs. Jordan, at Covent-garden. On
the 1st of June, 1814, she appeared as *Lady Teazle*, and
after the curtain fell on that night the London public saw
her no more. There was no leave-taking, neither was it
announced nor intended as a farewell. Pecuniary difficulties, not arising from any imprudence of her own, drove
her from England, and prevented her return. St. Cloud,
near Paris, was her haven of refuge, where she died
under the assumed name of Mrs. James, on the 5th of
July, 1816. Those who have never seen Mrs. Jordan,
and nearly all the living generation are included in the
number, would obtain but a very inadequate impression
of what she was, personally, from the two portraits by
De Wilde, in the collection of the Garrick Club. We
have been told by one (now dead) who knew her long
and intimately, and was a sound theatrical critic withal,
that her face had small pretensions to beauty, and was
more expressive and animated than handsome ; but her
figure in early life was faultless, and her voice most

exquisitely modulated. She was equally happy in the expression of pathos or humour. Her fine ladies and elegant heroines of comedy (according to this authority) lacked the grace and chastened manner of Mrs. Abington, and Miss Farren. It would, perhaps, have been better for her reputation if she had never attempted them ; but in hoydens and romps, in simple rustics, in scheming chambermaids, and characters of broad, exuberant humour, not Clive or Woffington in their best days could claim the superiority. Her laugh was irresistible, and carried all before it. Some have fancied that they heard it revived in the ringing tones of Mrs. Nesbitt. Her manner was perfectly original, and her articulation so distinct, that not a sentence she uttered was ever lost; but the most insignificant passage acquired importance, and stole upon the feelings of the audience through her exquisite delivery. Her attitudes and action were so expressive of the passions she delineated, that even had she not spoken, her story would have been perfectly intelligible to the audience. Hazlitt, who, when not under the influence of prejudice, could indite a good critical analysis, thus concisely sums up her theatrical attractions :—" Her face, her tones, her manner, were irresistible; her smile had the effect of sunshine, and her laugh did one good to hear it. Her voice was eloquence itself; it seemed as if her heart was always at her mouth —she was all gaiety, openness, and good nature. She rioted in her fine animal spirits, and gave more pleasure than any other actress, because she had the greatest spirit of enjoyment in herself."

The public career of Mrs. Jordan presented a series of triumphal processions, but in her private life there were some dark intervening clouds, and the close was melancholy in the extreme. We have no wish to raise the veil which shrouds these unexplained mysteries ; yet it

is painful to think that a being so gifted, who had so
often gladdened the hearts of admiring thousands, should
die in poverty, in obscurity, and extreme mental suffering, in a strange land ; and that the humble stone which
stands, or stood, at the head of her remains in the church-
yard at St. Cloud, should be scarcely recognizable when
looked for by a sympathizing tourist. A mound was
raised over the grave, shadowed by an acacia-tree, and
planted at the proper season with cypresses. This was
executed with taste at the time, but has since fallen into
dilapidation, in the absence of a small sum of money
necessary to keep it in repair. The inscription fixed her
age at fifty, but she must have been older, seeing that
she made her first public appearance under Ryder's
management, in Dublin, in 1777, as *Phœbe*, in " As You
Like It," when, if the record alluded to above be correct, she could only have been in her eleventh year, and
would necessarily have been announced as a child.
Boaden, in his " Memoirs," places her birth as far back
as 1762, which seems likely to be correct. This would
make her fifty-four when she died, and fifteen when she
went on the stage. Waterford may feel proud of having
been the birth-place of such a brilliant genius.

The effects which Mrs. Jordan possessed at St. Cloud
were taken possession of by the officers of police, and
after a certain time put up to auction. The proceeding
seems to have been official, in consequence of her dying
in France intestate, when it becomes the duty of the
public solicitor to collect and dispose of all property
belonging to persons deceased under such circumstances,
for the benefit of creditors. Even her personal wardrobe
was sold, amidst coarse jibes and vulgar mockery. The
fact rests on the evidence of an English gentleman who
was present, and purchased some trifling memorials.
This sad instance supplies a new and equally mournful

application of Pope's lines, in his celebrated " Elegy on an Unfortunate Lady : "—

> " What can atone, O ever-injur'd shade !
>   Thy fate unpitied, and thy rites unpaid !
>   No friend's complaint, no kind domestic tear,
>   Pleas'd thy pale ghost, or grac'd thy mournful bier.
>   By foreign hands thy dying eyes were clos'd,
>   By foreign hands thy decent limbs compos'd ;
>   By foreign hands thy humble grave adorn'd,
>   By strangers honour'd, and by strangers mourn'd."

It has been often said that Mrs. Jordan wrote the farce of the " Spoiled Child," which, through her admirable acting in *Little Pickle,* obtained more notoriety than it deserved. But there is stronger evidence to show that it is the production of Isaac Bickerstaff.

The loss of Mrs. Jordan to the stage was in some measure compensated for by the accession of two most accomplished performers, in very opposite lines—Miss Stephens and Miss O'Neill. The former appeared on the 23d of September, 1813 ; the latter on the 14th of August, in the year following, both at Covent Garden, which theatre thus obtained a counterpoise to the overwhelming attraction of Edmund Kean at the opposite house. In those days the great national establishments were rivals, but not enemies. They lent their performers freely. to each other when required, and carried on competition on liberal principles. The two last-named ladies have long retired from public life, and are enjoying the ease and happiness of domestic privacy : the one the widow of an earl, the other of a baronet. The Countess of Essex is the third enchanting *Polly,* whose sweet voice and gentle nature elevated her into the peerage she has so long adorned. The first was Lavinia Fenton, who became no less a personage than

Duchess of Bolton; and the second, Mary Katharine Bolton, who married Lord Thurlow.

Sweet is the remembrance of our early days, when we first heard the "Stephens" warble "her native wood-notes wild," at Covent Garden, before the invasion of foreign cadenzas and interminable flourishes which have since completely superseded the charms of simple melody. Her voice still vibrates in our ears, clear and ringing as the early carol of the lark, rich and spontaneous as the strings of pearls and diamonds flowing from the lips of the damsel in the fable, when rewarded for her good-nature by the benevolent fairy.

Miss O'Neill only gladdened the hearts of her admirers for five years—a short period in which to achieve histrionic immortality. Her appearance was loveliness personified; her voice the perfection of melody; her manner graceful, impassioned, and irresistible. Inferior to Siddons in grandeur, and in depicting the more terrible and stormy passions of human nature, she excelled that great mistress of her art in tenderness and natural pathos. She had also the additional attractions of youth, beauty, and novelty. In *Lady Macbeth, Constance, Volumnia, Margaret of Anjou, Euphrasia,* and *Lady Randolph,* she fell far below her predecessor; while in *Juliet, Belvidera, Isabella,* and *Mrs. Haller,* candour must admit that she surpassed her. You trembled before Mrs. Siddons, you wept with Miss O'Neill. You were awed by the one, and subdued by the other. Adoration was the sentiment produced by the first; the second you might venture to love. Mrs. Siddons presented a being exalted above humanity, to admire and gaze upon with wonder; but whom you hesitated to approach in familiar intercourse. Miss O'Neill invited sympathy, and while she suffered with intenseness, appeared incapable of retaliation. She embodied the gentle sacrifice of Aulis, rather than the sanguinary priestess of Taurica.   We do not say that she was more natural than Mrs. Siddons, but she was more like every-day nature—more closely resembling what you expected to meet in the common intercourse of life.   Some starched, mechanical old ladies, insensible to passion or feeling, whose blood had congealed with age and abstinence, or, perhaps, had never liquified, objected to her impas-sioned gesticulation and fervid utterance, as being, as they said, boisterous, extravagant, and bordering on indecorum.   It was perceived, after her first season, that she listened too much to such frigid criticism, and tamed down her impersonations accordingly.   A leading point of censure with this class of objectors, was her mode of acting the scene in which she recognizes *Biron*, in the fourth act of the " Fatal Marriage."   To us, with our young feelings as yet in their full flow, this appeared so exquisitely touching, so like reality, that we indulged in loud sobs, until frowned down and stared into their suppression.

For her own happiness, Miss O'Neill was doubtless right in quitting the profession she so eminently adorned, but her premature retirement occasioned a public lamen-tation, long indulged before she was forgotten.   Miss O'Neill's last appearance in London occurred on the 13th of July, 1819, as *Mrs. Haller*.   It was not announced as a final performance, but merely as her closing night before Christmas.   She acted afterwards in Edinburgh and Dublin, and, finally, at the private theatre in Kil-kenny, from whence she married Sir W. Wrixon Beecher.   Her portrait, by Joseph, as the Tragic Muse, fails to convey anything like an adequate idea of her personal attributes.   The best likeness is a full length, in *Juliet*, by Chalon, of which good engravings are now rarely obtained.

On the 1st of June, 1815, an actor of great and versatile powers, Jack Bannister, as he was familiarly called, made his last bow on the boards he had so long trod with universal admiration. His closing characters were *Echo*, in Kenney's comedy of the " World," revived for the occasion, and *Walter*, in the " Children in the Wood." In his farewell address to the audience, he said that his health warned him to retire (gout was his besetting malady), and that their patronage had given him the means of doing so with comfort. At the conclusion of his speech, he bowed respectfully to the house, and was led off by his brother actors, who attended for the purpose. No performer ever quitted the stage more deservedly respected or regretted. Bannister enjoyed the calm evening of his repose, and the social intercourse he so much loved, for twenty years. He died on the 7th of November, 1835, at his residence in Gower-street, being then in his seventy-sixth year. He was the last pupil of Garrick, and a scholar well worthy of the master who carefully instructed him in several leading characters.

When Bannister adopted the stage as a profession, he had only entered on his nineteenth year. His first essay was at the Haymarket, as *Dick*, in the " Apprentice," for his father's benefit, on the 27th of August, 1778. On the 15th of November following, he performed *Zaphna*, in, " Mahomet," at Drury-lane, followed in two months after, by *Dorilas*, in Aaron Hill's translation of Voltaire's " Merope," and *Achmet*, in " Barbarossa." In his next season, he restored " Hamlet " to its original form, and banished for ever the tasteless interpolations by which Garrick, not long before he resigned the managerial sceptre, had degraded Shakespeare and his own genius. Whether, in perpetrating this dramatic sin, he was moved by vanity, or by the criticisms of

Voltaire, it is difficult to say. In a letter to Sir William Young, preserved by Dibdin in his "Reminiscences," Garrick acknowledges, that his producing Hamlet " with alterations " was the most impudent thing he ever did: but he had sworn he would not leave the stage until he had rescued that noble play from all the rubbish of the fifth act. Garrick himself asserted that the alteration had been received with general applause; but there is reason to think, from less interested authority, that the public merely endured, and were glad to be relieved from it. Of the actor's two biographers, Davies is silent on the subject, and Murphy names it with unqualified censure, adding the pithy remark that, as Garrick never printed his alterations (contrary to his invariable custom in similar cases), it seems he saw his error. Boaden discovered the manuscript copy of the transformed tragedy in the library of the late John Kemble, to whom it had been presented by Mrs. Garrick, and describes it minutely in his memoir of that eminent performer.

Twenty-four years after Bannister had revived " Hamlet " at Drury Lane, he happened to fall into conversation on that event with Waldron (an enthusiastic admirer of Garrick), in the green-room at the Haymarket. " Do you know, Waldron," said he, " who first restored the scene of the grave-diggers, and played Hamlet on the occasion? It was I."

" Yes," Waldron answered, " and you ought to have known better; had Garrick been alive, he would have been justly angry with you; and I'll tell you what,— when you go to heaven, Bannister, and meet Garrick, his first expression will be, ' I am very glad to see you, Jack!—but why did you bring back the grave-diggers?' "

Strange are the mutations of an actor's career. Ten

years more rolled on after this conversation, and Bannister then found himself representing the first of these same grave-diggers, in the same theatre, when Edmund Kean personated the *Prince of Denmark*. One night, while he stood waiting to go on for this insignificant duty, he overheard an interesting discussion. A knot of ancient stage-carpenters were speaking of *Hamlet*, and each commented on his favourite performer. "You may talk of Henderson, and Kemble, and this new man," said one of them, "but Bannister's *Hamlet* for me; he was always done twenty minutes sooner than anybody else."

Honest Jack rendered full justice to the meteoric genius of Kean. Being asked what he thought of him as an actor, particularly as to his manner of playing *Richard the Third*, in comparison with the performance of the same character by Garrick, and whether he could recollect Garrick's *Richard*, he answered, "Yes; very distinctly." "For some time," he added, "I could not form a judgment, and yet was unable to account for it. I had only seen Kean from behind the scenes, so one night I seated myself rather beyond the centre of the pit, and there he appeared to me another man. You think this strange, but it is true. In this new and, as I suppose, proper station, I seemed at once to discover his merits, which grew upon my faculties, first to approbation of his powers, until I ended in surprise and admiration. Indeed, I found his conception of the character so entirely original and so excellent, that I almost forgot my old master, Davy Garrick."

On the night of Kean's first performance in *Richard*, a knot of fashionable loungers and unemployed actors were canvassing his merits in the green-room; some loud in panegyric, others qualifying their remarks with sarcasm. "This is really a wonderful man," said a warm admirer. "Yes," replied a sceptic, "I understand that he is an admirable harlequin." "I am certain of that," retorted Bannister, who was present, "for he has jumped over all our heads."

Bannister, during his early novitiate, was considered a tragedian of great promise, but it soon began to appear that his *forte* lay in a very opposite and peculiar line. He combined the serious with the comic in a manner difficult to understand. Those who recollect his *Walter*, his *Sheva*, in the "Jew," and *Storm*, in "Ella Rosenberg," have seen him elicit smiles and tears almost at the same moment. He had a noble countenance, capable of the most varied and rapid expression, a full, sonorous, flexible voice, and a sparkling animation in his eyes that rivalled the brilliancy of those of Garrick. His power of assuming distinct characters was nearly equal to that of the English Roscius. Of this, his *Colonel Feignwell*, in the comedy of "A Bold Stroke for a Wife," may be singled out as a remarkable instance. The part contains a compound of many different ingredients, and requires for each individual assumption, an opposite cast of features, manner, utterance, and action. All these Bannister exhibited with such masterly effect, that spectators unacquainted with the comedy would be led to believe that the various individuals he represented were not performed by one, but successively personified by different persons. This happy union of ease and versatility requires executive power, even more rarely accorded than mental conception. If an actor is able to assume youth, age, love, hatred, revenge, jealousy, joyous mirth, gloomy despair, and all the passions inherent in the human composition; if he can so completely change his voice, alter his features, and, with the aid of dress, persuade an audience that he is the identical character drawn by the author;

then, indeed, the perfection of his art is attained. But
to communicate all the little delicate but important
touches of nature, which are the physical qualities of
every man, often becomes too difficult for the most
accomplished actor to portray, although his hourly
intercourse with society calls forth all those feelings,
which he, nevertheless, is unable to depict with equal
fidelity when required to assume them on the stage.
The obvious reason appears to be, that what is most
natural is the most difficult to imitate; and, as Quintilian observes of eloquence, " Nothing is harder than
what every one imagines to be so easy that he could
have done it himself."   The same remark applies to a
beautiful composition which the reader often thinks he
could have expressed with equal elegance. We speak not
here of the inherent vanity which lurks in the corner of
every heart, and which induced honest, unsophisticated
Goldsmith to exclaim, in a burst of indignation, when
the dancing of the Fantoccini was praised, " Why, I
can jump higher than that little fellow myself! "—or of
the professional jealousy of Johnson, the machinist of
Drury Lane, who, when, by an unheard-of innovation,
the real Chunee was introduced into a pantomime,
growled out, as the animal made its entrance, " I should
be sorry if I could not make a better elephant than
that! "   When Imlac, in " Rasselas," under the excitement of professional enthusiasm, describes a great poet,
we may, without much exaggeration, apply his description to an accomplished actor. The materials requisite to constitute either are nearly the same. Before
the man of learning had enumerated half of them, the
Prince of Abyssinia exclaimed impatiently, " Enough,
thou hast convinced me that no human being can ever
be a poet." " To be a poet," said Imlac, " is indeed
very difficult." " So difficult," returned the Prince,

"that I will at present hear no more of his labours. Proceed with thy narration."

We conclude our brief notice of Bannister with an epigram addressed by an old friend, Sir George Rose, to the "Young Veteran," when he had passed his seventieth year :

> " With seventy years upon his back,
> Still is my honest friend ' Young Jack ; '
> Nor spirits check'd, nor fancy slack,
>   But fresh as any daisy.
> Though time has knock'd his stumps about,
> He cannot bowl his temper out,
> And all the Bannister is stout,
>   Although the steps be crazy."

The mortal remains of one of the most convivial hosts that ever dispensed hospitality lie in the parish church of St. Martin-in-the-Fields, and are deposited in a vault close by those of his father.

In little more than three months after Bannister had taken his leave of the stage, another " Honest Jack " presented himself, to fill his place, in the person of John Pritt Harley, who appeared at Drury Lane as *Lissardo*, in the comedy of the "Wonder," on the 10th Sept. 1815, followed on the 23d by *Dr. Pangloss*, in the " Heir-at-Law."   He soon became a general favourite, stepping with public approbation into many of the most important parts vacated by his predecessor.   For forty-three years he held his ground, in the language of the old tournaments, " against all comers."   Harley followed Bannister without resembling him either in person or style.   Both were original comedians, who seldom failed to come up to the full expectations of the audience.   Their names were often associated in comparison, although nothing could be more unlike than the manner in which they represented the same characters.   The retired veteran took a warm interest in the recruit whom he delighted to call his theatrical son and successor, bestowing on him, from time to time, much valuable instruction and friendly advice. Amongst other tokens of regard, he gave him, during his last illness, his Garrick mourning ring, his Shakespeare jubilee medal, set in a silver box, and a handsome walking stick, formerly used at Windsor by King George III. and which had been purchased for Bannister by Mr. Rundall, the jeweller.

On the 26th of September, 1816, an actor destined to fill an important place in theatrical history—William Charles Macready—made a highly successful first appearance at Covent-garden, in the character of *Orestes*, in the "Distressed Mother," which he repeated on the following Friday. He was then only in his twenty-fourth year, but had already won extended reputation in the leading provincial theatres, although, like others who have achieved high histrionic honours, he was not intended for the stage. A classical education, at Rugby, had amply qualified him for one of the learned professions. His second London part was *Mentevole* in " Julia, or the Italian Lover," a forgotten play by Jephson, first acted in 1787, and shelved after a few representations, in consequence of John Kemble's severe indisposition, brought on, it was said, by his great exertions in the repulsive hero. These opening parts were injudiciously chosen. The two plays had none of the ingredients of immortality, and could scarcely confer on the actor what they possessed not in themselves. Soon after, he appeared as *Othello* and *Iago*, alternately with Young. But the ground was too much occupied during his early seasons. He had to wait for opportunities which came sparingly and not always in the most desirable forms. In Shiel's tragedies, written expressly for Miss O'Neill, Young, C. Kemble, and himself, Mr. Macready evinced powerful and brilliant conceptions in what are generally termed "up-hill" characters, and contributed his ample share to the success which such an unusual combination of talent would have commanded for plays of inferior pretension. But ever and anon he was condemned to waste his strength, and driven from an advancing post, in support of such unprofitable nondescripts as " Proof Presumptive," " The Conquest of Taranto," " The Castle of Paluzzi," and others, of a similar cast. Such original parts as *Gambia* in the " Slave," and *Rob Roy*, added considerably to his rising fame; but still these were of a dubious character, and left an impression on the public mind that their representative was an actor of the melo-dramatic class, rather than a legitimate tragedian in the highest walk. It was not until he developed his full resources as the hero of Knowles's noble drama of " Virginius" (in 1820), that he came in sight of the position to which he aspired: and even then, and long after, there were severe critics who questioned his pretensions as a great delineator of Shakespeare, with one or two admitted exceptions.

CHAPTER V.

DURING the seasons of 1815, 1816, and 1817, Edmund Kean continued to uphold the fortunes of Drury-lane by his unaided attraction. He might say with *Coriolanus*, "alone I did it," for his coadjutors were of a very doubtful quality; while at Covent-garden, a phalanx of tragic talent was arrayed against him, in the combined strength of John and Charles Kemble, Young, Macready, and Miss O'Neill. The press materially assisted Kean, but had the true fire of genius not burned brightly within him, all the laboured panegyric in the world could not have kept him up against the army of disadvantages he had to encounter at the onset. There were many old dogmatic sticklers who could not believe in a first-rate tragedian, unless he had a tall person, a stentorian voice, a solemn, conventional deportment, and a measured tone of declamation. To these, Kean was perfectly unintelligible; but, fortunately, they comprised a minority in number, although vehement in censure. This class of judges disregarded, or, perhaps, had never felt the truth of Churchill's more discriminating appreciation :—

> " Figure, I own, at first may give offence,
> And harshly strike the eye's too curious sense :
> But when perfections of the mind break forth—
> Humour's chaste sallies,—judgment's solid worth !
> When the pure, genuine flame, by nature taught,
> Springs into sense, and every action's thought,
> Before such merit, all objections fly—
> PRITCHARD's genteel, and GARRICK six feet high."

Others discovered that because the manner of the new actor could be reconciled to no established rules, it was a dangerous heresy, and ought to be resisted. Exactly the same was said of Garrick when he erected nature on the ruins of formality. Kean was familiar, epigrammatic, and antithetical; he was, therefore, pronounced an actor of impulse rather than study, and his most original points were set down as happy accidents. But the great majority of the public thought differently, and crowded to see him. It could scarcely be expected that John Kemble should warmly admire, or admit the superiority of a manner so diametrically opposed to his own; but he spoke candidly on the subject, and said : "It must be acknowledged that Mr. Kean is terribly in earnest." In that earnestness lay his herculean strength, and the power it enabled him to wield over the passions of his audience. The pit does not now rise, in a body, and stand for minutes on the benches, waving hats and handkerchiefs, as it often did to Edmund Kean, in the days of his early vigour. Let those also who lament the size of large theatres, remember that he produced his greatest effects with the eye, and by the muscular workings of his face; and that Drury-lane was his arena.

In 1816, he achieved one of his greatest triumphs, in the performance of *Sir Giles Overreach*, Massinger's Satanic hero of " A New Way to Pay Old Debts." The character was said to be taken from a living model, and is drawn with great strength, although coarse and repulsive in the extreme. Kean's performance was masterly; but less grand than his *Othello*, because the elements of the part are not compounded of heroic materials. He repeated *Sir Giles* twenty-six times during the season, and to crowded houses. The last scene was absolutely terrific. It threw ladies in the boxes into hysterics, and gave Lord Byron himself a convulsive fit. It was on the first night of this great success, when he returned home, that the excited tragedian replied to his wife's anxious inquiry, "Well, what *did* Lord Essex think of it?" "D—n Lord Essex, the pit *rose at me!*" Either moved by professional vanity, or misled by injudicious advisers, John Kemble entered the lists with his young and vigorous rival in this tremendous part—unsuited to him in his best days, and utterly beyond his grasp in his decay. The attempt was grievous to his admirers; the result most mortifying to himself, and disgraceful to the audience. They absolutely hissed the majestic ruin on which, when in the maturity of its classical perfection, they had gazed with wonder and delight for thirty years. So much for popular favour or consideration! Kemble felt the insult deeply, and murmured, "It is time I should retire!" Why did he place himself in such a humiliating predicament? Whatever might be his deficiences, he had powers and faculties which no other actor on the stage possessed. He might have trusted to these instead of throwing himself upon the charity of criticism. Had he, after long experience, become so little acquainted with the gratitude of the world as to trust to its generosity?

During the period of which we are now treating, Kean followed up his success with persevering industry, and gave but few indications of the erratic habits which afterwards became so habitual and destructive. His escapades were confined to one or two absences from

" serious accidents ; " and now and then he indulged in a midnight ride on his favourite steed Shylock, which endangered his own neck, and greatly bewildered the drowsy custodians of the turnpikes. On these occasions, he and his brother equestrians rode without saddles, after the fashion of Astley's, and made as much clatter along the high roads as if they had been rehearsing the wild chase in the air, under the impelling power of the demon huntsman.

Kean was not fortunate in original characters—valuable auxiliaries in an actor's career, as they remove him beyond the hazard of comparisons and pre-conceived conclusions. His best were *Bertram*, in Maturin's turgid tragedy ; *Barabbas*, in Marlowe's re-vived " Jew of Malta ; " and *Brutus*, in a concoction from many preceding plays on the same subject, by Howard Payne. His strength lay in Shakespeare, and to Shakespeare he always retreated after a questionable advance on less substantial ground. In the summer of 1818, being then at the zenith of his reputation, he passed through Paris with his wife, on their return from a continental tour. Talma had seen him act in London ; and in spite of a strong personal regard for John Kemble, with his own habitual predilections in favour of certain classical conventionalities, he felt and acknowledged the power of the genius which had recently established an original and opposite school. Kean was not behind him in reciprocal admiration. He had not of the small jealousies of mediocrity, but was ever ready to acknow-ledge merit in others, and to express the delight which he derived from the exercise of congenial talents. He always spoke of Mrs. Jordan, Cooke, and the Kembles in terms of the warmest admiration, while he carried his worship of Mrs. Siddons even beyond enthusiasm. He was also liberal to an extreme in his encouragement of young actors who played with him during his country tours. On one occasion he was so pleased with an *Iago*, who had carefully attended to all his stage business, that he invited him home to supper; and while they were enjoying themselves with two or three other selected *convivæ*, the tragedian, suddenly addressing the tyro, said, " Fill your glass, and I'll tell you something. Here's your health. You are the best *Iago* I ever played with." *Iago* bowed, and smiled; but, being something of a wag, observed, in returning thanks, " I should value beyond measure such an unexpected compliment from so great an authority, only "—he hesitated—" Only what," interrupted *Othello* impatiently? " I can scarcely believe it, for I know seven other *Iagos* to whom you have said the same thing." " Do you?" retorted the host, thrown for a moment upon his beam ends; " then Edmund Kean is a greater humbug than I took him for."

The day after their arrival in Paris, Kean came home in a hurry to the hotel where he and his wife had taken up their quarters, and said, with great excitement, " I have secured a box for this evening, to see Talma in *Orestes*. Prepare yourself for such a treat as you have never yet enjoyed; he is the greatest actor living, and this is his finest part. They took their places, and the curtain drew up. At the end of the first act, in which *Orestes* has little or no passion to portray, Mrs. Kean expressed herself as rather disappointed both in the appearance and manner of the star of the night. " Non-sense!" replied her husband; " you don't understand what you are saying. Nothing was ever like him. John Kemble and I put together would not make half such an actor. He is unapproachable." The play went on, and still Mrs. Kean was cold in her approbation, as her spouse, irritated and disappointed at her apathy, became more and more extravagant in his eulogies. At length, when *Hermione*, in the fourth act, abruptly names *Pyrrhus* as the enemy she expects *Orestes* to remove by assassination, the total change of expression in Talma's face, and his attitude, as the single word was pronounced, and he repeated it in utter bewilderment, compelled Mrs. Kean to burst forth in the most unqualified praise. From that moment Kean's countenance lowered, and he became silent. When the play terminated after the mad scene, Mrs. Kean loudly proclaimed her delight, declaring that she had never beheld anything to compare with Talma's acting. "Indeed!" exclaimed her husband; "I'll let you see that I can do better than that. Wait till I give them my mad scene!" As soon as he reached his hotel, he wrote to the Drury Lane Committee of Management, and requested them to prepare the "Distressed Mother" for his return, assuring them at the same time that he could do wonders with it. The play which Kean had suggested was forthwith put in rehearsal; but the frigid translation of Ambrose Philipps conveys but a faint adumbration of Racine, and the experiment disappointed the actor himself, his admirers, and the public. He had studied *Orestes* in a hurry, and forgot the text as soon as the London repetitions, which were only six in number, had subsided. Some months later, in the course of an engagement at Edinburgh, Murray, the manager, anxious for the last novelty, induced Kean to appear once more as *Orestes*. When he came to rehearsal on the day of performance, he found that all his efforts to recover the words correctly were fruitless. He retained only a general impression, with here and there a few of the most impassioned speeches. Addressing the *Pyrrhus* of the evening (the same *Iago* whom a few nights before he had so highly praised), he said to him, "Are you a cue-hunter?" Cue-hunter, to the experienced in stage phraseology, implies a matter-of-fact actor, who cannot get on without the exact word; but the young beginner to whom the question was put, in his innocence, imagined that it meant, "Are you perfect?" to which he answered with eager acquiescence, "You may rely upon it, sir, that I am to the letter." "The devil you are?" rejoined the inquirer; "then we shall be in a precious mess to-night, for hang me if I can recollect six consecutive lines of this infernal stuff. However, we must get through it as well as we can."

The play begins with an introductory scene between *Orestes* and *Pylades*. Then follows the delivery of the embassy to *Pyrrhus*, who is seated on his throne in full council. *Orestes* has been deputed by all the sovereigns of Greece to demand the intentions of *Pyrrhus*, as to his reported marriage with the widow of *Hector*, and to insist on the surrender of the young *Astyanax*, as a hostage for his good faith. All this is detailed in a long diplomatic speech, to which *Pyrrhus* replies with fencing diplomacy of the same class. On the speech of *Orestes* what follows is based, and unless this exordium is made clearly intelligible to the audience, the whole play resolves itself into a mystery. *Pyrrhus* can neither say nor do anything, until he knows what is required of him. The speech begins with these prosaic lines, of no meaning beyond empty compliment:—

> "Before I speak the message of the Greeks,
> Permit me, sir, to glory in the title
> Of their ambassador, since I behold
> Troy's vanquisher, and great Achilles' son."

Orestes then goes on to the business of the embassy.

"Now," said Kean in the morning to the *Pyrrhus*, "I foresee that I shall stick in this speech at night, so as soon as I feel that I am breaking down, I shall wink my off eye at you, and you can then come to the front and go on with your answer."

When night came, the first scene went off smoothly enough. With the change, *Pyrrhus* entered and ascended his throne R. H.; *Orestes* was introduced L. H., and began deliberately :—

"Before I speak the message of the Greeks" (a strong wink of the eye, repeated several times, and then, after a pause, with a quick epigrammatic turn,) " I wish to hear what you have got to say."

The house rang with applause, which gave the astonished King of Epirus time to collect himself; and as it was evident the ambassador was determined that he should speak first, he had nothing left for it but to proceed with his reply to uncommunicated proposals, and which, as far as the audience were concerned, might as well have been delivered in Chaldaic.

In the great interview with *Hermione*, in the fourth act, where *Orestes* has more to act with his face than to speak in words, Kean brought down loud acclamations. In the mad scene he threw himself body and soul into the fulness of the situation, and when at fault for the exact words, substituted lines and speeches from the more familiar frenzy of *Sir Giles Overreach*.

On the following day the papers unanimously condemned the play, but lauded the actor to the skies. The part, they said, was unworthy of the talent he threw away upon it, and the English adaptation of Racine poor and uninteresting. One critic remarked, that towards the conclusion certain passages fell upon the ear as incongruous and unclassical, but this might be owing to the clumsiness of the translation. The same writer said of *Pyrrhus*, " Mr. —— looked his part well, and was splendidly dressed. This gentleman, who is new to our boards, has promise, but he was evidently imperfect. We would suggest to him the propriety of more careful study when standing by the side of so great an actor as Mr. Kean."

Othello was unquestionably Kean's masterpiece; and his third act, the climax of that glorious piece of acting. Perhaps his very best performance during his whole career, was in this great character, on the 20th of February, 1817, when Booth was pitted against him in *Iago*. This Junius Brutus Booth, as he was called, had some slight resemblance to Kean in certain points of personal appearance, and sedulously aped him in his peculiar manner. He had made an accidental hit at Covent Garden a few days before, but left suddenly, in consequence of a misunderstanding as to salary. His unexpected success completely turned his head. He had many partisans, and was loudly applauded when he made his entrance at Drury Lane on that eventful night. During the two first acts *Iago* has the advantage. Booth stood his ground fairly at the onset, but in the third act Kean put forth all his strength, and literally strangled his opponent, who went out like the snuff of a candle, and never again appeared on the same boards. His name was announced in the bills for the 22d, but he was too ill to perform, and returned back to Covent Garden, where, after the usual tumult, explanation, and apology, he was permitted to appear to the end of the season, and gradually merged into insignificance. Yet it is lamentable to think that, while he retained ephemeral popularity, men like Young, Macready, and Charles Kemble, were doomed by the caprices of management to play, and sometimes subordinate characters, with one who had little pretension to compete with their established fame, even in an inferior capacity.

Booth quitted England somewhat hastily in or about the year 1821, to avoid the consequences of an assault upon Il Diavolo Antonio, a noted rope-dancer of the day. After a short sojourn in the West Indies, he betook himself to the United States, which ever afterwards became his head-quarters. There he contrived to accumulate money and reputation, in spite of many evidences of constitutional insanity, aggravated by intemperance. He died at New Orleans in 1852. Amongst other offensive absurdities, he was accustomed to besmear his mouth in the last scene of *Sir Giles Overreach* with a sponge charged with rose pink, to convey the idea that he had burst a blood-vessel. Once he played *Oronoko* with bare feet, insisting that it was absurd to put shoes on a slave. At the Circus in Philadelphia he enacted *Richard the Third* on horseback, an example which has been imitated at Astley's within the last year.

We have often asked ourselves whether Edmund Kean, if he were to appear now for the first time in London, would produce the effect and attraction which he commanded forty-five years since? We find it difficult to answer the question in the affirmative. Modern audiences are less easily worked up to strong demonstration than they were at the beginning of the present century. Yet, we venture to think, true nature, genuine passion, and genius will never fail to vindicate their superiority, let taste, caprice, or fashion incline into what channel they may. Kemble and Mrs. Siddons used to say that the unsophisticated applause of the gallery gave them more pleasure than the critical "bravos" of the pit and boxes, and was a safer criterion of excellence. Kean thought differently. Neither the very high nor the very low were in his opinion judges of acting. "The only critics worth caring for," he said, "are doctors, lawyers, artists, and literary men." Audiences now-a-days are more numerous than ever; but they sit, for the most part, in silent admiration. A round of applause is as startling as a peal of thunder in a cloudless sky. Where is it to come from? The stalls, boxes, and even the pit, are too genteel to clap their hands; and the Olympian deities are awed into silence by their isolation, and the surrounding chill.

Lord Byron's opinion on the great actors of his day, was, that Cooke was the most natural, Kemble the most supernatural, and Kean the medium between the two; but that Mrs. Siddons transcended them all. In the preface to "Marino Faliero" he says (and the passage is worth transcribing): "The long complaints of the actual state of the drama" (when have there not been these complaints?) "arise from no fault of the performers. I can conceive nothing better than Kemble, Cooke, and Kean, in their very different manners, or than Elliston in *gentleman's* comedy, and in some parts of tragedy. Miss O'Neill I never saw, having made and kept a determination to see nothing which should *divide* or *disturb* my recollections of Mrs. Siddons." (Is this to be received as a compliment to Miss O'Neill?) "Siddons and Kemble are the ideal of tragic actors; I never saw anything at all resembling them in *person*. For this reason *we* shall never again see *Coriolanus* or *Macbeth*. When Kean is blamed for want of dignity, we should remember that dignity is a grace, and not an art, and not to be attained by study. In all but *super-natural* parts he is perfect; even his very defects belong, or seem to belong, to the parts themselves, and appear truer to nature. But of Kemble we may say, in reference to his acting, what the Cardinal de Retz said of the Marquis of Montrose, 'that he was the only man he ever saw who reminded him of the heroes of Plutarch.' "

Kean, as Lord Byron says, may have been deficient in dignity, but he was singularly graceful in his action, to which his skill in dancing and fencing materially contributed. We have seen his attitude, while leaning against the wing, listening to *Lady Anne*, in " Richard the Third," call down loud applause from its striking elegance. Not so with poor Conway, who was so bullied by the newspapers for being tall, that he twisted himself into all sorts of incomprehensible bends to diminish the height, which many other actors would have given one of their eyes for.

Conway was a remarkably handsome man, and so popular in society, that when ladies in Bath and Newcastle gave invitations to tea, they added to the cards, " Mr. Conway will be present," as an additional inducement. Conway and Warde, when rival heroes in the Bath theatre, had each a patronizing dowager, who sat in opposite stage boxes, and led the applause for their respective protégés. The red and green factions of the circus at Constantinople, in the reign of Justinian, or the feuds of the Ursinis and Colonnas, during the middle ages, at Rome, never raged with greater intensity than the "Vereker" and "Piozzi" parties, which divided " British Baiæ" in support of their respective favourites of the buskin. When Warde was locked up in " durance vile" under a merciless creditor, he was fed daily with eleemosynary turkeys, fowls, and rounds of beef. When Conway fell sick from over-exertion, three physicians were despatched daily to his door; and no sooner was he pronounced convalescent, than turtle, venison, and pine-apples poured in to re-establish his physical man. Before this, he had also been extremely popular in Dublin. Fortune smiled on him until he appeared at

Covent Garden in 1813, as *Alexander the Great*. He played many corresponding parts with Miss O'Neill in 1814 and 1815, and though the public received him well, several of the influential journals crusaded against him, which drove him from the stage in disgust. He declined into the office of prompter at the Haymarket, went to America, and threw himself overboard on a voyage from New York to Charlestown, in a fit of insanity.

Conway was most unjustly treated. Despite the persecution of *John Bull* (the newspaper of that name, not the public), and the unmeasured invectives of Hazlitt, he was not only an amiable, inoffensive man, but a good, sensible actor.

Edmund Kean and Miss O'Neill had performed together in Dublin, but they never trod the same boards after both became famous in the English metropolis. An opportunity occurred in Nov. 1817, which excited great · expectation, but the proposed arrangement fell through. Raymond, formerly stage-manager at Drury-lane, had died rather suddenly, and a benefit was announced for his widow and family. Miss O'Neill, being permitted by the management of Covent-garden, offered her services to play *Juliet*, which offer was gladly accepted. Kean had acted *Romeo*, the season before, at the request of the committee, but much against his own desire. In the banishment and death scenes, he produced some telling points, but as a whole, the performance was not one of his happy efforts, and he was glad to erase it from his list. The part, too, is theatrically inferior to *Juliet*. He declined, therefore, to match himself with Miss O'Neill on such unequal terms. It was said, that he proposed " Macbeth," " Venice Preserved," or even " Douglas," but none of these plays could be arranged within the required time. He was then on the sick list, and the benefit could not be postponed beyond a certain date. The great coalition, for one night only, never took place. The performance ended in "Oroonoko," and the "Maid and Magpie," with the ordinary company and no star; but interest and sympathy produced an overflow, in spite of one of the weakest bills that could possibly be selected.

CHAPTER VI.

RETIREMENT OF JOHN KEMBLE—PUBLIC DINNER AND PRESENTATION OF A VASE—TALMA'S SPEECH—KEMBLE AS AN ACTOR—HIS BLACK-LETTER LEARNING—HIS SPLENDID LIBRARY AND REASONS FOR ITS COLLECTION—REFLECTIONS ON " BIBLIOMANIA"—PUBLIC LIBRARIES AND THEIR UTILITY—KEMBLE'S ROMAN COSTUMES—TALMA'S TOGAS INTRODUCED AS MORE CLASSICAL—GARRICK'S ALTERATIONS OF SHAKESPEARE—HARD USAGE OF THE GREAT POET.

WE must retrograde a little in our chronological series to record the last appearance of John Kemble, which took place at Covent Garden on the 23rd of June, 1817. *Coriolanus* was the chosen part; and, as if he had collected all his powers for a final effort, he never played with more force or effect. The night was long remembered. He had previously bade adieu to his friends in Edinburgh, in a poetical address, written by Sir Walter Scott; but on this more momentous occasion he confined himself to a few valedictory sentences in simple prose: thinking, perhaps, with Garrick, that " the jingle of rhyme and the language of poetry" would but ill accord with the feelings of such a moment. The whole of the boxes had been taken a fortnight previously; and in order to gratify the enthusiastic admirers of Mr. Kemble, who thronged to the box-office, impatient in their demands for seats in front of the house, beyond all precedent, the ordinary music was played behind the scenes, the orchestra being set aside for persons of the first rank and literary celebrity; amongst the latter, Talma, the renowned French tragedian, was particularly conspicuous.

As the great English actor made his final exit after his concluding address, a gentleman in the pit handed to the French Roscius a white satin embroidered scarf, accompanied by a laurel wreath and a letter, desiring him to place them on the stage. His graceful compliance with this request was warmly applauded. The manager being called for, Mr. Fawcett appeared, took up the tribute, and, having stated his conjectures as to the intentions of the house, professed unqualified delight at being directed to convey it to Mr. Kemble. The letter contained a request that he would not entirely withdraw, but would consent to perform a few nights each season, as long as his health permitted. Kemble remained deaf to the flattering appeal; and thenceforward his great achievements in the art he had so eminently adorned lived only in the memory of his admirers. While feelings of mingled respect and regret were prevailing before the curtain, they were still more powerfully evinced by Mr. Kemble's professional associates behind the scenes. All contended to be foremost in their expressions of kind condolence, and were eager to obtain some trifling memorial of their long-cherished love and admiration. Mathews received from his hands the gift of his sandals, which he held aloft in triumph, and exclaimed, " Although I am proud to have his sandals, I can never hope to tread in his shoes." Miss Bristow obtained the handkerchief he had used that evening while uttering his farewell, which she playfully promised to keep with more true faith than *Desdemona* did the first gift of the Moor. On Mr. Kemble's leaving the theatre, the stage entrance was filled up by all ranks of the dramatic corps, anxious to offer a last salutation to their veteran commander; while the outside of the door was thronged by individuals of all descriptions, eager to catch a last glimpse of their tried and valued favourite.

It had long been determined to present Kemble with a vase commemorative of his great services in the cause of the drama. This intention was carried out at a public dinner, which took place at the Freemasons' Tavern, on Friday, the 27th of June, four days after the retirement, Lord 'Holland in the chair. Soon after the cloth was removed, and the chairman had spoken, Young rose and delivered, with remarkable energy and pathos, the celebrated "Ode" written for the occasion by the Bard of Hope, which was pronounced weak, though laboured, at the time, but has since been perpetuated as combining much poetical beauty with a just and graceful eulogium. Talma was there, and when his health was proposed, in due course, replied in a short speech, which, however, proved long enough to get him into hot water when he crossed back to his own side of the Channel. Some of the anti-English papers in Paris accused him of unnationality, of *Anglo-mania*, of time-serving duplicity, and almost of treachery, for the sentiments conveyed in the few words he had spoken. His popularity was in danger, and he felt it necessary to reply, which he did in a very gentlemanlike explanatory letter to the editor of the *Moniteur.**

* A whimsical anecdote has been connected with John Kemble's first London engagement in 1784. He was acting in Dublin, and his reputation had reached the English metropolis. Ambassadors were sent simultaneously from Drury Lane and Covent Garden to treat with the great Kemble. But there were two brothers of that name then on the same spot. The Drury Lane envoy singled out the right man, John, and secured him for his employer. The rival diplomatist of Covent Garden came back laden with the younger brother, Stephen, who certainly proved to be a *great* Kemble; but not exactly in the sense anticipated. Although only in his twenty-sixth year, he already developed symptoms of the extreme corpulence which rapidly expanded to twenty-five stone in weight, and qualified him to be yoked in a team with Daniel Lambert. Six days only before John appeared in " Hamlet " at Drury Lane, Stephen was exhibited at Covent Garden as *Othello*, and announced as *Mr. Kemble*. This attempt on the part of the managers

John Kemble only survived his retirement for six years, and died at Lausanne in 1823, aged sixty-six. He was, undoubtedly, in tragedy a great actor, the founder of an imposing school, and the leader of many eminent followers. Sir T. Lawrence has faithfully handed him down to posterity as *Hamlet* and *Cato*. In the latter portrait, no bust of antique sculpture can exceed the classic contour of that noble head. The picture is complete, and historically correct, down to the ornament on the sandal, the shape of the lamp, and the colour of the papyrus on which the republican stoic is meditating on the lucubrations of Plato. We never witnessed Kemble's performance of this part; but his *Brutus* and *Coriolanus* are present to our recollection, as clearly impressed as if we looked on them yesterday, although a chasm of forty-two years has intervened. The first time we ever saw him was in 1816, in *King John*, on which occasion Miss O'Neill appeared as the *Lady Constance*, Charles Kemble as *Falconbridge*, and Mrs. Siddons sat in a stage-box. She applauded the young and lovely actress, who supplied her place, with marked delight, to which the audience responded in the warmest manner, although *Constance* fell by no means within the range of

to mislead the public as to the real Simon Pure by no means assisted the first candidate. He had a handsome face, a fund of jovial humour, which made him a most desirable companion ; and was also a sensible elocutionist. But higher attributes were wanting for the fiery Moor, who "loved not wisely, but too well." The choice proved to be worse than injudicious. Not ten years had elapsed since many of the audience had listened with delight to the silver tones of Barry. The new-comer was coldly received. Applause came sparingly, and accompanied by an occasional titter which marred "the cunning of the scene." "Othello" commanded no repetitions. His representative lingered through the season, appearing in a few characters of second-rate importance, and then departed to push his fortunes elsewhere. The time had not yet arrived when a Falstaff without stuffing could be announced as an attraction. Henderson was still alive, and until he made a vacancy, the merry knight and he had become identified as Siamese twins. , parts in which Miss O'Neill approached the nearest to her illustrious predecessor.

Kemble's fortune received much injury from the burning of Covent Garden Theatre, and he died less wealthy than might have been expected. His habits, with the exception of a passion for buying scarce old books, were not expensive. His library, which contained many valuable editions, was sold by auction, with the exception of the theatrical portion, purchased entire by the Duke of Devonshire, and now at Chatsworth. He was universally reputed an accomplished scholar; but his pronunciation of many words was too arbitrary, singular, and pedantic, to justify a claim to sound erudition. For these eccentricities, he could neither adduce classical nor etymological authority, nor even the sovereign rule of custom,

> "Quem penes arbitrium est, et vis, et norma loquendi."

Colman evidently had Kemble in his eye when he described Sir Edward Mortimer :—

> " Edward is all deep reading and black-letter ;
> He shows it in his very chin.   He speaks
> Mere dictionary, and he pores on pages
> That give plain sense the headache.   ' Scarce and curious '
> Are baits his learning nibbles at ; his brain
> Is cramm'd with mouldy volumes, cramp and useless,
> Like a librarian's lumber-room."

The picture is overcharged as such pictures generally are.   Charles Kemble, in conversation with the writer of these pages, has more than once said that his brother delighted in collecting, exhibiting, and arranging his rare copies, but that he read them less than people supposed.

In Boaden's life of Mrs. Jordan (vol. ii. pp. 144-5,) we find a curious passage which bears directly on this subject—Boaden, it must be observed, though a weak biographer, was a devoted worshipper of his idols :—

"Kemble," he says, "had long enjoyed the reputation of being a scholar, and of being pedantic in scholarship; he was accused of playing the commentator, where it was of little moment, and of living upon points and pauses. It is astonishing what hatred was worked up against him; and amongst other absurdities, those who disliked him, gifted him with *black-letter* tendencies, which most certainly he never had, though some friend on such a presumption, gave him a MS. of Chaucer's "Canterbury Tales," which it was supposed had been the favourite volume of his own Hotspur, and which he read with difficulty I know, and I am confident never read throughout. The old plays of his country he collected, because Mr. Garrick had done so before him; and besides that, he thought there should be in some library at hand, every play that could by possibility be used; that if any impositions were practised, their source might be pointed out. If there was some ostentation in all this, it is surely a natural foible in any actor to possess the materials of his art. His plays cost him many thousand pounds, and were uniformly bound together in several hundred volumes of the quarto shape. We may be sure, as to Shakespeare, the god of his idolatry, he had everything that could be got for money."

Poor Nat. Lee, who was himself as insane a Bedlamite as ever raved in poetry, has said,—

> " Surely there is a pleasure in being mad,
> Which none but madmen know."

The frenzy of book-collecting has also a peculiar charm intelligible only to the collector. Of all the passions to which the human mind can surrender itself, there is none more absorbing than the " Bibliomania." Let those speak honestly who have indulged in it. It is a species of *bulimia*—an insatiable appetite, which grows by what it feeds on. The writer has purchased his experience in this matter rather dearly, having at one period of his life occupied much time, and laid out more money than he likes to think of, in collecting a library. Books formed his chief solace and amusement during many years of an active life. Circumstances induced him to part with them, and taught the owner practically the vast distinction between buying and selling. It was something to see placarded in imposing type, " Catalogue of the valuable and select library of a gentleman, containing many rare and curious editions." But, alas ! the sum produced was scarcely a third of the intrinsic value, and less than half of the original cost. There have been instances—but they are " few and far between "—when libraries have been sold at a premium. Take, for an example, the collection of Dr. Farmer, of Emanuel College, Cambridge,—he who wrote so learnedly of Shakespeare's want of learning; and whose " unanswerable " Essay has been repeatedly answered and refuted. This library, singularly rich in Shakespearean authorities, and black-letter lore, produced above 2,200*l.*, and was supposed to have cost the author not more than 500*l.* Many works are presents : when you get the character of a collector, a stray gift often drops in, and scarce volumes find their way to your shelves, which the quondam owners, uninitiated in the bibliomania, know not the worth of. An excellent and perfect copy of the quarto " Hamlet," of 1611, was not long since purchased from an innocent bibliopolist for five shillings. The conscience of the buyer smote him, but the temptation was irresistible. This small, dingy volume, originally published at sixpence, has sold for 12*l.* The best copy in existence of the Caxtonian edition of Gower's " De Confessione Amantis," fol. 1483, one of the rarest amongst printed books, was purchased by a Dublin bookseller, at Cork (in 1832), with a lot of old rubbish, for a mere trifle, and was sold afterwards for more than 300*l.* It is now in the celebrated Spencer Library, at Althorp.

Books in all ages have brought fabulous prices. St. Jerome says, he ruined himself by buying a copy of the works of Origen. A large estate was given for a Treatise on Cosmography, by King Alfred, in 872. Two hundred sheep, and five quarters of wheat, have been exchanged for a single Homily, in the thirteenth and fourteenth centuries. In our own times, an Illustrated copy of Macklin's Bible has produced five hundred guineas. A yet more superb copy is actually insured in a London office at 3,000*l.* The " Decameron," of 1471, was bought at the Duke of Roxburgh's sale in 1812, by the Duke of Marlborough, for 2,260*l.*

What time does book-collecting occupy! What anxiety it excites! What money it requires! What evil passions it sets in motion! It makes man exclusively selfish, and withers up Christian charity. As Burns says, of another, and more unholy indulgence—

> " It hardens a' within,
> And petrifies the feeling."

Under the influence of this insanity, we live in a perpetual breach of the tenth commandment, coveting our neighbours' goods, and anticipating the hour of his departure, when we may compete for his " Valdarfer Boccaccio," his unique " Game and Play of the Chesse," printed by Caxton in 1474, or his first folio Shakespeare, with genuine title-page and portrait.

The great use of books is to read them. The mere accumulation is an empty fantasy. Your thoroughbred collector seldom reads anything but catalogues, after the mania has fully possessed him, or such bibliographical works as facilitate his purchases. Antonio Magliabecchi is an exception, and cannot be quoted as a type of the species. If you are too poor to buy, and desire to read, there are public collections in abundance to which access may be obtained. There is a circulating library in every village, and there are plenty of private ones undisturbed by their owners. Subscribe or borrow; don't *steal!*—a common practice enough, and not without authority.* If your friends are churlish, and hesitate to lend; if your pockets are empty, and you have no cash even to subscribe, still you *can think*—you may try to remember what you *have* read, and live on your recollections of past enjoyment, as the *Wife of Bath* does in old Chaucer's tale. You'll save your eyes too, and, when you get on the shady side of life, you will find that point worthy of attention.

After all, what do we collect for? At most, a few years' doubtful possession of what we can very well do without. When Sir Walter Raleigh was on his way to execution, he asked for a cup of ale, and observed, as he quaffed it, "That is good drink, if a man could only stay by it." So are rare and curious libraries good things, if we could stay by them; but we cannot. When the time comes, we must go, and then our books, and pictures, and prints, and furniture, and china, go too; and are knocked down by the smirking callous auctioneer, with as little remorse as a butcher knocks a bullock on the head, or a poulterer wrings round the neck of a pullet, or a surgeon excises your arm out of the socket, chuckling at his own skill, whilst you are writhing in unspeakable agony.

Reader, once more, don't collect books, and envy not the possessors of costly libraries. Read and recollect,

---

* " This borrow, *steal,*—don't buy."
          Vide " Childe Harold's Pilgrimage."

how and when you can. Of course you have a Bible and Prayer-book. Add to these the "Pilgrim's Progress," Shakespeare, Milton, Pope, Byron (if you like), a History of England, Greece, and Rome, Boswell's "Life of Johnson," and Napier's "Peninsular War." A moderate sum will give you these ; and you possess a cabinet encyclopædia of religious, moral, historical, miscellaneous, and entertaining knowledge, containing more than you want for practical purposes, and quite as much as your brains can easily carry. Never mind the old classics. They may abound in wisdom and philosophy, but they are intolerably slow. Leave them to college libraries, where they look respectable, and enjoy long slumbers. The monthly periodicals and leading papers will place you much more *au courant* with the conversation and popular acquirements of the day. Should you happen to be in business of any kind, add, if you can, to the books we have named, *a Ledger*, with a good sound balance on the right side, and you will be a happier and perhaps a better read man, than though you were uncontrolled master of the Bodleian, the Imperial Library of France and the innumerable tomes of the Vatican into the bargain.

Don't collect books, I tell you again emphatically. Collect wisdom ; collect experience ; above all, collect *money ;* not as our friend Horace recommends, " *quo cunque modo,*" but by honest hard-working industry alone. And, when you have done this, remember who gave you the advice, and be grateful.

What is said here applies to private collecting only. Far be it from the writer to discourage great public libraries, which, under proper arrangements, are great national benefits, useful to society, and invaluable to literature. But, as they are regulated at present, fenced round with so many restrictions, and accessible chiefly to privileged dignitaries, or well-paid officials who seldom trouble them, they are little better than close boroughs with a very narrow constituency. Let it be remembered, however, on the other side, that the public misuse their indulgences, and are little to be trusted. Not one in twenty either knows or cares how to handle a book, not his own property, with becoming delicacy. It is easier to nurse a child.——But we have galloped away into a long and unpardonable digression, from which we must dismount, and resume our subject.

Kemble's widow, who was much younger than himself, and by whom he had no children, survived him for many years.* Like Garrick, he married for happiness rather than ambition, and made a most fortunate choice. Many stories have been told of the immediate cause and manner of his courtship; how he received a large sum from a noble lord whose daughter had fallen in love with him, on condition that he married within a given time; how he proposed to Mrs. Brereton, giving her a fortnight to deliberate; and how she considered that delays might be dangerous, and accepted him at once. Some of these, including his alleged absence of mind as to the important change of condition on his wedding-day, are humorous exaggerations, and others have been repeated *ad nauseam*.

It would be impossible to conceive anything finer than Kemble's appearance in the Roman costume, as introduced by himself. When he revived " Coriolanus" and " Julius Cæsar " at Covent Garden, his togas, then for the first time exhibited on the English stage, became the theme of universal admiration. They were pronounced faultless, minutely classical, even to the long-disputed *latus clavus*, severely correct, and beautifully

* She had been previously married to Brereton, an actor in the Drury Lane company, who died insane, in 1787.

graceful beyond precedent. But when the peace brought France and England together, and the treasures of the Louvre presented all the authorities under one glance which had been so long shut out from British eyes, it was found that Talma's senatorial robes were much nearer the truth. Whereupon they were, in due course, transplanted to the London boards, and the Kemble garments were deposed. Charles Young, the affectionate disciple of Kemble, was the first who adopted the new mode, which he studied under the restorer; and Charles Kemble himself, when attiring for *Marc Antony*, was wont to repair to Young's dressing-room before presenting himself on the stage, to be inspected, and assured that the folds of his toga were perfectly arranged according to the Talma model.

Kemble obtained great credit with the audiences of the day for his Shakespearean revivals; yet they cannot stand comparison for a moment, either in accuracy of text, costume, architectural details, or mechanical appliances, with the magnificent series we have all witnessed during Mr. Charles Kean's period of management at the Princess's Theatre. Of this, we shall speak more at large in the proper place. Half a century ago, the public were not ripe for the knowledge which they now imperatively demand, and the instructor himself was *unoculus inter cæcos*—the one-eyed teaching the blind. With all our traditional admiration of Garrick as an actor, we cannot close our eyes to the fact that he committed heavy sins against Shakespeare in the exercise of his managerial power, and the indulgence of his literary ambition. He never could forego the temptation of a clap-trap, and sacrificed consistency to what he considered effect without scruple or remorse. He literally pandered to, instead of attempting to amend or exalt, the vitiated tendencies of the million; his

" alterations," as he called them, were singularly auda-
cious ; and not less so was his prologue to one of the
most objectionable (the " Winter's Tale "), which he
winds up by saying,—

> " 'Tis my chief wish, my joy, my only plan,
> To lose no drop of that immortal man."

And with these jingling lines, he introduces a noble
drama, unmercifully cut down from five acts to three,
and in which dull platitudes are substituted for the
original inspiration.   There was justice in the severity
with which Theophilus Cibber reflected on Garrick in a
dissertation delivered at the Haymarket in 1756.   He
says, " Were Shakespeare's ghost to rise, would he not
pour indignation on this mender of poetry which wants
no repairs, who thus mangles, mutilates, and transforms
his plays ?   The ' Midsummer Night's Dream ' has
been minced and fricasseed into a thing called the
' Fairies,' the ' Winter's Tale ' mammocked into
a droll, and the ' Tempest ' changed into an opera.
Yet this sly prince would insinuate that all this ill-usage
of the bard is owing, forsooth, to his love of him ; much
such a proof of tender regard as the cobbler's drubbing
his wife."   Strange liberties were indulged in in those
days, which the superiority of modern taste utterly
repudiates.   John Kemble was a better scholar than
Garrick ; yet he sanctioned Dryden and Davenant's
monstrous interpolations in the " Tempest," calling them
Shakespeare's, transplanting the storm to the second
act, and removing *Prospero's* celebrated speech of " the
cloud-capp'd towers " from its natural position to the
end, for the sake of an effective tag.   He also perpetuated Tate's mawkish absurdities in " King Lear,"
with the loves of *Edgar* and *Cordelia*, and the unhappy
substitution of a happy catastrophe.   He retained

Garrick's weak additions to the " Winter's Tale " and " Cymbeline," his reduction of the " Taming of a Shrew " into a farce, together with Thompson's or Sheridan's last act of " Coriolanus."

It is really a matter of wonder, how a man of reputed classical mind and experienced judgment, could lend himself to such crying mistakes. Dr. Johnson observes with truth, " There is not, perhaps, any play of Shakespeare which could be represented on a modern stage as originally written." But, fortunately, his plays are very long ; and after the omission of all exceptionable passages, more than sufficient materials remain for five acts. The real friends of the immortal poet are no advocates for his faults, for even his transcendent genius has its blemishes. They are only desirous of seeing him represented with no changes but such as are absolutely necessary, and feel naturally indignant when influential followers, like Garrick and Kemble, who have given their sanction to the crudities of Tate, Cibber, and Co., are yet so inconsistent as to talk of their veneration for the great original. If Shakespeare encountered John Kemble in the Elysian Fields, unless he held aloof indignantly, as the ghost of Ajax did from the still living Ulysses, he might perhaps say to him, " I thank you heartily for your performance of my *Coriolanus, Hamlet, Brutus, Macbeth,* &c.—but did you never hear the good old proverb, ' Let every one stick to his trade ?' Why would you tamper with the text of my plays ? Why give many of my characters names which never entered my imagination ? Above all, what could induce you to restore such passages of Tate, as even Garrick had rejected when he revived ' King Lear ' ? Saint Lawrence never suffered more torture on his gridiron than I have endured from the prompt-book."

CHAPTER VII.

KEMBLE laboured under a constitutional asthma, which obliged him to husband his powers, and restrained him from daringly carrying out his own conceptions. He was ever apprehensive that his voice might fail him in an arduous part, and this sometimes imparted an appearance of languor and monotony to his best efforts. He was often compelled to check himself in the fullest tide of passion, from dread of a physical break-down. Churchill, in his encomium on Garrick, in the "Rosciad," dwells emphatically upon the advantages of the—

> " Strong expression and strange powers which lie
>   Within the magic circle of the eye ;"

and in this criticism he is right. But even the wonders of the eye will lose much of their charm if not supported by the still more imposing organ of the voice.   Of all the personal faculties which a great actor requires, the voice is that which above all others will, according to its strength or weakness, help or impede the execution of his conceptive genius. Where nature has bestowed the power, intonation will obey, with mechanical submission, the compulsive dictate of feeling. Edmund Kean's voice was melodious in the lower notes, but defective in the higher, under the exercise of violent emotion. Young and Macready were magnificently gifted in this respect; but Talma excelled them all; his intonation was wonderful; and his voice possessed a compass and a musical cadence which fell upon the ear with the effect of many well-tuned instruments blended together—a diapason more perfect than human mechanism has ever yet invented to improve and regulate sound. Dugazon, an actor of eminence on the French stage, under Louis XVI., held a theory peculiar to himself. He used to maintain that the nose was the most complete organ of expression, and wrote an essay, with diagrams, to show that there were forty distinct modes of moving this single feature with variety of effect.

Kemble paid great attention to the minutiæ of the stage, as they were understood in his day, and introduced many alterations of costume; but sometimes he fell into strange mistakes, and was so dogmatic, that he refused to rectify them on evidence. In *Hamlet* he wore an elephant suspended by a blue ribbon from his neck, and a modern star on his cloak, like that belonging to an English order of knighthood. Guthrie tells us, in his "Universal History," that the Order of the Elephant was instituted by Christiern I., of Denmark; but Christiern I. began to reign in 1448, whereas, Shakespeare has clearly fixed the time of the action of his play several centuries earlier. Besides, if it were proper for *Hamlet* to have the effeminate appendage of a badge and ribbon, *à fortiori* the King ought to be decorated after the same fashion.

In the early scenes of *Posthumus* in "Cymbeline," Kemble wore a half modern, open tunic, trimmed with spangles, a ruff, tight pantaloons, and boots of russet leather. This strange garb contrasted incongruously with the Roman togas and shirts of *Jachimo* and *Philario;* and still more so with his own military panoply, resembling that of *Coriolanus* or *Brutus*, in which he arrayed himself for the discovery in the last act.

Kemble, when playing *Hamlet*, always instructed *Guildenstern* to attempt to exit before him in one of the scenes; this breach of etiquette he checked by a severe look, and then walked off with much dignity. He did something of the same kind with *Campeius*, in the second act of " Henry the Eighth;" and both these arrangements of what is called "stage-business," were greatly lauded as profound readings of the author. They might have stood for such had there been one syllable in the text to warrant them, but as no such interpretations are there to be found, they must be looked upon as stage trickery, below the practice of a great actor. In *Leon* he made no scruple of kicking *Cacafogo*, but *Cacafogo* was not allowed to give the original provocation, which utterly destroys the gist of the retort. If he had played *Stukely*, he might equally have objected to being struck by *Lewson*. When Mrs. Siddons assumed the part of the termagant *Lady Loverule*, for a benefit freak, she left out the strapping as the cobbler's wife. If performers of the first class descend, for their own advantage, to what conventional critics call inferior *rôles*, assuredly they ought to discharge them in their " severe integrity," or let them alone altogether.

Kemble's best parts may be considered, *Coriolanus, Brutus, Cato, Hamlet, King John, Wolsey, Jacques, Leontes, Macbeth, Hotspur, Leon, Zanga, Octavian, Penruddock*, the *Abbé De l'Epée*, the *Stranger, Rolla*, and

De Montfort. Not long before his retirement, he was for several days underlined for *Falstaff,* and wore the dress in his room to become accustomed to it. His friends wisely saved him from what must of necessity have proved a pitiable mistake. The actor who could play eighteen such characters as those we have enumerated above, better than any other living representative, might be satisfied with ranking as a rare exception which scarcely occurs once in a century. Universality of genius is given to no one. Garrick failed comparatively in *Marplot* and *Othello.*

John Kemble was convivial in his habits, fond of late hours, and given to indulge freely in post-prandial libations when his company pleased him. But he had the systematic prudence never to exceed when there was business in hand. "A man," he would say, "should get drunk occasionally; it gives nature a fillip." He was a humorist, too, after a peculiar fashion; but his jokes and his laugh were somewhat sepulchral. Even when completely under the influence of wine, he never relapsed from his habitual solemnity of manner, and stately mode of speech. When young on the stage, he fancied, under the strange hallucination by which actors are frequently possessed, that he was gifted with the attributes of gay, dashing comedy. Tate Wilkinson tells us that he selected *Plume, Doricourt, Archer, Ranger,* and similar parts, to please himself, and not by the desire of either manager or public. A smile on his countenance appeared to wonder how it got there. As John Wilson Croker said in the "Familiar Epistles," it resembled the plating on a coffin. He then goes on to say—

> "Young *Mirabel* by Kemble play'd,
> Look'd like *Macbeth* in masquerade,"

and adds, in a note, "I have had the misfortune to *see* this exhibition; truly it was, as Shakespeare's clowns say of their interlude of "Pyramus and Thisbe," 'very tragical mirth.'"

Reynolds tells an amusing anecdote, for which he quotes the authority of Kemble himself. In 1791 the great tragedian chose to act *Charles Surface*. Some time afterwards Reynolds and Kemble met at a dinner: the flattering host asserted that *Charles Surface* had been lost to the stage since the days of Smith, and added, that Kemble's performance of the part should be considered as *Charles's Restoration*. On this a less complimentary guest observed, in an under tone, that it should rather be considered as *Charles's Martyrdom*. Kemble overheard the remark, and said, with much good humour, "I will tell you a story about this, which proves that you are right. Some few months ago, having unfortunately taken what is usually called a glass too much, I inadvertently quarrelled with a gentleman in the street. On the next morning, when I came to my senses, I felt that I was in the wrong, and offered to make him any reasonable reparation. 'Sir,' interrupted the gentleman, 'at once I meet your proposal, and name one—promise me never to play *Charles Surface* again, and I shall be perfectly satisfied.' I gave the promise, and have kept it; for though Mr. Sheridan was pleased to say he liked me in the part, I certainly do not like myself." Kemble, when he told this story, had seen his error, and put the best face he could on it; but certain it is that when he first acted *Charles*, he was very desirous of having his performance lauded in the papers. Mrs. Wells has printed in her "Memoirs," a letter from Kemble to Captain Topham, in which he says, "I hope you will have the goodness to give orders to your people to speak favourably of the *Charles*, as

more depends on it than you can possibly be aware of."
Topham, in reply, declared that he could not sacrifice
the credit of his paper by puffing either Mrs. Siddons or
Kemble in comedy.

Mrs. Siddons used sometimes to sing comic songs in
private (we have been told that "Billy Taylor" was
her favourite) with admirable effect; but on the stage
she was out of her element entirely when she laid down
the bowl and dagger of Melpomene. The author of
"Familiar Epistles" again says, with humour that
atones for the satire, "I have heard of a lady who wept
plentifully throughout the whole of 'As You Like It,'
when Mrs. Siddons played *Rosalind*, from an unhappy
impression that it was 'Jane Shore.' I am glad to relate the anecdote that so much good tears should not go
for nothing." Promiscuous audiences are capable of
very rich flights in erudition. The same writer tells us
that in witnessing a performance of Betty, the Young
Roscius, as he was called, his neighbours in the pit
began to argue as to who this Roscius could be. Some
said it was one Garrick's Christian name; but the general voice decided that he was a French actor, who had
been guillotined in the early days of the Revolution.
We ourselves once heard a sapient critic inform an
inquiring brother, that the "Merchant of Venice" was
written by Sheridan, and the "School for Scandal"
conjointly by Beaumont and Fletcher.

Boaden, in 1825, published a "Life of John Philip
Kemble," in two volumes, 8vo. His intimacy with
the subject of his biography, enabled him to give some
information which few other persons could have obtained; but this information is little in quantity and less
in value. Garrick and Kemble have been unfortunate
in their historians, of whom it is difficult to say which
has the worst.

On September 18th, 1818, William Farren made his first appearance at Covent Garden, as *Sir Peter Teazle*, followed in quick succession by *Lord Ogleby, Sir Bashful Constant,* and *Sir Anthony Absolute.* A loud flourish of trumpets preceded him from Dublin, where he had long been a universal favourite, and for several seasons stage-manager. He at once established himself as the legitimate successor of King, and held his ground against all rivals during a career of thirty-seven years. When he became known to the London public he was a young man, although he had long accustomed himself to play old characters.

The 28th of June, 1820, witnessed the last performance but one, in London, of Jack Johnstone, the celebrated representative of Irish characters. He took a formal leave of the stage at Liverpool, in the August following; but returned for one night, at Drury Lane, May the 18th, 1822, when he volunteered his services as *Dennis Bulgruddery,* for the benefit of his distressed countrymen.* He was then in his seventy-fifth year. Whether in or out of his stage clothes, Johnstone was a remarkably handsome man, with a bearing so innately gentleman-like that it was impossible by any external travesty to change him into a clown. But his constitutional humour made up for that strange deficiency in his rustics—a want of natural vulgarity. His acting was ease personified, without the slightest appearance of study or labour. In a military character, or a travelled Irish gentleman, he stood above all rivalry; but Tyrone Power, who filled his place within a very few years, excelled him in the line of rollicking dare-devils, which

---

* Edmund Kean gave up the proceeds of his Benefit on the 3d of June following, for the same benevolent purpose, and acted three parts:—*Paris,* in the " Roman Actor," *Octavian,* and *Tom Tug,* in the " Waterman," with all the songs.

admitted of greater breadth and depended more on physical elasticity and exuberant spirits. In their drunken men both were equally happy, and hit the difficult point of rich merriment without verging on disgust.

Irish Johnstone, as he was commonly called, was one of the pleasantest table companions that ever gladdened society. He realized a handsome fortune, and lived to see his eighty-first birth-day *—another eminent instance that the exercise of the art histrionic is in itself highly conducive to health, happiness, and longevity. Much of the true spirit of Irish fun and eccentricity, departed, and apparently "never to return," with Johnstone and Power. Of some later representatives, the less that is said the better. Hudson and Barney Williams must, however, be quoted as praise-worthy exceptions. They are always agreeable, animated, and natural. But when we witnessed the heavy, measured, hard, mill-grinding attempts of the greater number of the so-called successors of the two great artists of whom we are now speaking, we thought of the past with redoubled regret, and a feeling very similar to what the late Daniel O'Connell meant to convey, when we once heard him say of a tiresome long-winded talker (the son of a great orator), at a public-meeting, " that young man does not remind me of his father." Irish fun is either the best or the worst thing on the stage. It admits of no medium. The richest, the most varied, and the most exhilarating of all imaginable humour, when truthfully and tastefully depicted ; but when, as Shakespeare says, " overdone, or come tardy off," it becomes in equal proportion wearisome, vulgar, and anti-national.

The association of John Johnstone and Tyrone Power,

---

* He died on the 26th December, 1828, at his residence, No. 5, Tavistock Row, Bedford Square, and lies buried in a vault in St. Paul's, Covent Garden.

which naturally presents itself here, although not in chronological keeping, suggests also an estimate of their relative pretensions. They were unquestionably the two greatest actors of Irishmen the stage has produced, within the range of surviving experience. Which of the two is entitled to take precedence of the other, or whether they stood on an equality, are questions open to endless argument and opinion. Their style and qualifications differed in essential particulars, however the general merit might be evenly balanced. We know of no other candidate to be admitted into the competition. Charles Connor, who died suddenly on the 7th October, 1826, was next on the list; but, although good, he scarcely stood beyond first in the second class. His early death made way for Power, before he had himself reached the point of excellence, Of those who preceded, we have but scanty records; and to classify the pretensions of the living would be unprofitable. The step from mediocrity to greatness is wide and impassable except to the chosen few. Moderate talent may please, but high genius alone can delight to enthusiasm.

Johnstone, although perhaps less habitually familiarized to first class society, had on the stage a more commanding air, and a more imposing personal deportment than Power possessed. Never wanting in the spirit and humour which his part required, he indulged more in repose. He flashed out occasionally and then subsided for a time. Sometimes he ambled or cantered gently along; but Power dashed away in a continual gallop. As George the Third said of Garrick, when asked to describe his peculiar manner, " he was unlike anybody else, always doing something, and always keeping the whole audience on the alert." With Johnstone the laugh was long and loud at intervals. With Power it was incessant. An occasional round shot, as distinguished from the rattling fire of musketry. Johnstone, although rich in his clowns, was scarcely so distinctly identical as his successor. His *Dennis Bulgruddery, Looney Mactwolter, Murtoch Delany,* and *Teague,* were more nearly related than Power's *Rory O'More, O'Flannigan, Larry Hoolagan,* and *Teddy the Tiler.* Johnstone's " brogue " was purer, indigenously Milesian, and engrafted on his natural attributes. Power could assume or divest himself of his Hibernian dialect and cadence, as he pleased. But absence and a foreign education had mixed up with it some discrepancies which a practical native ear might discover, although not prominently perceptible to ordinary observation. Johnstone excelled in characters where a high-bred tone blended itself with military ease and polish, such as *Sir Lucius O'Trigger,* and *Major O'Flaherty.* We are not sure that he would not have surpassed Power in certain points of " The Irish Ambassador," *Sir Patrick O'Plenipo,* admirable as that representation proved in the hands of the actor for whom it was invented. But we question whether he possessed physical energy enough to support a whole play instead of now and then an insulated scene. With Power the point was settled beyond dispute by repeated experiment. Up to his time` the Irishman in a comedy or farce had been a feature, and a highly amusing one, thrown in to relieve, rather than a central pivot, on which the entire action revolved. Johnstone brought to perfection an existing style, but Power created a new one for himself. Both studied from nature ; but Power, although by much the younger man, had opened more leaves of her polyglot volume, as he had seen greater varieties of human character, in different and far-distant countries, and had led a life of superior travel and adventure. He introduced a new school of acting, founded on his own inexhaustible energy. Authors began to write pieces for him which partook of the monodramatic class. In these he was the alpha and omega, seldom absent from the stage, while the laugh never ceased, and the audience never yawned. As the curtain fell, after three or four hours of joyous excitement, there stood Tyrone Power, fresh, smiling, and untired, as when he bounded on the stage under the first burst of acclamation which greeted his entrance. Natural spirits made his labour light, and doubled the satisfaction of the spectators, who felt that he entertained them without effort. It seems rather an odd contradiction, although a common case, that professed comic actors are often constitutional hypochondriacs—men unconscious of a joke, except those set down for them, and who never laugh out of character— bending under morbid melancholy, until relieved by brandy-and-water, or fidgetting in a state of nervous depression, not many degrees removed from lunacy. "Go and see Liston," said an eminent physician to a patient who consulted him as to the best cure for low spirits. "Alas! I am the man," replied the sufferer in a despairing tone. The story has been fathered on Liston, whom it fits appropriately enough, but we have seen it in earlier print, recorded of a celebrated French comedian, who flourished more than a century ago. Johnstone and Power were remarkable exceptions to this rule—as merry and entertaining in private as on the stage, full of rich anecdote and conversible on many topics. They taught us to believe practically in the value of a "light heart," which, according to the old song, with the accompaniment of light marching order, will carry us triumphantly through the world and all its battles.

Power realized more money, and in less time, than Johnstone; he received higher salaries and was more individually attractive. He was fortunate, too, in a larger and more brilliant list of original characters; but this marks the extent of his popularity. Dramatic authors write for the actors who can give their works the greatest currency. Johnstone far excelled Power as a vocalist (he had appeared for several years as a singer); and was unrivalled in a *chanson-à-boire:* but Power sang pleasingly, and always introduced his songs with taste and effect, both on the stage and in private society. He sometimes supplied the words himself, and adapted them to well-known national airs which suited the compass of his voice. We are not aware that Johnstone ever meddled with authorship in any shape. Power wrote much, and distinguished himself in more than one branch of ornamental literature. Both were prudent in worldly affairs, honourable in all their dealings, and systematically gentlemanlike in their habits.* Each was the son of an officer in the army, left under the care of an indulgent mother, and intended for the military profession. Each imbibed a fondness for the stage from intimacy with two managers who gave them the *entrée* of their respective theatres in early youth—Johnstone with Ryder of Dublin, and Power with Adamson in Cardiff. Each encountered the strong opposition of parent and friends in the course he had resolved on, and each came out and persisted for years in a line contrary to that for which his attributes were especially moulded. Their ultimate success was equal, but here the parallel ceases; Johnstone lived to extreme old age, while Power was cut off in his prime. This slight comparison of two very superior men is attempted less in the character

---

* Johnstone was twice married. By his second wife, a Miss Bolton, he left an only daughter, to whom he bequeathed a considerable fortune. She was a lady of great beauty and accomplishments, married Mr. James Wallack, and died, we believe, in 1850.

of a critic than as a recorder of impressions uninfluenced by prejudice, and formed on personal observation. Power, as our readers will remember, was lost in the *President,* which foundered with all on board, as it is supposed, on the night of the 13th March, 1841. For a considerable time the fact was disbelieved, and such was the prevailing impression of the good fortune attached to the name of Tyrone Power, that it was still confidently expected that the missing steamer would be heard of, long after all reasonable ground for such expectation had ceased to exist. It was singular enough that Power had a prejudice against the *President,* and gave up the idea of taking his passage in her, as he intended, on her first outward voyage, saying she looked unlucky, and had a broken back.

More than eighteen years have passed over since she disappeared in that destroying tempest of March, 1841, and not even the smallest vestige of the ill-starred vessel, or aught that it contained, has been disclosed to human eye. This event stands recorded in its shroud of doubt and darkness, amongst the impressive tragedies of history, and will often be referred to, and called up in illustration—

> " To point a moral, or adorn a tale."

What Dr. Johnson, with some exaggeration of feeling, arising from the memory of long friendship, said of the decease of Garrick after his retirement, may with more strict fidelity be applied to the untimely fate of Power, in the full tide of his popularity :—" His death eclipsed the gaiety of nations, and impoverished the public stock of harmless pleasure."

During the early part of 1818, there appeared alarming indications of a revival of the *Rosciomania.* A child named Clara Fisher, warranted to be only six years old, astonished the town with a performance of *Lord Flimnap,* in Garrick's romance of "Lilliput, and

wound up with the tent scene of " Richard the Third."
The exhibition was wonderful for so young a creature ;
but when she grew to be a woman, her talent fell to a
very moderate standard. It had been so before with
young Betty, who, as a youth, evinced an extraordinary
aptitude for acting ; but his partisans, not content with
lauding him up as a boy of great promise, insisted that
he was actually at that moment a first-rate performer,
and would soon eclipse all competitors. The public, as
usual, suffered themselves to be carried away in the
whirlpool. As Cumberland says, he was caressed by
dukes, and, what is better still, by the daughters of
dukes, flattered by wits, feasted by aldermen, stuck up
in the windows of print-shops, and wafted to his morning's rehearsal in coronetted carriages, attended by
powdered lackeys. One of the prints alluded to exhibited Master Betty and John Kemble on the same
horse, Betty in front. He was represented as saying to
Kemble, " I don't mean to insult you, but when two
persons ride on a horse, one must ride behind."

George the Third, who was a determined play-goer,
could never be induced to see the young Roscius. When
told that he was a wonderfully clever boy, " Pooh,
pooh !" said his Majesty, " I don't care for clever boys ;
I'll wait till he's a man." He waited and never went ;
for with manhood came disappointment and mediocrity.
When Betty acted at Covent Garden, in 1813, the
public had recovered their senses, and the manager
never offered to renew the engagement. There have
been a legion of youthful *Roscii* and *Rosciæ* on the
stage, besides Master Betty and Clara Fisher, but none
that ever rivalled the first either in popularity or profit.
There was the little girl, Miss Mudie, who, at eight,
told the audience with the most perfect self-possession,
when they hissed her, that she knew it was an organised
conspiracy, and claimed the protection of the British

public. Then came Master Balfe, and Master Burke, and lately the Batemans, and little Cordelia Howard, and little Anna Maria Quinn ; with infant Viottis, Lyras, and Sapphos without number; some of whom clung pertinaciously on to childhood, till they were proved to be thirty, and were only driven away by a combined assault of baptismal registers.

Premature talent is not confined to the dramatic art, but many instances have been recorded in higher and more complicated sciences, which leave the early prodigies of the stage at a contemptible distance. Gassendi, according to Bernier, delivered lectures at four, taught astronomy to the boys of his village at seven, and harangued his bishop in Latin at ten. Pascal made discoveries in mathematics at eleven ; Grotius lisped law in his cradle; Joseph Scaliger spoke thirteen languages at twelve; and Ferdinand of Cordova was such a sage at nine, that the monks of Venice publicly denounced him as antichrist. Samuel Wesley, on the testimony of Dr. Burney, composed music before he could write. Mozart was a proficient on the harpsichord at four, and when just turned of five, wrote a concerto so difficult that nobody could execute it but himself; William Crouch, of Norwich, played " God save the Queen," at little more than two years old, without any previous instruction, and a month or two after, astonished his father by a voluntary on the organ of his own composition. But these examples of precocity are nothing to that of the learned Lipsius, who, as we are assured by Mr. Shandy, senior, composed a work the day he was born. We must refer our readers to the book for my Uncle Toby's matter of fact commentary on the hypothesis, as being more natural, though far less profound, than that of the erudite Baillet.*

* See " Tristram Shandy," and " Jugement des Savans."

CHAPTER VIII.

EDMUND KEAN IN KING LEAR AND DE MONTFORT—REFERENCE TO THE ORIGINAL PERFORMANCE OF THE LATTER PLAY—CAUSES OF ITS NON-SUCCESS—SUPERIORITY OF THE STRANGER AS AN ACTING DRAMA—MISS BAILLIE'S PLAYS ON THE PASSIONS—"RAYNER" AND "CONSTANTINE PALÆOLOGUS"—MRS. HEMANS'S "VESPERS OF PALERMO"—RETIREMENT AND DEATH OF JOHN EMERY—ROMEO COATES, THE AMATEUR OF FASHION—EDMUND KEAN AND YOUNG TOGETHER AT DRURY LANE—RETIREMENT OF JOSEPH MUNDEN—DEATH OF TALMA—EARLY EDUCATION OF CHARLES KEAN—HIS FIRST APPEARANCE ON THE STAGE.

IN 1820, Edmund Kean accomplished what had long been a leading object of his ambition, the performance of *King Lear*. The play continued under suspense from feelings of delicacy, during the last mental derangement of George III.; but the death of the good old King, on the 29th of January, in the year named above, removed the *taboo*. Great things were expected from this revival, and by none more sanguinely than by the actor himself. "I will make the audience," he said, "as mad as I shall be." The play drew crowded houses, and was repeated twenty-eight times in that season, but even Kean was not quite satisfied with the effect produced. The curse was tremendous, and there were other points of great excellence, but something was wanting to the completeness of the picture. Perhaps the cause might be that Shakespeare was still enfeebled by Tate's incongruous alterations. Towards the close of the year, Kean paid his first visit to America, where he was received with a ferment of enthusiasm, and returned in September, 1821, with increased reputation and an overflowing harvest of dollars.

On the 27th of November, Miss Baillie's tragedy of " De Montfort," was disinterred for him, with a newly arranged fifth act. Five unattractive repetitions limited the success; but it is no reproach to Kean that he failed to render a play popular, which, adorned as it is by powerful writing, is so inherently heavy, that even John Kemble and Mrs. Siddons combined were unable to give it dramatic vitality. The authoress complimented Kean on his acting in the warmest terms, and the professed critics were almost unanimous in his favour. The poet, Campbell, who was present, was so enraptured with Kean's performance, that he sought his acquaintance in consequence, and talked of writing a play that he might represent the hero. In his " Life of Mrs. Siddons," he says, " There was so much silence, and so much applause, that though I had had my misgivings to the contrary, I was impressed, at the end, with a belief that the play had now acquired and would henceforth for ever retain stage popularity. But when I congratulated Kean on having rescued ' De Montfort,' he told me that, though a fine poem, it would never be an acting play."

When " De Montfort " was originally announced for representation at Drury Lane, in 1800, the public roused up from the periodical apathy which ever and anon comes over them; the critics prophesied the approach of a new era in dramatic literature, and the talents of the two great artists, then in their zenith, left no doubt that the conceptions of the authoress would be fully realized. The expectation was great, and the disappointment commensurate. The audience yawned in spite of themselves, in spite of the exquisite poetry, the vigorous passion, and the transcendent acting of John

Kemble, supported by Mrs. Siddons. There was a total absence of underplot or skilfully interwoven subordinate characters; no variety, no relief. It was all De Montfort, through five long acts, with his deadly hatred, his unsatisfactory arguments, his gloomy meditations, and their inevitable catastrophe. There was a dreary unredeemed monotony, which coiled round the entire *dramatis personæ* like a sepulchral shroud, and reduced to suffering what should have been enjoyment. It was a positive reprieve when the curtain closed all in, and though the spectators felt that they had been dealing with a very superior production, many doubted if they understood it; few shed tears (the most genuine test of tragedy), and still fewer cared to undergo the operation a second time. The play was consigned to the shelf after a short and unproductive run of eleven nights.

More than twenty years later, the same result ensued from the same cause. The play, as we have seen, was still found to be a ponderous monodrama, and its resurrection was even more transient than its first brief existence. All this is very discouraging, and somewhat extraordinary when there is such undoubted excellence in the writing, and that writing has been so ably illustrated by the best performers of modern days. Look at the " Stranger," which keeps the stage, and never fails to interest the audience, although recent critics have entered into a league against this and other dramas of the same class. It scarcely possesses a tithe of the merit or pretensions of " De Montfort," yet it is a far more effective play, and the same great actors, Kemble and Mrs. Siddons, immortalized this German impropriety, this daring outrage upon our social feelings, while they failed in giving permanent life to the purer and more legitimate English tragedy. It must be (as we think) that the one, with all its faults and inferiority, is more natural than the other, more intelligible to the mass of spectators, more likely to happen to-day or to-morrow. The one is simple, the other strained. It is the rule opposed to the exception. We sympathise more readily with what is likely, than with what is barely possible. Many are inclined to think that the authoress of "De Montfort" has gone beyond nature in colouring hatred so strongly, when arising from an insignificant cause, and cherished pertinaciously after so long an interval. For one case of romantic or highly wrought incident, either of crime or virtue, and which only happens to peculiar natures under peculiar contingencies, there occur twenty common ones in the ordinary incidents of every day life; and in which, as everybody can understand them, they take a greater interest. If this reasoning is correct, it may be applied as a general rule, although introduced here to bear on a particular instance, and proves that a mere skilful playwright may carry away the public suffrage, which is sometimes refused to higher genius and far more profound conceptions.

Miss Baillie having written her double series of "Plays on the Passions,"—which were generally pronounced more adapted to the closet than the stage,—published, in 1804, an additional volume of "Miscellaneous Plays," intended expressly for representation, and all of which, at different times, had been offered to, and rejected by the London managers. She was evidently solicitous that her dramas should be acted, and says in the Preface, "It has been, and still is, my strongest desire to add a few pieces to the stock of what may be called our national or permanently acting plays, how unequal soever my abilities may be to the object of my ambition." And again, "I have wished to leave behind me, in the world, a few plays, some of which might have a chance of continuing to be acted even in our canvas theatres and barns, and of preserving to my name some remembrance of that species of amusement which I have, above every other, enjoyed." She says, very justly too, that the failure of her attempts to add to the acted drama is the more to be regretted, as having no opportunity of seeing any of her productions on the stage, many faults respecting effect, arising from want of practical experience, would remain undiscovered, and thus render improvement in her subsequent productions almost impossible. This Preface was published after the first production of " De Montfort," although written probably at an antecedent date. That she had, even without experience, some idea of what are called stage effects, or *coups de théâtre*, may be evidenced by several instances from her dramas :—such as the arrangements for the execution of *Ethwald ;** the sawing asunder of the planks supporting the scaffold by *Ohio*, the negro, in " Rayner," and the contrivance of *Othoric* to escape death with torture, in " Constantine Palæologus."

" *A propos des bottes*," as somebody says in an old French farce, and everybody quotes when they want an apt sentence—there is a passage in a letter from Sir Walter Scott to Mrs. Hemans (in Lockhart's " Life "), on the production of her tragedy, called the " Vespers of Palermo," in Edinburgh, in 1824, which supports so strongly the argument that construction supersedes language with our present audiences, that we venture to insert it. He says, " they care little [that is, audiences] about

---

* A very similar effect was long afterwards copied from this, and introduced in a play at Drury Lane, called the " Red Mask," adapted from Cooper's novel of the "Bravo," when the execution of Jacopo was transacted much after the same fashion.

poetry or fine writing, on the stage. It is situation, passion, and rapidity of action which seem to be the principal requisites for ensuring the success of a modern drama; but I trust by dint of a special jury, the piece may have a decent success; certainly I should not hope for much more." This play did succeed moderately in Edinburgh, although it had been an outside failure in London, but never became popular or attractive, and most probably from a deficiency of the qualities so strongly insisted on in Sir Walter's letter.

On the 29th of June, 1822, the boards of Covent Garden were trodden for the last time by John Emery, who died in the course of the following month, at the comparatively early age of forty-five. He has left no successor in his peculiar line, which expired with him. No actor ever evinced more power blended with rich humour than Emery did when portraying the rough and simple nature of unpolished country life. He was great in all he undertook, even down to such small but defined sketches as *Barnardine* and *Justice Silence*. He was a painter, too, as well as an actor, and brought his knowledge and taste in the one art to bear on the other. In such opposite characters as *Caliban, Dogberry,* and *Barnardine* he appeared to be inspired with the very genius of Shakespeare; but *Tyke*, in the "School of Reform," was the part with which he peculiarly identified his name. It was an impersonation of tremendous energy and truth, equal in the impassioned scenes to the highest efforts of the first tragic actors. Emery could produce effects out of the slenderest materials, and give prominence to parts which, in the hands of a common artist, would have been held of no importance—such as *Gibbet* and *Lockit*. He usually visited the provinces in conjunction with Irish Johnstone. They worked well together, and the combined talents of two comedians so distinct in their walk produced a corresponding attraction. Emery was sometimes encored iu the jealous scene of *Fixture*, in " A Roland for an Oliver,"—a compliment, except in this case, and *Mawworm's* sermon, when delivered by Liston, invariably confined to singers. Romeo Coates would sometimes gratify the audience by a voluntary repetition of his dying agonies; and the celebrated Dublin amateur, Luke Plunkett, once essayed to repeat the fight at Bosworth after he was killed; but the victorious *Richmond* held him forcibly down, and refused again to " stand the hazard of the die " against such a desperate adversary. The mention of the celebrated " amateur of fashion," Robert, or, as he was more generally called, Romeo Coates, from his favourite character, may excuse a line or two in our reminiscences. A West India proprietor, and the owner of extensive estates in the Island of Antigua, he possessed ample means for indulging a whimsical taste, and, some forty years ago, was a man upon town of the first order of singularity. We recollect him a constant appendage to Bond Street, while that yet favoured locality was still the fashionable lounge, and before Regent Street was thought of. He drove a light claret-coloured curricle, in shape like a cockle-shell, with beautiful bay horses and two splendidly-mounted outriders. He was usually attired in nankeen tights and white silk stockings, to display his legs, on the symmetry of which he greatly prided himself. His harness, panels, and liveries were bedizened with silver cocks, his adopted armorial bearings, with the motto, " Whilst I live I'll crow." These unlucky cocks furnished an apt cue to his ridiculers, for, as soon as he died in *Romeo* or *Lothario*, there arose from the gallery of the Haymarket, a simultaneous burst of crowing, which sounded as if every farm-yard in England had furnished its quota for the gratulation. A cruel trick was once played off upon Coates, by sending him a fictitious invitation to one of the Prince Regent's grand fêtes at Carlton House. When his name was announced, and he appeared in gorgeous costume, the Prince, who at once recollected that he was not included amongst the guests, whispered to those about him, " This poor man has been hoaxed, but I will disappoint them." He then advanced to Coates with that peculiar urbanity by which he was distinguished, and welcomed him in the most cordial manner. Divested of his theatrical mania, Mr. Coates was perfectly rational in conduct, and well informed ; while in disposition he was harmless, amiable, and charitable to a degree. He lived to a great age, and owed his death, at last, in some sort, to the theatre. Coming out of Drury Lane, he was run over by a street cabriolet, and died from the effects of the accident on the 4th of March, 1848. There have been many absurd theatrical amateurs, but none to compete with Romeo Coates, who always seemed insensible to the ridicule he excited.

During the season of 1822-3, at Drury Lane, a great sensation was produced in the theatrical world by the combined performances of Kean and Young. They appeared together for the first time on the 27th of November, 1822, as *Othello* and *Iago,* followed in due course by *Jaffier* and *Pierre, Posthumus* and *Iachimo.* These three plays were very attractive. Both performers were roused by the competition, and played their very best. On two benefit occasions they acted *Lothaire* and *Guiscard* in " Adelgitha," and *Alexander* and *Clytus,* in " Alexander the Great."

On the 31st of May, 1824, Joseph Munden left the stage. His retiring characters were *Sir Robert Bramble,* in the " Poor Gentleman," and *Dozey,* in " Past Ten

O'Clock," with the usual valedictory address on similar occasions. He came out at Covent Garden in 1790. Reader, he was a great actor, and, if he sometimes coloured a little beyond nature, it was impossible not to laugh at him. He had not simply a face, but an endless gallery of faces. He has been called a grimacer, but this very extravagance added power to what he uttered. When he appeared to have exhausted all his humour, he had ever a stroke or two in store. He possessed also the peculiar merit of playing serious old men as well as comic ones. His *Captain Bertram* and *Old Dornton* were equal to his *Sir Francis Gripe* and *Old Rapid.* His *Marall* was inimitable, and his *Nipperkin* and *Christopher Sly* never to be forgotten. No living man could wonder or see a ghost like Munden. The old Spanish proverb says, "He who has not seen Seville has lost a miracle." So have you lost a marvellous treat, such as you will never have provided for you again, if you began to frequent playhouses after Joseph Munden had departed. You are as unlucky as Darteneuf, the great epicure of Pope's day, who died just before turtle was first imported from the West Indies. Shall we attempt to describe this incomparable comedian and his vagaries? If we were to write for a hundred years, we could never emulate the brilliant sentences of Charles Lamb, in " Elia ;" and to them we must refer for the better edification of those who may like to read of what they can never hope to look on.

Munden was careful, and fond of money, even to extreme parsimony. He died in 1832, aged seventy-four, leaving a widow, one son (an officer in the army), and a daughter. His personal effects were sworn under £20,000. He was supposed to be much richer, but the emoluments and savings of actors are invariably overrated.

During the summer of 1824, Edmund Kean visited the Continent for the second time, and seems to have made a great impression on the monks of St. Bernard. They spoke with delight of him to many subsequent travellers, and he so thoroughly reciprocated the sentiment, that he inscribed in their book that he had there passed the happiest day of his life. On his return, he became involved in the well-known trial from the result of which his health and popularity never recovered. A second visit to America again recruited his funds; but his memory began to fail, and, though he could retain his old parts, he had lost the faculty of acquiring a new one. He was much too young in years to feel the inroads of time through lawful wear and tear, but he had impaired his powers by reckless indulgence.

On the 19th of October, 1826, the celebrated French actor, Talma, died at his house, in Paris. His age was supposed to be sixty-three, but on that point he was mysterious. Whenever asked to decide the question, he replied, with a smile, that "actors and women should never be dated. We are old and young," added he, " according to the characters we represent." This great artist belongs not to the history of the English stage, but he associated much with Englishmen; and, in a theatrical record, it would be an unpardonable omission not to give him a few tributary passages.

Francis Joseph Talma may be ranked amongst the most remarkable men of the age and country in which he lived. His theatrical eminence was only one of his many claims to distinction. The Garrick of the French stage, combined with the powers of a first-rate actor, the man of literature, the well-bred gentleman, the honest citizen, the steady friend, the affectionate husband and father, and the agreeable companion, endowed with ample stores of knowledge and unrivalled conversational powers. His memory resembled a vast magazine from whence he could draw supplies at will, without danger of exhausting the hoard.

A short time before his death, Talma was asked by an admiring friend why he did not write his own biography, as La Clairon, Le Kain, Preville, and Molé had done before him. He answered that he had not time ; and, that having so incessantly studied and repeated the thoughts and words of others, he could find no original phrases in which to express his ideas. On a just comparison of pretensions, it may be admitted that Talma was the greatest tragic actor that France has ever produced. Men of high stamp preceded him—such as Baron, Le Kain, Monvel, La Rive.* He excelled them all ; and none of his successors, to the present year inclusive, are worthy to rank in the same file. There is not a shadow of Talma amongst the living men. Inferior to Garrick in versatility, he excelled him in classical acquirements, and had built himself more on the ancient models. He was the only French actor who had the good taste and courage to disregard the measured monotony of the rhyme, in which all their tragedies were written, and to break through the fetters of conventional declamation. His first attempts were comparative failures. He was pronounced too natural and familiar—not sufficiently imposing for the million. There were a few discerning exceptions, however, who saw that the true spirit was in him ; and Ducis, who has been called the " French Shakespeare," was amongst the number. He introduced himself to the debutant,

* Monvel had great sensibility, but no advantages of person or face. La Rive was handsome but cold. It was said of the first, that he was a soul without a body ; and of the second, that he was a body without a soul. " To make a perfect actor," said Champfort, " La Rive should be compelled to swallow Monvel."

and proffered a friendship which terminated only with his life. Talma and Ducis have been materially indebted to each other for much of the reputation they both enjoy.

In 1789, Talma being then in his twenty-sixth year, a play, called "Charles the Ninth," was presented to the Théâtre Français, by Chenier. Many were opposed to the production of this drama. The political sentiments were considered dangerous and inflammatory. The managers thought they contained the elements of a tumult, but the friends of the author had a predominant influence, and compelled its production. St. Phal, the leading tragedian of the company, was afraid of undertaking the terrible hero of St. Bartholomew, and rejected the character. The next in rank, one by one, as a matter of course, considered themselves treated with indignity, in being applied to as substitutes or stop-gaps, and peremptorily refused. As a last and desperate resource, Talma was thought of, and eagerly embraced the opportunity. Here was the chance he wanted — an original part, which might make him for ever. The opposite extreme lay in the balance, but the hazard gave him no concern. "He is quite mad enough to risk it," thought his companions; and when it was known that he had so decided, many pronounced his funeral elegy. "Here will be an end of Talma," said they; "the play and the actor will be condemned together."

The result falsified their wishes and expectations. Talma had closely studied the historical descriptions and pictures of Charles IX.; had impressed himself with a perfect knowledge of his personal appearance, dress, manners, and peculiarities. He presented himself upon the stage a resuscitated portrait of the weak and blood-thirsty Valois.

In 1791, Talma married. The wife of his choice,

Mademoiselle Vanhove, was fifteen years older than himself, but still a very attractive, charming woman; an actress in the same theatre, and the possessor of a considerable fortune. The latter circumstance induced many to say that on his part the marriage was one of interest rather than inclination; but the affectionate life they led, and the happiness of their union, contradicted the rumour by the most convincing evidence.

Much idle gossip, which has no foundation in truth, has been propagated relative to the early acquaintance of Talma with the first Napoleon; how they were at school together, and afterwards young men upon town in Paris; and how, when they dined at a restaurateur's, the actor paid the reckoning, because the future emperor had no cash in his pocket. According to memoranda left by Talma himself, their first meeting took place on the 18th of June, 1792, in the green-room of the Théâtre Français. Napoleon, then Captain Buonaparte, had been brought there by Michaud, an actor of the company, and at his own particular request introduced to Talma, to whom he paid several flattering compliments on his performance of *Charles IX.* During a short conversation at this interview, Talma discovered that his new acquaintance had read much and reflected more, and that he was no ordinary man, although neither of heroic stature, nor imposing in personal appearance. There can be no doubt that then, and afterwards, Napoleon was in great pecuniary distress; but it does not appear, although often asserted, that he received aid from Talma. Their acquaintance, at that time, was too slight. The actor relates the following anecdote:—

Napoleon, to obtain immediate support, while vainly soliciting employment, had successively pledged whatever trinkets he possessed, rings, brooches, and watches, and his resources were entirely exhausted. The man of destiny was reduced to despair, and resolved to end all by a plunge in the Seine. On his way to the Pont Neuf, he ran against some one in his abstraction, and raising his head, recognised an old school-fellow of Brienne. The latter had just received from his notary the sum of 20,000f.; the former was intent on suicide, because he had no longer the price of a dinner. They divided the money between them, and Napoleon returned to his lodging. If that warm-hearted comrade of the college had accidentally passed down another street, the history of the next twenty years would have been written without the names of Lodi, Marengo, Austerlitz, Jena, Friedland, Moscow, Leipzig, and Waterloo.

The acquaintance between the great actor and future emperor gradually ripened into friendship. When the Egyptian expedition was planned, Talma, in his enthusiasm, volunteered to accompany the commander-in-chief. Napoleon, the only person who could by authority prevent this enterprise, set himself entirely against it. "You must not commit such an act of rash folly, Talma," said he. "You have a brilliant course before you; leave fighting to those who are unable to do anything better."

When Napoléon rose to be first consul, Talma, with the modesty of his nature, and the good sense of a man of the world, made his visits less frequent at the Tuileries. His reception was, however, as cordial as in the days of their nearer equality. With the progress of events Napoleon became emperor, and the actor naturally concluded that the intimacy of the sovereign and the subject must then entirely cease. But in a few days a note was addressed to him by the first chamberlain, couched in these words: "His Imperial Majesty has felt much surprise at not receiving M. Talma's personal felicitations. It appears as if he intended to withdraw himself from his Majesty, which is far from his Majesty's wish. M. Talma is hereby invited to present himself at the Tuileries as soon as he finds convenient." It may be supposed that such an invitation was not declined. He waited on the Emperor, was received with his former friendship, repeated his visits constantly, and never without being welcomed with peculiar distinction.

All who enjoyed Talma's society are unanimous in praise of his amiable qualities. Lady Morgan (in her book on France) says: "His dignity and tragic powers on the stage are curiously but charmingly contrasted with the simplicity, playfulness, and gaiety of his most unassuming, unpretending manners in private life." He was thoroughly an honest man, with a cultivated mind, an unerring taste, and a warm, true heart. He dispensed his affluence with hospitality devoid of ostentation. His principal residence was at a villa which he had purchased at Brumoy, in the neighbourhood of Paris, with extensive grounds and prospects, where he maintained a splendid establishment, and delighted to pass his time secluded from the noise and bustle of the metropolis. Twice a-week he went to Paris to perform.

Talma's superiority was never contested by any ambitious rival, yet he suffered much during a series of years (not in popularity, but in personal annoyance), from the severe and unjustly depreciatory criticisms of Geoffroy, a celebrated Aristarchus of his day, who had checked the success of St. Prix, lacerated the decline of Molé, and driven La Rive prematurely from the stage. He had a double infusion of the waspish acerbity of Freron (the antagonist of Voltaire), with ten times his erudition and tact in the art of tormenting.

Talma writhed under these assaults, which constantly revived at regular intervals, but he was too old then to change his style, and too proud to adopt lessons so dogmatically administered.   He derived consolation, however, from the enthusiastic encomiums of Madame de Staël, liberally bestowed in her work entitled, " Germany ; " and in the letters addressed to him by Corinna, from her involuntary exile at Coppet.

Talma, so late as December, 1821, when he was verging towards his sixtieth year, achieved one of his greatest triumphs, in Jouy's Tragedy of " Sylla." Napoleon had been dead only a few months.   The actor determined to recall the living image of his early friend and subsequent patron, by the closest resemblance which art could enable him to present. He dressed his hair exactly after the well-remembered style of the deceased emperor, and his dictatorial wreath exhibited an accurate facsimile of the laurel diadem in gold with which the first Napoleon was crowned at Notre Dame.   The. intended identity was recognised at once ; and when, in the last scene, he descended majestically from the rostrum, and, laying down the coronet, pronounced the line—

" J'ai gouverné sans peur, et j' abdique sans crainte,

the whole audience imagined that they saw the embodied spirit of Napoleon standing in awful majesty before them, and demanding their judgment on his actions.   The effect upon such an excitable public may be easily conceived.   The government trembled, and thought of interdicting the play ; but they confined themselves to a private communication, in which Talma was directed to curl his hair in future, and adopt a totally new arrangement of the head.

Something similar to this occurred in England in

1835, when Tallyrand was ambassador. In a play called "The Minister and Mercer," W. Farren, who acted the *Minister*, wished to present a fac-simile of the old time-serving diplomatist. His intentions transpired, and he was ordered to send his wig for the inspection of the Lord Chamberlain, who suggested certain changes, to prevent the rupture of the *entente cordiale* between the two countries, which such a palpable insult might have endangered.

Talma's last original character, *Charles the Sixth* (in the tragedy of M. Delaville), proved also to be his final performance. While representing this aged monarch, imbecile, demented, and worn out by sufferings and misfortune, he himself was struggling with the mortal disease which came as the herald of death, and was soon destined to close his earthly career. He was taken ill in Paris, and wished once more to revisit his country seat at Brumoy, but his strength failed so rapidly, that removal was found to be impossible. He expired gradually, and without pain, on the 19th of October, 1826, at his own house in the Rue de la Tour-des-Dames. His last words were, " The worst of all is that I cannot see." His sight had completely failed during his illness. Within a few hours after his death, two painters took sketches of his head, and David, the sculptor, was employed on a cast, from which was afterwards executed, in marble, the statue destined to occupy a prominent position in the hall of the Théâtre Français. Two days later, on the 21st of October, the body of Talma was borne to its final resting-place on earth, in the cemetery of Père la Chaise, attended by a concourse of at least one hundred thousand admiring mourners ; and as the coffin was lowered, his friend, comrade, and rival, Lafont, deposited on the lid a wreath of *immortelles*, and pronounced a funeral oration which was long remembered for its affectionate sincerity.

The annals of the French stage embrace three distinct epochs, signalized by three great masters, each remarkable for an opposite style; Baron, Le Kain, and Talma. A close parallel presents itself in our own dramatic history, when we turn to the ages, schools, and names of David Garrick, John Kemble, and Edmund Kean.

Our chronological series now reaches 1827. Thirteen eventful years had elapsed since that decisive evening in February 1814, when Edmund Kean, the father, had, on the boards of Drury Lane Theatre, identified himself with Shylock. Charles Kean, the son, in due course of time was despatched to school, preparatory for Eton College. His father resolved to give him a good education, an advantage which he fully appreciated, though it had not fallen to his own lot. The boy was first sent to the preparatory establishment of Mr. Styles, at Thames Ditton, and was subsequently placed under the Reverend E. Polehampton, at Worplesdon, in Surrey, and afterwards at Greenford, near Harrow. At this seminary he remained several years; the number of scholars being limited, and principally composed of noblemen's sons. In June, 1824, he entered Eton as an "Oppidan," his father fixing his allowance, for board and education, at £300 per annum. His tutor was the Reverend Mr. Chapman, since Bishop of Colombo: Dr. Goodall, Provost; and Dr. Keate, Head Master. He remained at Eton three years, being placed as high as the rules of the institution, having reference to age, would allow. When taken away, he was in the upper division, and had obtained considerable credit by his Latin verses.

Boating and cricket matches have ever been the

two great amusements of the Etonians during summer ; but the abolition or modification of these time-honoured, manly exercises, is now menaced by short-sighted, mistaken reformers, who, in the rabid furor of instruction, forget the practical truism that—

> " All work and no play,
> Make Jack a dull boy."

Charles Kean became so expert a leader in aquatics, that he was chosen second captain of the " Long Boats," as they are called—no insignificant honour in Etonian eyes.   Under the tuition of the celebrated Angelo, he also won distinction as an accomplished fencer, a valuable acquirement in the profession he was destined to pursue. His contemporaries and associates included many youths of rank and promise, who have since risen to marked eminence amongst the " men of the time."   In the list we may enumerate the Duke of Newcastle, the late Marquis of Waterford, Lords Eglinton, Sandwich, Selkirk, Boscawen, Canning, Walpole, Adare, Alford ; Messrs. W. Gladstone, Somerset, Cowper, Holmes, Saville, Craven, Wentworth, Middleton, Watts Russell, Alexander, Eyre, &c.*

Up to the period at which we have now arrived, everything appeared outwardly happy and prosperous in the Kean family.   The domestic skeleton was there, but, as yet, invisible. Charles was repeatedly assured by both his parents that he would inherit a splendid fortune, and be brought up to a distinguished profession. His mother preferred the church ; his father inclined to the navy ; but his own predilection was decidedly for

* A series of highly interesting articles entitled " Recollections of Eton College in the days of Charles Kean," have recently appeared in the *Era* and attracted much attention.   They abound in characteristic anecdotes.

a military career. There can be no doubt whatever, that
Edmund Kean might have maintained himself and family
in all the elegancies of life, and have left behind him a
sum amounting to 50,000*l.* Since the days of Garrick,
no actor had received so much money in the same short
space of time. But clouds had long been gathering,
and a crisis was at hand. Habits of irregularity and
reckless extravagance had gradually settled upon him.
Ill-chosen associates estranged him from his wife and
son. He had still a few sincere and anxious friends,
who stepped in and endeavoured to arrest his down-
ward course; but a legion of evil counsellors hemmed
him round, and the warning voice passed by unheeded.
He was falling from his high position; his popularity
was on the decline, his physical powers were sink-
ing under premature decay, and his finances were
exhausted.

Charles, who had for some time suspected the total
derangement of his father's affairs, was startled into
conviction by a pressing letter from his mother, received
during his last half-year at Eton, in the early part
of 1827, entreating him to come to her immediately.
He obtained permission to absent himself for a few days,
and hastened to London. He found her suffering the
most intense anxiety, and she implored him not to leave
her. It appeared that Mr. Calcraft, a member of Parliament, and one of the most influential of the Drury
Lane Committee of that day, had offered to procure
for him a cadetship in the East India Company's
service. His father thought the offer too eligible to be
declined, and in giving notice that he intended to accept
it, ordered his son to make instant preparations for his
departure. Mrs. Kean had been entirely separated
from her husband for two or three years; she was
reduced to a broken, pitiable state of health, nearly

bed-ridden, helpless as an infant, and without a single relative to whom she could look for succour or consolation. Weighing these circumstances well, Charles Kean formed his determination, and sought an interview with his father, at the Hummums, Covent Garden, where he resided at that time, to bring matters to a final understanding.

Edmund Kean was then precariously situated. He had dissipated his realised capital, and was living from day to day on the uncertain earnings, which might cease altogether with increasing infirmities. He still commanded a large salary when able to work, but his power of continuing that supply was little to be depended on. He told his son that there remained no alternative for him but to accept the offer of the cadet-ship; that he would provide his Indian outfit, and this being done, he must depend thenceforth entirely upon his own exertions, and never apply to him for any future support or assistance. Charles replied that he was perfectly contented, and willing to embrace these conditions, provided something like an adequate allow-ance was *secured* to his mother. Finding that his father no longer had it in his power to promise this with any degree of certainty, he respectfully, but firmly, told him, that he would not leave England while his mother lived, and declined, with thanks, the kind proposal of Mr. Calcraft.

This answer excited the anger of the elder Kean to the highest pitch; he gave way to the most intemperate passion, and a painful scene ensued.

"What will you do," said he, "when I discard you, and you are thrown entirely on your own resources?"

"In that case," replied the son, "I shall be compelled to seek my fortune on the stage (the father smiled in derision); and though I may never rise to eminence, or be a great actor, I shall at least obtain a livelihood for my mother and myself, and be obliged to no one."

The father stormed, repeating, almost with inarticulate fury, what he had often said before, that he was resolved to be the first and last tragedian of the name of Kean. The son endured a torrent of vituperation without losing his temper, or forgetting the respect which, under any circumstances, he felt to be still due to a parent. They parted, and from that hour all intercourse between them was suspended.

The result of this conversation was communicated through Mrs. Kean to Mr. Calcraft, and drew from that gentleman the following reply :—

" Hanover Square,
" February 27th, 1827.

" DEAR MADAM,—

"I confess it was a great disappointment to me, that you and your son refused (if it could be obtained) the cadetship to the East Indies; for, after what you had said, I did not expect it. Yet, having been much pleased with your son's manner, and appearance, and being thoroughly sensible of his unprotected situation, I shall not withhold from him any services which may be in my power. Always wishing you to keep in mind that I am entirely without official interest,

" I am, dear Madam,
" Your obedient servant,
" J. CALCRAFT."

In the following July, when the Eton vacation came on, Charles Kean was informed that his accounts were paid up, his allowance stopped, and that he was not to return. A short time before this, a young nobleman, one of his intimate associates, with whom he had first become acquainted at Mr. Polehampton's preparatory school, seeing him unusually dejected, inquired the cause. Kean, in the fulness of his heart, told him the result of his interview with his father, and that, in all probability, he should be driven to adopt the stage as his profession. " I quite approve of your resolution," said his aristocratic friend, " and commend you warmly for it; but recollect this, if you do so, from that hour you and I must be strangers, as I never did, and never will, speak to or acknowledge an actor." He kept his word. About a year or so afterwards, when Charles Kean was fulfilling an engagement at Leamington, in Warwickshire, the noble lord, finding himself in the same hotel, moved off instantly, bag and baggage, to avoid the unhallowed propinquity; thus, at least, carrying out the consistency of his prejudice, without regard to personal convenience.

Very fortunately, Charles Kean had contracted no private debts, a rare occurrence in an Etonian, and particularly in one who had hitherto been well supplied with pocket money. He made his way to London, and hastened immediately to his mother's lodgings. He found her in sickness, in sorrow, and in poverty. A small yearly income, hitherto allowed by her husband, had been entirely withdrawn. They were without cash, and utterly destitute of resources. A more forlorn condition can scarcely be imagined.

Precisely at this juncture, a misunderstanding arose between Edmund Kean and Mr. Stephen Price, the well-known American lessee of Drury Lane Theatre, and for the first time the great tragedian left his old theatrical home, the scene of his early triumphs, to engage with Mr. Charles Kemble at Covent Garden. Mr. Price, having heard how the son was situated, and thinking the name of Kean a powerful talisman, immediately made him an offer of an engagement at Drury Lane Theatre for three years, with a salary of 10*l.* a-week, to be increased to 11*l.* and 12*l.* during the second and third years, in case of success. Such an offer appeared to drop from the clouds; the heart of the young man bounded with hope, and the proposal was gratefully accepted. He stipulated, however, that he must first write to his father, who was then absent from London, and make him acquainted with the circumstance. Price approved of this, received the letter, and undertook to forward it; but no answer was returned; and there is reason to believe that the missive never reached the hands for which it was intended.

Thus Charles Kean became an actor. Necessity, and not choice, determined his lot in life. How little does the world in general know of the secret springs of our actions. It judges by the surface only, and can seldom penetrate the hidden depths, or sound the under-currents, which, with controlling power, impel us on a course we otherwise might avoid, and never would have selected. For this act he was generally condemned. Mr. Calcraft considered him as rash and ill-advised. His father's partisans denounced him as flying in the face of parental authority, wilful, thankless, and disobedient. Some shrugged their shoulders, while others shook their heads, but none whispered a word of encouragement. And all because he would not leave a helpless mother without protection; who, if his father had died suddenly during his absence, might have starved in her bed !

The future course of the young adventurer being now marked out, his first appearance on any stage took place at Drury Lane Theatre, on the opening night of the season, Monday, October the 1st, 1827. *Young Norval,* in Home's tragedy of " Douglas," was the character selected for the occasion. He was yet under seventeen, and so complete a stripling in appearance, as well as in years, that the authorities of the theatre sat in council on the question of, whether he should be announced as Mr. Kean, *junior*, or *Master* Kean. He settled the point by rejecting the latter designation with the utmost disdain.

On the Saturday night previous to his appearance, a dress-rehearsal was suggested by the manager, that he might " face the lamps " for the first time, and familiarise himself with his stage costume. Many personal friends of Mr. Price, with some members of the committee, were present, who complimented him warmly on the success of this, his preliminary essay. While supping afterwards in the manager's room, with true boyish feeling, he expressed a wish to show himself to his mother in the stage habiliments of *Norval.* The manager consented, but wondering that he still lingered in the theatre, drew from him, in a whisper, the reluctant confession that he was without the means of paying for a hackney coach. Price supplied the money, and young Kean flew to his mother's lodgings to display his finery, relate the encouragement he had received, and cheer her with the hopes and expectations with which he panted for the following Monday.

The expected night arrived. Curiosity to see the son of the great actor, Edmund Kean, filled the vast theatre to overflowing. A first appearance before a London public, in those days, and at one of the great national establishments, was a much more serious affair than it is at present—a trying ordeal even for the experienced veteran, who might feel confident in his powers, and had often tested their effects. What then must it have been to the unpractised novice, trembling at the sound of his own voice, and unnerved even by the sight of his own name for the first time exhibited in print? The awful moment is come—he stands before the audience, fairly launched on the experiment of his life—he has no time to think of all that hangs on the issue of the next two hours, but must brace his spirits to the task, and sink or swim, according to the measure of his own unaided courage.

The play was cast as follows:—

Young Norval	Mr. CHARLES KEAN.
(*His first appearance on any stage.*)	
Lord Randolph	Mr. MUDE.
Glenalvon	Mr. WALLACK.
Old Norval	Mr. COOPER.
Lady Randolph . . .	Mrs. WEST.
Anna	Mrs. KNIGHT.

Young Norval does not appear until the opening of the second act. His entrance is preceded by that of the retainers of Lord Randolph, bearing in custody the faithless servant, "the trembling coward who forsook his master." The audience unluckily were led to mistake the latter worthy for the new candidate, and greeted him with the rounds of applause intended for the hero of the evening. Here was another damper, for, in such situations, the veriest trifles have their effect. The debutant recovered himself notwithstanding, and went through his part, at the opening, with hesitating doubt, but as he warmed into the business of the scene, with courage and gradually increasing animation. Some unprejudiced judges (and more than one were present who took an interest in his fate) could detect, even through all the rawness of an unformed style, and the embarrassment of a novel situation, the germs of latent ability, and the promise of future excellence. The audience received him throughout with indulgence, encouraged him by frequent approbation, and called for him when the tragedy concluded. It was success certainly, but not decided success. Charles Kean felt, that although he had passed his examination with tolerable credit, he had neither carried away " high honours," nor achieved what in theatrical parlance is termed " a hit." On the following morning he rushed with feverish anxiety to the papers, and, without pausing, read them to his mother. His fate and hers, their future subsistence, the hope that sustained them, the bread they were eating, the roof that covered them—all lay in the balance—and all depended on the dictum of the all-powerful press! It was unanimous in condemnation. Not simple disapproval, or qualified censure, but sentence of utter incapacity—stern, bitter, crushing, and conclusive. There was no modified praise, no exceptional encouragement, no admission of undeveloped faculties, no allowance for youth and inexperience. The crude effort of a school-boy was dealt with as the matured study of a practised man.

The papers gave no quarter, but went in unanimously, to burn, sink, and destroy — an overwhelming fleet against a little light-armed gunboat. The hearts of both mother and son were struck with dismay—they wept in concert; and Charles Kean's first impulse was to abandon the stage in despair. He hastened to Mr. Price, and proposed to cancel the engagement, but this the manager considerately declined, and urged him to persevere. Hope is ever strong in the heart of youth. In the morning of life the voice of cheering approbation impels more than the leaden tongue of censure can impede.

For good or evil, to make or mar a fortune, the press, as an organ of critical opinion, is invested with tremendous power. How important then is it that such power

should be exercised by able delegates, with sound dis-
cretion, and strict impartiality! If ever there was a
case in which the slow but unerring award of time has
reversed a hasty judgment, that case stands prominently
conspicuous in the position which Charles Kean has
won for himself, in defiance of many obstacles, and in
the teeth of reiterated discouragement.

CHAPTER IX.

ON the day following Charles Kean's first appearance,
a strenuous partisan of his father, supposed to be a
writer of some critical ability, addressed the following
letter to Edmund Kean, containing an account of what
had taken place, with a prognostic as to the future.
The letter becomes remarkable when compared with the
sequel.

"London, 2d Oct. 1827.

" MY DEAR KEAN,—

" I am sure you feel no otherwise than anxious
to know the result of last night's effort on the part of
your son. 'I pray you, Sir, take patience,' nor let the
knowledge of the fact that he failed to attain, as he was
taught to think he should, in one night, and with a
single exertion,* that eminence which his father took

* How could the writer, who was unacquainted with the boy, dive
into thoughts which he never uttered even if he conceived them ?—
so much for prejudice.

years of labour to secure, cause you one moment's uneasiness. I went to see his performance; and send you by this post, in the *Times* newspaper, the best critique thereon : it is strictly correct. Every performer that came on the stage in the first act was, by the *favourable* audience, taken for your son, and applauded. Even the 'trembling coward,' who, as you remember, enters a short time previously to *Young Norval*, was loudly and vehemently greeted for 'Mr. Kean, jun.' When Charles first came on the scene, he was heartily received. He trembled exceedingly, supported himself on his sword, and appeared to have much ado to retain his self-possession. He bowed to the audience several times, gracefully, and like a young gentleman of education. He gained his composure wonderfully, for in ten minutes he was so far recovered, that one would have supposed him to have been accustomed to the boards from his cradle. His voice is altogether puerile; his appearance that of a well-made genteel youth of eighteen. His speech, 'My name is Norval,' he hurried, and spoke as though he had a cold, or was pressing his finger against his nose. His action, on the whole, better than could have been expected from a novice—I may say, in many instances graceful. He made no points; and copied your manner in attitude as much as possible. The particular applause bestowed was only in two instances, when he imitated your voice and style; and his exit in the fourth act, with the words, 'Then let yon false Glenalvon beware of me,' bordered upon the extreme of ludicrous. My conclusion is, that it was just such a performance as would have been highly creditable to a schoolboy acting in conjunction with his companions, for the amusement of their parents on a breaking-up day, and nothing beyond this. After the play he was called, and appeared, led on by

Wallack, and bowed gracefully to all parts of the house. So much confidence had he by this time acquired, that he smiled, and smiled again, as though the laurelled crown were already on his head. I have given you as near a report as is in my power; and I will add, that, even with this well-mustered audience, he would have left the stage for ever, but for the name he bore. He will draw one or two more good houses, and then, I fear, sink into nothingness. Though your son has, I suspect, completely failed to make a great, or even a good actor, the name of Kean will be handed down to posterity, as long as Shakespeare's play of 'Othello' is remembered."

The youthful actor lingered at Drury Lane through the season of 1827–8, occasionally repeating the character of *Norval,* varied by *Selim,* in "Barbarossa," *Frederick,* in "Lovers' Vows," and *Lothaire,* in Monk Lewis's tragedy of "Adelgitha," which last was revived when Mrs. Duff, an American actress, made her first appearance. The houses had ceased to be crowded; his attraction dwindled to nothing; the audience grew cold in their applause. The papers, whenever they condescended to notice him, continued their censure; and, at length, almost heart-broken, he left London for the provinces, that he might have a better opportunity of obtaining the constant practice he so much required.

On the 20th of April, 1828, Charles Kean presented himself to his warm-hearted countrymen, in Dublin, as *Young Norval,* and met with the cordial reception which might have been anticipated. His father had ever been one of their especial favourites; and they remembered, with gratitude, how in 1822 he had given the proceeds of his benefit to relieve their starving peasantry. The humour of the Dublin gallery has long been proverbial; but latterly it has received heavy checks from the

" exodus" and the temperance movement. To fun succeeded propriety, the police, politics, and poverty—
poverty of wit engendered by vacuity of purse. Nothing
checks the play of imagination more effectually than
empty pockets. In 1827, there was yet fun enough left
amongst the merry Olympians of the Irish capital, to
astonish and amuse a stranger. No sooner had the play
terminated, on Charles Kean's opening night, than he
was unanimously demanded; and having, under similar
circumstances in London, merely made a silent bow and
retired, he naturally thought the same pantomimic acknowledgment would pass muster elsewhere. Most
unexpectedly, he was greeted by a general demand for
" a speech." Completely taken by surprise, he hummed
and hawed for a moment or two; then endeavoured to
look grateful, placed his hand on his breast, and stam-
mered out a few incoherent sentences, nearly as intelligible as the following :—" Ladies and Gentlemen, I
am deeply sensible of your being quite unprepared—no,
I don't mean that—I mean, of my being quite unprepared—overwhelming kindness—incapable of thanks—
totally unmerited—never to be effaced—when time shall
be no more." Here a friendly auditor cried out, " That
will do, Charley; go home to your mother;" which
produced a universal burst of approbation, during which
he bowed himself off. As he disappeared at the wing,
and the applause was dying away, a stentorian shout
arose of " Three cheers for Charles Kean's speech!"
which was taken up with overpowering effect.

A volume might be filled with characteristic anecdotes
of the Dublin gallery. Perhaps the introduction of two
or three may not be considered irrelevant.

On an occasion when the gods were overcrowded on a
benefit night, a loud clamour arose for relief, or more
accommodation. After becoming diplomatic delay, the

tardy manager appeared, and addressed them with the usual formula, " What is your pleasure? "   " None at all!" roared out a dozen at once ; " but a d—d sight of pain, for we're all smothering here."

A new piece by Power had not made a very successful impression ; however, as usual, he was vociferously called for at the close, and announced it for repetition with the customary plaudits.   As he was retiring, an anxious admirer in the gallery called out, in a confidential tone, " Tyrone, a word in private—don't take that for your benefit ! "

In those days they had an indirect mode of *hinting* opinions, which they considered less personal than overt hostility.   As thus : if Cobham was acting one of Warde's characters, in Warde's absence, after what he intended for a great effect, they would cry, " A clap for Warde !" in that particular speech, and *vice versâ*.   If a new piece bored them, they would demand " A groan for the performance *ginirally !*" or tell the actors to " cut it short;" or fall back upon their never-complied-with cry for " Garry-Owen !" a tune which has been a bone of contention between the audience and the management ever since the memorable " races of Castlebar," in 1798. Mrs. Siddons was once interrupted in one of her greatest scenes by a vociferous demand for this same " Garry-Owen."   She was utterly unconscious of what it meant ; but, anxious to gratify the " celestials," if possible, she paused, and asked solemnly, " What is Garry-Owen ? Is it anything that I can do for you ?"

There was an old actor at the Dublin Theatre, still living in 1825, named Michael Fullam, who died on the stage during the following year.   He had outlived his powers, and was on very familiar terms with the galleries, who, knowing the tetchiness of his temper, perpetually tried to excite him, by shouting, " Speak up !"

a favourite practice of theirs from time immemorial, and
a natural one enough, when people have paid their
money to hear, and the actors are mysterious. "Arrah,
then, Mick Fullam, the divil a word can we·hear!
Speak up, ould boy!" The first time he would reply,
sharply, but without halting in the scene, "I can't." If
the call was repeated a second time: "I won't," angrily.
If a third time: "Be quiet, fools!" in a burst of indignant reproof. Then ensued a roar of laughter, in which
the whole house joined; and, by-and-by, a *da capo* of
the same composition.

This call was once urgently addressed to John
Kemble, during his performance of the philosophic
Prince of Denmark. Finding it impossible to comply,
as his asthmatic tendency always compelled him to
husband his lungs, he came forward at once, and said,
"Gentlemen of the gallery, I can't *speak up;* but if you
won't speak at all, you'll hear perfectly every word
I say."

On the first night of a new play by Sheridan
Knowles, not many seasons ago, a heavy explanatory
scene was "dragging its slow length along," between
two still heavier actors, who had no effects to·produce,
and were unable to elicit them if they·had. The audience were evidently tired, though patient from respect
to the name of the author, and now and then relieved
themselves by an expressive yawn. There happened to
be a momentary pause, when a voice from one of the
gallery benches called out, in parliamentary cadence,
"I move that this debate be adjourned to this day six
months." This·sally woke up the house, and prepared
them to enjoy the more telling scenes which were
about to follow. Every public has its own particular
mode of expressing satisfaction or disgust, the usual
symbols being applause or hissing, and sometimes

general somnolency. The latter is the most fatal. "You see they don't hiss," said a disciple of Voltaire to the great master, who had accompanied his pupil to witness the expected condemnation of his first tragedy, which the cynical wit had confidently predicted,—" you are mistaken for once, there is not a single hiss." "Not at present," replied Voltaire, "for they are all asleep."

A troublesome customer in a thin pit, once adopted a strange mode of vindicating independent opinion. He amused himself and disturbed the rest of the audience, by lying nearly at full length, and hissing and applauding every speech from every actor, at the same time. After a desperate struggle he was removed to the police-office, and when interrogated by the local authorities as to why he had thus interrupted the performance, he said, "he didn't know, he meant no offence; but he had always understood that any one who paid his money in a theatre had a right to hiss or applaud according as he pleased; and he thought the fairest way of exercising his privilege was to keep on doing both together."

It is amazing what the public will sometimes endure without anger, from favourite performers, when they are either taken by surprise, or the good-humoured vein predominates. George Frederic Cooke told the people of Liverpool to their teeth that they were a disgrace to humanity, and that every stone in their city was cemented by human blood—a figurative mode of conveying that their commercial prosperity sprang from encouraging the slave trade. They saw that he laboured under his "old complaint," and forgave the actor while they pitied the man. At Washington, in America, when the President had come expressly to see him in "Richard the Third," he flatly refused to commence his character, or act before the "King of the Yankee Doodles," as he called him, until the band had played " God save the King," in addition to their own national air. And in this extravagance the stiff republicans actually indulged him! During Elliston's management of the Surrey Theatre, a very poor play was one night unequivocally condemned. He rushed from his dressing-room on the stage, under a tempest of disapprobation, and when silence was with difficulty restored, exclaimed, with a face of bewildered astonishment, " I thought I heard a hiss—unusual sound! Ladies and gentlemen, you are under a very lamentable mistake here. I can assure you (and I think you will allow my opinion is worth something) this is a most excellent piece, and so you will find out when you exercise your unbiassed judgment, and have seen it three or four times. A British audience invariably gives fair play. With your kind permission, therefore, I shall announce the new drama for every evening until further notice." This address was received without a dissentient voice, and procured for the doomed play a long and successful run.

But the climax of public endurance occurred with Edmund Kean, at the Victoria, formerly the Cobourg, on the Surrey side of the water. He had been tempted into the engagement by the large terms of 50*l.* per night. He opened in " Richard the Third " to an enormous house, and all passed off with great effect. On the second night he appeared as *Othello*, on which occasion *Iago* was personated by Cobham, a prodigious Victoria favourite. The house was crowded as before, but noisy and inattentive. There were nearly twelve hundred persons in a gallery measured for about half the number. The best speeches in the most striking scenes were marred by such unclassical expletives and interruptions as a Cobourg audience were given to dispense, in those days with more freedom than politeness

—by the incessant popping of ginger-beer bottles, and by yells of "Bravo, Cobham!" whenever Kean elicited his most brilliant points. The great tragedian felt disconcerted, and by the time the curtain fell, he overflowed with indignation, a little- heightened by copious libations of brandy and water. He was then loudly called for, and after a considerable delay came forward, enveloped in his cloak, his face still smirched, not more than half cleansed from the dingy complexion of the Moor, and his eyes emitting flashes as bright and deadly as forked lightning. He planted himself in the centre of the stage, near the footlights, and demanded, with laconic abruptness, "What do you want?" There was a moment's interval of surprise, when, "You! you!" was reiterated from many voices. "Well, then, I am here." Another short pause, and he proceeded: "I have acted in every theatre in the United Kingdom of Great Britain and Ireland, I have acted in all the principal theatres throughout the United States of America, but in my life I never acted to such a set of ignorant, unmitigated brutes as I now see before me." So saying, he folded his mantle majestically, made a slight, contemptuous obeisance, and stalked off, with the dignity of an offended lion. The actors, carpenters, and property men, who listened to this harangue, stood aghast, evidently expecting that the house would be torn down. An awful silence ensued for a moment or two, like the gathering storm before the tempest, when suddenly a thought of deadly retaliation suggested itself, and pent-up vengeance burst out in one simultaneous shout of, "Cobham! Cobham!" Cobham, who was evidently in waiting at the wing, rushed forth at once, bowed reverentially, placed his hand on his heart again and again, and pantomimed emotion and gratitude after the prescribed rules. When the thunders of applause subsided, he delivered himself as follows :—" Ladies and gentlemen, this is unquestionably the proudest moment of my life. I cannot give utterance to my feelings ; but to the latest hour of my existence I shall cherish the remembrance of the honour conferred upon me by one of the most distinguished, liberal, and enlightened audiences I ever had the pleasure of addressing."

During the course of Charles Kean's first provincial tour, he found himself, while fulfilling an engagement at Glasgow, in close proximity to his father, who was then enjoying a term of relaxation in a cottage he had built in the Isle of Bute. Notwithstanding their estrangement, the heart of the son yearned towards his parent, and he made an overture, through a third person, to pay him a visit. The proposal met with a ready assent, and his reception was more cordial than he an-. ticipated. Little allusion was made to the past, and a temporary reconciliation took place. This led to a proposition from the elder Kean to act one night in the Glasgow theatre for his son's benefit, on the 1st of October, 1828—by singular coincidence, the anniversary of his first appearance in London. They appeared as *Brutus* and *Titus*, in Howard Payne's tragedy of " Brutus." The house, as might be anticipated under such circumstances, presented a complete overflow, the receipts amounting to nearly £300. The strong interest of the play, combined with the natural acting of father and son, completely subdued the audience. They sat suffused in tears during the last pathetic interview, until *Brutus*, overpowered by his emotions, falls on the neck of *Titus*, exclaiming in a burst of agony, " Embrace thy wretched father ; " when they broke forth into the relief of loud and prolonged peals of approbation. Edmund Kean then whispered in his son's ear,

"Charley, we are doing the trick." This may appear strange and inconsistent, perhaps unnatural, to those who persuade themselves that the accomplished actor must of necessity feel, at the moment, the full influence of the passion he is so eloquently expressing. Garrick may be cited as an eminent instance to the contrary. His superiority over Barry in *Lear* consisted chiefly in his power of simulating tears and sobs without suffering them to impede his utterance, a perfection of art which his rival could never attain, from yielding too much to natural emotion. An enthusiastic admirer of Talma once said to him, "You must be deeply affected to produce such painful impressions on your audiences. How intensely you identify yourself with every character you represent." His reply embraced a lecture on his art. "Acting," said he, "is a complete paradox;" we must possess the power of strong feeling or we could never command and carry with us the sympathy of a mixed public in a crowded theatre; but we must at the same time control our own sensations on the stage, for their indulgence would enfeeble execution. The skilful actor calculates his effects beforehand. He never improvises a burst of passion or an explosion of grief. Everything that he does is the result of pre-arrangement and fore-thought. The agony which appears instantaneous, the joy that seems to gush forth involuntarily, the tone of the voice, the gesture, the look, which pass for sudden inspiration, have been rehearsed a hundred times. On the other hand a dull, composed, phlegmatic nature, can never make a great actor. He who loves his profession and expects to excel in it, must study from himself, and compare his own proved sensations under grief, happiness, disappointment, loss, acquisition, anger, pain, pleasure, and all the ordinary variations of human events and feelings, with the imaginary emotions of the character he is supposed to represent." "Not long ago," he added, " I was playing in ' Misanthropy and Repentance' with an admirable actress. Her natural and affecting manner, deeply studied nevertheless, quite overpowered me. She perceived and rejoiced in her triumph, but whispered to me, ' Recover yourself, Talma; you are excited.'* Had I not listened to the caution, my voice would have failed, the words would have escaped my memory, my gesticulations would have become unmeaning, and the whole effect would have dwindled into insignificance. No, believe me, we are not nature, but art producing nature, and in the excellence of our imitation lies the consummation of skill."

We have recorded the substance of similar opinions as expressed by Edmund Kean in more than one conversation. He and Talma are great authorities on the art which they so eminently illustrated, although in this point both dissent from Horace, who, speaking poetically, says, " You must first weep yourself if you wish to excite compassion in others."

> " Si, vis me flere, dolendum est
> Primùm ipsi tibi."

"Do you believe, Sir," said Boswell to Dr. Johnson, " that Garrick, as he says himself, is so carried away by artistic enthusiasm that he actually fancies he is *Richard*

---

* Charles Young related to Campbell the poet, a similar effect produced upon him by Mrs. Siddons, in the last scene of the " Gamester," when as a young actor he was performing with her in that play in Edinburgh. He was so carried away by her intensity that he totally forgot his part, until she whispered to him in a low tone ; " Mr. Young, recollect yourself." Elliston really persuaded himself that he was George IV., when he personated that monarch in the pageant of the Coronation. As he crossed the platform along the front of the pit, he invariably paused, and extending his hands benignly, said to the audience, " Bless you, my people !"

the Third, every time he performs the character?" "No, Sir," replied the Leviathan, "David talks nonsense, and he knows it. If such a metamorphosis were possible, he would deserve the penalty of hanging every time it occurs." The philosopher knew his man; and when Garrick rebuked him for talking loud with his friends during the performance, alleging that it disturbed his tragedy feelings, he replied with a laugh, "Pooh, pooh, Davy; Punch has no feelings."

But although Dr. Johnson delighted in teazing Garrick, by pretending to undervalue the actor's art, and spoke slightingly of him in conversation with others, he never would suffer any one else to do so in his presence. "If I choose to decry David, Sir, is that any reason why I should suffer you to do so?" This was his stern rebuke to more than one "triton of the minnows" who thought to curry favour with him by echoing his sentiments. When Garrick died, Dr. Johnson caused it to be conveyed to his widow that, if she expressed a wish to that effect, he would undertake the editorship of the works, and also write a memoir of his deceased friend. The lady, from whatever cause, remained silent, and the biography, which, in beauty of composition, and literary value, might have rivalled the life of Savage, or Dryden, or Milton, was doomed to execution by the hands of Tom Davies and Arthur Murphy.

An anecdote has escaped the diligence of Boswell, which may be found in a note to Sir W. Forbes's "Life of Beattie." At Garrick's funeral, which moved in ostentatious display, attended by much that was dignified in rank, wealth, and literature, from his residence in the Adelphi to Westminster Abbey, Dr. Johnson rode in the same coach with Sir William Jones, to whom, and the rest of his companions, he talked incessantly, as was his habit; his theme being an uninterrupted eulogium on the departed actor, both in his public and private capacity. "Garrick," said he, "to my knowledge, gave away more money than any man in England, with the same means. He was proud of his profession, and had a right to be so. Each owed much to the other. His profession made him rich, and he made his profession respectable."

Actors, naturally enough, have an exalted idea of their own calling. But in this harmless vanity they are fully emulated by professors of the kindred arts. Baron, the great French tragedian, said "a tragic actor ought to be born amongst princes, and nursed on the laps of queens." The sentence is well rounded, and reads with an imposing air. Of him, the following hyperbole is gravely recorded. In pronouncing the two lines—

> " Et dans le même moment par une action sévère,
> Je l'ai vu *rougir* de honte, et *pallir* de colère ;

his panegyrist tells us that as he uttered the words *rougir* and *pallir*, his face alternately grew red and white. This was suiting " the action to the word" to an extent that Shakespeare never contemplated—a muscular trickery quite impossible, and utterly absurd if it could be contrived. The actor is merely repeating of another what he is by no means supposed to feel in his own person. This flight may stand side by side with the still higher one of a living theatrical critic, Alison, who, in one of his volumes, mentions that Garrick so studiously copied nature, that he acted *King Lear* on *crutches*, but threw them away to give more complete effect to the *great scene*. Where on earth did the ingenious essayist and historian find his authority for this extravagance ? We are told by many contemporaries that Garrick used a *stick* in acting *Lear*, such as is carried to this day by *Shylock, Sir Giles Overreach*, and other elderly characters ; and for which Edmund Kean, and afterwards Macready, substituted a Saxon sceptre, or hunting-spear.   When he came to the curse, if this is what is implied by the *great scene*, he dashed down this stick, with his cap, and clasped his hands convulsively together, as he fell on his knees in the agony of passion.   Henderson, John Kemble, and Young, who followed in succession, adopted the same stage business, which appears to have descended lineally from Betterton, through Booth and Quin, to Barry and Garrick.

Davies' "Life of Garrick" is little more than a dull register—a mere record of performances, unenlivened by incident or profitable reflection.   Murphy's consists of little more than the margin.   Galt's is a meagre sketch ; well supplied with erroneous particulars, and, if possible, of less value than Murphy's.   Compilations of personal anecdotes are always popular and entertaining, but not of necessity authentic.   Sometimes they are confounded, or misapplied, or break down under the most conclusive of all evidences, when substantiated—an *alibi*.   Your professed anecdote hunter is a dangerous individual to depend on, or quote from.   He is, in fact, often a clap-trap actor, ready at any time to yield up the sense for the applause, or to dally with severe truth for the sake of a brilliant period, or an epigrammatic point.   Let us look for an instance or two, by way of illustration.   How often have we read that when the great Duke of Marlborough was observed to shed tears at the imaginary woes of *Indiana*, in Sir Richard Steele's weeping comedy of the "Conscious Lovers," it was remarked by the lookers on that " he would fight none the worse for that."   Now, how stands the fact?   The case falls through on an *alibi*.   The illustrious warrior died a few months before the play was produced, and was thus clearly otherwise engaged ; added to which, his fighting days were over long before his death, and the last years of his existence passed in strict domestic privacy, clouded by mental prostration.

Ireland, the biographer of Henderson, says, that in the winter of 1780, he appeared at Covent Garden as *Sir John Brute;* but Mr. Garrick observed, " it was the city Sir John, for egad he had neither the air nor the manner of the rake of fashion." The anecdote slays itself, for Garrick died on the 20th of January, 1779, and thereby was incapacitated from giving an opinion on anybody's acting in the winter of the following year. Another clear case of *alibi.* Lord Byron sings in " Childe Harold," in imperishable verse, how the so-called Convention of Cintra was negotiated in the palace of the Marquis of Marialva, at that place; and the entertaining author of the " Diary of an Invalid," improving on the story, detected on the table the stains of ink spilt by Junot on that occasion. The more accurate Napier (Peninsular War) destroys both fables, by showing to a demonstration that the preliminaries, details, and all particulars connected with the treaty, were discussed and arranged at a distance of twenty miles from Cintra, and had no more connexion with the abode of the Marquis of Marialva than with the imaginary Promontory of Noses, to which the traveller, on the dun-coloured mule, with the huge proboscis, was bound, in Sterne's indecent rhapsody.

The Italian chronicler, Gregorio Leti, who came to reside in England during the reign of Charles II., soon gave out that he intended to employ himself in collecting materials for an anecdotal history of the reign of the merry monarch. The subject was fertile in incident, but likely to be very objectionable in substance. The King, observing him at one of the levées, asked him how his work went on. " I understand," said his Majesty, " that you intend to deal largely in anecdotes of the English court; take care there be no offence." "Sire," answered the Italian, "I will do what I can, and will be as careful as possible; but if a man were as wise as Solomon, he could hardly publish historical anecdotes without giving *some* offence." "Why, then," retorted Charles, "do you copy the wisdom of Solomon; write proverbs, and leave history and anecdotes alone." It would have been well for Leti had he followed this sound advice from one of whom Rochester has recorded in a well-known epigram, that "he never *said* a foolish thing." But he followed his own bent instead, and published his book under the title of "Teatro Britannico." It gave outrageous umbrage in certain high quarters, and raised such a clamour about his ears, that he was ordered to quit the kingdom, which he forthwith did, and betook himself to Amsterdam, where he died in 1701.

This same Gregorio Leti, however defective as a compiler of annals or biography, is entitled to the praise of a most industrious labourer, in more fields than one. He boasted that for twenty consecutive years, without intermission, he presented the world annually with a child and a volume. As a writer of history, his authority is naught. His works of this class are too much overloaded with error and fiction to rank above ingenious romances. But many of his anecdotes are infinitely racy and amusing. In all probability they are founded on truth, which may account for their being so ill-received. All traders in anecdotes, particularly personal "Ana," should keep a constant eye on the caution which Leti disregarded.

Garrick, with every allowance for his great merit, was undoubtedly what is called a lucky man. Life ran smoothly with him, for success was his constant companion. He suffered much in his latter days from more than one painful infirmity; and his retirement in affluence and credit was cut short by the hand of death in three years, and at by no means an advanced age. He began to accumulate the fortune at an early period, which went on continually increasing. His favour with the public never declined; and though he was always in dread of rivals, none ever shook his acknowledged supremacy. His labour was comparatively light, and his performances far less numerous than the drudgery of the modern stage imposes on a leading actor and manager. From thirty to forty comprised the maximum during an average of many seasons. He made two professional visits to Dublin before his purchase of a share in Drury Lane; but, with these exceptions, he never performed in any theatre out of London, after his fame was securely established. He was happy in his domestic life, although not blessed with children. He had his enemies and waspish detractors in common with all other men of talent. These annoyed him more than he should have permitted. Macklin, from personal pique, both wrote and spoke of him disparagingly; and Macklin, in so doing, was ungrateful as well as spiteful. Tate Wilkinson records a specimen of his colloquial conversation, too coarse and vulgar for the pages of an otherwise respectable book; and Kenrick, whose hand, like Ishmael's, was against everybody, provoked him by groundless insinuations, which were unworthy of notice. He had one or two riots in the theatre during a management of twenty-eight years, and sundry squabbles with the Cibber and the Clive. But his term of existence was nearly all sunshine, darkened only by passing clouds. Few who live by a profession have been so uniformly fortunate. That he deserved his good fortune is equally certain. With many trifling faults, such as vanity, and love of adulation, inseparable from his position, Garrick was a kind-hearted, charitable man, an affectionate husband and relative, a firm friend, and far from an implacable enemy. As an actor, he stands unrivalled in the wide scope of his versatility. Others may have equalled, or even excelled him in particular characters or passages, but his range was more extensive than that of any individual who either went before or came after him. He was, perhaps, greater in comedy than in tragedy; but of the two leading divisions of the dramatic art, it is easier to obtain a high degree in the college of Thalia than in that of Melpomene.

CHAPTER X.

FALL OF THE BRUNSWICK THEATRE—LAMENTABLE LOSS OF LIFE, AND MANY SEVERE CASUALTIES—RELIGIOUS INFERENCES—CHARLES KEAN RETURNS TO DRURY LANE—APPEARS IN ROMEO—DISCOURAGEMENT OF THE PAPERS, AND COLDNESS OF THE PUBLIC—VISITS THE COUNTRY AGAIN, AND ACTS WITH HIS FATHER IN DUBLIN AND CORK—AT THE HAYMARKET IN THE AUTUMN OF 1829—SUCCESS IN SIR EDWARD MORTIMER—THE PRESS PRAISE HIM FOR THE FIRST TIME—VISITS AMSTERDAM AND THE HAGUE—THE MANAGER LEAVES THE COMPANY TO SHIFT FOR THEMSELVES—THEY ARE EXTRICATED BY A BENEFIT—CHARLES KEAN'S FIRST VISIT TO AMERICA IN 1830—HIS WARM RECEPTION AND SUCCESS—DEATH OF ROBERT WILLIAM ELLISTON—HIS FIRST GREAT BENEFIT AT THE OPERA HOUSE—HIS EXTRAVAGANT PROPENSITIES—EMBARRASSED AFFAIRS OF COVENT GARDEN THEATRE—APPEARANCE OF MISS FANNY KEMBLE—SHE RETRIEVES THE PROPERTY FROM BANKRUPTCY.

ON the 28th of February, 1828, a lamentable event occurred in the east end of London, by the falling in of the iron roof of the New Brunswick Theatre, erected on the site of the old Royalty, which had been burnt down in 1827. This occurred, most providentially, in the day-time, about half-an-hour previous to a rehearsal, when there were comparatively few persons within the building. Eleven dead bodies were dug out of the ruins, and twenty-two still living sufferers; more than one of whom died afterwards in hospital of the injuries they had received. Had this catastrophe taken place at night, during the performance, it is awful to think of the hundreds, perhaps thousands, that would have been immolated.. Some overheated pietists, who are ever ready to "saddle with a judgment" (as Thwackum dealt with Square) whatever they happen to disapprove, loudly declared this accident to be a manifest instance of Divine anger, excited by the horrible profligacy and impiety of the stage. Similar sentences are pronounced without scruple, whenever any sudden calamity befalls a theatre or an actor. The Rev. John Duncan, Rector of Wimborne Minster, Dorset, in a treatise entitled "The Lawfulness of the Stage Inquired Into," published in 1787, quotes the burning of the great theatre at Amsterdam, while the audience were in it,—the Burwell Tragedy in 1727, when eighty persons were burned in a barn, while looking at a puppet-show—and a terrible fire in Wapping, by a pitch-kettle boiling over, all hands belonging to the yard having run into the street to see a dancing bear. He sums up as follows: —"If God had no hand in any of these evils, it is evident he had none in preventing them." It is certainly not easy to parry this mode of reasoning, which affords a specimen of the antithetical style, sufficiently wide to embrace all imaginable casualties.

When Covent Garden and Drury Lane were burnt in 1808 and 1809—when Palmer died on the stage at Liverpool, and Cummins at York,—on these and similar occasions, homilies were delivered and pamphlets printed, all declaring in plain terms that every case was "a judgment from Heaven!" When the Brunswick Theatre fell, a sermon was actually preached in the ruins before all the sufferers were removed or the extent of the mischief ascertained. But accidents such as these have happened to churches and chapels dedicated to holy worship, to ministers in the exercise of their sacred office, and to individuals at their private devotions. It would be difficult to find any voice sufficiently bold or blasphemous to say, that the wrath of offended Heaven speaks in these instances also; or to deduce from thence, arguments against preaching or praying. Yet, on what ground shall such conclusions be demanded in the one case and denied in the other? What says Minutius Felix, in an early defence of Christianity?—"Fulmina passim cadunt; sine delectu tangunt loca sacra et profana; homines noxios feriunt, sæpe et religiosos." * Thunderbolts fall indifferently; they light upon places profane and sacred without any choice; they strike good men and bad alike. Occurrences of sudden death or misfortune are powerful arguments to arouse the thoughtless to reflection, or the profligate to repentance; for such purposes we may suppose them to be intended, but we have no warrant to make arbitrary distinctions, or to build conclusions founded on bigotry or prejudice.

A letter from Mr. Percy Farren, stage-manager of the Brunswick Theatre, printed with the farce called " An Uncle Too Many," contains some interesting particulars relative to the sudden destruction of the building. He says:—" Previously to relating my share in the occurrences of that memorable morning, I must most distinctly state that, for myself, I never apprehended the slightest insecurity, nor did I ever hear an opinion that led to such a belief in others. It was about half-past eleven o'clock, after I had been for some time conversing with Mr. Maurice, the proprietor, in the front of his private box, on the opposite prompt side of the stage, upon the subject of some theatrical arrangements, that our attention was arrested by an almost indescribable discordant sound, which must have been heard in every corner of the building, and continued for several seconds. Upon looking upwards, whence it seemed to proceed, I observed the lustre falling. My poor friend rushed towards the centre of the stage, apparently to ascertain the cause of alarm, whilst I, almost without a

* Minutius Felix, Octav. p. 14. Edit. Oxon. 1631.

consciousness of what I did, sprang into the box, and supported myself by the outward pillar of the proscenium.   In an instant, the whole fabric fell before me with an awful crash ; the iron roof buried all beneath it, and the sky was entirely open to my view.   So complete appeared the work of death and destruction around me, that for some time I considered myself the only survivor of this fearful ruin, until, through the cloud of dust, I distinguished Mrs. Vaughan's daughter, Miss Yates, severely wounded in the head, and heard her imploring me to save her.   With some difficulty I succeeded in rescuing her from her perilous situation, and, on placing her by my side in the box, urged her grateful acknowledgments to the Almighty for her preservation up to that moment.   The exact period that we remained in this precarious safety, every moment expecting destruction, I cannot conjecture : but my fervent gratitude may be conceived, when I at length saw some carpenters and other workmen climbing wounded and bleeding through the rubbish.   Upon their recognizing me, I expressed my joy at their escape with life, and inquired if our danger was yet over.   Their replies convinced me of the necessity of instant exertion, and amidst horrors and difficulties, which I shall not attempt to describe, I descended and found myself on my knees at the bottom of the ruins, with Miss Yates locked in my arms.   Having recovered from the oppression on my feelings by a violent flood of tears, I was at length enabled to place my interesting charge in a place of safety, and, thank Heaven ! providentially escaped myself without any personal injury.   I first informed Mrs. Vaughan of the preservation of her daughter, and then, in a state of mind more easily conceived than described, went to inform my brothers of my own miraculous rescue.   On my return to the scene of terror I learned the confirmation of my worst fears in the irreparable loss of my most esteemed friend Mr. Maurice, and of the many others who died with him. At the moment when the calamity occurred I was too horror-struck, and my mind too entirely occupied with my own preservation for me to be competent to speak with any accuracy of the escape of those who happily, like me, live to be grateful for it. The number of persons then in the theatre I am also unable to state with any confidence ; though there certainly could not have been more than from twenty to thirty-five on the stage ; and, I should say, scarcely more than the same number in other parts of the building."

Charles Kean resumed his engagement at Drury Lane a few days before the Christmas of 1828. His country tour had given him practice and confidence. On the 15th of December, a young lady of great promise (a pupil of Mrs. St. Ledger), named Phillips, was announced as a first appearance in *Juliet*. Price, the manager, thought that it would be injudicious to risk the appearance of two novices on the same night; and intimated to the expectant *Romeo* that a more experienced hand must be selected for the first performance, but that he should take his place on the second. The mortification was great, but inevitable; so nothing remained but to digest it, and feed on hope. The chosen Montague was of the genus *respectable*, a term hateful to the actor to whom it is applied, but popular with some critics, who thereby think they express considerable excellence. He was neither youthful, nor fascinating, nor elegant, but he was *safe;* and nothing more was required or expected. Kean sat in the front of the house, and looked on with interest, and something of the natural jealousy which arose from seeing his post occupied by another. He marked, with inward satisfaction, that the slaying of

Tybalt passed off without notice. It was tame and business-like. He, however, expected to produce a great point here, by rapid, graceful fencing, and a striking attitude. On that day week he came to the trial. When he rushed furiously on *Tybalt*, and after two or three tremendous thrusts, stood bewildered over his fallen enemy, the house thundered down their plaudits, and the actor's heart beat high with exultation. On the following morning an influential paper, speaking in general condemnation of Mr. Kean, junior, observed of this particular passage, that Mr. ―― would have been a much more effective representative of *Romeo*, judging by the immense applause he received in the fall and death of such a comparatively inferior part as *Tybalt*. On Boxing-night, as it is called, " Lover's Vows " was revived, when Miss Ellen Tree, the future Mrs. C. Kean, acted *Amelia Wildenhaim ;* this being the first time of their meeting together on the stage.

Fortune was not yet prepared to smile on Charles Kean's efforts. The press continued to discourage, and the public neglected him. He remained a member of the company, but his services were seldom required. He was evidently of no importance to the management, and felt that he was losing his own time. He, therefore, took the first opportunity of again visiting the provinces, for the sake of hard study and frequent practice. In the course of the summer he acted with his father in Dublin and Cork, appearing as *Titus, Bassanio, Wellborn, Iago, Icilius,* and *Macduff.*

In October, 1829, he accepted an offer from Mr. Morris, of the Haymarket Theatre, to play six nights, during the concluding fortnight of the season, for which he was to receive 20*l.* He commenced as *Reuben Glenroy;* acted *Romeo* twice to Miss F. H. Kelly's *Juliet ; Frederick,* in " Lovers' Vows ;" and *Sir Edward Mortimer* in the

" Iron Chest."   For the first time he felt that he had succeeded.   The latter play was repeated on the closing night of the season, with increased effect and attraction. The papers afforded him positive praise.   He could scarcely believe it real.

Mr. Morris was so struck with the effect he produced in *Sir Edward Mortimer*, that he offered to engage him permanently for such parts in heavy tragedy as *Richard* and *Macbeth*, telling him that he would find his true bent in that line.   Charles Kean, with sound judgment, declined the tempting offer, and replied to the manager's proposal that, though such was his ambition, he knew that he required more experience before he could encounter the risk.

During the early part of 1830, he visited Amsterdam and the Hague, with an English company, under the management of an adventurer named Aubrey ; being tempted by an offer of 20*l.* per week, which his employer evidently had no intention of paying, and of which, with the exception of a few pounds at the commencement, he never received a penny.   After a short experiment of about three weeks, Aubrey decamped, leaving his actors without funds, and in rather an awkward predicament, to shift for themselves.   As their only resource, they announced a general benefit at Amsterdam, to which the King of Holland contributed by a handsome present. The receipts were doled out in due proportion, and the modicum allotted to Charles Kean enabled him to return to England, by way of Calais.   He now began to feel his strength ; his powers were called forth by exercise ; and he had obtained a mastery over the mechanical part of his profession—a knowledge of " stage business," which severe apprenticeship only can accomplish.   He therefore determined to try his fortune in America ; and, accordingly, crossed the Atlantic, and appeared at the

N 2

Park Theatre, New York, as *Richard the Third*, in the early part of September, 1830.

The name of Kean was already well known to our transatlantic descendants ; not only by the voice of fame, but by the two visits of his father, who had produced a most powerful and permanent impression throughout the United States. They were prepared to greet the son with warm cordiality. His reception was all he could desire. Everywhere he attracted numerous audiences, and gained applause, with a solid accompaniment of dollars. His hopes revived in proportion. It was no small triumph for a lad, still under twenty, to establish an enduring American reputation, in such characters as *Richard the Third, Hamlet, Romeo, Sir Edward Mortimer,* and *Sir Giles Overreach*.

Some few years later, at a public dinner in Waterford, he spoke thus of the encouragement which hailed him on his first visit to America :—

"Thrown before the public by untoward circumstances, at the early age of sixteen and a-half, encompassed by many difficulties, friendless, and untutored, the efforts of my boyhood were criticised in so severe and spirit-crushing a strain, as almost to unnerve my energies, and drive me despairingly from the stage. The indulgence usually extended to novices was denied to me. I was not permitted to cherish the hope that time and study could ever enable me to correct the faults of youthful inexperience. The very resemblance I bore to my late father was urged against me as an offence, and condemned as being 'strange and unnatural.' Sick at heart, I left my home and sought the shores of America. To the generous inhabitants of that far land I am indebted for the first ray of success that illumined my clouded career."

During Charles Kean's absence in America, an actor

of great and varied abilities, Robert William Elliston, " shuffled off this mortal coil." He died July the 7th, 1831, aged fifty-seven, and was buried on the 15th of the same month, at St. John's Church, Waterloo Road. At the time of his decease, he was manager of the Surrey Theatre, where he made his last appearance as *Sheva*, on the 24th of June. He was announced in the bills for *Megrim*, on the 28th, but his rapid illness interfered, and the public saw him no more.

Elliston, in his best days, was a most fascinating, brilliant performer, with powers nearly as universal as those of Garrick. Perhaps this universality injured his fame. His comedy was superior to his tragedy, although he succeeded in the arduous character of *Sir Edward Mortimer*, in which John Kemble had signally failed. His early reputation, like that of Henderson and Mrs. Siddons, was won in Bath. During the height of his popularity he was engaged in London, and through a part of the same season, acted in both places, running backwards and forwards as he was wanted. This rapidity of locomotion, in the old days of heavy coaches, obtained for him the name of the " Telegraph," or " Fortnightly Actor." But the arrangement was found to be inconvenient as well as unprofitable to all parties, and was soon abandoned.

Having performed at the Haymarket for several seasons during the summer, he at length appeared at Drury Lane, to contest supremacy with Kemble, as *Rolla*, in " Pizarro; " being engaged to assume the leading line in both departments of the drama. His success was so great that he took his first benefit at the Opera House —Drury Lane not being large enough to accommodate the expected overflow. The house was literally carried by assault. At every entrance the rush was so overwhelming that the door-keepers, money-takers, and assistants, were swept before it, and a scene of confusion ensued, not easy to describe or understand. Fortunately no accident occurred. An address was made from the stage by the actor, and hats were handed round to collect the price of admission from those who had been forced in without the option of disbursement. The receipts reached 600*l.*; but if all the places occupied had been fairly paid for, they would have exceeded 1000*l.*, being the largest sum ever levied on the public by any performer on the occasion of his benefit.

Elliston was the original *Duke Aranza* in the "Honeymoon:" a part exactly suited to him in all its points, and in which he has never been equalled. He had a fine, full-toned voice, and though sometimes inflated and extravagant in tragedy, he delivered a sentiment, or an occasional didactic speech in comedy, with an effect peculiar to himself. Mrs. Inchbald, a professed theatrical critic, engaged to write prefatory notices for an edition of the " British Theatre," says, in her remarks on the "Honeymoon," "Mr. Elliston's *Duke* is most excellent through all his different scenes; and the character requires abilities of so varied and forcible a nature, that to represent him perfectly in all the vicissitudes of his honeymoon is to possess powers of acting equal to the personation of every comic, and almost every tragic hero on the stage." When we consider that this is written of a part that never soars beyond level speaking, of which the leading attributes are ease, elegance, humour, and firmness mingled with affection—but, at the same time, utterly untinctured by a scintillation of the terrible passions which rend *Othello*, *Macbeth*, *Lear*, or *Richard*—we lift up our hands in wonder at the hyperbolical summary, and think what strange judgment it must be that could run into such a ridiculous extreme. You may cull a hundred first-rate *Duke Aranzas* before you reach one passable

Hamlet, Shylock, or *Jaffier.*   A criticism delivered on Edmund Kean, when he played the *Duke* in the "Honey-moon," is almost as good as Mrs. Inchbald's.   "Well, Tom, how did you like it?"   "Oh! it was magnificent: Kean's dancing is glorious itself, by Jupiter!"

Elliston's last appearance at Drury Lane occurred in May, 1826, when he twice performed *Falstaff,* in "King Henry the Fourth."   Great expectations were excited which were not realized.   He possessed every requisite for the part, and ought to have surpassed Henderson, or any living representative.   He rehearsed splendidly, but failed when it came to the acting.   Long habits of dissipation had impaired his powers before their legitimate time of decay—for he was then only fifty-two; but he had become careless, vulgarized in style, and slovenly in his delivery of the text of his author.   In the same manner he had dilapidated his fortune by an inveterate indulgence in gambling—a vice in itself sufficient to exhaust the treasury of Crœsus down to the most imperceptible residuum.   Amongst his best parts, while in his zenith, may be reckoned, *Vapour, Captain Absolute, Sylvester Daggerwood, Walter, Sheva, Octavian, Rolla, Fitzharding,* in the "Curfew," *Sir Edward Mortimer, Young Rapid, Dr. Pangloss, Rover, Ranger, Vapid, Abednego, Bob Handy, Tangent, Belcour,* the *Three Singles, Jeremy Diddler, Duke Aranza, Felix,* in the "Hunter of the Alps," and *Mercutio.*   He failed utterly in *Wolsey* and *Lord Townly.*   So did Garrick in *Marplot, Gil Blas,* and *Othello.*

Elliston was treated very shabbily by the Drury Lane proprietors, or committee.   He laid out many thousands in remodelling and improving the theatre; but because he fell into a small arrear of rent, they kicked him out unceremoniously, for which act of gross injustice, retribution came on them in due course.

It has too often been the destiny of large theatres to become a prey to the Fire King, or to be engulphed in the devouring whirlpool of the Bankruptcy Court. The latter fate had nearly anticipated the former, at Covent Garden, in the year 1829. The newspapers said in August, " The affairs of Covent Garden continue in a bad state. Yesterday the magistrates at Bow Street signed distress warrants for 896*l.* for arrears of parish rates, and the King's Collector is now in possession for assessed taxes, due to the amount of above 600*l.*" Then the ground landlord came in, and the walls were placarded with bills of sale by auction. The hammer of George Robins stood ready elevated, and the " incomparable stock" appeared to be on the very eve of dispersion. The proprietors made a last cogent appeal to the public, and the appeal was responded to. In September new paragraphs appeared, to this effect :—

" It is said that the ruin which would be consequent on the sale of the fine wardrobe, splendid scenery, glasses, chandeliers, and decorations of Covent Garden Theatre, is likely to be averted, by the interference of three or four persons of high rank and consideration."

And again :—

" The subscription for opening Covent Garden Theatre proceeds admirably. Several persons of rank and respectability sent various sums yesterday to the Committee."

" The King's Theatre was thronged to an overflow on Friday, in aid of the Covent Garden subscription fund. The net proceeds amount to 750*l.*"

Charles Kemble, on the 9th of September, wrote to the author of these pages as follows :—

" You will, I know, be delighted to hear that my appeal has been answered with even more success than our most sanguine hopes had anticipated. The stone is set rolling, and, I doubt not, will gather marvellously."

On the 5th of October, the theatre opened, when Miss Fanny Kemble made her first appearance as *Juliet*—her father as *Mercutio*,—and her mother, Mrs. C. Kemble, returning to the stage for that night, to support her daughter,—as *Lady Capulet*. Abbott, in the absence of a better, was specially retained for *Romeo*. At the bottom of the bill it was said,—" Miss Kelly has consented to perform gratuitously for ten nights. Miss Foote has also given her services for ten nights. Mr. T. P. Cooke has offered to act six nights, and Mr. Kean will act three nights gratuitously, on his return to London."

Miss F. Kemble proved so attractive that she enabled the proprietors of Covent Garden, in a single season, to pay off 13,000*l.* of pressing debt. Her characters were *Juliet, Belvidera, Euphrasia, Mrs. Beverley, Portia,* and *Isabella.* The papers were extravagant in her praise, and the public received her with enthusiasm, bordering on affection. The impression that she came forward to save the theatre, and to retrieve the affairs of her father and family, added materially to the interest of her performances. Her talent was extraordinary, and her success well-merited; but it was impossible that at nineteen, without an apprenticeship, she could be either Mrs. Siddons or Miss O'Neill, although there were not wanting over-heated admirers who said she was both.

What somebody christened her *Canova*, in *Juliet*, we always considered a terrible mistake. In the fourth act, when during the soliloquy which precedes her taking the potion, she fancies that she sees the ghost of her cousin *Tybalt*, she ran down from the back of the stage to the right-hand corner of the proscenium, under the stage-box ; and there threw herself into an attitude upon one knee as if driving the apparition before her. Even so under the old conventional system, *Macbeth* was accustomed to bully the spirit of the intruding *Banquo* at the royal feast (the said spirit being usually personated by a stout gentleman), step by step, from O. P. to P. S. In both cases nature was equally forgotten. We recoil from an object of terror instead of rushing madly to grapple with it. But, to redeem the false reading, Fanny Kemble's "*Do it!*" in the "Hunchback" was really magnificent.

CHAPTER XI.

DURING the season of 1829-30, at Covent Garden, Mrs. Davenport and Fawcett took leave of the stage. The lady was an excellent actress in her proper line of comic old women, which she never stepped from, either through vanity or the occasional exigencies of the theatre. She originally acted, as a child, at Bath, when Miss Harvey, as far back as December 21st, 1784. As Mrs. Davenport, she appeared in London, in the character of *Mrs. Hardcastle,* on the 24th of September, 1794. On the 29th of May, 1830, she retired, after thirty-six years of faithful and unremitting service. The last performance was for her own benefit, as the *Nurse* in " Romeo and Juliet."

John Fawcett was the son of an actor who held a situation of minor importance at Drury Lane. At the age of fifteen he was apprenticed to a linen-draper, but left the shop clandestinely for the Margate theatre, where he assumed the name of Foote, and commenced a business more congenial to his taste. He afterwards joined Tate Wilkinson in the York circuit, and in 1791, made his bow to a London audience, at Covent Garden, as *Caleb* in " He would be a Soldier." His reputation advanced rapidly by his performances of *Ollapod, Dr. Pangloss,* and *Caleb Quotem.* Volubility and distinctness of utterance were amongst his natural requisites, and these were particularly essential in the above-named parts. There is an admirable portrait of him, by Clint, in the collection of the Garrick Club, as *Captain Copp*, with Charles Kemble as the *King*, in a scene from " Charles II." In this character, which he had played with great success, he bade farewell to the public on the 20th of May, 1830.

Fawcett was the original *Job Thornberry*, in " John Bull," a part which furnished an excellent specimen of his peculiar style. Munden was called to the reading, having been told by Colman that he had measured him to a hair. He expected *Job Thornberry*, and chuckled with delight as the reading proceeded ; but great was his indignation when, at the close, *Sir Simon Rochdale* was put into his hand. This he peremptorily refused, and it was then transferred to Blanchard, to whom it proved a valuable step in the ladder of promotion.

The original cast of " John Bull " is worth remembering, as a sample of how plays were acted at Covent Garden under the government of the elder Harris ; *Job Thornberry*, Fawcett ; *Hon. Tom Shuffleton*, Lewis ; *Peregrine*, Cooke ; *Dennis Brulgruddery*, Johnstone ; *Sir Simon Rochdale*, Blanchard ; *Frank Rochdale*, H. Johnston ; *Dan*, Emery ; *Lord Fitz-Balaam*, Waddy ; *Mary Thornberry*, Mrs. Gibbs ; *Lady Caroline Braymore*, Mrs. H. Johnston ; and *Mrs. Brulgruddery*, Mrs. Davenport. All these were first-rate artists in their respective lines. No single theatre in the present day could produce anything like a parallel. The play, brought out in March, 1803, ran forty-eight nights the first season—an enormous longevity fifty years ago. The name (" John Bull ; or, an Englishman's Fireside ") was happily chosen at the time, as the whole nation was in arms to resist the threat of French invasion at the commencement of the war; but the piece contained not the most remote allusion to politics or public affairs.

Cooke said of this comedy (in Dunlap's "Memoirs"), "We got 'John Bull' from Colman, act by act, as he wanted money, but the last act did not come, and Harris refused to make any further advances. At last, necessity drove Colman to make a finish, and he wrote the fifth act in one night, on separate sheets of paper. As he filled one piece after the other, he threw them on the floor, and finishing his liquor, went to bed. Harris, who impatiently expected the conclusion of the play, according to promise, sent Fawcett to Colman, whom he found still in bed. By his direction, Fawcett picked up the scraps, and brought them to the theatre." An improvement on this story is told of Sheridan and "Pizarro." It has been said, that the last act was not finished when the curtain drew up on the first night, and that the parts were delivered to the actors before the ink was dry, and during the progress of the performance.

Those were halcyon days for managerial exchequers, when a single comedy such as "John Bull," the "Heir-at-Law," and the "Poor Gentleman," was considered novelty enough for an entire season. No new scenery was looked for, and the dresses were a mere nothing. There was no previous outlay of two or three thousand pounds, before a shilling could revert to the treasury.

Fawcett succeeded Lewis as stage-manager at Covent Garden, and filled that unenviable office for many years, with as much popularity as belongs to the post. The stage-manager is the adjutant of the establishment. If he does his duty to the commanding-officer, he is hated by the corps. If he sides with the rank and file he becomes suspicious to the chief. In private life Fawcett was kind-hearted and irreproachable; but in his official capacity there was a quickness of manner which sometimes appeared like intentional rudeness. A performer in his own line, and of equal talent, once said to him that he disliked a new part; " You are not engaged to like your part," replied Fawcett, " you are engaged to act it." He was not profound in erudition, and some whimsical stories have been told of his proposed amendments in the elocutionary defects of careless actors : amongst others, the late William Abbott used to declare that the stage-manager publicly rebuked him at a rehearsal for saying " imminent danger," informing him that the adjective should be " eminent."

Fawcett possessed much versatility, and many of his delineations were as perfect as art and strong conception could render them. He could either melt the heart with pathos, or stimulate mirth with keen discriminating humour. As an instance of the homely pathetic, his *Rolamo*, in " Clari," was excellent. His *Falstaffs* were loudly praised; while his *Touchstone* was considered by many equal to King's. Neither were his *Lord Ogleby* and *Sir Peter Teazle* much behind in the race; until William Farren, in a sharp contest, left him in the rear, and came in at least neck-and-neck with the original.

We may here ask permission to step aside a little from our regular course, to mention a most extraordinary phenomenon who visited England for the first time in 1831; and though not a member of the English stage, becomes connected with its history from having exhibited his rare talent in several leading theatres. We allude to Nicolo Paganini, the inimitable violinist. He came with a prodigious introductory flourish, a vast continental reputation, and a few personal legends of the most exciting character. It was said that he had killed his wife in a fit of jealousy, and made fiddle-strings of her intestines; and that the devil composed a sonata for him in a dream, as he formerly did for Tartini. When you looked at him you thought all this and more very likely to be true. His talent was almost supernatural; while his "get up," or *mise en scène*, as the French have it, was original and unearthly—such as those who saw him will never forget, and those who did not can with difficulty conceive. The man and his performance were equally unlike anything that had ever been witnessed before. No picture or description can convey an adequate idea of his mode of entrance and exit. To walk simply on and off the stage appears a common-place operation enough; but Paganini did this in a manner of his own, which baffled all imitators. When he placed himself in position to commence, the crowded audience became hushed into a death-like silence; and the thousands present gazed in motionless fascination on that strange epitome of many contrasted attributes. They took in at a glance his black habiliments; his sallow, attenuated visage; his chiselled features, Satanically expressive; his long, silky, raven tresses, and the flash of his dark eye as he shook them back on his shoulders; his thin, transparent fingers, unusually long; the fashion after which he grasped his bow, with the tremendous length to which he drew it; and, climax of all, the antithetical suddenness with which he jerked both bow and instrument under his arm, while he threw his hands behind him, elevated his head, his countenance almost writhing under what was meant for a smile of ecstacy, and his very hair instinct with life, at the conclusion of a bewildering fantasia! And there he stood, immovable and triumphant, while the theatre rang again with peals on peals of applause, and shouts of the most excited enthusiasm! None who witnessed this are likely again to see the same effect produced by mere mortal agency.

The *one* string feat was unworthy of this great master

in his art. It has been performed by fifty others, and is at best but an imperfect exhibition on a perfect instrument; a mere piece of charlatanerie, or theatrical "gag," to use a professional term, sufficiently intelligible. There have been, and are, mighty magicians on the violin. Spagnoletti, De Beriot, Ole Bull (who, according to some, plays without any string at all), Sivori, Joachim, Ernst, and others, are all in the list of fine players; but there never was a second Paganini.

In Dublin, during the autumn of 1831, Paganini saved the musical festival, which would have failed utterly but for his individual attraction, although supported by an array of talent in every department. The festival was held in the Theatre Royal, then, as now, the only building in the city capable of accommodating the vast numbers which alone could render such an experiment remunerative. The arrangement was to have oratorios kept distinct on certain mornings, and miscellaneous concerts on the evenings of other days. The concerts were crushers, while the first oratorio was a break-down. Many who would listen to sacred music in a church, or hall, objected to enter a theatre; but both cathedrals had been refused on application. The committee became alarmed; the expenses were enormous, and heavy liabilities stared them in the face. There was no time to be lost in hesitating scruples, and at the second oratorio, duly announced, Paganini appeared, violin in hand, in front of the orchestra, on an advanced platform overhanging the pit, not unlike orator Henley's tub, as immortalized by the satiric poet. Between the acts of the "Messiah" and the "Creation," he fiddled "The Witches at the great Walnut-tree of Benevento," with other equally appropriate interpolations, to the extatic delight of the applauding majority, who cared not a pin for Haydn or Handel, but came to hear Paganini alone;

and to the no small scandal of the pious few, who looked upon the episode as too much on the north side of consistency. But expediency carried the day; the money was thereby forthcoming, everybody was paid in full, the committee escaped without damage, and a hazardous speculation undertaken by a few spirited amateurs was wound up with deserved success.

When the festival was over, the town empty, and a cannon-ball might have been fired down Sackville-street without doing much injury, Paganini engaged himself for a series of five concerts, in the theatre. For these he received 1,143*l.* His dividend on the first night amounted to 333*l.* The terms he demanded, and obtained, were a clear two-thirds of each receipt; twenty-five guineas per night for Pio Cianchettini, a poor pianoforte player, and a Signora Pietralia, a vocalist who could not sing at all; the full value for every free ticket, and an express codicil to the agreement, that if he required a rehearsal on a dark morning, when extra light might be indispensable, the expense of candles should not fall on him;—a contingency which by ho possible contrivance could involve a responsibility exceeding five or six shillings.

Paganini was in all respects a very singular being, and an interesting subject for study. His talents were by no means confined to his wonderful powers as a musician. On other subjects he was well informed, acute, and conversable, of bland and gentle manners, and in society perfectly well bred. All this contrasted strangely with the dark stories that were bruited abroad, touching some passages in his early life. But outward semblance and deportment are treacherous quicksands, when taken as guides by which to sound the real depths of human character. Lord Byron has told us that his pocket was once picked by the civilest person he ever conversed with, and that by far the mildest individual of his acquaintance was the remorseless Ali Pacha of Yanina. The same has been said of Djezzar, the butcher of Acre, who, as Mrs. Flockhart says of Fergus M'Ivor, was reputed to be "a quiet, weel-spoken gentleman, when not in ane o' his deevilish tirrivies."

The expressive lineaments of Paganini's face told a powerful tale of passions which had been fearfully excited, which might be raised again from temporary slumber, or were exhausted by indulgence and premature decay, leaving deep furrows to mark their intensity. Like the aggregate of his countrymen, he looked much older than he was. Born at Genoa in 1784, he was in his forty-seventh year at the time of his first visit to England. With Italians in general, the elastic vigour of youth and manhood rapidly subsides into a protracted and joyless old age, numbering as many years, but with far less of physical and mental faculty to render them endurable, than the more equally poised gradations of our northern clime. It is by no means unusual to meet a well-developed Italian, whiskered to the eyebrows, and "bearded like the pard," who tells you, to your utter astonishment, that he is scarcely sixteen, when you have set him down from his appearance as, at least, five-and-thirty. The women are full grown at thirteen, begin to decay at two or three and twenty, and then become speedily old, but never die. An ancient marchesa, or duchess, is as immortal as her diamonds.

Paganini's father, who was a commission broker by trade, but a great admirer of music, initiated his son in the principles of the art at a very early age, and as he grew up, placed him successively under the able instructions of Costa, Rolla, and Paer. His first professional appearance was at Lucca, where he found a zealous patroness in the Princess Elisa Bacciocchi, sister of Napoleon. The following extract from Colonel Montgomery Maxwell's book of military reminiscences, entitled, " My Adventures," dated Genoa, February 22d, 1815, supplies the earliest record which has been given to the public respecting Paganini, and affords authentic evidence that some of the mysterious tales which heralded his coming, were not without foundation:—

" Talking of music, I have become acquainted with the most *outré*, most extravagant, and strangest character I ever beheld, or heard, in the musical line. He has just been emancipated from durance vile, where he has been for a long time incarcerated on suspicion of murder. There is something scriptural or Jewish in the *tout ensemble* of the strange physiognomy of this uncouth and unearthly figure. Not that, as in times of old, he plays, as Holy Writ tells us, on a ten-stringed instrument: on the contrary, he brings the most powerful, the most wonderful, and the most heart-rending tones from one string. His name is Paganini; he is very improvident, and very poor. The D——'s and the Impresario of the theatre got up a concert for him the other night, which was well attended, and on which occasion he electrified the audience. He is a native of Genoa, and if I were a judge of violin playing, I should pronounce him the most surprising performer in the world."

That Paganini was either innocent of the charge for which he suffered the incarceration Colonel Maxwell mentions, or that it could not be proved against him, may be reasonably inferred from the fact that he escaped the galleys or the executioner. In Italy there was then, (whatever there may be now), an exclusive law for the rich and another for the poor. As he was without money or friends, and unable to buy immunity, it is charitable to suppose he was entitled to it from innocence. A nobleman, with a few *zecchini* to bribe the court, was in little danger from the law, which confined its practice entirely to the lower orders. In 1814, a Sicilian prince, who afterwards became a sort of fashionable lion in London for a season, most wantonly blew a vassal's brains out, merely because he put him in a passion. The case was not even inquired into, although it happened at the time when we were supposed to have conferred on the inhabitants of Trinacria the blessings and benefits of the English constitution, and to have abolished the feudal privileges and abuses. The prince sent half a dollar to the widow of the defunct (which, by the way, he borrowed from the writer of these memoirs, and never repaid), and there the matter ended. Lord Nelson once suggested to Ferdinand IV. of Naples to try and check the daily increase of assassination, by a few salutary executions. "No, no," replied old Nasone, who was far from being as great a fool as he looked, "that is impossible. If I once began that system, my kingdom would soon be depopulated. One half of my subjects would continually be employed in hanging the remainder."

Amongst other peculiarities, Paganini was a living compound of avarice and parsimony, with a most contradictory passion for gambling. He would haggle for sixpence in an engagement, and stake a rouleau on a single turn at *rouge-et-noir*. He screwed all who dealt with him in a bargain as tightly as if they were compressed in a vice; yet he had intervals of liberality, and occasionally deviated into a generous action. In this he bore some resemblance to the celebrated John Elwes of miserly notoriety, who debarred himself from the common necessaries of life and lived on a potato-skin, but had been known to give a cheque for 100*l*. to a public charity, and to contribute largely to private subscriptions. It is not on record that Paganini went so far as this; but once or twice he played for nothing, and sent a donation to the Mendicity Association when he was in Dublin.

Paganini had a faithful attendant called Antonio, who tried to ape his master, but without success, in some of his peculiarities. He affected silence, solemnity, and eccentricity, but these attributes sat uneasily upon him, and he frequently abandoned them, and became social and communicative. Voltaire says, " No man is a hero to his *valet-de-chambre*," meaning thereby, as we may suppose, that, being behind the scenes of every-day life, he finds out that Marshal Saxe or Frederick the Great is as subject to the common infirmities of our nature as John Noakes or Peter Styles. Whether Paganini's squire of the body looked upon his master as a hero in the vulgar acceptation of the word, it is now useless to inquire; but, in spite of his stinginess, which the lackey writhed under, he regarded him with mingled reverence and terror. " A strange person, your master," once observed a visitor. " *Signore*," replied the faithful Sancho Panza, " *è veramente grand 'uomo ; ma da non potersi comprendere.*" He is a truly great man, but quite incomprehensible. It was edifying to mark the awful importance with which Antonio bore the instrument nightly entrusted to his charge to carry to and from the theatre. He considered it an animated something, whether demon or angel he was unable to determine; but this he firmly believed, that it could speak in actual dialogue when his master pleased, or become a dumb familiar by the same controlling volition. This especial violin was Paganini's inseparable companion. It lay on his table before him as he sat meditating in his solitary chamber; it was placed by his side at dinner ; and on a chair within his reach when in bed. If he woke, as he constantly did, in the dead of night, and the sudden *estro* of composition seized him, he grasped his instrument, started up, and, on the instant, perpetuated the inspiration which otherwise he might have lost for ever. This marvellous Cremona, valued at four hundred guineas, Paganini, on his death-bed, gave to De Kontski, his nephew and only pupil,—also an eminent performer,—and in his possession it lately remained.

Paganini, having received enormous sums of money in France and England, returned to Italy, to take up his abode. His last years were spent at his villa Gajona, near Parma, but he died at Nice in 1840. Not long before his decease, he purchased the title of Baron, with a patent of nobility, from some foreign potentate, we believe, the King of Bavaria. These, with his accumulated earnings, somewhat dilapidated by gaming, he bequeathed to his only son. He was the founder of his school, and the inventor of those extraordinary tricks, with which his endless successors and imitators are accustomed to astonish the uninitiated. But he still stands at the head of the list, although it includes many eminent names, and is not likely to be pushed from his pedestal.

We turn from our digression on this singular exotic to speak of the retirement of one of the most popular of English actors, who justly merited the esteem in which he was held both in his private and professional character. We allude to Charles Young, who closed his public career at Covent Garden, on the 30th of May, 1832. The character he selected on this occasion was *Hamlet*, always considered one of his best performances, and in which he originally presented himself to a London audience at the Haymarket, on the 22d June, 1807. Matthews, who had played *Polonius* with him on his entrance, resumed the same character at his exit, and Macready complimented him by appearing as the *Ghost*. Every place in the boxes had been taken for some days;

and the first rush filled the pit and galleries to such excess that, from the former, several females were handed over the boxes as they could not endure the dreadful pressure, notwithstanding they had been able to undergo the annoyance of waiting for hours at the doors, and the positive suffering of getting through them. The extremely crowded state of the audience occasioned much confusion and discontent; so much so, that the earlier part of the tragedy was inaudible, and the actors made symbols of speech, and stared at each other with the most edifying expression. Egerton first came forward, bowed, spread his arms, and retired to the wing, to consult; bowed, spread his arms again, and finally withdrew without being able to obtain a hearing. Young then appeared. He had hoped to be allowed to go on with his part, and that his presence would have stilled the storm, but he was mistaken. He advanced to the orchestra, and at last was made to understand that more had been admitted than the house would hold without risk of suffocation. He expressed his regret, and promised that the money should be returned to all those who " would have the kindness to take it and quit the theatre." But, by this time, the inconvenienced had wedged themselves into a few yielding inches of space, nobody thought fit to depart, and the disturbance gradually subsided. Notwithstanding the discontent, Young was loudly and unanimously greeted on his entrance, and he acknowledged his reception with becoming grace. He left off acting in the full vigour of his powers, before they evinced the slightest symptoms of decay, and before he began to feel the inroads of age. In his case, there was no coquetting with last appearances, no recalls for a few nights " by special desire," no longing aspirations to hear once more the applause of former days. When remonstrated with by some zealous admirers who wished him to postpone his resolution, he replied, with the true spirit of a philosopher, and in the words of *Penruddock* which he had so often delivered, " When I am quietly retiring from the stage of this vain world, call me not back to lose the little grace that I have gained; I would not be made a spectacle in my decline and dotage." To his last audience he repeated the same sentiment in his farewell address. "It has been asked of me," he said, "why I retire from the stage while I am in possession of all the qualifications I could ever aspire to, unimpaired? I will give you my motives, but reason and feeling are not always cater-cousins. I feel the excitement and toil of my profession weigh more heavily upon me than formerly; and, if my qualifications are still unweakened, so I would have them remain. I know that they were never worthy of the degree of approbation with which you honoured them; but, such as they are, I am unwilling to continue before my patrons until I can offer them only tarnished metal."

Young was in easy, independent circumstances, and enjoyed his *otium cum dignitate* for twenty-six years, happy in himself, until his last long and painful illness, which he bore with Christian resignation, and contributing much, by his social accomplishments, to the happiness of a large circle of personal friends. He was ever most popular with his professional brethren, from his unvarying urbanity of manner and kindliness of disposition, and may be quoted as a rare instance of one

> " Bless'd with temper whose unclouded ray
> Could make to-morrow cheerful as to-day."

He was constitutionally light and humorous as a school-boy, and had nothing of the tragedian in his composition except the power of embodying the tragic passions, in imitative art. Not long before he left London for his final residence at Brighton, he called with one of his grandsons to see the writer of these pages, who had long enjoyed his personal friendship, and who happened at the moment to be at dinner with his family. "Tell them," he said to the servant, "not to hurry, but when they are at leisure, there are two little boys waiting to see them." Beginning life with advantageous prospects, and receiving a good education at the Merchant Taylors' school, and afterwards at Eton College, Charles Young might have pursued fortune through many channels, but the stage was his fascination. He proved himself to be the most eminent disciple of the Kemble school, and a worthy successor of the founder on whom he built his style. His genius was imitative rather than creative : he had no stage trickery ; his manner was invariably sustained ; his cast of features commanding; his voice of a noble quality, and beautifully modulated; his discrimination excellent. If he seldom astonished, he never disappointed an audience. Whatever he did was done well, and altogether he may be pronounced the safest and most reliable actor that ever assumed leading characters. There was no apprehension that his physical powers would ever fail or that his judgment would be at fault. He was equally suited to represent the heroes of the classic drama and of the recent stage. Whether in Roman, Oriental, or modern fashionable costume, his appearance satisfied the eye and fixed the attention of the spectator. It has been repeated that Lord Byron pronounced Young the quintessence of mediocrity. If the noble poet said so, the phrase was more smart than just, more depreciating than true. There was no mediocrity in his performance of *Zanga, Pierre, Iago, Hamlet, The Stranger, Rolla, Rienzi, Brutus* and *Cassius*, both so excellent, that it was difficult to assign the palm to either; and, above all, in his *Sir Pertinax Macsycophant*, in which he trod close on the heels of Cooke.   In semi-serious characters, vibrating between tragedy and comedy, such as *Falkland, Lord Townly, Joseph Surface, Penruddock*, and others of that class, he maintained a high reputation.   His comic performances abounded in rich humour, and he sang with a pleasant compass of voice, which he never attempted to force, and with good taste and execution.

CHAPTER XII.

CHARLES KEAN RETURNS FROM AMERICA—LONG PASSAGE CONTRASTED WITH PRESENT SPEED—SERIOUS ACCIDENT ON LANDING—ENGAGED BY LAPORTE AT COVENT GARDEN AND APPEARS AS SIR EDWARD MORTIMER—QUALIFIED SUCCESS—ACTS IAGO TO HIS FATHER'S OTHELLO—LAST PERFORMANCE OF EDMUND KEAN— HIS DEATH AND PUBLIC FUNERAL AT RICHMOND—TABLET ERECTED TO HIS MEMORY BY HIS SON—SALE OF HIS EFFECTS BY AUCTION—FATE OF THE DRURY LANE VASE—CHARLES KEAN LEAVES LONDON AND DETERMINES NEVER TO RETURN UNTIL HE CAN COMMAND HIS OWN TERMS— REFLECTIONS ON THE PERISHING NATURE OF THE ACTOR'S ART, WITH ITS RELATIVE ADVANTAGES AND DISADVANTAGES—ANECDOTES OF ANCIENT AND MODERN ACTORS.

CHARLES KEAN'S successful tour in America continued for nearly two years and-a-half. Sailing for England in the *Ontario*, he arrived at Portsmouth, on the 11th of February, 1833, having been forty days on the voyage. This was before the broad Atlantic had been spanned by steamers as with a bridge, reducing to hours what had formerly occupied days, and multiplying life and energy with increased locomotion—a feat which the great philosopher and mechanician, Dr. Lardner, had recently declared to be impracticable, but which he was not long afterwards amongst the first to refute by personal experiment. A voyage of three thousand miles is now scudded over rapidly, and with infinitely less discomfort than it took our ancestors a few generations back, to rumble in a lumbering *diligence* from Edinburgh to London.

As if to prepare the young adventurer for a cool reception at home, in descending into the boat which

was to convey him on shore, he fell overboard and narrowly escaped drowning.   Such was his anxiety to
reach London, and see his mother, after a long separa-
tion, that he travelled all night from Portsmouth in his
wet clothes, but fortunately sustained no injury from
this act of imprudence.   Very soon after his arrival, he
was engaged by Monsieur Laporte, at that time manager
at Covent Garden, with a salary of 30*l.* per week, and
stipulated as a *sine quâ non,* in opposition to the wishes
of the theatrical authorities, that he should make his
first appearance in *Sir Edward Mortimer*—his former
success in that character at the Haymarket, in 1829,
appearing a sufficient guarantee for a similar sequel in
1833.   But he found himself mistaken.   He was but
coldly welcomed by the audience; the press veered
round again, and the same papers which had formerly
lauded his efforts in the same character, rescinded their
opinions, and fell back on the old tone of condemnation.
There seemed to him, in this, "something more than
natural," which his philosophy was unable to fathom.
He had acted only a few nights with qualified success,
when his father was engaged by Laporte, and in the
month of March appeared as *Shylock.*   But time and
dissipation had done their work.   The powers of the
elder Kean had long been on the decline, and it was
now painful to behold the " poor remains " of the once
great delineator of Shakespeare's noblest characters.
He was reduced to a mere shadow, the wreck of what he
had formerly been.   There was still the occasional flash,
which, as usual, electrified the audience, but the effect
was momentary; the piercing eye, the varying expression, the epigrammatic distinctness, the sustained passion,
were gone for ever.

Laporte thought, with sound managerial tact, that
the appearance of the father and son in conjunction,

would be likely to attract money to his almost empty treasury. They acted together for the first, and, as it was so fated, the only time in London, on the 25th of March, 1833. The play was " Othello." The *Moor*, as usual, by Edmund Kean, *Iago* by Charles Kean, and *Desdemona* by Miss Ellen Tree. This eventful performance, the last appearance of the father on the mimic scene, and the rapid precursor of his final exit from the stage of life, is thus graphically described by the pen of Barry Cornwall.*

"There was no rehearsal, nor any arrangement as to the mode of play; but when the son arrived at the theatre in the evening, he was told that his father desired to see him. He went accordingly to his dress-ing-room, and found him shivering and exceedingly weak. 'I am very ill,' he said; 'I am afraid I shall not be able to act.' The actors who were present cheered him up; but to provide against the worst a servant was desired to air a dress (such as *Othello* wears), in order that Mr. Warde might take up the part, in case Kean should actually break down before the conclusion. The play commenced. After the first scene, Kean observed, 'Charles is getting on to-night— he's acting very well; I suppose that's because he is acting with me.' He himself was very feeble. He was, however, persuaded to proceed, and brandy and water was administered to him as usual. By this help he went on pretty well until the commencement of the third act; but before the drop-curtain rose, he said to his son, 'Mind, Charles, that you keep before me; don't get behind me in this act. I don't know that I shall be able to kneel; but if I do, be sure that you lift me up.' Still, he pursued his way without faltering. He went off with *Desdemona*, and no one observed any

* Life of Edmund Kean, London, 1835, vol. ii. pp. 239 et seq.

change. But, on entering again, when he says, 'What, false to *me*, &c.,' he was scarcely able to walk across the stage. He held up, however, until the celebrated 'Farewell,' which he uttered with all his former pathos; but on concluding it, after making one or two steps towards his son (who took care to be near him), and attempting the speech, 'Villain, be sure, &c.,' his head sank on his son's shoulder, and the tragedian's acting was at an end. He was able to groan out a few words in Charles's ear, 'I am dying—speak to them for me;' after which (the audience refusing in kindness to hear any apology) he was borne from the stage. His son, assisted by other persons, carried him to his dressing-room, and laid him on the sofa. He was as cold as ice ; his pulse was scarcely perceptible, and he was unconscious of all that was going on around him. In this state he remained some time, when the remedies which were applied having restored him to his senses, he was taken to the Wrekin tavern, near the theatre, and Messrs. Carpue and Duchez (the surgeons) were sent for."

After a week's stay he was removed to Richmond, when he rallied a little, and was soon enabled to go out in a carriage. But the weather was cold, and he fancied that this airing gave him his death-blow. On the 15th of May he died. A short time before his death, during an interval of serious reflection, he wrote a penitential and affectionate letter to his wife, entreating her forgiveness and obliteration of the past. " If I have erred," he said, " it was my head and not my heart, and most severely have I suffered for it. Come home, *forget* and *forgive*." The letter produced the desired effect. " Mrs. Kean answered this appeal by proceeding at once to Richmond. She saw her husband once more after seven years of estrangement, and the most perfect reconciliation followed. She went to him again repeatedly, and the best understanding prevailed between them. All this was the work of their son." *

The character of this great original actor, apart from his professional merits, is thus summed up by his biographer :—

"As a man, Kean, with all his faults, possessed redeeming points. He had an independent spirit; he was proud in his own way. He gave away large sums of money to his fellow-actors in distress. He exerted himself for charities. He stood up for the cause of his profession. If his delinquencies be retorted upon us, we may reply that his unchecked childhood was of itself sufficient to extenuate many errors ; that years of penury and suffering should also be taken into the account in his favour ; and that the sudden and almost unparalleled fortune that met and lifted him, in a moment, from obscurity and want to the very summit of prosperity and fame, was such as scarcely any man, with the common weakness of humanity, could have encountered without rendering himself liable to some little reproach."

Edmund Kean died deeply involved in his pecuniary affairs. He was ever careless of money, paying bills without examining them, and trusting to others in all matters of finance. It is no exaggerated calculation to say, that he gave away, or was fleeced out of half his earnings. Sometimes he wrote cheques at night, when he was in a state of intoxication. These he desired to recall in the morning, but found they had already been presented and honoured, as soon as the doors of Coutts' bank were opened. The holders dreaded the repeal of their documents.

The career of this remarkable man—his indomitable genius, long contending with adverse circumstances, but

* Life of Edmund Kean, vol. ii. p. 243.

finally forcing its way in spite of every obstacle; his reiterated weaknesses and wasted opportunities,—all supply many subjects for painful meditation, but this is not the place in which they may be indulged. His funeral was most respectably conducted. Nearly all the leading members of the different London theatres were present, with a large proportion of the principal inhabitants of Richmond. The shops were closed in respect, as the procession passed along the green, and through the streets, to the western portal of the old church, near which his remains are deposited. His son, as soon as he was able, erected a tablet to his memory, with a medallion portrait, bearing the following inscription :— "EDMUND KEAN, DIED MAY 15TH, 1833, AGED FORTY-SIX. A MEMORIAL ERECTED BY HIS SON, CHARLES JOHN KEAN, 1839."

The theatrical wardrobe and properties, furniture, plate, and other moveables, either at Richmond or the cottage in Bute, were seized and sold for the benefit of creditors. Included amongst these articles were some of peculiar interest—a snuff-box and two swords, gifts of Lord Byron, with the splendid silver cup (made after the celebrated Warwick vase), which cost three hundred guineas, presented to Edmund Kean in 1816 by the Committee and Company of Drury Lane. It was sold to a silversmith for the weight of the silver. In July, 1834, this cup was standing in the window of a carver and gilder's shop in Duncannon Street, Strand. Charles Kean, accidentally passing by, saw it, and walked in. He had a conversation with the shopman (the master being out), told him who he was, and begged him to say, that if not parted with for a reasonable time, the first money he earned should be applied to the purchase. On the following evening it was stolen from the window, as the handbills stated, which were published in consequence, offering 20*l.* reward for its recovery. In all probability it was melted down forthwith, and had ceased to be in existence. Far better would it have been if the play-going public, admirers of the late possessor, or a few personal friends, had thought of securing the relic by subscription, as a present to his widow and son. This more desirable object might have been accomplished by a timely suggestion.

The sale of Edmund Kean's valuables took place on the 17th of June, 1834. The world wondered, or affected to wonder; and it was said beyond a whisper, by more than one, that Charles Kean *ought* to have bought in the personal effects of his father, and prevented a public auction. A hasty opinion uttered by those who either knew not, or, what is more likely, chose to forget, that the young man was still struggling for his own subsistence, that he had his mother to support, and that he had not as yet had sufficient time to accumulate store. Could he have commanded the necessary funds, a comparatively small sum might have redeemed the Bute estate, on which two or three years' ground rent had accumulated. This unprofitable purchase comprised twenty-four acres of bog and rock, on which his father, dreaming that he loved rural retirement, had expended 4,000*l.* in the building and furniture of a house, in the construction of a road by which it could be reached, and in other expensive improvements. It was generally rumoured that the noble Marquis, to whom the island belonged, had presented Kean the elder with an estate, from mere admiration of his genius. There was no foundation for this, as his lordship had never set himself forward as a Mæcenas; neither was there any reason why he should affect the character on an insulated occasion, and in favour of a person with whom he was personally unacquainted, who then possessed the means of indulging his fancies. The property at Bute fell with the rest to the creditors of the deceased actor, and was bought back from them by the Marquis for a mere trifle.

Shortly after the interrupted representation of "Othello," Sheridan Knowles' play of the "Wife" was produced at Covent Garden, and met with a success almost equal to that of the "Hunchback," which had been the great stay of the house during the preceding year. Charles Kean was the original *Leonardo Gonzaga*, Miss Ellen Tree, *Mariana;* Knowles himself playing *Julian St. Pierre.* The latter was determined to show the world, even if they required demonstration of the fact, that a great author might be a very insufficient reflector of his own creations. This piece, notwithstanding, ran for the remainder of the season, and was continued with undiminished attraction long after the Covent Garden company removed to the Olympic theatre. But Charles Kean saw he had as yet made little or no permanent impression. Causes were in operation which time and absence might remove. Knowing that, without difficulty, he could obtain profitable engagements elsewhere, he resolved to "bide his time," and to act no more in London until he could place himself at the "top of the tree." He had encountered rebuffs and disappointment; as often as he made a step in advance, some opposing influence dragged him back again; still the conviction of ultimate success was strong within him, and he felt satisfied that, sooner or later, he should attain the object of his ardent desire. One day he accidentally met Mr. Dunn, the treasurer of Drury Lane Theatre, who, on the part of Mr. Bunn, at that time the lessee, proposed a benefit for his mother, as the widow of Edmund Kean. The offer was a kind one, but Charles declined it, feeling that he was now able to support his surviving parent by his own exertions, and unwilling to let her be considered an object of public charity. Mr. Dunn then suggested, that in all probability he could readily obtain an engagement at Drury Lane at 15*l.* per week. "No," replied the young actor, "I will never again set my foot on a London stage until I can command my own terms of 50*l.* a night. "Then, Charles Kean," rejoined Mr. Dunn with a smile, "I fear you may bid a long farewell to London; for the days of such salaries are gone for ever." Time rolled on, and, at the expiration of five years only, during which he had received 20,000*l.* by acting in the country, he drove to the stage-door of Drury Lane Theatre in his own carriage, with a signed engagement at 50*l.* a night in his pocket, and which engagement, for upwards of forty nights, was paid to him by the very man who had predicted its impossibility.

It would be difficult to cite a more striking instance of a strong internal conviction leading to the anticipated end, or of industry and perseverance so amply crowned by a corresponding result. There was talent of no ordinary quality, beyond doubt, with some assisting circumstances, in this individual case; but a valuable lesson and a powerful moral of general application are here combined. In struggling through the journey of life, some are doomed to toil perpetually on a rugged path, while others glide with railroad regularity on a smooth one. But the goal is open to all. What one has accomplished another may hope to achieve also, and no one should despair, while retaining health and unclouded faculties to sustain an honourable resolution.

A word or two here on the large salaries received by members of the theatrical profession. In all ages successful actors have been an uncommonly well paid community. This is a substantial fact which no one can deny, however much opinions may differ as to the comparative value of the histrionic art, when ranked with poetry, painting, and sculpture. From hence we may infer that the world places a higher estimate on the ornamental accessories than on the bald realities of life. The actor complains of the hard conditions inseparable from his most successful efforts—that they fade with the decay of his own personal capabilities, and are only preserved for a doubtful interval through the medium of unfaithful imitation—very often a bad copy of an original which no longer exists to disprove the libel. In the actor's case, then, something must certainly be deducted on the score of posthumous renown; but this deficiency is amply balanced by living estimation and a realized fortune. There are many instances of great painters, poets, and sculptors (aye, and philosophers, too), who could scarcely gain a livelihood; but we should be puzzled to name a great actor without an enormous salary. Managers are not included in this category. They are unlucky exceptions; and not unfrequently lose in sovereignty what they had gained by service. An income of 3,000*l.* or 4,000*l.* per annum carries along with it many solid enjoyments. The actor who can command this by labouring industriously in his vocation, and whose ears are continually tingling with the nightly applause of his audience, has no reason to consider his lot a hard one, because posterity may assign to him in the temple of Fame a less prominent niche than is occupied by Milton, who, when alive, sold "Paradise Lost" for 15*l.* or by Rembrandt, who was obliged to feign his own death, before his pictures could provide him a dinner. If these instances fail to content him, let him recollect what is recorded of "Blind Mæonides."

> " Seven Grecian cities claim'd great Homer dead,
>   Through which the living Homer begg'd his bread."

No doubt it is a grand affair to figure in the page of history, and to be recorded amongst the foremost men of our generation. But there is good practical philosophy in the homely proverb which says, "solid pudding is better than empty praise." The reputation which wins its current value during life, is more useful to the proprietor than the honour that comes after death, and comes, as *David* says, in the "Rivals," "exactly when we can make a shift to do without it." To have our merits appreciated two or three ages hence, by generations yet unborn, and to have our works, whether with pen, pencil, or chisel, admired long after what was once our mortal substance is "stopping a beer-barrel," are very pleasing, poetical hallucinations for all who like to indulge in them; but the chances are we shall know nothing of the matter, while it is quite certain that if we do we shall set no value on it. Posterity, then, will be the chief gainers, and, of all concerned, the only party to whom we owe no obligations. The posterity, too, which emanates from the nineteenth century is much more likely to partake of the commercial than the romantic character, and to hold in higher reverence the memory of an ancestor who has left behind him 30,000*l.* in bank-stock or Consols, than of one who has only bequeathed a marble monument in St. Paul's, or "Westminster's old Abbey" a flourishing memoir in the "Lives of Illustrious Englishmen," or an epic poem in twenty-four cantos.

Let it not be supposed that we are disciples of *Pizarro,* who calls the applause of future ages "renown for visionary boys to dream of;" or that we depreciate the love of posthumous fame with "those longings after immortality," which are powerful incentives to much that is good and great; but we are led into this train of thought by hearing it so constantly objected as a misfortune to the actor, that his best efforts are but fleeting shadows, and cannot survive him. This, being interpreted fairly, means, that he caunot gain all that genius and perseverance toil for; but he has won a preponderating share, and ought to be satisfied. Perhaps, too, the indistinctness of tradition may be more favourable to his memory than the stereotyped, matter-of-fact accuracy of contemporary evidence.

Formerly the actor had to contend with prejudices which stripped him of his place in society, and degraded his calling. This was assuredly a worse evil than perishable fame; but all this has happily passed away. The interdict is removed, and he takes his place with kindred artists, according to his artistic pretensions. His large salary excites much wondering comment, and more jealousy; but he is no longer exposed to obloquy and insult. When the elder Sheridan appeared as an evidence on the trials resulting from the celebrated "Mahomet riot" at the Smock Alley Theatre in Dublin, in 1754, he happened to use the term gentleman as applied to himself. On this one of the opposing counsel took him up, and said, "I have often heard of a gentleman poet, a gentleman painter, and a gentleman architect, but I never yet saw a gentleman player." "Then I hope, Sir," replied Sheridan calmly, "that you see one now."

Le Kain, the French Roscius, once received a heavier affront than this, which he was obliged to swallow as he might. Dining one day at a *restaurateur's*, he was accosted by an old general officer near him. "Ah! Monsieur Le Kain, is that you? Where have you been for some weeks? we have lost you from Paris." "I have been acting in the South, may it please your excellency." "*Eh, bien!* and how much money have you earned?" "In six weeks, Sir, I have received four thousand crowns." "*Diable!*" exclaimed the general, twisting his moustache with a truculent frown. "What's this I hear? A miserable *mimic* such as thou can gain in six weeks double the sum that I, a nobleman of twenty descents, and a knight of St. Louis, am paid in twelve months! *Voila une vraie infamie!*" "And at what sum, Sir," replied Le Kain, placidly, " do you estimate the privilege of thus addressing me?"

In those days, and long after, in France, an actor was denied Christian burial, and would have been broken alive on the wheel if he had presumed to put himself on an equality with a gentleman, or dared to resent an unprovoked outrage.

The large salaries of recent days were even surpassed amongst the ancients. In Rome, Roscius, and Æsopus his contemporary, amassed prodigious fortunes by their professional labours. Roscius was paid at the rate of 45*l.* a-day, amounting to more than 15,000*l.* per annum of our currency. No wonder he was fond of his art, and unwilling to relinquish its exercise. He became so rich, that at last he declined receiving any emolument, and acted gratuitously for several years.* A modern manager would give something to stumble on such a star. Æsopus, at an entertainment, produced a single dish stuffed with singing birds, which, according to Dr. Arbuthnot's computation, must have cost about 4,883*l.* sterling. He left his son a fortune amounting to 200,000*l.* British money.† It did not remain long in the family, as, by the evidence of Horace and Pliny, he was a notorious spendthrift, and rapidly dissipated the honest earnings of his father.

---

* Plin. lib. vii. cap. 39 ; Macrob. Sat. lib. ii. cap. 10 ; Middleton's Life of Cicero :—Cic. Orat. pro Q. Roscio.

† Macrob. Sat. lib. ii. cap. 10.

Decimus Laberius, a Roman knight, was induced, or, as some writers say, compelled, by Julius Cæsar to appear in one of his own *Mimes*, an inferior kind of dramatic composition very popular amongst the Romans, and in which he was unrivalled, until supplanted by Publius Syrus. The said Laberius found consolation for his degraded dignity in a good round sum, as Cæsar gave him twenty thousand crowns and a gold ring for this, his first and only appearance on any stage. Neither was he " alone in his glory," being countenanced by Furius Leptinus and Quintus Calpenus, men of senatorial rank, who, on the authority of Suetonius, fought in the ring for a prize. We are inclined to think the money had its due weight with Laberius. He was evidently vain, and in his prologue, preserved by Macrobius, and translated by Goldsmith, he laments his age and infirmities quite as pathetically as the disgrace to which he was subjected. " Why did you not ask me to do this," thus he remonstrates with Cæsar, " when I was young and supple, and could have acquitted myself with credit ? " But, according to Macrobius, the whole business was a regular contract, with the terms settled beforehand. " Laberium asperæ libertatis equitem Romanum, Cæsar *quingentis millibus invitavit*, ut prodiret in scenam."* Good encouragement for a single amateur performance !

Garrick retired at the age of sixty, having been thirty-five years connected with the stage. He left behind him above 100,000*l.* in money, besides considerable property in houses, furniture, pictures, plate, and articles of *virtû.* He lived in the best society, and feasted archbishops, bishops, and noblemen, with becoming splendour. But he had no family to educate

---

* Macrob. Sat. lib. ii. cap. 7.

or provide for, and was systematically prudent in expenditure, although charitable to the extreme of liberality when occasion required. Edmund Kean might have saved a larger fortune than Garrick, had his habits been equally regular. George Frederick Cooke, in many respects a kindred genius to Kean, threw away a golden harvest in vulgar dissipation. The sums he received in America alone would have made him independent. John Kemble and Mrs. Siddons both retired in opulence, although less wealthy than might have been expected. She had through life heavy demands upon her; and he, in an evil hour, invested much of his savings in Covent Garden theatre. Young left the stage in the full tide of his fame, with a handsome independence. Macready did the same under similar circumstances. Liston was always accounted one of the richest actors of his day, and William Farren is generally set down as "a warm man." Miss Stephens, the Keans (father and son), Macready, Braham, and others, have frequently received 50*l.* per night for a long series of performances. Tyrone Power bade fair to hold one of the highest places in the list, such was his increasing popularity and attraction, when the untimely catastrophe occurred which ended his career, and produced a vacancy *we* are not likely to see filled up.

John Bull has ever been remarkable for his lavish encouragement of foreign artists. The largest remuneration awarded to native talent bears no comparison with the salaries given to French and Italian singers, dancers, and musicians. This love of imported prodigies is no recent passion, but older than the days of Shakespeare. *Trinculo*, in the "Tempest," thus apostrophises the recumbent monster, *Caliban*, whom he takes for a fish: "Were I in England now, as I was

once, and had but this fish painted, not a holiday fool
there but would give a piece of silver. There would
this monster make a man. Any strange beast there
makes a man."

Catalani, Pasta, Sontag, Malibran, Grisi, Taglioni,
Rachel, Rubini, Mario, Tamburini, Lablache, Paganini,
cum multis aliis, have received their thousands and tens
of thousands; but the Jenny Lind mania left all prece-
dents at an immeasurable distance. What the Swedish
nightingale drew from England during her last public
appearance, in concerts alone, has never authentically
transpired, but we can scarcely exaggerate when we set
the figure at a sum sufficient to buy up the fee simple of
half the hereditary baronies in any given country on the
continent.

CHAPTER XIII.

IN October, 1833, Charles Kean, after leaving London, performed twelve nights in Dublin, during which engagement he personated the arduous and varied characters of *Sir Giles Overreach, Sir Edward Mortimer, Othello, Jaffier, Reuben Glenroy, Richard the Third, Romeo,* and *Macbeth.* In all he was well received, and laid the basis of a reputation which from that hour increased rapidly with every succeeding visit. The characteristic warmth with which he was welcomed in Dublin received no impulse from national partiality, because the candidate for their favour happened to be an Irishman—the fact was either unknown or disregarded. But, naturally quick, they saw and encouraged the rising merit, uninfluenced by preconceived opinions or fostered prejudices.

Before the close of the year, Charles Kean accepted an offer to perform, with a well-selected English company, in Hamburgh, under the direction of Mr. Barham Livius. The experiment promised successfully, as far as general patronage was concerned; but in a few weeks it came to a premature close, through the interference of the local authorities, to whom a representation was made that the attraction of the " foreign intruders " interfered with and injured the regular establishments. Upon this hint, the English actors received notice to quit.   Some governments are less tenacious of the interests of their fellow-countrymen.

The heroine of this company was Miss Ellen Tree, a young lady equally distinguished by her amiable character, personal attractions, and high professional ability. A friend, well acquainted with both, predicted to Charles Kean, when dining one day with his family, that he would infallibly lose his heart, exposed to such combined temptations, and has lived to see his prediction most happily accomplished in the marriage of the parties. The visit to Hamburgh led to an intimacy, increasing a mutual attachment previously commenced in London, and they became engaged to each other.   But the projected union was broken off, and for some years appeared anything but a likely event, the mothers on both sides deeming it equally ineligible.   At this time all the advantages were clearly on the side of the lady.   The young actor had yet the world before him, with his fortune to make ; while the object of his choice was in the full tide of her fame, with worth, beauty, and accomplishments which might have added lustre to a coronet.

When Charles Kean returned from the Continent, engagements in all the leading country theatres presented themselves in abundance.   During a visit to Exeter, a ludicrous incident occurred.   He had a favourite Newfoundland dog, named Lion, who accompanied him everywhere, and usually remained in his dressing-room while he was on the stage. One evening, during *Richard the Third*, the door happened to be left open, and Lion heard the well-known voice in loud excitement. He trotted out, and appeared at the wing just as *Richard* and *Richmond* were on the point of engaging in the last scene. Lion growled at his master's antagonist, exhibited his teeth, and rushed furiously forward; whereupon the terrified *Richmond*, deeming the odds too serious, fled from the field, and was seen no more. Kean, being left without an antagonist, was obliged to fall and die unwounded. Lion bestrode his master in triumph, licking his face, and barking vociferously while the curtain fell, amidst a roar of laughter and applause. *Richard* was then unanimously summoned before the curtain; presented himself, made his bow, and retired. Loud calls continued for " the dog;" but Lion, having finished his unstudied *rôle*, declined a second appearance.

On another occasion, in the same city, and while acting in the same play, Charles Kean had to deal with a tall, ungainly *Richmond*, who knew nothing of fencing. He pressed him into a corner, until he fell backwards into the orchestra, and remained fixed in the kettle-drum, through which he partially disappeared. *Richard* again found himself without an opponent, until the musicians helped the latter out of his narrow prison, handed him his sword, and he renewed the fight, so inopportunely impeded. The roars of the audience may be more readily imagined than described. But still *Richard* remained invulnerable, and at last succumbed without a wound. *Richmond* then avenged himself by showering deadly thrusts upon his fallen foe.

Amongst Charles Kean's early and warmest patronesses, we must enumerate the late Duchess of St. Alban's, from whose kindness he obtained many valuable introductions. He had no particular claim on her notice, beyond the sympathy naturally excited in a generous mind for a young man of talent struggling with difficulties, and in want of patronage. ⸱Exalted in rank, and possessed of boundless wealth, she had herself in earlier days gone through the ordeal of adversity; and when selected by fortune for one of her especial favourites, encountered every species of abuse which slander and detraction could invent, to terrify her into the purchase of silence by bribes which would have exhausted the treasury of Crœsus, without accomplishing the desired object. She had the good sense and firmness to pay no regard to these attacks, while her heart remained ever kind and her hand extended.

The portals of fashion being thus opened through interest, Charles Kean made his own way by gentleman-like bearing and unassuming demeanour. During his probationary *lustrum* in the provinces, Edinburgh vied with Dublin in encouragement and remuneration. In each of these great cities he was invited into the best society. In Dublin he became a frequent guest at the Castle and the Park, under the viceroyalty of the Marquis of Normanby, and the chief secretaryship of the Earl of Carlisle (then Lord Morpeth). These two distinguished noblemen and statesmen have ever been remarkable for their admiration of the dramatic art. The late venerable ex-chancellor, Lord Plunkett, although beyond his seventieth year, was generally to be seen in the dress boxes on the nights of Kean's performance. Chief Justice Doherty (whose wife was his mother's second cousin), a most accomplished scholar, was seldom absent. In Edinburgh, in the year 1837, he cleared, by a single engagement, nearly 1,000*l.* All the leading members of the bench and bar, including many names of first-rate literary celebrity, were to be seen amongst his constant auditors. In the list we may enumerate the Lords of Session (as the Scotch judges are called), Meadowbank, Medwyn, Jeffery, Fullerton,

Cockburn, Moncrieff, Robertson, and Mr. Maitland, afterwards Lord Dundrennan. The professors of the university also came forth, and many learned and distinguished scholars, who seldom frequented the ordinary performances of the theatre. During the same year (1837), an engagement in Glasgow, similar in duration to that of Edinburgh, even exceeded it in profit; Charles Kean's dividends reaching an average of 115*l.* While this was going on, a Baillie of influence in the city, remarkable for his non-theatrical tastes, called upon him at his hotel, and with many preliminary flourishes and compliments, invited him to set aside the proceeds of one of his nights for the advantage of a local charity.

"Sir," replied Charles Kean, "I live by my profession, and I cannot afford to give up considerably above 100*l.* for the purpose you name; but oblige me by a sight of your subscription-list, and I will contribute accordingly."

"Oh—ah!" said the functionary, a little taken aback. "I didn't view the matter in that light, certainly. Here is the list."

"And here, Sir," rejoined Kean, "are ten guineas—the highest sum I find there from any of your richest citizens."

"Oh—ah!" ejaculated the Baillie a second time, and departed with many thanks. On his way home he called at the box-office, and, for the first time in his life, took a ticket for the play on the actor's benefit.

The residents of the Northern Metropolis, or modern Athenians, as they delight to be called, have ever been slow and cold when sitting in critical judgment on new candidates for their favour; but they are warm and steady when once that judgment is pronounced. On Mrs. Siddons's first appearance, the crowded pit sat in

solemn silence throughout four-fifths of " Isabella."
Point after point, which had electrified the more susceptible Londoners, fell upon them without enkindling
a flash, or exciting an exclamation. Eyes looked dull,
and hands were quiet. The great actress was in despair,
and had scarcely courage to go on. One burst more,
with concentrated energy, and she paused for the result.
Still a moment of silence, when a dictatorial voice from
the pit exclaimed, " That's no bad." This settled the
question, and roused the whole house to applause, which
fell " fast and furious," with scarcely any intermission,
to the end of the play.

The three letters from the late Lord Meadowbank, here
inserted, may be read with interest, as conveying the
opinion of a very competent judge on the merits of a
young performer; and also as bearing on the much
disputed question of the real or assumed mental aberra-
tion of *Hamlet*. The two first letters are addressed
to Mr. Murray, the manager of the Edinburgh Theatre.
The third to Charles Kean himself :—

" 13, Royal Circus,
" March, 1836.

" DEAR SIR,—

  " I have spoken with a good many persons
who were not fortunate enough to have seen Mr. C. Kean
play *Hamlet*, and who are very desirous of having it in
their power to do so. Can this be obtained by inter-
cepting him on his way back from Aberdeen? Perhaps
the *eclât* of having been solicited to play another night
might induce him to change his plan of not returning
by Edinburgh; and if you think it desirable either for
him or you, there will be no difficulty in getting up a
requisition to Mr. Kean making the request. To this I
shall be ready to subscribe most willingly, as, though I
have seen him twice in *Hamlet*, I shall be most glad to

see him perform that noble character again. The only night until the 28th on which I could not do this is the 22d.

"I remain, dear Sir, yours faithfully,

"A. M. MACONOCHIE.

"William Murray, Esq."

"13, Royal Circus,
"March 31st, 1836.

"DEAR SIR,—

"Having availed myself last night of your kindness in giving me seats, I have been so much delighted again with Mr. Kean's personification of *Hamlet*, that I cannot resist the temptation of requesting that I may have a box, should the character be repeated, or should Mr. Kean play *Othello*, and, above all, *Lear*.*

"I have never seen *anything* on the stage so perfect as Mr. Kean's *Hamlet*. We may rise from reading the criticisms of Johnson and Malone, without fully comprehending the precise character which Shakespeare intended to delineate. But no one can have seen the representation of Mr. Kean, without having all his difficulties removed, and his doubts cleared away. From the beginning to the end, *Hamlet* is a gentleman and a prince ; but a gentleman the equilibrium of whose brain has been deranged, and who, for the purposes of revenge, feigns that madness in a greater degree. But he is not sensible himself of this derangement. I could not detect a single emphasis improperly placed. The recitation of all the speeches was exquisitely fine. Nothing was lost to the sense which the most finished study could convey, and yet the audience were, to all that appeared, entirely lost sight of. In short, the identification was complete ; and it was impossible to fancy that it

* This letter led to a renewed engagement with Charles Kean in Edinburgh, when he had finished his northern tour.

was not the Prince of Denmark who himself occupied the scene.

"I could not help observing, in the scene with the *Ghost*, that, since the days of Garrick, the observations of Partridge, in 'Tom Jones,' on that part of the play, never could have been so well applied.* I have to offer an apology for yielding to the impulse of the feelings of gratification which were excited last night, by troubling you with these remarks. But having lived long enough to have seen *all* the *Hamlets* who have appeared on the stage for forty years, and never before having seen the character embodied as I felt it, I thought it might afford satisfaction to Mr. Kean to know (should you think it worth while to tell him) what an old and early admirer of his father thought of his performance of the finest and most difficult of Shakespeare's manifold creations. It is now twenty-three years since I went to Glasgow for no other purpose than to see the late Mr. Kean play *Othello*.

"I remain, dear Sir,

" Yours faithfully,

" A. M. MACONOCHIE.

" W. Murray, Esq."

Mr. Murray, as might be supposed, handed this letter, with much alacrity, to the subject of its eulogium. It now lies on the table of the writer of these pages while his hand traces them. The third letter, addressed to Charles Kean, runs thus :—

---

* Dr. Johnson, who lost no opportunity of finding fault with Garrick, thought his terror in this scene exaggerated and unnatural. "Do you think, Sir, if you saw a ghost," said Boswell, " you would start as Garrick does in *Hamlet?*" " No, Sir ;" replied the cynic philosopher, " If I did, I should frighten the ghost."

" 13, Royal Circus,
" April 15th.

" MY DEAR SIR,—

" Some time ago I ventured to give an opinion that you were endowed with powers to excel equally in the higher walks of comedy, as in tragedy; an opinion formed on the observation of occasional *glimpses* of what appeared, in some of the characters in which I had the high gratification of seeing you, as well as from your manner in the ordinary intercourse of society. That opinion has been confirmed beyond all doubt, by what I saw in your representation of *Hotspur* last night, which, allow me to add, considering the nature and extreme difficulty of the part, has left no doubt on my mind, that if you do not throw away your health, as I fear you are doing, by over-exertion, you will very speedily rival the fame and reputation of Garrick. But the parts which more forcibly struck me as supporting the opinion I have referred to, were, not only the scene after the first interview with the *King*, as well as I remember it, but also that with *Lady Percy*, in which the playfulness of manner and the comic effect produced both from voice and expression, satisfied me entirely that you could not fail in *Don Felix*, and the like range of characters, if you would only set your mind to them. It is but failing, at the most; and if you succeed, then, as I said, you rival Garrick.

" Why did you leave out the scene with *Glendower?* *

" Yours ever,

" A. M. MACONOCHIE.

" To Charles Kean, Esq."
&c. &c.

---

* This fine and characteristic scene has never been acted. Perhaps from a desire not to let any portion of the play detract from or interfere with the humorous prominence of *Falstaff.*

On a later occasion, Lord Meadowbank, in forwarding to Charles Kean a complimentary note from an old gentleman of the name of Strange, accompanied it by these remarks—"Mr. Strange is son of Sir Robert Strange, the eminent engraver. Being above eighty-four years of age, he was a living play-goer in the days of Garrick, and saw him more than once play *Hamlet*, which, in his opinion—and he is highly accomplished, and perfectly entire in his faculties—was not equal to Mr. Charles Kean's representation. He is married to a daughter of the late Viscount Melville."

Lord Jeffrey, so long known and celebrated as the editor of the *Edinburgh Review*, and the dispenser of literary reputation before he became a judge, introduced himself to Charles Kean in the year 1836, and soon became one of his warmest admirers. In the *Caledonian Mercury* of Thursday, the 24th of March, 1836, we find this notice of " Richard the Third," in which the name of the great critic is introduced :—" During the encounter with *Richmond*, which Mr. Kean sustained, not only with wonderful energy and lofty daring, but with a character and truth that were truly natural, the excitement of the audience was raised to the utmost pitch ; and his attitude, look, and whole expression, after he received the fatal thrust, were appalling to such a degree, that the audience seemed to feel a relief when the proud spirit was for ever quenched. Not the least interesting feature of the scene was the presence of Lord Jeffrey. His lordship was in a private box, and unseen during the earlier part of the evening ; but during the last spirit-stirring scenes, he presented himself in front, and warmly joined in the general acclaim to the commanding genius of the actor."

In a letter to Lady Gifford, about this time, Lord Jeffrey thus speaks of the impression made on his experienced and critical mind by the fervour of the rising actor :—

"You are possibly aware how highly I think of Charles Kean's talents, and how much I shall be gratified to see him attain the success which I am persuaded he deserves, and to which I believe he is destined. Independent of my admiration of his professional excellence, I have much esteem and regard for him as an individual."

These and similar opinions from judges of the same weight, counterbalanced in the mind of Charles Kean the strong censures which had been so unsparingly dealt out to him by a majority of the London papers,* and encouraged his fond hope that prejudice and not justice had dictated their severity. At a later period, when he had triumphantly passed the London ordeal, and was preparing to visit America for the second time, Lord Jeffrey addressed him as follows :—

" Craig Creek,
"July 11th, 1839.

" Dear Mr. Kean,—

"I now inclose you a line of introduction to my brother-in-law, Dr. Wilkes, which will open to you, I make no doubt, the houses of all his family and the rest of that circle. I can scarcely say that I have now any acquaintance at New York, but with your reputation you can really need no introduction. I have accordingly confined my testimony rather to your agreeableness as an individual, and the modesty with which you bear your high and hard-won fame, than to the gifts and attainments by which you have deserved it.

"I hope you will have a prosperous voyage and a bril-

* At this very time, and in the midst of his Edinburgh triumphs, a local paper, inoculated with the hostile feeling, said, "When will our public be weary of the contortions of this galvanized carcass ?"

liant success, and that you will come back to us loaded with wealth and honours, before I am too old to understand and rejoice in your prosperity. But I must be very far gone indeed if I am not most happy to see you. With kind remembrances from Mrs. Jeffrey, believe me always, very faithfully yours,

J. JEFFREY.

" To Charles Kean, Esq.'

Liverpool proved to Charles Kean another stronghold, almost equal in value to Dublin or Edinburgh. Manchester, Bath, Exeter, Plymouth, with many of the larger towns, followed the example. In the summer of 1836, he visited his native city of Waterford, and was greeted by the compliment of a public dinner. A silver claret jug, valued at 100*l*., and voted on this occasion, was afterwards presented to him in London, by a deputation of gentlemen from Waterford, inscribed as follows :—

" PRESENTED TO CHARLES KEAN, ESQ.

AS A TOKEN OF ESTEEM FOR HIS PRIVATE CHARACTER, AND

ADMIRATION OF HIS TALENTS,

BY A FEW FRIENDS,

IN HIS NATIVE CITY OF WATERFORD,

JUNE 28TH, 1836."

He was now making rapid strides towards fame and fortune; establishing himself in the best society, and acquiring hosts of influential friends in every place in which he appeared. The theatres were almost invariably crowded wherever he acted. He presented the unique instance of an actor without metropolitan popularity, proving himself the safest speculation and the most attractive " star " that a manager in the country could venture to engage.

In the meantime the two great national temples of the

British drama, in London, were undergoing the usual vicissitudes. Before the expiration of 1833, Mr. Bunn became lessee of both Drury Lane and Covent Garden; a Napoleonic sovereignty which no single head or hand could possibly wield with satisfaction or permanent success. But this temporary union, which was repealed in 1835, gave rise to much discussion and squabbling on the subject of a third patent theatre. The application, although defeated at the time, led to the ultimate abolition of all patents, and the establishment of the present free trade in theatres, under the control of the Lord Chamberlain. When Mr. Bunn gave up the lease of Covent Garden, it passed into the hands of Mr. Osbaldistone, of the Cobourg, or Victoria, who removed thither the transpontine prices, system of management, and style,—with what effect the result of two short seasons most unsatisfactorily demonstrated.

During the season of 1835, the British operatic stage received a memorable although fleeting addition, in the person of an enchanting foreigner—Madame Malibran de Beriot, *née* Garcia, as the continental formula runs. She was engaged by Mr. Bunn to appear at both his theatres, and for twenty-six performances, at the rate of three per week, received no less than 3,463*l.*, secured beforehand—an average of rather more than 135*l.* per night. Her attraction was so great that the daring speculator escaped from his liabilities without being absolutely smothered under them; but the defalcations on the off-nights of a telling "star," when the costly exotic lies in abeyance, make terrible inroads on the receipts of any given week.

Poor Malibran died rather suddenly, during the Manchester festival, on the 23d of September, 1836. She was then only in the twenty-ninth year of her age. She sank under exhaustion, produced by exertions beyond her physical capability; and not as was generally and maliciously circulated at the time, in consequence of the mistaken treatment of her own foreign physician, who was also an intimate friend, and in whom she placed the most unbounded confidence. Her death-warrant was signed before the arrival of Dr. Belluomini, and his system could neither accelerate nor retard its execution. Her remains were in the first instance consigned to the church-yard of the cathedral in Manchester, but not long after exhumed and transported to Lacken, near Brussels, where she and her beloved De Beriot possessed a park and château. In a book purporting to be memoirs of the deceased vocalist, by the Countess de Merlin, it is stated that, "The committee of the Manchester musical festival wished to pay De Beriot the full amount of his wife's engagement, though she had only performed twice. This he refused!" Mr. Bunn, in commenting on the numerous mis-statements in this pretended biography, says, in his work entitled "The Stage; Before and Behind the Curtain" (and he was likely to speak from certain knowledge), with reference to this particular passage—"De Beriot did no such thing, for he received every farthing of it."

Malibran may be pronounced one of the greatest artists the world has ever produced. It is difficult to say whether she excelled most in acting or in singing, in tragedy or in comedy. There was a reality, an earnestness, an identity in all she did, which have seldom been equalled, and never surpassed. She was fond of money, and exacting in the terms of a bargain, but enthusiastically attached to her art, and jealous of even the shadow of rivalry. Her mind was in a perpetual fever of excitement. Cut off in the full bloom of youth, fortune, and professional reputation, to her may be aptly applied the impressive lines of Dryden:—

> " A fiery soul, which, working out its way,
> Fretted the puny body to decay,
> And o'er inform'd the tenement of clay."

On the 28th of June, 1835, died, on his fifty-ninth birthday, the inimitable Charles Mathews. We call him inimitable, for, though he had many followers, he left no successor, while he himself imitated all the world. He possessed also the faculty of ventriloquism in a rare degree.

Mathews was the son of a Wesleyan bookseller in the Strand, who placed him for education in Merchant Taylors' School, where, we believe, he was a fellow-student with Charles Young. It was intended that he should follow his father's business; but the stage seduced him into its more flowery paths. He obtained much celebrity in the York circuit; and made his first appearance at the Haymarket on the 16th of May, 1803, as *Jabal*, in the " Jew," and *Lingo*, in the " Agreeable Surprise." For many years before his death, he had ceased to practise as a legitimate member of any company, and became joint proprietor of the Adelphi, in conjunction with his friend and pupil, Frederick Yates. The latter managed the theatre, while the former went round the country with his budget. Both were supposed to be eminently successful; but read the " Memoirs of Charles Mathews," and will it not be found written there, how, at the close of what was proclaimed one of the most successful seasons the Adelphi Theatre had ever witnessed, when the house could scarcely contain the crowds who nightly thronged the doors, the proprietors wound up their accounts with a surplus on the left-hand side, simply because the expenses exceeded any possible receipts? Let all theatrical speculators lay this salutary lesson to their hearts: the great secret of profitable management consists less in the sum you can take than in the balance you can contrive to keep. The song says :—

> " How happy's the soldier that lives on his pay,
> And spends half-a-crown out of sixpence a day ;"

We have never yet heard of any manager disposed to join chorus in this canticle. At the Adelphi, Mathews exhibited regularly his annual "At Home," and never were audiences more delighted than by the endless variety of portraits which he so accurately sketched for them. But because Mathews established unrivalled fame in this exclusive line of entertainment, and was admitted to be an imitator beyond parallel, it was usual with many to assert, that for this very reason he could not be an actor : and when he gave up appearing as a part of the whole, to take the entire task of entertaining an audience for three successive hours, without interval, on his own shoulders, exceptious criticism endeavoured to place him in a lower grade than when he formed merely an item in a combined *dramatis personæ*. As an actor, he would have been deemed greater, had not his peculiar vein given a handle to ready detractors to call that mimicry, which was, in fact, creation. The conclusion appears to us as illogical as it was ungenerous.

Entertainments entirely supported by one person had often been given before the days of Charles Mathews. Foote, Tate Wilkinson, Henderson, and Bannister, were each celebrated and successful in their way : but Mathews was the first who added the *Monopolylogue*, and wound up with a drama of many characters personated by his single self. In this, the rapidity and completeness of the changes, either as to countenance or costume, far surpassed anything of the kind attempted by the ablest of his predecessors. Harry Stoe Van Dyk summed up the character of his professional powers in one comprehensive line : —

" Thou *live* kaleidoscope, thou single *Co.!*"

Mathews was irritable and eccentric to a proverb, full of crotchets and fancies, but withal warm-hearted, unsuspecting, and liberal; a most amusing companion, and a steady friend. He enjoyed the intimacy of Sir Walter Scott, Lord Byron, Moore, Rogers, and all the *literati* of his day; was not unfrequently the guest of George IV.; and his society was courted by the highest and noblest in the land. He was as much respected in his private, as applauded in his public life; and few men were more generally beloved by all who had an opportunity of becoming acquainted with his worth. He died poor, for which many causes might be assigned, including unsuccessful speculations; although, with the exception of Edmund Kean, he received more money in a given period than any performer of his day. His widow and biographer, who knew him better than any one else, says, in an affectionate tribute to his excellence, " he was one of the most unassuming possessors of genius that ever graced it with a life of undeviating rectitude and goodness." He was twice married, and had one child only, the present Charles Mathews, who inherits much of his father's genius, though not exactly in the same line.

During the early part of William Abbott's first season as manager of the Dublin Theatre, Mathews, who was an intimate friend of his, accepted an engagement there, and commenced with the characters of *Goldfinch* and *Morbleu*, in Moncrieff's popular farce of " Monsieur Tonson." On the nights when he appeared in the regular way, the houses were thinly attended. When he gave his " At Home," they were filled to suffocation. In the farce of " Monsieur Tonson," the part of *Morbleu* had been originally personated with great success by Montague Talbot, a favourite of long standing in the Dublin company, and still remembered by the patriarchs of the expiring generation.* During the first scene, when Mathews was beginning already to make a favourable impression, some half-dozen malcontents in the gallery raised a cry of " Talbot! Talbot!" which operated like an epidemic, and was speedily caught up by a few more. Mathews paused, appeared astonished, and at length said, " I hear a cry of 'Talbot! Talbot!' but I am unable to follow the meaning." " We want Talbot," was the reply. " You may have him," muttered the indignant actor, *sotto voce*, bowed, and walked off the stage, under considerable excitement.

---

* Talbot was a gentleman of good family and education, and a graduate of Trinity College, Dublin. His *forte* lay in light comedy and Frenchmen ; but his attempts in tragedy were ineffective. He is greatly lauded in Croker's "Familiar Epistles," where it is said of him :—

> " By art and nature chastely fit
> To play the gentleman or wit ;
> Not Harris's nor Colman's boards,
> Nor all that Drury Lane affords,
> Can paint the rakish *Charles* so well,
> Give so much life to *Mirabel ;*
> Or show, for light and airy sport,
> So exqusite a *Doricourt*."

Talbot was the original *Rezenvelt* in " De Montfort," at Drury Lane ; a character unsuited to him, and in which he made little impression. In his decline, his notions of acting had become " very peculiar." Amongst other eccentricities, he discharged the duties of the *Ghost* in " Hamlet" with tin eyes, fastened over his own, to do away with speculation, and a sort of revolving, ambient motion, under the idea that an immaterial, disembodied spirit should not stand as if fixed to earth, but float etherially. More than one *Hamlet* has been sadly disconcerted by this strange demeanour of his father's spirit. In 1826, Talbot's partizans concocted the last of the Dublin " Rows," which lasted several nights, the object being to compel Mr. Henry Harris, the manager, to engage him contrary to his wishes.

The interruption then increased to an uproar. The manager came forward, and stated that his friend Mr. Mathews was merely there for a short engagement, to serve and oblige him ; that he performed, as a matter of course, his usual round of characters ; and that he was not come to displace Mr. Talbot, or succeed to his position. This address was received with universal acclamations, which redoubled when Mathews entered, immediately afterwards, and resumed his character. But, in a few moments, the mischievous spirits again shouted "Talbot! Talbot!" Mathews, never the most patient of men, now lost his temper entirely. He came forward and said, with brusque irritation, " Either you want to see this farce, or you do not ; so make up your minds at once. If I am interrupted again by this cry of 'Talbot! Talbot!' I shall relieve you from my performance ; but it is rather too good, after having acted this part with universal applause in London and all the principal theatres in England, to come here and be annoyed by you and your Talbot." It was thought he had now committed himself beyond recovery, and would be pelted off; but the audience suddenly veered round to the humorous point, took it all in good part, and there was no more "Talbot!" during the remainder of the engagement. A theatre has been sacked upon less provocation. But Mathews visited Dublin no more, and never forgot the affront. To all subsequent applications he replied laconically, " Talbot, Talbot."

. The celebrated gallery of theatrical portraits which now graces the walls of the " Garrick Club," was originally formed by Charles Mathews. These pictures he collected with great taste and perseverance, and without any regard to the cost of such an expensive hobby-horse. For years they constituted the pride of his existence, and comforted him under many disappointments. This is the only complete series of the kind ever formed, and devoted to one exclusive subject. For those (and there are many) who delight to live on retrospection, and to multiply present enjoyments by a revival of the past, they possess a charm irrelevant of and superior to their pretensions as works of art; and a power over the imagination and feelings which can be felt more easily than described. We may sit or stand for hours in dreamy abstraction, looking on the familiar faces and costumes which have so often thrilled the soul with high-wrought sentiment, or convulsed the faculties with immoderate mirth, until they step from their frames in animated reality, surround us in a band, and carry us far away into the realms of fancy. We persuade ourselves that we hear, and are mingling with the social intercourse, the lively green-room gossip, the professional jealousies, the sparkling jest, the biting sarcasm, or the pungent anecdote. The little, busy world becomes instinct with life, variety, and conflicting passions. These musings are as salutary as they are delightful; and, like the sleeping *Caliban*, when enjoying visions of pleasant sights and sounds, we are almost ready to weep on awakening from them.

The number of pictures collected by Mathews amounted to 388, according to the printed catalogue. In the original purchase he sunk nearly 5,000*l*. He built a room expressly for their accommodation, at his residence, Ivy Cottage, Kentish Town, and took much delight in showing them to his friends. He was frequently bored by vapid, unmeaning curiosity-hunters, many of them perfect strangers, who almost forced themselves in, and would have scarcely left him an hour to himself, had he admitted them all. But nothing afforded him more pleasure than to exhibit his gallery to friends, or even simple acquaintances, who were attracted by true taste, and a rational desire to see what was known and admitted to be one of the lions of the day. Mrs. Mathews says, in her Memoirs of her husband:—" So many came, whom to reject would have been personally mortifying to us, that our peaceful retreat was converted almost into a fatigue to us, too often having all the character of a show-place (from which I pray heaven to defend me!) where we lived more for others than for ourselves."

When the pressure of circumstances compelled Mr. Mathews to break up his suburban establishment and live in London, it became absolutely necessary to part with the pictures. He could not endure the idea of their dispersion. The Garrick Club, it was said, *ought* to have them. Pleased with the idea of seeing them kept as an unbroken collection, where he could still look at his old associates whenever he felt inclined, the transfer was proposed at 3,000*l.*; but the sum which the finances of the club at that time enabled them to offer, was so small (about one-fifth of the original cost), that the idea of their disposal was for the present wholly given up. The owner was then strongly advised to exhibit them, to which with reluctance he consented, thinking their deserved popularity would assist and enhance the ultimate sale. It was well that he contemplated no immediate gain. In May, 1833, the exhibition was opened to public view, the price of admittance being one shilling. When the accounts were closed at the end of the period announced, it was found that the loss exceeded 140*l.* Thus it became evident, upon an unanswerable arithmetical calculation, that the troublesome curiosity, the rabid appetite of thousands, had been excited more by a desire to see the unrivalled Mathews, than Mathews' unrivalled show. When the original proprietor and collector died, in 1835, his widow sold the pictures to Mr. John Rowland Durrant, the well-known and wealthy stock-broker, who purchased them for the Garrick Club, they paying him five per cent. interest until convenient to reimburse the capital. At his death, he bequeathed them as a free legacy to the club; and thus they are permanently fixed (with many subsequent and valuable additions) in the most eligible of all resting places, which appears as if specially provided for their reception, and secured against the probability of being diminished or dispersed.

In the course of the season of 1836, Mr. Bunn introduced to the London public, in Drury Lane, the renowned hero of the buskin from America, Edwin Forrest. He came out in a native tragedy, written by Dr. Bird, of New York, entitled, the "Gladiator"—a sort of "rawhead and bloody-bones" affair, with here and there a vigorous passage approaching to poetry. But the hero, *Spartacus*, well suited the physical attributes of his representative. Forrest had a noble, muscular figure, with stentorian lungs. He might have stood for a model of the Farnesean Hercules. When commanded in the arena to kneel to the consul by the attendant officer, and he replied indignantly—

> " Kneel thou whose craven soul was form'd for crouching ;
> I am here to FIGHT !"

every one present felt that the athletic individual before them splendidly embodied the purpose for which he was produced. When called forward at the end of the play, to receive the congratulations of the audience, he thanked them very warmly for his reception, not only on his own account, but on the part of his friend, the author of the " Gladiator." But Mr. Bull gave him distinctly to understand that the welcome was intended for himself

personally, and that the compliment by no means included the literary importation.

Forrest was a bold, rough, manly actor, always in
earnest, though frequently incorrect in his Shakespearean
readings. His curse in *Lear* was tremendous, and his
sustained palsy natural, though painful to an extreme
degree. His dialect was occasionally tinctured by
American provincialisms, and he was too confirmed in
his elocution and style—too dogmatic in temperament to
alter or improve by London experience. Had he been
brought up in a good classic school of acting, there was
that within him which would have placed his name
high in the foremost list. He lost much in the estimation of all well-thinking people, by going into the boxes
of the Edinburgh theatre, after the termination of his
own engagement, and hissing Mr. Macready during his
performance of *Hamlet*. If he disliked the "*pas de
mouchoir*," as he chose to call it, in the third act, good
taste might have suggested to him to refrain from any
public expression of his contempt for the conceptions of
a brother actor. But our transatlantic brethren have
very bewildered notions of etiquette or delicacy.

The death of the facetious George Colman, in October,
1836, opened to Mr. Charles Kemble the appointment
of " Examiner of Plays," to which office he succeeded
through his personal interest with the then Lord Chamberlain, the Marquis Conyngham. A better selection
could not have been made. Charles Kemble was a fine
scholar, an experienced artist, well versed in all the arcana
of theatrical business, a dramatic author himself, and an
accomplished gentleman in every sense of the word.
But the post was incompatible with his position as an
actor still before the public. He therefore determined
to retire, and went through a round of his favourite
characters, winding up on the 3d of December, with

Benedick, in which he had long been without a competitor. On the 24th of March, 1840, he returned to the stage for five nights, at the express desire, it was said, of her present gracious Majesty. The characters he appeared in were *Don Felix, Mercutio, Benedick, Charles Surface,* and, finally, *Hamlet,* which really closed his theatrical career on the 10th of April. These performances produced enormous receipts, but the revived actor gave his services gratuitously, and thereby rendered considerable service to the theatre in which his brother had sunk a large sum of money for a very unprofitable return. Charles Kemble lived to a good age, dying so recently as the 12th of November, 1854, when he was within a few days only of completing his seventy-ninth year. He was by much the youngest of the gifted race; and being intended for one of the learned professions, was sent at a very early age, by his brother John, to the same continental seminary at which he had himself been educated—the English college at Douay. He afterwards obtained a situation in the Post-office; but finding the duties irksome, unintellectual, and monotonous, resolved to follow the family bent, and try his fortunes on the stage. He came out as *Malcolm,* in "Macbeth," in 1794. His progress was slow. For several seasons he was considered little better than a walking gentleman; but, by time and perseverance, he succeeded in placing himself in the highest rank. Through a mistaken ambition, when managerial power enabled him to do as he pleased, he constantly thrust himself before the public in *Hamlet, Macbeth,* and *Othello.* In these, and the loftiest walk of heavy tragedy, he never soared beyond respectability; while in *Romeo, Macduff, Edgar,* and *Cassio,* he evinced an excellence which no other actor ever contested. In his own line, a more elegant and finished performer never graced the boards. Those who remember him in the full vigour of his manly beauty, in such parts as *Faulconbridge, Marc Antony, Jaffier, Benedick, Mirabel, Mercutio, Charles Surface,* and *Don Felix,* have seen specimens of acting in the best school, never surpassed, and which they may despair of seeing approached in these " fast" days, when the young aspirants of the stage hold themselves superior to the trammels of study, experience, or example, and expect to achieve 'sudden fame and fortune by a sort of impromptu inspiration.

In 1837 the stage lost John Liston, of whom it may be said in the words of Ariosto, " *Natura lo fece e poi ruppe la stampa,*" — Nature after compounding that ineffable physiognomy broke the mould.   No human visage, no, not even Munden's, ever resembled or came up to the rich comic powers of Liston's.   Heraclitus could not have looked upon that marvellous assemblage of features without being moved to laughter, while the proprietor himself would have remained imperturbable. His great and distinguishing excellence lay in the ease and apparent unconsciousness of effort with which he convulsed an audience.   There was no hard straining, no deep delving for a joke which came up by reluctant instalments and produced a consumptive half-strangled laugh, dying in its own echo.   The image is somewhat laboured like the humour it deprecates.

Liston was originally a pedagogue of humble pretensions, a teacher's assistant in a day-school.   How is it possible to fancy boys looking seriously for a moment on that magazine of fun which his countenance must ever have exhibited !   By some strange infatuation he imagined himself destined to excel in the heroes of ˙tragedy, and was not a little mortified when on benefit nights he played *Romeo* and *Octavian* in sober seriousness, and the audience insisted on receiving them as burlesques.   George IV. encored him from the royal box in *Mawworm's* sermon, which ever afterwards stamped that unbecoming mummery with a singular reputation and a similar call. It appears strange that the laughter-loving public of Dublin should never have fully understood or tasted the humour of Liston It was a complete mystery to them, although they are (or rather were) entirely compounded of humour; they neither enjoyed the style nor the pieces written for its peculiar illustration. Being invited in 1832 to make a farewell visit to the Irish metropolis:—" No," replied he, " they have seen me for the last time; they don't laugh at my jokes; they hiss all my new pieces, and I am rich enough not to expose myself to unnecessary mortification." His last appearance in Dublin was in the latter part of 1824, under the management of his friend William Abbott, when he felt so vexed at his cold reception, that he declared he would never come again, and kept his word. Liston died on the 22d of March, 1846, aged sixty-nine, in ne possession of a handsome fortune—the natural consequence of living within a large income, and of never having been led to engage in any hazardous speculations.

Another rich comedian, John Reeve, but of a class and character quite distinct from Liston, died within two years after him, on the 24th of January, 1848. He was more of a droll than a legitimate or classical actor, and excelled in burlesque. He had only entered on his fortieth year. Habits of free living proved his bane, and brought him to an early tomb; his style was somewhat coarse and exuberant, but it must be admitted that he was the personification of fun, jollity, and good humour.

CHAPTER XIV.

CHARLES KEAN MAKING RAPID GROUND IN THE PROVINCES—CORRESPON-
DENCE WITH MR. MACREADY RELATIVE TO AN ENGAGEMENT AT COVENT
GARDEN—ENGAGES WITH MR. BUNN—APPEARS AS HAMLET AT DRURY
LANE—UNPRECEDENTED SUCCESS—WARM EULOGIUMS OF THE LEADING
PAPERS—CONTRAST OF POSITION AND PROSPECTS BETWEEN 1827 AND
1838.

FROM 1833 to the close of 1837, Charles Kean
steadily pursued the course he had laid down for
himself; his eye was ever on the metropolis, but the
road through which he expected to reach it once
more had many windings, and he resolved to traverse
them with patience, and not to jump hastily at any
opportunity, no matter under how specious a form it
might present itself. He now approached the culmi-
nating point of his theatrical life—the apex, as it
might be called, of his career. He had achieved great
marvels in the country; his hold on all the leading
provincial theatres was well secured, and, to a certain
extent, he was perfectly independent of London. But
still London success was the key-stone of his ambition,
the crowning glory to which he aspired. The time had
come when the question was to be decided whether he
had formerly been held down by prejudice, or really
had not the abilities by some so pertinaciously denied
to him. He was twenty-seven years of age, and had
served an arduous apprenticeship of more than ten
years. He was now to take his degree permanently
amongst the masters of his craft, or to sink for ever

into the ranks of mediocrity. His enemies (and they were numerous, as well as pertinacious) loudly predicted his failure. To use their own favourite and elegant expression, he was nothing but a "lucky humbug," trading on his name and resemblance to his father. "Let him only face a London audience," said they, "and he will be found out at once." If *they* were right, all the audiences in the principal theatres throughout the kingdom, all the provincial press, were in a conspiracy to be wrong. His many friends, on the other hand, were equally confident of his triumph. Mr. Macready had entered on the management of Covent Garden in 1837; he was naturally anxious to secure all the strength he could muster, and invited Charles Kean to enter under his standard. The views of both are clearly set forward in the correspondence which took place between them :—

" 8, Kent Terrace, Regent's Park,
"London, July 22d, 1837.

" *To* CHARLES KEAN, ESQ.

" DEAR SIR,—

" The newspapers may, perhaps, have informed you that I have taken Covent Garden Theatre. I have embarked in this hazardous enterprise, congenial neither to my habits nor disposition, in the hope of retrieving, in some measure, the character of our declining art, or at least of giving to its professors the continuance of *one* of our national theatres, as a place for its exercise, which most persons despaired of. The performers have met the sacrifice I am prepared to make, with a spirit highly laudable to their feelings, and I trust the event will prove not discreditable to their judgment. Every one has consented to a reduction of his or her claims, and I believe the names of all our principal artists are entered on my list. Your celebrity has, of course, reached me; in the most frank and cordial spirit, I invite you to a participation in the struggle I am about to make. I understand that your expectations are high; let me know your terms, and, *if it be possible*, I will most gladly meet them, and do all in my power to secure your assistance, and give the completest scope to the full development of your talents.

" I will not further allude to the cause for which I am making this effort, than to express my belief and confidence that your own disposition will [so far suggest to you its professional importance, as to insure us against any apprehension of your becoming an antagonist, should you decline (as I sincerely trust you will not) enrolling yourself as a co-operator.

" I remain, dear Sir.

" Very faithfully yours,

" W. C. MACREADY."

" Cork, July 27, 1827.

" *To* W. C. MACREADY, ESQ.

" DEAR SIR,—

" I have had the honour to receive your very courteous letter; and permit me, before I answer that portion of it which relates to myself, to congratulate you on the assumption of the Covent Garden management.

" I assure you, with great sincerity, I think it a most fortunate circumstance for the drama and the public, that you have placed yourself at the head of this theatre, and that you occupy a position where your energies will sustain, your taste improve, and your influence elevate the stage. No one could be more fitly chosen to preside where you do now. I say this without hesitation, and distinctly; because, from your well-understood predilection for our classical plays, and your own range of parts, you will give those plays every possible preference; and thus (to use your own words), ' retrieve in some measure the character of our declining art.' Connected as you now are with Covent Garden, controlling its business, and set over its destinies, allow me to wish you, for your own sake, and that of the profession, a long term of prosperous management.

"For your offer to me of an engagement, and your assurances of giving ' ample scope to the full development of my talents,' I thank you very much. Your invitation, and the kind and handsome manner in which you offer it, are most flattering to me; and though neither my inclination nor my interests point to London just now, still I set due value upon your encouraging proposal. But, let me tell you *frankly*, that, *were* I to go to London, there have occurred some circumstances between Mr. Bunn and me, whereby he might hold me bound (were it only partially so) to *him*; and even in a case where a contract was perhaps but *implied*, if Mr. Bunn made it a question of *honour* with me, I should, of course, be governed by the absolute and arbitrary dictate of such a monitor. I repeat, however, I do not contemplate a movement towards London for the present.

"Another point in your letter demands a few words. You express your confidence that my own disposition will so far suggest to me the professional importance of your present enterprise, as to insure you against my becoming an antagonist elsewhere, should I decline your offer to co-operate with yourself. You may indeed believe that I *could not*, neither *would* I, oppose myself to the interests of any establishment or any individual.

But surely you could never suppose that my acceptance of an engagement at any time, with any manager of the other great theatre, would involve hostility to you. The interests of both the national theatres are alike important to the public. I should naturally consider my own advantage in connecting myself with either, consistently with my rank in the drama, and its welfare generally; and were I to assent to your idea of the case, I should necessarily shut myself out of a large sphere of action; I might deprive myself of those professional associations I most valued; I should, in fact, compromise my professional freedom and independence; and it does not belong to the proud eminence you have yourself attained, to narrow my efforts in working out my individual fame. I labour hard in my profession, and, in doing this, if I can in any way, or at any season, contribute to your success, while honourably zealous for my own, it will gratify my feelings and my heart.

" I remain, dear Sir,

" Truly yours,

" CHARLES KEAN."

" Theatre Royal, Covent Garden,
" August 2d, 1837.

" To CHARLES KEAN, ESQ.

" DEAR SIR,—

" I beg my observations may not be considered in the light of a desire to limit you in any way. I intended to convey to you my intention to concede as liberal terms as I supposed either you could demand, or any manager, with the means or purpose of paying you, could grant. Any expectation founded on such an intention was not meant to make a part of

the *business* of my letter. In inviting you to London,
I fulfil a duty that devolves on me with my office, and
I do so in the most frank and liberal spirit.

"I shall regret your absence, should you think it
right to reject my overtures; and with my very cordial
thanks for the kind expressions of your letter,

"I remain, dear Sir,

"Yours truly,

"W. C. MACREADY."

In this correspondence, conducted with marked cour-
tesy on either side, we find it difficult to understand
why Mr. Macready fell into the diplomatic error of
expecting from Charles Kean a promise or pledge that
if he declined coming to him, he would at least abstain
from going elsewhere. It was false policy without the
chance of success; as the other, unless he were insane,
would surely pay no heed to such a suggestion. He judged
that, according to the plan laid down by Mr. Macready,
it could not possibly come within his views to place him
in the exclusive position at which he had so long aimed.
He, therefore, paused to deliberate well before he
hazarded the London venture, and finally closed with
the offer of Mr. Bunn, to act twenty nights, at Drury
Lane, with a salary of 50*l.* per night. That he decided
wisely in preferring an arena entirely unoccupied, was
evidenced in the most conclusive manner by the result.
Had he fallen into the ranks at Covent Garden, he
might have proved a valuable recruit, but he would
never have risen to a truncheon of command.

On the 8th of January, 1838, he appeared as *Hamlet*,
—a memorable evening in his own history—with a triumphant issue, never surpassed in the history of the
stage.

The play was cast thus :

Claudius, King of Denmark . . .	MR. BAKER.
Hamlet	MR. CHARLES KEAN.
Polonius	MR. DOWTON.
Laertes	MR. KING.
Horatio	MR. H. COOKE.
Rosencrantz	MR. F. COOKE.
Guildenstern	MR. DURUSET.
Osric	MR. BRINDAL.
First Actor	MR. MC IAN.
Second Actor	MR. T. MATTHEWS.
First Gravedigger	MR. COMPTON.
Second Gravedigger.	MR. HUGHES.
Ghost of Hamlet's Father . . .	MR. COOPER.
Gertrude, Queen of Denmark . .	MRS. TERNAN.
Ophelia	MISS ROMER.

The house was crowded from orchestra to upper gallery.
The new *Hamlet* was received with enthusiasm.   From
his entrance to the close of the performance the applause
was unanimous and incessant.   The celebrated " Is it
the King?" in the third act, produced an electrical effect.
To use a favourite expression of his father's, " *the pit
rose at him.*"

At the conclusion he was called for, and hailed with
reiterated acclamations.   " Caps, hats, and tongues
applauded him to the clouds."   The success was solid,
substantial.   There was no array of hired *claqueurs*, no
packing in the pit, no pre-arranged signals, no managerial influence to forestall or misrepresent unbiassed
judgment.   It was an honest verdict by an impartial
jury.   The day following, the most influential journals
corroborated the opinion of the public.   The articles
were elaborately written with sound critical acumen,
and with candour, kindness, and ability.   The *Times**
spoke thus :—

* Mr. Michael Nugent, at that time theatrical critic of the *Times*,
and a writer of much experience, was the author of the article.

" After a very successful probation in the provinces, Mr. Charles Kean appeared last night again on these boards, where, a few years since, when a mere boy, he endeavoured to conciliate public favour. That was an immatured and ill-judged attempt, and, as might be expected, ended in failure. The mind of the play-going public was still filled with a vivid recollection of the transcendent talents of the elder Kean, who had temporarily retired, and however kind their feelings might be towards the young aspirant, they could not avoid showing their discontent at the incapacity of the *nominis umbra*, who thus early sought, or more probably, perhaps, was solicited, to vault from the school-room into the then vacant tragic chair. Defeated in the first instance, he did not abandon the profession. He laboured to improve himself, and subsequently appeared at Covent Garden and the Haymarket. At each of these theatres his exertions effected nothing for the manager in the way of money; nothing for the actor in the way of fame; still he was not disheartened. A long course in the provinces he thought would do him service. If he succeeded there, he felt that much of the trepidation and awe, which, before a London audience, in a great degree paralysed his powers, would be removed, and he would have a fair and honest hold on the feelings of those who came in a just and honest spirit to witness his performance. We like these strugglings against untoward circumstances. They speak the workings of a determined mind, which thinks, however the world may have been inclined to slight it, that there are within itself seeds not merely of talent but of genius. Thus much for the early efforts of Mr. Charles Kean.

" Now for what we may call his real *debût*, when experience and judgment have come to the aid of his natural faculties, and made him, in one character certainly, that of *Hamlet*, an accomplished, elegant, and, when the scene requires it, an energetic actor without bombast. Such we think were the leading features of his performance last night. He has taken a fine, philosophical view of the part. The groundwork is melancholy abstraction, sometimes diverted from its vein by the recollection of circumstances which elicit passion, or by the interference of court-flies, who sting a gallant nature to sarcasm and reproach by their sinister actions. The sombre hue of the character was well preserved by Mr. Kean, and those occasional bursts of tearful emotion which are directed by *Hamlet's* knowledge of his father's fate, and his own irresolution in not at once doing execution on the murderer, were finely contrasted with the prevailing melancholy.

Mr. Kean delivered the soliloquies with great feeling, and consequently with corresponding effect. We look, however, for his excellences in the more active scenes of the play. His rencontre with his father's spirit, where astonishment, awe, and reverence were commingled, was finely acted. The celebrated scene with *Ophelia* was well imagined, and was as well played before the audience. Here Mr. Kean was wholly different from any person we have ever before seen in the character. There was enough of violence in his manner to justify the grossly lascivious king in saying,

" Love ;—his affections do not that way tend ;"

but there was also enough of tenderness and delicacy to show to tenderer and more delicate minds that his very heart-strings were breaking, while in his assumed frenzy he was saying unkind things to one whom he entirely loved.

The closet scene with his mother was acted with great power. His attitude and look when, having slain

Polonius, he rushes in exclaiming " Is it the King ? " fully deserved the immense applause which followed one of the most striking scenic exhibitions we have witnessed for a long time. In the play scene, Mr. Kean was good ; but though at the conclusion he received much applause, there was less marking about it, less force, less power, than we have seen manifested by others. His last scene was very good. He fences not merely gracefully but skilfully. We need not say that the house was on this occasion crowded from the pit to the ceiling. The jury before whom Mr. Kean appeared was not a packed one. There was no indiscriminate applause. Assuredly where applause was given, and the instances were very frequent, it was well merited.

Looking to the whole of Mr. Kean's performance we are greatly pleased with it. It may, however, be rendered even better. His pauses are in many instances so long that he fails to make the point at which he is aiming. Again, he carries the weeping sentimentality of *Hamlet* into situations where he is a mere abstract speculator. The beautiful lines commencing, " Imperious Cæsar, dead and turned to clay," do not want tears to enforce their moral—the nothingness of defunct mortality.

Mr. Kean's reception was of the most cheering description. When he appeared, the applause from every part of the house was enthusiastic ; and throughout the evening the same anxious wish to encourage (we hope now no longer struggling) merit was observable. At the conclusion of the tragedy he was loudly called for, and he made very gracefully his obeisance to a much delighted audience. He certainly has succeeded in giving a very elegant and finished portrait of *Hamlet*. What he will do with the *Richards* and *Macbeths* is yet to be proved. That he has mind for them we can imagine, but yet we cannot speak with anything like decision of his physical powers."

The notice in the *Morning Post* ran thus :—"The old times of Drury seemed last night to have come back again. Never, in its most palmy days, did we witness a greater crowd—never more enthusiasm in an audience—and scarcely ever more success in a performance. It was gratifying to witness once more such a house assembled, to delight themselves with one of Shakespeare's plays, and that play, *Hamlet*—the most refined, perhaps, and most touching of them all. The house was crowded to the roof, and gave Mr. Charles Kean as warm a reception as it is possible to imagine that an actor could receive. He might well say, as his father did before him, that "the pit rose at him." But it was not the pit alone, but the whole house which rose, and by acclamations loud and long continued, by waving of hats and handkerchiefs, and by every possible demonstration of welcome, testified their gladness to see Mr. Kean, or (as his Irish friends would say), to see his father's son. From the beginning to the end Mr. Kean's performance was brilliantly successful. We never saw an audience which seemed better pleased, and though we do not hold this by any means an infallible criterion of an actor's merit, it is one upon which much dependence may generally be placed; and in the present case we think the decisive judgment of the audience was well borne out.

" We do not think, indeed, that the performance of Mr. Kean was without fault, or that all the parts of it which brought down great applause were entitled to the praise of the considerate and judicious ; but, as a whole, the performance was striking, energetic, skilful, and undeformed by any such marked blemish as would mar this general impression in the mind of even the most fastidious. Our readers are aware that there are two styles of performing *Hamlet*, which, like the two great divisions in the modern French literature of fiction, may be called the classic and the romantic. Within the memory of present audiences the late Mr. Kean was the most prominent representative of the *romantic* style; and the late actor—but we are happy to say the still-living private gentleman—Mr. Young, was the most distinguished professor of the *classic* style. We shall not now enter upon the controversy as to which of the two general modes of performance ought to be preferred; both have undoubtedly their excellences, and both their defects. An even, uniform performance, however well considered, however dignified in its energy and delicate in its pathos, may be said to be scarcely applicable to one whom Shakespeare certainly intended should exhibit strong contrasts :—

> " This is mere madness,
> And thus awhile the fit will work on him.
> Anon, as patient as the female dove,
> When that her golden couplets are disclos'd,
> His silence will sit drooping."

On the other hand, the imagination of most readers of sensibility has been so apt to associate the character of *Hamlet* with melancholy meditation, that persons of a pensive temperament are almost offended at any departure from the serious dignity and philosophic scenes which are the prevading characteristics of *Hamlet*. He is the man so weary of the world and its sin that he wishes he was dead—who looks upon all the uses of this world as weary, stale, flat, and unprofitable. In this key is the character pitched; and however airy, fantastical, satirical, may be its occasional flights, to this deep note of melancholy does it ever return, and we feel that he has that within, of killing grief, 'that passeth show.'

"Of Mr. Charles Kean's performance we should say that he tries to combine the two styles to which we have alluded; but he is an hereditary actor, and his nature leads him to the *romantic*. That style materially preponderates. He has evidently studied much, as well as gained much experience, since he last appeared in London, and the result has been remarkable improvement. In height, in gait, in expression of countenance, and especially in voice, he bears the strongest resemblance to his father. We should not say that the features of his face are like his father's, or so good; but the shape of the forehead is the same—the piercing dark eye is the same—and, above all, the voice, husky in its energy, and soft, distinct, and clear in its lower and more subdued tones—is exactly that of his father. There were many passages—not those, we confess, which we liked best—in which the mannerisms of the old favourite were so vividly brought to mind, that the house rang again with applause. Indeed, it struck us occasionally that the audience were determined to enjoy two poets on the one evening—that Rogers as well as Shakespeare had something to do with their delight, and ' The Pleasures of Memory,' as well as ' Hamlet, Prince of Denmark,' occupied their attention, and contributed to their satisfaction.

" We believe that, at the very commencement, Mr. C. Kean was somewhat overwhelmed with the enthusiasm of his reception ; and the extreme slowness of his enunciation, together with a certain tremulousness which may not have been intended, threw an expression of grief—almost sobbing grief—into his first speeches that the best interpreters of the character have not, we think, contemplated. *Hamlet* speaks, indeed, of the 'fruitful

river in the eye,' as one of the shows of grief to which
the *Queen* had referred, but it is scarcely consistent with
his appearing in public at all that he should then, while
speaking, be almost weeping too. Mr. Kean's soliloquies,
though well delivered, are not the happiest parts of his
performance: and it was not until the interview with
Horatio, Marcellus, and *Bernardo,* in which the appearance of the *Ghost* is related to him, that the spirit of the
actor fairly showed itself.   The

'In my mind's eye, Horatio,'

which was, indeed, most like Edmund Kean's manner
of delivering that passage, was loudly applauded; and
thenceforward, through all the action of the play,
similar applause was elicited. It struck us that nothing
could be more admirable than the conception of Mr.
Kean's performance when his companions find him after
his interview with the *Ghost.* He played it as if when
first speaking to them of secrecy he had intended to
tell them all that he had heard, and with that intention begins,—

'There's ne'er a villain dwelling in all Denmark,'

but then, suddenly remembering the prudence of keeping
his own secret, he turns it off with—

'But he's an arrant knave.'

Mr. Kean paused between these two lines, and delivered the second in quite an altered tone.
    "The third act is the great trial of a performer of
Hamlet, and Mr. Kean came well through that trial.
Not that we think the famous soliloquy beginning, 'To
be or not to be,' was given as well as Mr. Young used
to give it; but from that forward the performance
throughout the act was admirable, unless we should

except what seemed to us a much too rapid delivery of that most Shakespearean passage :—

'I am myself indifferent honest; but yet I could accuse me of such things, that it were better my mother had not borne me : I am very proud, revengeful, ambitious ; with more offences at my beck than I have thoughts to put them in, imagination to give them shape, or time to act them in. What should such fellows as I do crawling between heaven and earth ! We are arrant knaves, all ; believe none of us.'

"This was hurried over with such rapidity that the quickest ears could scarcely follow the words. But the speech to the players was given with delightful ease and nature. The intensity with which he regarded the *King* at the play, and the exulting conviction with which he leaped up as the *King* bursts away, conscience-struck, from the scene, were also most natural and vivid; and the whole of the scene with his mother was a triumph of bold, vigorous, judicious, and delicate acting. The voice of anxious inquiry—the attitude—the depth of eager expression with which, when returning from slaying *Polonius* behind the arras, he asks,—

'Is it the King?'

was as successful as any piece of performance we ever saw.

"In the dying scene we thought there was rather a needless protraction of the hideous pantomime of dissolution. *Prince Hamlet* died rather too elaborately, especially as Mr. Kean had presently after to appear before the curtain, to receive the renewed shouts of applause, and to witness once more all manner of encomiastic gesticulation. We learned after we had left the theatre —we own to our very great astonishment—that Mr. Kean had certainly never seen his father play *Hamlet*. We should have concluded from his performance that he must have seen him represent the character often. Upon the whole, the performance of last night at Drury

Lane was, in technical phrase, so decided a *hit* that we apprehend few who ever go to a theatre at all will be satisfied without seeing it, and we expect that the engagement of Mr. Kean will be of the utmost advantage to the establishment."

The tone of the *Globe* was equally laudatory with that of the *Post*, but the respective critics differed a little in their estimate of particular points. The *Globe* said :—

" The second *avatar* of Mr. Charles Kean took place last night, when the rich promise given by the crude efforts of his boyhood was amply redeemed. The reports which have for some time past reached us from the provinces, had prepared the public mind for a more than ordinary display of talent, and the house, in consequence, was so full that the management, we conceive, are now able to calculate to a fraction what it will contain. Nothing could be more cheering than the first reception given to the *débutant* (for in this light we consider him) ; the applause lasted full three minutes by ' our stop watch,' and seemed to act powerfully on the object of it, as the first few words he had to utter were tremulous and indistinct. This agitation, however, was but momentary, and *Hamlet* was ' himself again.' Minutely to criticise the performance of such a character would carry us into a wider field than our limits would afford ; but as all our readers are familiar with the part, it will be sufficient for us to mention a few of the chief excellences (for most excellent Mr. Kean's personation was throughout) displayed on this occasion ; and we content ourselves with so doing, the rather that, unquestionably, every admirer of Shakespeare will take an early opportunity of judging, in this instance, for himself.

" Mr. Kean's conception of the part was good ; the

melancholy abstraction, the vacillation, the derangement of 'a noble mind o'erthrown,' partly affected and partly real, were finely delineated. In the first scene with the *Ghost*, he reminded us much of his father; it was, however, no servile imitation, but evidently a similarity of conception similarly embodied. The interview with his mother in her closet, too, was admirably sustained, and the effect of his exclamation, 'Is it the King?' electrical. If, however, we were to analyze minutely Mr. Kean's performance, we should not hesitate to give the palm to the soliloquies. In the first place, they were real soliloquies, and not a sort of '*asides*' to the pit, as is too generally the case. In that fine burst of indignation at his own want of firmness — 'O, what a rogue and peasant slave am I!' he was eminently successful, and with great good taste restored many of those brilliant lines of the poet which fashion or convenience has of late years banished from the speech. The scene with *Ophelia* was well worked out, though he received but little support from her fair representative, whose excellence was confined to the musical part of the character. In the fencing match his elegance and skill were displayed to great advantage. We need scarcely add, that Mr. Kean was called for, and cheered with the greatest enthusiasm, at the fall of the curtain. It was impossible that his triumph could have been more complete, and we take our leave of him for the present, with the sincerest congratulations upon his success—a success which has stamped his character, and made his fortune."

It refreshes the spirit to read these honest, straightforward expressions of opinion, from men who, while they knew how to criticise, wrote without a bias, and felt what they described. We have selected the extracts from many of the same tone, and could multiply them readily, but too much space would be occupied, and enough are given to show that the impression of this first performance was most flattering to the actor, and fully vindicated the judgment of his friends. Had he been endowed with the united ambition of Alexander, Cæsar, and Napoleon, his loftiest aspirations must have been more than realized by the result of the 8th of January, 1838. Far different were the feelings of his mother and himself, when, on the morning following, their breakfast-table was strewed with the encomiums of the leading journals, from that deep mortification with which they had been overwhelmed ten years before from the same source which now conferred their happiness. Presently, there arose a few dissentient cavillers, but their censure passed unheeded and innocuous amidst the overwhelming torrent of approbation.

CHAPTER XV.

COMPLIMENTARY AND CRITICAL LETTERS.

THERE could now no longer be any doubt as to the position Charles Kean was thenceforward to hold. His place in the foremost rank of his profession was established. He had received the diploma for which he had so ardently toiled. His performances were continued for forty-three nights with undiminished attraction, and would have been protracted to a much longer period without intermission, but that a previous engagement in Edinburgh interfered, and compelled his temporary absence from London. Increased terms were offered to him if he could effect a compromise, by which that absence might be suspended. He felt the full disadvantage of the break, but determined not to disappoint his northern friends, to whom he was under many obligations.

Attentions were now lavished on him from every side —his society was courted by persons of the highest rank—his desk literally groaned beneath the weight of cards, invitations, and congratulatory letters. From the latter, a few selections may not be considered inappropriate :—

From LADY MORGAN.

> "6, Stafford Row, Buckingham Palace,
> "Jan. 10th, 1838.

"MY DEAR MR. KEAN,—

"I trust I am amongst the *earliest*, as I am certainly amongst the *sincerest*, to congratulate you on a success which I prophesied. I am so blind that I shall reserve further observations and congratulations till we meet, which I trust will be soon. Sir Charles and myself will be delighted to see you, at present in Stafford Row, and in a few days, more comfortably in our own house, which is at present in the hands of the workmen. We are always at home from two till five. Alas! for our poor Duchess!* How proud she would have been of your triumph. Tell Mrs. Kean I envy her her feelings. How far sweeter is the success of those we love, than our *own*, I can well tell. With Sir Charles and my niece's best compliments,

"My dear Mr. Kean,

"Most truly yours,

"SYDNEY MORGAN.

P.S. "I confide this to the most worthy two-penny, as I am ignorant of your address, and my footman is Irish."

From LADY BURDETT.

"LADY BURDETT'S compliments to Mr. Kean, and begs to offer him her very best congratulations on his distinguished success on his first appearance last evening.

"St. James's Place, Tuesday, Jan. 9th, 1838."

From LADY BLAKENEY.

"Royal Hospital, Dublin,
"Jan. 18th, 1828.

"MY DEAR MR. KEAN,—

"It is impossible to express how much gratified both Sir Edward and myself have been by hearing of your

----

* The Duchess of St. Alban's, one of Mr. C. Kean's steadiest friends and patronesses, who had died five months before, on the 6th August, 1837.

complete and unbounded success in London. We have read the newspapers with the greatest pleasure, containing, as they all do, such delightful accounts of your reception and triumph. Had it been otherwise, we should have been greatly surprised, feeling how deeply indebted we, and all your numerous friends in Dublin, have frequently been to you, in witnessing your splendid talents. That prosperity, health, and happiness may ever attend you, is, my dear Mr. Kean, Sir Edward's and my most sincere prayer, and believe me,

" Very sincerely yours,

" MARY BLAKENEY."

From the late GENERAL SIR G. D'AGUILAR.

" Dublin, 13th Jan. 1838.

" MY DEAR KEAN,—

" I congratulate you with all my heart on the brilliant success of your *debût*. You must never complain of the Press again. Take it all in all I think it is most laudatory. I like the *Times* critique best. To be ' an accomplished, elegant, and energetic actor of Hamlet, without bombast,' is the highest praise.

" I am full of business at this moment, but I cannot refrain from sending you this line, and requesting you to make my best respects acceptable to your good mother, whose existence will, I trust, be lengthened by many years more of pleasure and of pride.

" Ever faithfully yours,

" GEORGE D'AGUILAR.

" Have you seen Mr. Bulwer ?"

From LORD VISCOUNT MORPETH, *now* EARL OF CARLISLE.

" Jan. 9, 1838.

" MY DEAR MR. KEAN,—

" As one not the least interested amongst that crowded and fervid audience which witnessed your appearance last night, allow me to wish you joy on its complete and unequivocal success, and on the entire self-mastery and command of your powers, which you exhibited under circumstances naturally trying.   Do not trouble yourself to acknowledge this, but accept my most cordial wishes for your welfare in every possible respect.

" I am,
" Your faithful servant,

" MORPETH."

From EDWARD GOULBURN, ESQ.

" 21, Park Street, or Serjeant's Inn,
" Chancery Lane.
" Friday, Jan. 12, 1838.

" MY DEAR SIR,—

" When at Brighton, I understood that you would have been good- enough to let me know when your appearance in London was to take place.   I truly, however, rejoice to hear (as I do from all quarters) of its entire success.   I hear from my friend, Serjeant Talfourd, a most gratifying account.

" I am anxious to have the pleasure of making you known to him, and also to Lord Denman (for whom I was commissioned to procure a box to witness your performance), and I wish you would name some early day, or, perhaps, in order to secure their presence, two days, on which I could have the pleasure of seeing you at dinner, at my house, which, I need not add, would give me great gratification ; and I hope on one of these to find them disengaged, and able to meet you. I send this to Drury Lane, where I take it for granted it will find its way to your hands; and believe me, with hearty congratulations,

> "Yours most sincerely,
>
> "EDWARD GOULBURN."

From SIR THOMAS DICK LAUDER, BART.

> "The Grange House, Edinburgh,
> "12th Jan. 1838.

"MY DEAR KEAN,—

"I hope I need not use many words to convince you how much delighted all in this family have been, by the agreeable intelligence we have heard of your triumphant appearance at Drury Lane. It comes upon us by no means as matter of surprise; for, in fact, it is no more than I have been all along most sanguinely anticipating —and I think that I do not now anticipate too much, when I say, that if it pleases God to spare you to a reasonable span of life, you will yet be reckoned the first actor since Garrick's time. Instead of writing thus drily, with this abominable iron pen, I wish I was within reach of your hand, to give it such a hearty shake as my feelings at this moment would dictate. God bless you, and may your career from henceforward be as glorious as you deserve.

"I hope that we in the provinces are not to be cut out of our usual visit from you, because you have now climbed to the top of the tree. I long to see you again amongst us. I was at Howick lately, and had a long talk about *you* with Colonel Grey, as well as about all our old friends of the 71st. The Colonel is now in constant attendance at Windsor, and I think it looks very like as if his corps was destined for Canada. What a delightful person Mrs. Grey is! I fell quite in love with her.

"I begin to think that it is a piece of great presumption in me to have ventured on such an intrusion as this at such a time, when no doubt millions of *billets doux* from fair damsels are brought to you every hour, and when it cannot be supposed that such an epistle as mine may hope for consideration. But treat it as you may, it is a poor offering, but an honest offering of the heart, and as such it deserves to be forgiven.

With our united best wishes and hearty congratulations, believe me,

"My dear Kean,

"Ever yours most sincerely,

"THOS. DICK LAUDER."

From LORD MEADOWBANK.

" 11, Hanover Terrace, Edinburgh,
" Thursday.

" MY DEAR KEAN,—

" I enclose you a copy of Lockhart's letter, just as I received it. He said to me that he had no doubt you had the power of equalling any actor who had ever lived. He is, in short, as friendly a critic as you could have, but he is sometimes severe. Knowing well the London audience, his remarks are worth your having. In haste,

" Yours faithfully,

"A. MACONOCHIE."

From J. G. Lockhart, Esq.* *to* Lord Meadowbank.

" London, Jan. 17th, 1838.

" My dear Lord,—

"I saw young Kean in *Hamlet,* and was not disappointed in the main; though I did not recognize what had been described to me as the chief merit of his performance of that most difficult part; and I wish you, who have I believe very great authority with him, would caution him that, if he has altered what was so much admired in Scotland, from apprehension of his physical powers being inadequate to do full justice to his own conceptions, in our great theatres here, he is mistaken totally, and may incur a sad risk of marring his destiny. His whisper is as effective as ever Mrs. Siddons's was, and, though I was near, I think his features must tell equally at a distance, as the lines are cut with singular decision. I had been told that he was distinguished from other actors of Hamlet by his ordinary demeanour and tone being quiet, as certainly would best become a prince who had been ' the glass of fashion,' into whatever state of melancholy abstraction he might have fallen. Kean realized this admirably in his advice to the players, and I could not but think, ' Oh, if he would but stick *throughout to his own rules as he now practises them!*

" He injured, to my feeling sadly, the effect of his most beautiful scene on the battlements, by having previously given various parts with a too theatrical vehemence; and, in general, I thought he often uttered

---

* Many years editor of the *Quarterly Review;* the son-in-law, literary executor, and biographer of Sir Walter Scott. He was a caustic critic, very difficult to please, and full of strange conceits ; but keen and shrewd withal.

with passionate gesticulation, what Shakespeare meant
to be scarcely beyond a whisper. This must be the case
with all soliloquies; and I take it the same rule holds
as to all such involuntary expressions of desolate regret
over youth and hope departed, as occur throughout
Hamlet—nowhere more than in the lamentation over
the loss of all power to see beauty in the external world.
He acted that passage. I think he should have whispered it, with hardly a gesture, except to cast his eyes
upwards to the 'golden fires.' Perhaps the truth is,
however, that he attributes a more prominent madness
to *Hamlet* than I take the poet to have designed. If so,
I saw too well his deep study of the play, to be rash
or bold in my dissent from his judgment. I can only
speak my own feeling, and it was, that occasional un-
called for energy and violence disturbed the general
effect of a very graceful and touching performance.

" He cannot know how infinitely superior the sweet,
melancholy tones of his voice are to all the rest. His
pathos and tenderness in many places were never excelled. He will never declaim like Kemble, but he
may go beyond any actor I have seen in sober, simple,
gentleness of effect, if he will—and I think rival any,
even his father, in easy variety. I was much gratified;
for, in truth, I never could see any merit in any tragedian of late years, and I thought I should never see
any of Shakespeare's higher parts done the least justice
to again. I shall certainly go to see ' Hamlet ' again
very soon, and whatever of that file he takes up next.
I am anxious especially for the *Macbeth* and the *Lear*.
The theatre used to be one of my chief delights, and I
feared it was lost to me for ever, like ' many others.' I
think I may add that something of the general objections I have hinted, seemed to be felt by the ladies I
was in company with, and they are, as he won't deny,

the most delicate of all critics on matters of deportment and gesture.

"I hope Mr. C. Kean may have a long and prosperous career, and die with a fortune like Garrick's, and a character like John Kemble's.

"Ever truly yours,
"J. G. LOCKHART.

"P.S. Do you remember what Goëthe says—that Hamlet's sensibilities are like a rose-tree that has grown too big for its china vase?"

Some time after the date of the foregoing letter, when Charles Kean was balloted for, and admitted as a member of the Athenæum Club, Lockhart wrote the following note to Colonel Gore, one of the Committee :—

"Athenæum, March 21st.

"DEAR COLONEL,—

"Do be kind, and introduce young Kean as a child of the Committee, therein gratifying his high and laudable ambition; and showing your own skill in the recognition of true merits—professional, moral, and social.

"Yours most truly,
"J. G. LOCKHART."

—————

From SERJEANT, *afterwards* JUDGE, TALFOURD.

"Temple, 29th Jan. 1838.

"MY DEAR SIR,—

"The flattering terms in which you were so kind as to speak of my dramatic poem ('Ion') when I had the pleasure of meeting you on Saturday, encourage me to request your acceptance of one of the very few remaining copies of the unpublished edition, which in type and paper may be less unworthy a place in your library than the play as printed for sale. I am proud that it should meet with any share of the approbation of one whose rich hereditary claims on the sympathy of the English people, have been superseded by the triumphs of his own genius, and who is entering on a brilliant career, which I trust will long be associated with the noblest efforts of the great writers of past times, and with the hopes and successes of those who may humbly seek to follow them.

"Believe me, my dear Sir,

"Very truly yours,

"T. N. TALFOURD."

————

"56, Russell Square,
"14th Feb., 1838.

"MY DEAR SIR,—

"If you should be disengaged on Saturday, the 24th, and can allow me the honour of your company at dinner, at a quarter before seven, I shall very highly esteem the favor of your company. As I shall leave town for the Circuit on Sunday or Monday following, I have not the opportunity of offering you a choice of days—mine being limited to Saturdays and Sundays—which otherwise I should prefer; but I should be extremely sorry to postpone the pleasure of your society until after my return from my sad prosaic duties, and yours from the delightful welcome which I know awaits you in the beautiful city where your success was predicted and ensured. I have not yet been able to see you in *Richard*, but I rejoice to hear of your triumph from those on whom I can rely; and I hope, before the day when I solicit the pleasure of seeing you at my house, to realize the picture they have given me.

"Believe me, my dear Sir,

"Very faithfully yours,

"T. N. TALFOURD."

From J. H. MERIVALE, ESQ.*

"Sunday, Feb. 26, 1838.

"MY DEAR KEAN,—

"I endeavoured to find you at the stage-door last night, to tell you how highly I had been gratified by your performance of the *Prince of Denmark*, which, I can safely assure you, in many points, I never saw personified so much in accordance with my own conception of the part as by yourself. But the porter did not know how to direct me to you, and seemed to think you had already either left the house, or adjourned to one of the private boxes. Herman was with me, and we were both in the pit, for the sake of seeing you to the best advantage. If I were to specify the parts of your performance that pleased me most, they are these: the first scene, in which the soliloquy 'Oh, that these,' &c., was spoken far more suitably, to what I judge to have been the poet's own intention, than by any other actor I have seen, not excepting your father or Kemble —the scene with the *Ghost*, which was full of strong and earnest feeling, and gave evident marks of original genius—and that with the *Queen Mother*. Those in which I fancied you less successful, and in which I think you may still greatly improve, are the scenes with *Ophelia* and with the *Gravediggers*. In the first, though much of it was well and strongly imagined, I thought you too harsh and abrupt, even for assumed madness. In the latter you appeared to me too solemn and

* The friend and schoolfellow of Lord Byron; a staunch advocate and wholesome adviser of Edmund Kean. Amongst other literary works he adapted to the stage the three parts of *Henry the Sixth*, under the title of *Richard Duke of York*, which was played with great effect by the elder Kean, at Drury Lane in 1819. Mr. Merivale translated the Greek *Anthology* in conjunction with the Rev. Robert Bland, and wrote a poem called *Orlando in Roncesvalles*. He became subsequently a commissioner in the new Bankruptcy Court.

studied. The moralizing reflections on the skull, though prompted by deep feeling, and habits of philosophical thought, being intended to be rather sportively, or, if I may say so, whimsically, than sententiously or gravely uttered; especially the extravaganza of Cæsar stopping a beer barrel, which is a mere piece of grotesque work, like the grinning heads or faces on the roof of an old Gothic cathedral, and illustrating what is often met with in real life—a propensity to jest with one's own wretchedness. *You*, on the contrary, spoke it as if it was a grave sermon, than which nothing can be more unlike.

"Now will you show that you forgive me the freedom of these observations, by saying that you will come and take your dinner with us on Wednesday the 6th, or if you should be engaged on that day, on Friday, the 8th of March, at six o'clock, and let me know which it shall be.

" Yours very truly,
" J. H. MERIVALE."

From SERJEANT ADAMS.

" Court of Exchequer,
" Nov. 17, 1836.

" MY DEAR SIR,—

"Mrs. Adams has this morning sent me your message. I can quite understand your scene with *Laertes*, in which I should have forgiven you, if you had displayed as much feeling, though of a different nature, as you did with your *Queen Mother*. The case was desperate.

"I am inclined to trouble you with a few of my opinions on your *Hamlet*, because, as an old admirer of your father, and so nearly connected with the history of your family, they may derive a value in your eyes, to which they are not intrinsically entitled. *Hamlet* is a character which I have studied more deeply than any other in our immortal poet. I have seen every great actor who has appeared in it, from John Kemble downwards. I remember them all. The first characteristic of your performance is its originality. The second, its depth of feeling and pathos. Your conceptions on these points are so just, that they seem as if they were the real feelings of a youth called forth by actual circumstances. The only doubt I have is, whether a *prince*, accustomed to a court, would express them in a manner so true to nature. Your answer will be—they are expressed in solitude, where the prince gives way to the man.

"The whole of your scene with the *Ghost* is beyond praise. It had the same *truth*—it was the *son* awe-struck by his father's spirit. I observed that you adopted Young's reading of 'But you'll reveal it,' &c., which I am sure is the correct one. Are you quite at liberty to cut out 'my tablets,' &c.? It certainly makes the character harmonize better.

"With respect to the scene with *Ophelia*, I admit now that I never before thoroughly understood it. The clapping and banging the doors, and the maniac ravings of the old school, I always protested against; but I never could read the scene to my own satisfaction. Little was wanting here to render the illusion perfect. A noble mind obliged to feel that his mother has committed incest, and thinking that if *she* fails, all womankind must—distracted and unsettled, looks at the object of his love, and, with all the variety of passion so beautifully delineated, wishes to save her from the fate which he thinks awaits her, and to send her from the inevitable corruptions of the world into retirement. How different was your 'Go to a nunnery, go,' from the bullying tones of older days.

"The address to the players was very pleasing. I think in the play scene you somewhat over-acted the watching of the *King*, and were a little too *familiar* with *Ophelia*. You were from the beginning *too* confident of the *King's* guilt. *Hamlet*, you know, is confident of nothing. Doubt and irresolution are his besetting weaknesses. You began to move towards the *King* too soon. The whole of the subsequent part of the scene was excellent.

"Why did you curtail any part of the first beautiful soliloquy, ' Oh, that this too, too solid flesh would melt,' &c.? I know it is usual, but I am sure it impairs the effect. I confess I was a little alarmed when you first appeared—you looked *vacant*, not *sorrowful*—and I wanted more expression, with a ' a little more than kin,' &c.; but the soliloquy redeemed it. I think I have seen the closet scene played to greater advantage. If I remember right, John Kemble's hand was always on his mother's arm, her eyes fixed on him—his own on the *Ghost*; and when the *Ghost* desired him to address her, he did so *mechanically* without looking at her, or moving a muscle.

"With the third act, my criticisms cease, as does the character of *Hamlet*. There certainly are some points in the last two acts, but they must fall flat with such a *Laertes*. In the grave scene it was like a kite pouncing upon a sparrow. The poor man looked as if he thought you were actually going to eat him. You have heard praises of your fencing too often to need any more.

"After this lengthened disquisition I should say— the conception of your *Hamlet* is splendid. That is, all those parts of the character in which the workings of the heart are to be portrayed; your exhibition of these is powerful and true to nature. But the same may also be said of your *filial* feelings, and especially of your feelings for *Ophelia*; and that your faults are, that you are not enough of the prince—or somewhat deficient in the mixture of condescension and ease which marks the intercourse of a prince of kind and affable disposition with his inferiors. Those who are born to command, acquire a manner which never deserts them even in their most familiar moments. You are always the *gentleman*, but not always the *prince—Hamlet* is both.

"I need not say how highly gratified I was with your performance, or how anxious, too, it made me to see your conception of other characters. If you preserve your present style of *playing to the pit and boxes*, you must continue to rise in public favour, in spite of all the minors and melodramas in the world.

"I have in these remarks avoided all allusion to your father. It was only occasionally that you reminded me of him, and I do not think they were the happiest parts of your performance—for *Hamlet* was not a character which particularly suited him.

"Pray make my best remembrances to Mrs. Kean, and excuse this hasty essay, which is written in Westminster Hall pending the argument in Vandenhoff *v.* Bunn.

"I am, my dear Sir,
"Yours faithfully,
"JOHN ADAMS."

————

From LORD VISCOUNT MORPETH.*

"Nov. 8th, 1838.

"MY DEAR MR. KEAN,—

"I want to tell you, with my parting good wishes, that I think your recitation of a *continuous* passage

* Written in Dublin, on the conclusion of C. Kean's engagement there, after his London success.

very beautiful; and I mention this, because I fancy that you rather slight it yourself, in comparison with the more abrupt and jerking passages, which I cannot value so highly, but which I sometimes think you may learn to indulge from the splendour of hereditary recollections. I am more and more confirmed in wishing you to do some *lover* parts. I see you have all 'the arts of soft persuasion.' Excuse my intolerable presumption. May God bless you with success, and many better things.

> " Very sincerely yours,
>
> " MORPETH."

It will be perceived that the notices and critical letters we have inserted, deal with Charles Kean as avowedly a master in his art, and one who by long service had vindicated his claim to the post he now occupied. They furnish, too, a diversified study of the complicated character, respecting which the best judges of dramatic literature have long been divided in opinion.

CHAPTER XVI.

CONTINUED SUCCESS— RICHARD THE THIRD—SIR GILES OVERREACH—
PUBLIC DINNER AND PRESENTATION OF A SILVER VASE, IN THE SALOON
OF DRURY LANE THEATRE—ENGAGEMENT AT EDINBURGH—RESUMED
PERFORMANCES IN LONDON — OTHELLO — COMMENCEMENT OF A HOS-
TILE CLIQUE—CORRESPONDENCE WITH THE COMPANY OF THE ENGLISH
OPERA-HOUSE—WITH THE SECRETARY OF THE GENERAL THEATRICAL
FUND—WITH THE BATH COMPANY.

WE have seen that the new performer's first London
engagement ran on in one continuous stream of success,
exceeding the number of nights originally proposed,
and greatly to the reciprocal satisfaction of the public,
the manager, and himself. But *"surgit amari aliquid"*
even in life's most honied intervals. He was beset, from
morning till night, by innumerable petitions for relief,
from unemployed hangers-on of the stage, decayed
actors and artists, and semi-genteel professional mendi-
cants; claims from parties he had known and often
assisted before; with demands, sometimes authorita-
tively urged, from others whose names and pretensions
he had never heard mentioned. Between the 8th of
January and the close of March, he received 2,100*l.*,
and was asked to lend or bestow at least 6,000*l.*! These
worthy applicants undoubtedly looked upon him as the
public conduit of supply; and considered that having
made a fortune in less than three months, he had
nothing to do but to give it away again.

Within the period named above, Charles Kean
appeared in only three different characters—*Hamlet,*

Richard the Third, and *Sir Giles Overreach.** The first of these he acted twenty-one nights, twelve of which were without intermission. The following extract from Mr. Bunn's work, " The Stage Before and Behind the Curtain,"† supplies some interesting information, extracted from the account-books of the theatre, with respect to the receipts of that engagement, as compared with those of his father's first performances in 1814.

" In the first chapter of these volumes will be found a recapitulation of the receipts attracted by Mr. Kean, *senior,* on his *debût* before a London audience; and it will be a matter of theatrical curiosity to contrast them with those produced by his son on the present occasion. The difference, when all things are considered, will be found so trifling as to be scarcely worth notice. Between the 8th of January, and the 3d of March, 1838, Mr. Charles Kean played forty-three nights; twenty-one of them in *Hamlet,* seventeen in *Richard the Third,* and five in *Sir Giles Overreach.* The following is a genuine recapitulation of the receipts, with the nightly average of them as well :—

	£.	s.	d.
21 Nights of *Hamlet* produced	6,236	0	0
Nightly average	296	19	0
17 Nights of *Richard the Third* produced .	5,516	14	0
Nightly average	324	10	0
5 Nights of *Sir Giles* produced	1,536	8	0
Nightly average	307	5	0
43 Nights in all produced	13,289	2	0
Nightly average	309	10	0

---

* These were also the three characters in which John Kemble made his first appearances at Drury Lane, in 1783, and he acted them in the same order.

† Vol. iii. pp. 26-8.

"The nightly average Mr. Charles Kean's father played to in 1814 was 484*l.* 9*s.*; exhibiting an apparent nightly excess over that his son played to, of 174*l.* 19*s.* But it must not be forgotten that the prices of admission in 1814 were 7*s.* to the boxes, 3*s.* 6*d.* to the pit, 2*s.* to the one gallery, and 1*s.* to the other, and the half-price was in proportion; whereas, in 1838, the prices were 5*s.* to the boxes, 3*s.* to the pit, and 2*s.* and 1*s.* to the galleries, with a corresponding reduction in the half-price. That the reader may judge of the difference such a deduction makes, a statement shall be submitted to him. The largest receipt Mr. Charles Kean played to was 464*l.* 3*s.* 6*d.*; on which occasion 770 people paid to the boxes—which number, at 5*s.* each, makes the sum of 192*l.* 10*s.*; but had the price been 7*s.* the amount would have been 269*l.* 10*s.*, a difference of itself of 77*l.* Then, 768 persons paid to the pit—which number, at 3*s.* each, makes a sum of 115*l.* 4*s.*, whereas, at 3*s.* 6*d.*, the amount would be 134*l.* 8*s.* 6*d.* In these two items alone arises a difference of 96*l.* 4*s.*, which added to 3*l.* 18*s.* difference in the half-price to boxes and pit, make a total of 100*l.* 2*s.* In addition to this, it must be taken into consideration that the father played only three nights per week, while the son played four nights during the greater part of this engagement; and that consequently by a more frequent repetition the attraction becomes somewhat lessened. Between the 8th of January and the 3d of March, 1838, the son played forty-three nights, as just stated; whereas in a corresponding period of 1814, following his *debût*, the father played, between the 26th of January and the 21st of March, only twenty-two nights. The father in that period played *Richard the Third* ten times, *Shylock* ten times, and *Hamlet* twice; whereas the son played *Richard* seventeen times, *Hamlet* twenty-one times, and *Sir Giles*

Overreach five times.   Thus, in the same period of two months, though each of them only played three characters, yet, barring one night, the son played twice as often as the father.   Weighing, therefore, all these points together, it will be found, that in the outburst of their London career, there was but a slight difference in the attraction of either: a coincidence without any parallel in the annals of the stage."

It has often been argued that the enormous salaries paid to individual performers in recent times, have had a very damaging effect on the interests of the drama. This may be quite true in the abstract, and sound, as a general principle; but instances such as that of which we are now treating, furnish unanswerable exceptions. The matter reduces itself to a commercial speculation, and viewed in that light, no one will deny that the intrinsic worth of any commodity is the purchaseable value at which it is quoted in the market.

We believe Charles Kean was the first actor of *Hamlet*, of any note, who gave up the old traditionary custom of having a stocking "down-gyved to the ankle," during that part of the play when he assumes a disordered intellect—a piece of literal rendering sufficiently vulgar, and certainly " more honoured in the breach than the observance."   Garrick, though a professed reformer, indulged freely in these stage trickeries.   It is recorded that in the closet scene with the *Queen*, he had a mechanical contrivance by which his chair fell, as if of itself, when he started upon the sudden entrance of the *Ghost*.   Henderson, his immediate successor in the part, rejected this practice, and his doing so was called, by the critics of the day, a daring innovation. Garrick, with all his brilliant genius, was a very methodical actor ; when he had once settled in what is technically called " business " of a part, he never altered it."

In the play-scene, when he satisfies himself that he has detected the guilt of the *King*, he wound up his burst of exultation at the close by three flourishes of his pocket-handkerchief over his head, as he paced the stage backwards and forwards. It was once remarked, as an extraordinary deviation, that he added a fourth flourish.

The popularity of Charles Kean's *Hamlet* was by no means on the decline at the twenty-first repetition, but the public were naturally anxious to see the new performer in another Shakespearean character, of a different cast; and accordingly, in compliance with incessant applications at the box-office, *Richard the Third* was brought forward on the 5th of February. The receipts of that evening amounted to 409*l*. Her Majesty was present throughout the entire performance, and commanded the manager to express to Mr. Kean her extreme approbation of his performance. The Queen was so pleased that she repeated her visit within a week or two after. The *Times* spoke thus on the 6th of February :—

" Shakespeare's historical play of ' Richard the Third,' as altered by Colley Cibber, was last night represented before a most crowded audience. Many plays of our great dramatist have, from time to time, been altered by various hands; but Cibber's alteration of this piece is undoubtedly the best effort of the kind that has yet been made. He has lopped off superfluities, which, however beautiful in the closet, were not calculated to produce a powerful effect on the stage; and he has condensed within a reasonable compass, more of interest, of striking situation, and of stirring action, than is to be found in almost any other drama. Mr. Charles Kean sustained the character of the crook-backed tyrant. It is not often that the son inherits any great portion of the genius of the father. In this instance, however, the mantle of the father has fallen gracefully on the son. When we witnessed his *Hamlet*, we saw that he had mind ; that he could perform, and finely, that which was quiet, contemplative, melancholy; but we certainly did feel a doubt whether his physical powers would enable him successfully to enact characters where great bodily as well as great mental exertion, was required. His performance of last night has dissipated the doubt. His vigour seemed to grow with the exigency of the scene. The tender, lowly, and in some parts somewhat sarcastic wooing of *Lady Anne*, was finely contrasted with the bold audacity of the successful tyrant in the fourth and fifth acts of the play. These are general remarks : we now wish to devote a few lines to particulars. *Richard's* opening soliloquy was given with great point and effect; the latter part more especially, where the mis-shapen monster expresses his belief that dogs bark at him as he halts by them. In his delivery of this sentence there was much concentration of bitterness. It told you at once of something like hatred to himself, but certainly of hatred towards the rest of mankind. The courtship scene with *Lady Anne* was, on the whole, good ; but there was, in the sly sarcasm with which it was sprinkled, too much straining after epigrammatic effect. The audience enjoyed it ; but had *Richard*, in his wooing, so much exposed his natural aptitude to ' snarl and bite, and play the dog,' he would have never won the widow of his murdered victim.

" With the soliloquy in the fourth act, when the murder of the young princes is on foot, we were greatly pleased. *Richard*, for a moment, is assailed by remorseful pangs, but they are quickly expelled by the more powerful feelings of an exorbitant ambition. The momentary penitence and the subsequent hardihood of the usurper were forcibly depicted by Mr. Kean. He met with commensurate vigour the busy, bustling scene at the end of the fourth act, where *Richard* is assailed alternately by good and bad intelligence; when he falters at the idea of *Lord Stanley's* defection, and rejoices in the overthrow of *Buckingham* and his rash levied crew. The tent-scene in the last act was ably performed. Instead of sliding on his knees when, terrified by the ghosts of his murdered victims, *Richard* rushes from his couch, Mr. Kean staggered and fell, cowering and conscience-stricken, to the earth. This departure from the old routine was as strikingly effective as it was natural.

" Speaking of the entire performance, we should say that Mr. Kean has studied the character thoroughly; that he understands it, and plays it in a manner worthy of his name. We again, however, object to the length of many of his pauses. They give you, at times, an idea that he has forgotten his part, and is pondering to refresh his memory. We equally object to the manner in which he occasionally weighs out and measures his syllables, when they ought to come trippingly from the tongue. These, nevertheless, are matters of little moment, and with a wish may be corrected. Mr. Kean's reception was of the most flattering kind. At the end of the play, he was loudly called for. He appeared, after considerable delay, occasioned, we believe, by exhaustion, and having made his obeisance to the audience, retired."

The friends and admirers of Charles Kean, having determined to mark their opinion of his professional ability by a specific compliment, a public dinner was given to him, on the 30th of March, in the saloon of Drury Lane Theatre, on which occasion he was also presented with a magnificent silver vase, value 200*l.*

The workmanship of this gratifying testimonial was exquisitely designed and finished ; the lid being surmounted by a model in minature of Roubilliac's celebrated statue of Shakespeare, left by Garrick to the British Museum (at the death of his wife), a cast from which stands in the entrance rotunda of Drury Lane Theatre.   On the front, the following inscription was engraved :—

PRESENTED

TO

CHARLES KEAN, Esq.

BY THE ADMIRERS OF HIS DISTINGUISHED TALENT

AT

A PUBLIC DINNER

GIVEN TO HIM IN THE SALOON AT THE

THEATRE ROYAL, DRURY LANE,

MARCH 30TH, 1838 ;

THE RIGHT HON. LORD VISCOUNT MORPETH, M.P.

IN THE CHAIR.

At this dinner, Lord Morpeth, now Earl of Carlisle, had, in the kindest and readiest manner, undertaken to preside ; but two days before the appointed evening, political duties interfered, and compelled him to write thus to Mr, Bunn, who superintended the arrangements :—

" Wednesday Evening,
" March 28, 1838.

" SIR,—

      " It is with extreme regret and disappointment that I find myself compelled to announce to you, that, in consequence of a new arrangement of the business of the House of Commons, and the certainty of the debate upon Negro Emancipation, from which I cannot absent myself, extending over Friday, it will be wholly impossible for me to attend the dinner to be given on that day to Mr. Charles Kean.

"I ought, perhaps, to have guarded myself more strictly against such a contingency, when I agreed to discharge the honourable office' of chairman on this auspicious occasion. I was misled by the anticipation of other business in the House, and by my anxiety to bear a part in the tribute which I thought so well deserved.

"I am conscious, however, that almost all there is of privation in this matter belongs to myself. I beg to inclose my contribution to the vase, which it is intended to present to Mr. Kean, as a humble mark of my admiration for his talents, and of my regret that I am debarred from this occasion of giving it oral expression.

"I have the honour to be, Sir,

"Your most obedient servant,

"MORPETH.

"To A. Bunn, Esq."

This unexpected disappointment threatened to derange the whole plan, but the difficulty was surmounted by an application to the Marquis of Clanricarde, who was to have officiated as vice-president, but now promptly consented to supply the place of his noble colleague. The dinner took place as appointed, and all went off in the most satisfactory manner. Above one hundred and fifty persons were present, including many names eminent by their rank, talent, and literary reputation. The speeches, as may be supposed, were eloquent and characteristic. That of Charles Kean, in particular, was remarkable for the modest and unassuming tone in which he spoke of himself and his pretensions.

The chairman, in his address to the guest of the evening, after expressing his regret at the unavoidable absence of their mutual friend Lord Morpeth, who, he said, would have performed the duty which had in consequence unexpectedly devolved upon him with much superior grace and ability, went on to say :— " But I know your kindness will overlook any deficiency, and that you will not measure the depth of my feeling, and that of the gentlemen I represent, by the inadequate language I can command, or by the value of the offering which is before you. At the same time, I trust you will receive this cup with satisfaction; for sure I am, there is no tribute which could be offered to you, either from your friends or the public, that you may not attribute to your own merits and your own abilities. Perhaps one source of the high position to which you have attained, is the fact of your having entered upon your professional career with no circumstance or advantage that I can recollect or call to mind. The name you bore, the similarity in form, in feature, and in voice, which nature had impressed you with, and which proved to every beholder that the genius of the father was transmitted to the son, counteracted the indulgence usually manifested to a youthful beginner; but you have overcome all obstacles. You knew the toil, the study, and the perseverance that it would require to attain to eminence in your profession. By study I mean that diligent examination of the variety of delicate and almost imperceptible shades and tints of character, which our mighty bard has infused into all his heroes, so as not only to create corresponding ideas in your own mind, but to be able to convey those ideas to an audience, and make them feel and recognise the character which Shakespeare drew. In this you have succeeded, and, in doing so, you have raised the character of the stage, while you have earned the admiration of your friends and the public. It is a circumstance not only singular, but I believe unprecedented, that a performer should have appeared forty-three nights in one season, and played only three parts, and those old stock parts, so well known to the public that they could receive no new impression from them, and no gratification, except in the way in which they were performed."

The noble chairman then referred to the estimation in which actors had been held in ancient Greece and Rome, and to the low condition of the stage in this country until its character was vindicated by Garrick, and sustained by the Kemble family; names with which that of Kean was well calculated to stand associated. Having then enumerated amongst Mr. C. Kean's principal claims upon the respect and admiration of his supporters, his unblemished integrity, high honour, and refined taste in private life, he concluded by expressing a hope that the object of his eulogy would long continue the ornament of the stage, the delight of his friends, and, above all, the pride of that surviving parent who lived to bless him as the joy, the stay, and the comfort of her declining years.*

This complimentary address and the accompanying gift were thus acknowledged:—

"MY LORDS AND GENTLEMEN,—

"The situation in which your kindness has at this moment placed me, I feel to be the most arduous and difficult I have ever yet encountered. It would be unbecoming affectation were I to pretend that I was not in some measure aware of the high and unmerited compliment you intended to confer on me. I had thought and hoped, that when the proper time arrived I should have been able to express myself in terms suited to the occasion. The opinions and wishes of the distinguished company by which I am surrounded, have been conveyed to me by the noble chairman in a manner so

---

* See " The Stage, Before and Behind the Curtain," vol. iii. pp. 33–4.

unexpectedly kind, so flattering, and so overwhelming, that even a practised orator might falter in his reply; but lest I should appear cold and ungrateful, while my breast is throbbing with contrary emotions, let me entreat you to receive the language of the heart, in place of the set phrases of studied eloquence; and to believe in the sincerity of those feelings which, by their own intensity, have deprived me of adequate expression.

" The distinguished honour I am now receiving at your hands, is one which artists of the highest name and pretensions have hailed with delight, when in the decline of life, and at the close of a long and brilliant career, as the reward of their honourable exertions. How, then, must I appreciate your kindness, young in years, standing almost on the very threshhold of my professional life, my pretensions untried by the purifying test of time, the station I am ultimately to fill unascertained; upheld, as I now am, by the partial judgment of enthusiastic friends, and above all, by a name which has been my most powerful introduction to the notice and favour of the public.

" I cannot and do not wish to blind myself to my true position; but I feel that an affectionate remembrance of the father has, in your eyes, invested the son with attributes to which he has no personal claim, and has placed him in a situation, brilliant indeed and dazzling, but full of difficulty and danger. I shrink from the consciousness of my own inability to realize the expectations of those friends who have so kindly and incautiously committed themselves in my favour; yet to the latest hour of my existence, the remembrance of this, the proudest day which that existence has yet witnessed, will serve as a stimulus to unremitting exertion, and make me feel as if I had given a pledge which it is my incumbent duty to redeem.

"My lords and gentlemen, the place where we are now assembled is associated in my mind with feelings of hereditary interest. Within these walls the name of Kean first became known to the London public, and the success of my father created an epoch in the history of the British drama, which will not soon be forgotten. After an interval of twenty-four years, on the same boards, and by the same public, my humble efforts have been received with a degree of favour and indulgence far indeed beyond my merits and expectations, and which has engraved on my heart one paramount impression of lasting gratitude. My lords and gentlemen, I will occupy your attention no longer. What I have said is totally unworthy of the occasion, and conveys but faintly what I feel. The conduct of my future life can alone convince you how I estimate the honour I have received."

A few days after the dinner, Charles Kean took his departure for the northern capital, where he was received with the old enthusiasm, and a succession of the same crowded houses. He returned to London on the 9th of May, when his performances at Drury Lane were resumed, but with something of diminished attraction. The season was advancing, and the interruption (as all persons experienced in theatrical matters anticipated), had given a check to the flowing tide. In Mr. Bunn's published diary, we find the subjoined note :—

"Charles Kean has been absent but five weeks; yet in that time he has allowed those who *have* seen him to forget him in the folly and fashion of a London season, after Easter ;—and those who have *not*, want to know if he is a fine actor, and keep back until *they're told*. There comes a new world into Babylon when this period of the year arrives. At the same time nothing can be more injudicious than to break the thread, and, too often, the chain of anything, particularly if connected with public life. I doubt me if he will rouse up the Cockneys to any great extent until next Christmas hath waned, and then much will depend upon whose hands he gets into. He will, however, at all times do more than any of the dogs who venture to snarl at him."

On the 16th of May, Charles Kean essayed the difficult character of *Othello*, a touchstone, if possible, more trying than any he had yet handled. The performance was most satisfactorily welcomed by a crowded house. The notice in the *Morning Post* ran thus :—

"DRURY LANE THEATRE.—Mr. Charles Kean appeared here last evening for the first time, as *Othello*. Under any circumstances, the character is an arduous one, but was rendered more so on the present occasion, from its having been considered the *chef-d'œuvre* of his lamented father. Mr. C. Kean, however, sustained the burthen most manfully, and achieved so complete a victory over all obstacles (amongst which reminiscences of by-gone days were not the least embarrassing), as to warrant us in pronouncing *Othello* as entitled to a foremost rank in his range of parts. On his first appearance he evinced by his manner a consciousness of the difficulties he was about to encounter, which created some apprehension that physically he might be unequal to the task; but as the play progressed, and level speaking gave place to bursts of feeling, the genius of the actor shone forth in its brightest colours, and elicited from a crowded audience such manifestations of applause, as might fairly lead to an anticipation of the revival of the most flourishing days of the drama. When everything was so deserving of praise, to particularise may seem invidious; but we should imperfectly fulfil our duty were we not to select a few passages in the delivery of which Mr. Kean achieved his greatest triumphs. In the first scene of the third act, after *Iago* has first awakened his jealousy, the soliloquy expressive of his resolve as to what course to pursue in the event of *Desdemona* proving false to him, was given with an alternate power and pathos to find a parallel to which we must revert to the days of his father. The passage commencing—

> ' If I do prove her haggard,
> Though that her jesses were my dear heart-strings,
> I'd whistle her off, and let down the wind,
> To prey at fortune,'

was delivered with an effect really appalling; and the transition from the frenzied manner which accompanied the utterance of the above lines, to the thrilling tone of deep despondency with which he uttered—

> ' Haply, for I am black,' &c.,

drew tears in abundance from the eyes of the larger portion of his fair auditory. The concluding scene demands a word, were it only for the death, which was true to nature, inasmuch as in such a predicament, a man does not usually study attitudes ; and, albeit, the falling of Mr. Kean may have been premeditated, it was hardly planned with a due regard to life and limb. For the safety of the last we certainly felt no small degree of apprehension. The play was announced for repetition on Friday, amidst vehement applause."

On the 4th of June following, the engagement terminated, when Charles Kean appeared for his own benefit, as *Sir Edward Mortimer*. This second series of performances was less productive than the first ; for which some reasons have already been assigned. A change, too, had suddenly " come o'er the spirit " of the press ; more than one of the most influential journals assumed an altered tone, and condemned the identical " points" which they had a short time before so warmly praised. It was impossible that a few weeks of absence could have produced any variation in the actor's style, or the measure of his pretensions. A *hostile clique* was forming ; but how, wherefore, or by whom suggested, fostered, and matured, it would be fruitless now to inquire. These hidden enemies, whoever they might be, had the merit of keeping counsel with the secrecy of a freemason's lodge, and evinced a pertinacity of purpose which perpetual defeat during a long series of years seems only to have had the effect of sharpening into augmented virulence. The subjoined letter received at a period somewhat later than that of which we are now treating, bears upon the progress of the conspiracy, or coalition, or combination, or whatever it may be called, and was written by Mr. Michael Nugent, for many years the theatrical reporter of the *Times*, and a critic of acknowledged repute.

" New Street, Covent Garden,
" June 9, 1839.

" MY DEAR SIR,—

" I regret sincerely that severe illness, which has confined me to my bed for nearly the whole of the bygone week, prevented me from seeing you, when you were good enough to honour me with a call.

" It gave me a true and honest satisfaction to perceive by the statements in the country journals, that your career through the long range of the provinces was a continued triumph. That it should be so everywhere, requires, in my mind (and I have expressed the sentiment and defended it too, in public and in private, before those to whom it was little palatable), nothing more than a fair, candid, and impartial spirit.

" That during your last London engagement such a

spirit was not entertained towards you, by certain partisans, I can testify. But you may, and ought to laugh at their miserable malice. What have you to fear from the petty malevolence of *judges* (?) who lauded to the skies and worshipped as stars such *ignes fatui* as ———? Rejoice in their censure.

" Were I engaged in the theatrical arena just now, your talents, for talents' sake, should receive my warmest support. As it is, I am obliged, at this critical period of political strife, to attend to the sayings and doings of the great actors at St. Stephen's. I can only, therefore, offer you my sincere good wishes, whether you pursue fame and fortune in this country, or in the great Western Republic.

" Suffer me to subscribe myself

" Your admirer and friend,

" MICHAEL NUGENT.

" To C. Kean, Esq."

If professional jealousy, in any shape, or through any influence, had anything to do with this growing hostility, it never was exercised upon less justifiable grounds. Charles Kean had ever proved himself a kind and generous friend to his less prosperous brethren. Many instances have fallen within the knowledge of the writer, from which two or three are selected, to establish by evidence what might otherwise be treated as mere assertion.

A Letter from MR. PEAKE *on behalf of the English Opera House Company.*

" English Opera House,
" Sept. 22d, 1838.

" DEAR SIR,—

" We, the undersigned, crave your attention for a few moments, in the hope that you may be induced to favour us with an act of kindness which would certainly relieve us from a position of great embarrassment.   We ask this boon, knowing your attachment to your profession, and your liberality to the less fortunate brethren thereof.

" The undersigned, apprehending that the English Opera House could not, for want of a speculator, open for the summer season, and seeing that a large number of their brothers and sisters must literally starve, by being out of employ, subscribed a little fund and commenced a season.   We have produced no less than ten new dramas, successful as to their representation; but such has been the state of public apathy as regards the theatres, that every effort of ours has proved a failure. We have paid all the humble classes employed, but at the expense of our own salaries; and we have also a heavy arrear of rent to meet, with exhausted means.

" In great anxiety of mind we ask of your kindness to come and act *one night* for us.   The cause to be assigned openly to the public, and your liberality to be as openly recorded.

" Pray, dear Sir, take our wishes and hopes into your favourable consideration, and confer a lasting obligation on

" Your obedient servants, &c.

" To Charles Kean, Esq."

Here follow the signatures, sixteen in number.

MR. KEAN'S *answer to* MR. PEAKE, *from Leeds.*

" Scarborough Hotel, Leeds,
" Sept. 24th, 1838.

" MY DEAR SIR,

" I received last night the letter signed by the members of the English Opera House, and was deeply pained to hear that the Company are in such embar-

rassed circumstances. I am equally grieved that it is
totally out of my power to comply with their request
of performing a night for their benefit, and refer you to
the list of my engagements left with Mr. Hughes, lest
occasion should render my direction necessary, to show
that I have not a single day at my command from the
present time until Christmas. Presuming, however,
that a benefit will be announced for the purpose of
removing the present difficulties, I trust that in place
of my professional services, you will accept the enclosed
cheque for 100*l.* to be placed at the disposal of the Company.   With every wish for their better success,

"I remain, my dear Sir,

"Very truly yours,

."CHARLES KEAN."

MR. PEAKE *to* CHARLES KEAN, *in reply :—*

"English Opera House, London,
"Feb. 27th, 1838.

"MY DEAR SIR,—

"I beg to acknowledge the receipt of your kind letter,
and a bank note for 100*l.*

"Accept the grateful thanks of all who addressed you
for this mark of liberality, which will prove a great
relief under the circumstances. I have not adequate
words to express my astonishment at this act of princely
generosity.   The warm feelings of your heart will in
some measure repay you ; but may constant and deserved
prosperity attend you.   We, one and all, fervently say,
God bless you !

"I am, my dear Sir,

"Your faithful and obliged servant,

"R. B. PEAKE.

"To Charles Kean, Esq.,
    "Scarborough Hotel, Leeds."

It has seldom fallen to the lot of a biographer to transcribe a more satisfactory correspondence than the foregoing.

From Mr. E. W. Elton.*

" Dear Sir,—

" I have great pleasure in acknowledging the receipt of your very liberal donation (of 50*l.*) to the General Theatrical Fund, and of forwarding the grateful thanks of the directors for so generous an assistance of the object they have in view. At the same time allow me to inform you that if no personal application has been made to you on the subject, the omission has not been through any slight, or forgetfulness of the rank you hold in the profession, but simply because no such application has been made to any one. Our donors have all been, like yourself, volunteers in the cause, and I need not say how happy I am at seeing your name added to the corps. I inclose you a formal receipt for your donation, and have great pleasure in subscribing myself,

" Dear Sir, yours very truly,

" Edward William Elton.

" To Charles Kean, Esq."

* A tragic actor, of good, second-rate reputation, who was unfortunately lost in the *Pegasus* on the 19th of July, 1843, which ill-fated vessel struck on the *Gold Rock*, during a voyage from Leith to London. Of fifty-five persons on board, all but six perished. Poor Elton had repeatedly expressed the greatest possible horror and commiseration of the similarly sudden fate of Tyrone Power, in March, 1841. A sum of 2,700*l.* was realised for his family by subscriptions and benefit performances. Whatever may be the professional jealousies of actors, how often are we called upon to note that when a fraternal appeal is made to them, they are ever ready to respond with generous warmth.

From the COMMITTEE OF THE BATH COMPANY.*
To CHARLES KEAN, ESQ.

"Theatre Royal, Bath,
"1st June, 1842.

" SIR,—

" We, the Committee of Management of the Bath Company, beg to acknowledge the receipt of your kind letter, with its very handsome and liberal donation (20*l.*). In applying to you for your valuable name and assistance, we did so in the conviction that both would be of the highest importance to our interests; and however we must regret your inability personally to aid us, accept our very sincere and grateful thanks.

" We remain, sir,

" Yours most gratefully,

" J. WOULDS,

"*Chairman of the Committee, &c.*

" Charles Kean, Esq."

Other signatures follow to the amount of eight.

* The Bath company had been left in great distress by their runaway manager.

CHAPTER XVII.

CORRESPONDENCE WITH SIR EDWARD BULWER RELATIVE TO A NEW PLAY —ENGAGEMENT AT THE HAYMARKET—HAMLET—SIR GILES OVERREACH —SECOND VISIT TO AMERICA—BURNING OF THE NATIONAL THEATRE AT NEW YORK—ATTACK OF BRONCHITIS, AND PERFORMANCES SUSPENDED IN CONSEQUENCE—VISIT TO THE HAVANNAH—LETTER FROM THENCE—RETURN TO ENGLAND IN JUNE, 1840—SECOND ENGAGEMENT AT THE HAYMARKET—HAMLET—RICHARD THE THIRD—SHYLOCK—SIR GILES OVERREACH—MACBETH—ARTICLE HEADED " CHARLES KEAN AND HIS LONDON CRITICS "—ENGAGEMENT AT THE HAYMARKET FOR THREE SUCCESSIVE SEASONS.

CHARLES KEAN had always been anxious for an original character, which greatly assists the actor's progress, by placing him on his own ground, freed from the disadvantage of comparison. Now that fortune had given him the means, he was ready to pay any sum within reason for a new play. Money he regarded as secondary to fame, and valuable as a medium through which the nobler acquisition might be won. With this impression, he applied to Sir Edward Bulwer, in the hope of being aided by his powerful genius. We insert the letter and reply :—

" *To* SIR E. LYTTON BULWER, BART.

"Liverpool, Nov. 13th, 1838.

" SIR,—

"The flattering success which has attended my attempts in the provinces to do justice to the character of *Claude Melnotte*,* and the debt of gratitude I owe you

---

* The hero of Sir E. L. Bulwer's highly-popular play of the " Lady of Lyons "—one of the most successful of modern dramas. The original representative in London was Mr. Macready, by whom the play was produced at Covent Garden in 1838, and who personated *Claude Melnotte* with great ability.

for the means thus afforded me of advancing my professional career, must be my apology for addressing you; if a better excuse did not exist in your character as an author, and the deserved influence you possess over our dramatic literature. I am most anxious to appear in London in a new part; and I feel that your assistance would be invaluable in the promotion of this purpose, and of my desire to carry out all the objects of the legitimate drama in a spirit of honourable competition. If it should suit your views to give me the benefit of your great talents on this occasion, I shall be sincerely grateful; and though pecuniary considerations can be no object with you, I think it right to add, as a matter of business, that I place myself and a *carte blanche* at your disposal. I trust there is no indelicacy in saying this, when I reflect how much I should still remain your debtor, by the honour I might hope to derive from the representation of any character from the pen of Sir Lytton Bulwer.

"I have the honour to be, Sir,

"Your most obedient servant,

"CHARLES KEAN."

"*To* CHARLES KEAN, Esq.

"8, Charles-street, Berkeley-square,
"Nov. 14, 1838.

"MY DEAR SIR,—

"Believe me sincerely obliged and flattered by your letter, and the request it contains. The manner in which you express your wish cannot but make me anxious, sooner or later, to comply with it. I fear, however, that, at present, heavy engagements, and other circumstances too tedious to enter upon, will not allow me an honour, otherwise sincerely to be desired, and which you will permit me to consider not sacrificed, but deferred. For the rest, allow me to assure you that the pecuniary considerations to which you so delicately allude, are not likely to form an obstacle against any future arrangement; and that—

" I am, dear Sir,

" Very truly, your obliged

" E. LYTTON BULWER."

On Thursday, the 3d of June, 1839, Charles Kean returned to London after a tour round the kingdom, in which praise and profit accompanied him as inseparable travelling companions. His performances were now transferred to the Haymarket, under the management of Mr. Webster, from whom he received, as previously at Drury Lane, 50*l.* per night, and a benefit. The engagement was for twelve nights, but the success extended it to twenty-two, *Hamlet* being acted on ten out of the number, and proving, as before, the most popular representation. The other characters were, *Richard the Third*, repeated five times; *Sir Giles Overreach*, three times; and *Othello* and *Sir Edward Mortimer*, each twice. His reception was everything that he could desire, although he had now to contend occasionally with a captious criticism and a dissentient opinion. The unfriendly *clique* was gaining strength: still an overwhelming majority were with him; enough to satisfy the most ambitious candidate for that most uncertain of all acquisitions—although so universally courted—public favour. The press began to be more divided and qualified in their notices than during the preceding year. In the *Times* and *Morning Post* there was no alteration. The former said: "When Mr. Charles Kean commenced his career at Drury Lane Theatre, with the character of *Hamlet*, it may be remembered that our opinion of him was most favourable. On the occasion of his first appearance last night at the Haymarket, in the same character, it will be sufficient to remind our readers of the opinion, and to state that that opinion is entirely unaltered, as is decidedly the case. The house was crowded, and at Kean's first appearance the applause was so immoderate, and lasted so long, as to impede for some minutes the progress of the piece. At the fall of the curtain he was loudly called for, and made his bow before a mass of waving hats and handkerchiefs."

The *Morning Post* spoke thus, after noticing his enthusiastic reception:—"In regard to Mr. Kean's performance of *Hamlet*, there will be always conflicting opinions. Our own is, that it is of a very high order. Unequal, it is true, but at times full of fire, at others of feeling; never violating proprieties, and often producing fine effects. Let us, however, add, that *Hamlet* is to our mind the most difficult part within our knowledge of all the conceptions of Shakespeare; that Mr. Kean's own father misread it, and gave us a startling performance instead of a true one; that John Kemble did not master all its subtle delicacies; and that Charles Young alone, of all whom we have seen play it, brought it nearest to anything like an even and equable perfection. The acting of Charles Kean last night was well sustained throughout. The points he intended to make came out forcibly. He was much applauded in his address to *Guildenstern*, previous to the entrance of the players; and the scene with the players itself he acted carefully, crowning their departure with the truly splendid and powerful declamatory soliloquy with which Shakespeare at this juncture fills the mind and soul of *Hamlet*. His reproachful comparison between the energy and feeling of the player without a cause, and what his own should be, who had so much and such agonizing incitement, was kindling, vehement, and passionate, and told eloquently with the audience. But Mr. Kean's greatest, and most effective episode of acting all through the tragedy was in the scene in which the play is represented before the *King* and *Queen*, and *Hamlet* is reclining on the ground at the feet of *Ophelia*. All the minor points which occur in the strongly-applied incidents of this scene were admirably brought out; and at the conclusion, when the *King* hastily departs, calling in hurried terror and anger for '*some light*,' he rushed up with a glorious burst of half-frantic triumph, to the utterance of the lines—

> ' Why, let the strucken deer go weep,
>   The hart ungallèd play ;
> For some must watch, while some must sleep ;
>   So runs the world away ! '

This was the most loudly-applauded effort during the whole performance. The tragedy was, after Kean had been called for, and vociferously cheered, announced for repetition on Wednesday and Friday, amidst general applause."

The same paper thus warmly eulogizes a subsequent performance of *Sir Giles Overreach*—" Notwithstanding the qualified praise of some critics, and the stern opposition of others, the brilliant success which has attended Mr. Charles Kean's late engagement at this theatre (Haymarket), proves that the public voice has confirmed his right to wear the mantle of his father. Although it must be confessed that the drapery continues to display something like its former folds, they fall easily and naturally into their position, and have none of the stiffness of artificial arrangement. That which would be imitation in another, is, in the younger Kean, obedience

to the law of nature. Even when the son strives successfully to avoid his father's style of speaking a remarkable passage, the similarity of their tones compels
the auditor to blend his recollection of past enthusiasm
with his present enjoyment. But if his celebrated precursor had never appeared before a London audience,
Mr. Charles Kean's embodiment of *Sir Giles Overreach*
last night would have caused him to be hailed as a
star of no ordinary brilliancy in the dramatic firma-
ment. To enter into an analysis of a performance which
has very lately been much dilated upon, would indeed
be a work of supererogation. Mr. Kean's attributes for
the personification of this painful conception of the poet,
are extraordinary in so young a man. Last night his
spirit and energy were unfailing ; no point ' came tardily
off.' Perhaps a fastidious observer might say that the
actor's efforts to produce effect are sometimes too obvious;
but this is a fault which experience will not fail to
remedy completely. Time will, doubtless, give to the
filling up of Mr. Kean's bold outlines that mellowness
which age gives to the productions of masters in a rival
art. After the hero of the night had been called forward,
to be complimented with the now customary cheerings,
waving of hats and handkerchiefs, bouquets, &c., an
announcement was made that his engagement is renewed
for six nights, in obedience to the wishes of the patrons
of the theatre. As the demands for places have lately
increased beyond the possibility of accommodating the
applicants, the enterprising lessee will, no doubt, profit
by the extension of this exceedingly popular young
actor's engagement."

In a report on the last night, the *Morning Post* again
spoke, as follows :—" Mr. Charles Kean took his ' farewell benefit ' last night before one of the most crowded

and brilliant audiences we ever saw in this or any other theatre. The play selected for the occasion was *Hamlet*, the tenth time of its performance during an engagement originally proposed to be but for twelve nights, but which has been extended to nearly double that number, in consequence of Mr. Kean's extraordinary attraction. It would be superfluous to make any remarks on a performance so well known and highly appreciated. It is sufficient to say, that Mr. Kean exhibited even more than his usual care and energy, and was rewarded by a corresponding enthusiasm on the part of his auditors. On being summoned before the curtain at the conclusion of the tragedy, by often-repeated calls from every part of the house, Mr. Kean was greeted with the most flattering demonstrations of favour—'bravo!' waving of hats, handkerchiefs, showers of bouquets, wreaths, &c. As soon as silence could be obtained, he, evidently in a state of considerable emotion, addressed the house in the following words :—

'LADIES AND GENTLEMEN.—The simple but sincere expression of my thanks is all the poor return I can make you for your continual kindness. The pride and happiness I feel at this moment are darkened by the thought that I am on the eve of departure. I quit you for a country endeared to me by many recollections—a country where in my early professional struggles I found a home to receive and friends to cheer me. If since that period my position be changed, how can I acknowledge the debt of gratitude I owe the British public? Encouraged by this success, I venture to announce that on my early return from the United States I am engaged again at this theatre, till when, ladies and gentlemen, I most respectfully and gratefully bid you farewell.' "

Mr. Kean's announcement of his return to the Haymarket was received with an unanimous burst of approbation; and he left the stage cheered by the reiterated plaudits of the audience.

During the following September he appeared at the National Theatre in Church Street, New York, then under the management of Mr. J. Wallack. The house was crowded and enthusiastic, but after this auspicious commencement clouds gathered rapidly, and a series of fatalities seemed to attend Charles Kean's second visit to the United States. When he began to act he was suffering from an affection of the throat; exertion made his voice give way, and on the fourth night he entirely broke down. The theatre was soon after destroyed by fire. Such burnings are often suspicious, and on this occasion rumours of foul play were loudly disseminated. Wallack himself made no secret of his impression that a rival manager had some share in his misfortune. That rival was seen conspicuously posted on the roof of the Astor House Hotel, watching the progress of the destroying element, and no one heard him utter expressions of sympathy or regret. We naturally think of Nero, who played the lyre on the terrace of his own palace, as an accompaniment to the conflagration of his own imperial city, fired by his own hand or by the hands of his emissaries. At Boston, in December, 1839, Charles Kean narrowly escaped a frightful catastrophe. While acting *Rolla*, in " Pizarro," and standing between the wings, preparatory to his entrance for the dying scene, the child was brought to him; he stepped a pace forward to receive it; the leader of the supernumeraries, named Stimpson, who was also waiting to go on as one of the Peruvian soldiers, moved into the spot he had left vacant : at that moment a heavy counter-weight fell from the machinery above, broke through a slight scaffolding, and crushed the unfortunate underling, who was killed on the spot, his blood profusely sprinkling the dress of *Rolla* as he rushed on from the wing to finish the tragedy. This shocking disaster was immediately communicated to the crowded audience, who at once departed from the theatre. A gloom was thus unavoidably thrown over the remainder of the engagement. A renewed attack of bronchitis soon after this compelled Charles Kean to suspend acting until rest should remove the complaint. Loss of time to a man who lives by his profession is loss of money. Hoping to benefit by change of air and variety of climate in a milder temperature, he visited the Havannah. From thence, the subjoined letter, written to the author of these pages, detailed his proceedings up to that date :—

" Matanzas, Island of Cuba,
" March 20th, 1840.

" MY DEAR C——,

" I have been long intending to write to you a full account of my transatlantic visit, but have procrastinated so long from one cause and another, especially as I wished to be able to give you a better account of myself, that I dare say you will be surprised to hear from me at all, after so long a silence, and particularly from the West Indies; unless the newspapers have informed you that ill health obliged me to seek the benefit of this climate, which already has so much improved me, that people smile to hear that I came to Havannah on the sick list. Away from the cares and troubles of my American campaign, where I have been subjected to a succession of annoyances, accidents, and unsatisfactory transactions with managers and others, here I am, occupied in visiting an island so novel and interesting to an English eye, and have for the first time since I left home enjoyed those sensations which accompany an unshackled mind and healthful body.

"After I had secured a passage with other English travellers, and agreeable companions, from Charleston, in a very small American brigantine, a steamboat arrived with the ex-governor of Cuba, and having landed his Excellency, was as glad to receive us back as passengers, as we were to forego our previous quarters, and avail ourselves of a chance that gave us so good an opportunity of visiting the Havannah. On one of the most lovely mornings since the creation, we passed under the frowning battlements of the Moro castle, and the light-house at the entrance to the harbour, and soon set foot in the capital of the Western Indies. I cannot describe the delicious temperament of the morn and evening; although it is considered rather dangerous to walk much abroad under the scorching influence of the meridian sun.

"Imagine me in the costume of a planter, white jacket and trousers, and straw hat about four feet in the circumference of the brim. In the evenings, however, you must change to something more European, to attend a capital opera. On the other night this large and handsome building was crowded to the roof on the occasion of De Begnis's benefit. A most singular, and, as I think, degrading custom, although a very lucrative one, exists here, of the performer, whose night it is, sitting at the door, dressed for the character he is to represent, with two silver dishes before him to receive the doubloons and dollars the visitors may think proper to bestow. Sometimes, I am told, as much as 500l. is collected in this manner by a popular actor or actress. De Begnis told me he cleared *four hundred*, on this occasion, and from the appearance of the house, he could not have exaggerated.

"Unfortunately I am deprived of the pleasure of the bull-fights, and a Spanish play, as both these amusements are prohibited during the Lent season; but a masquerade ball gave me an opportunity of seeing one of the finest theatres, perhaps, in the world. Eight thousand persons were assembled within its walls, while the streets presented the appearance of a carnival. In consequence of the slave trade, which is carried on here to a frightful extent, in spite of all British exertion to the contrary (being privately encouraged, or, I should rather say, permitted, by the Spanish government), several of our ships of war are either in port or cruising about in the neighbourhood; and one of the captains in his uniform was accosted by a masked lady, who so fascinated the gallant commander, that after much solicitation and the assurance of a good supper, she exhibited her features to the astonished officer, who gazed with wonder on the face of one of his own midshipmen.

" The city is finely situated, with one of the best harbours in the old or new world. It is strongly fortified, intrenched and walled. The antique and venerable looking churches, convents, prisons, forts, &c., give an appearance of age. The streets are very narrow, without side-walks, and crowded with carriages and carts, besides multitudes on foot, of every colour and variety of the human species, from the potent Spanish Nabob, to the miserable mulatto and slave. The buildings are generally from two to three stories high, without any window glass, and built of stone. The population is about 180,000, nearly half of which, however, live without the walls. There are several fine public squares, ornamented with and supplied by fountains of water. In one of these squares, opposite the Governor's palace, one of the finest military bands I ever heard plays by moonlight; and such sounds in such a climate render the scene perfectly enchanting.

" Formerly, the government of this important island, containing above a million of inhabitants, with a standing army of 22,000 capital troops, was intrusted to men totally unworthy of such an important charge, and in consequence, it became little better than a nest of pirates, swindlers, and common thieves; but under the vigorous administration of Tacon, who was sent out by the Spanish authorities at home, about twelve years since, as Captain General, Havannah, and indeed the entire colony has become a very different place;— and although Tacon has ceased to be governor, the community are still enjoying the blessings of his laws and regulations.

"I travelled by railroad about fifty miles into the interior, and there our party engaged riding horses, and a *volante*, as their carriages are called, to carry us to Matanzas. I wish I had time and space to give you a full description of our two days' journey through cocoa-nut, palm, and orange trees, sugar and coffee plantations; armed, according to the custom here, with pistols and swords nearly as long as ourselves. I have suffered greatly from the musquitoes, who appear to have formed a far stronger affection for me, than for any of my companions.

"On Sunday I return to Havannah, and shall sail for New York early in April, and steam to England by the *Great Western* on the 9th of May. Perhaps I may have the pleasure of seeing you in London during my Haymarket engagement, but at any rate you may expect me at the time I usually visit Dublin, from about the end of November to the middle of December. Nothing has reached me from England since the 1st of January, and you may imagine how anxiously I am anticipating my return to the States, where I expect to find a post-office full of letters, waiting my arrival. You cannot think how much I shall miss Colonel D'Aguilar, who, I presume, has by this time received his brevet rank, and has in consequence, removed from Ireland. Commercial business in the States has been in a deplorable condition, and of course theatricals have not flourished. Mrs. Fitzwilliam has been perhaps the most attractive star, take her for all in all. I have acted so seldom, in consequence of ill-health, and partly from the manner in which I have been treated in money matters, that I may say in truth 'I have lost a year.'

"Pray remember me most kindly to Mrs. C——, and give my love to the children, and do not forget to mention me to C——, to whom I send every kind wish. Let me hope that I have not exhausted your patience, as completely as I have filled this paper, having hardly space left to assure you how delighted I shall be to see you again, or to subscribe myself, your sincere friend,

"CHARLES KEAN.

" Not having my writing-desk with me, and finding it impossible to get sealing-wax, pray excuse the wafer."

On the 1st of June, 1840, Charles Kean commenced his second engagement at the Haymarket, which continued for thirty nights. *Hamlet*, as usual, was his opening part, followed by *Richard*, *Shylock*, and *Sir Giles Overreach.* On Monday the 6th of July, he added *Macbeth*, for the first time, to his list of London characters. In this, the most metaphysically complicated, perhaps, amongst all the mighty conceptions of Shakespeare, his performance equalled the sanguine expectations of his friends, and it has ever since been considered one of his ablest delineations. In the last act, in particular, he was singularly majestic: his death scene was entirely original. *Macbeth* had never been ranked amongst his father's greatest efforts. It had magnificent passages, but they were insulated. As a whole, there was something wanting of sustained power, with indications of incomplete study. On the present revival at the Hay-market, the play was very carefully produced; it ran fifteen nights, and materially served both the theatre and the actor of the leading character. On the first night, the applause was enthusiastic and unanimous; on the second, a few expressions of disapprobation were heard, which were ever after continued by the exceptious minority who thought proper to indulge in them. That this was a systematic opposition became so evident, that the most strenuous efforts were used to detect the parties who so obviously placed themselves in direct opposition to the general voice of the public. But these efforts led to no result, beyond the actual conviction that a planned conspiracy was in existence, the authors and agents of which conducted their proceedings with an impenetrable mystery, not even surpassed by the *Vehme gericht* of the middle-ages, or the more recent *Tugend-bund* of modern Germany. They enjoyed their malice and escaped exposure, but this was all the advantage they gained; while on the other hand, the duration of Mr. Charles Kean's engagement, which ran to thirty nights, was more than doubled by the corresponding attraction.

After the first representation of *Macbeth*, which Charles Kean selected for his benefit on the 3d of July, we find this notice in the *Morning Post:*—

"'Bravo! bravo! Kean! Kean!' the congratulatory cheers which greeted the *beneficiare* last night, are still ringing in our ears. We never remember to have witnessed a more signal triumph. The stage at the fall of the curtain presented the appearance of a *vendange* of *bouquets*. The horticultural *fête* which is to take place this afternoon will not be able to compete with the Haymarket show of flowers; and well did Mr. Kean deserve the tributes which were so plentifully bestowed upon him by his fair admirers. As for obtaining a place in the theatre, that has been out of the question ever since the announcement of Mr. Kean's first appearance in *Macbeth*. The private boxes were crowded to excess, the dress circle was densely thronged, and the upper regions appeared to groan under the weight of the countless masses who came to see whether the son would inherit the transcendent talents of the father in his conception of this great character, which has time out of mind been universally acknowledged to be the most magnificent production of Shakespeare's fertile genius.

" On his first coming forward, Mr. Kean was enthusiastically received, and appeared somewhat embarrassed and thrown off his balance at making his first appearance before the English public in this difficult part. In a moment, however, he cast aside all hesitation, and plunged headlong and gallantly into the yawning gulf and fearful whirlpool of conflicting emotions and passions, which soured the milk of human kindness in the breast of *Macbeth*.

" Mr. Kean's success last evening was one of the most brilliant which has ever been recorded in the annals of the drama. Throughout the whole play he continued to achieve a succession of triumphs, far too numerous for us to record; and at the last, instead of being exhausted by the stupendous exertions he had undergone, he appeared to have gained fresh vigour and inspiration with every successive effort, and fought his last fight, and died, like a stern soldier, with his harness on his back—just as Edmund Kean did before him; and it would be impossible to accord higher praise. But of Mr. Kean, as the actor of last night, we saw or thought nothing. It was *Macbeth, Macbeth, Macbeth*. Ever and anon he appeared before us. First, attired in the plaid of the wild highlander, with the weird sisters on the heath; next, led on by the diabolical instigation of his wife to stain his hands with the blood of his confiding sovereign; and then—we yet shudder and quail at the hideous workings of remorse which tore his heartstrings asunder in the spectre-dagger scene—he threw his words upon us like thunderbolts, and not a soul within the confines of the theatre but felt a weight off his mind when he discovers that he is the dupe of his own disordered brain. It were vain to attempt giving any description of the effect produced by Mr. Kean's utterance of the few simple words—'There's no such thing.' This and the closing scene are the two grand *coups de main* by which he carried away such a splendid harvest of admiration and congratulation. The various costumes worn by Mr. Kean last evening, were some of the most superb ever seen upon the stage. When he appeared in the robes of usurped majesty, his sumptuous attire was well worthy of a monarch.* It consisted of a rich crimson velvet tunic, or gaberdine, on which hung a mantle of dark green velvet, lined with ermine. His other dresses, though necessarily not gorgeous, were remarkable for elegance and simplicity.

"Mr. Kean derived great assistance from, and was very ably seconded by, Mrs. Warner, who sustained the character of *Lady Macbeth* with great intenseness and energy. At the fall of the curtain, Mr. Kean was loudly called for, and at length came forward, and received a tremendous fire of applause. He had 'to bide the pelting of a pitiless storm' of *bouquets*. An announcement was then given forth that the manager had entered into a fresh engagement with the attractive star for

* Such commendation would not now, nineteen years later, be bestowed upon a very inappropriate costume, which, however rich and graceful, was quite out of character.

ten more nights. This led to a second ebullition of Bravo ! "

The variety of opinions delivered by the press on Charles Kean's acting, during his round of performances at the Haymarket, and the biassed disposition by which some were so transparently dictated, called forth the following article in an Edinburgh paper of Monday the 6th of July, entitled,—

"CHARLES KEAN AND HIS LONDON CRITICS.

"The age of true criticism, like the age of chivalry, is gone. The legitimate drama is- neglected by parties interested in the success of the illegitimate; and tragedians, comedians, and vocalists are now written down or up, in London, not according to their demerits or deserts, but in proportion as they are identified with parties sensitively alive to extraneous considerations. The criticism of the London press, as a whole, and in the light of a guide to judgment, is unworthy of perusal, otherwise than as a matter of composition; and the reason is, that it has become sectarian, and is influenced in what it puts forth or suppresses, by party spirit. In this state of things, the rising generation, whose opinions are unformed in respect of great plays and talented performers, is not fairly dealt with, while the public is cavalierly treated. It now forms its own estimate of performances and "stars," and leaves interested flatterers to their adulation, and detractors to their spleen, unheeded; except to be smiled at with the remark, 'Oh, yes; we understand !'

"We have ever been of opinion, that the best star-actor in any age, is he who, in his day, draws the best houses. It is to no purpose that we can be talked at to the contrary. Taste and fashion are incapable of mathematical demonstration, and are seldom, if ever, reformed by the laboured analysis of special pleaders. What Mr. Macready is, he yet is, in spite of the London press being for or against him; and whether Charles Kean be an intellectual performer or not, is a question which it is too late in the day to agitate. Its purpose is seen by the public, who have made up their minds, and who persevere in going in crowds to see him in well-known parts.

"The *Polytechnic* of this month has an article, ably written, *as writing*, cutting up Mr. Charles Kean's *Hamlet*, and exposing, at the same time, the animus of a party writer at war, less with the popular tragedian, than with the public, who, by their crowded audiences on his nights of playing, show the uselessness of such isolated scolding and raving at merits which they gladly pay to see the exhibition of, and cheer and applaud into the bargain! How, in the name of fortune, could, or would, a prudent, thorough man of business like Mr. Webster give Mr. C. Kean a large weekly revenue, unless the public, who go along with him in his engagements, enable him to do so, and by the most convincing of all proofs of public appreciation—liberal payment, and praise besides? Some critics write and abuse managements, as if a management drove people into their theatres, and fleeced them of money at the point of the bayonet!

" We question much if all the writing *at* Mr. Kean, in some of the papers in an opposing interest, has kept a shilling out of the Haymarket treasury. On the contrary, it may have put it into people's heads to go and see the phenomenon of a ' bad actor,' being supported by crowds of all grades of a metropolitan population, and at the west end of London, too! Well, they go; and, instead of agreeing with the critic, they join in feeling double interest in the actor, who they think must be somebody to be so abused, and to be able to withstand the shock on the support of full pockets and applauding houses.

" In his manners off the stage, Charles Kean is a *gentleman;* and precisely what is his recommendation to good society, is the secret cause of that perfect hatred which the vulgar and low-minded cannot conceal that they are eaten up with towards him. Those who win may well laugh on the resource of smiles and a princely income. We have pleasure in quoting the *Morning Post's* statement of Mr. Kean's reception, and the house which he drew last Friday. Had the article been a modern 'critique,' we should not have read it through; but as it reports what actually took place by an eye-witness of the facts, we have perused and herewith extract it."

Then follows the notice in the *Morning Post*, which we have given above. About this time, Madame Vestris, who had assumed the sovereignty of Covent Garden Theatre in the preceding autumn, expressed a desire to engage Charles Kean, to perform with Miss Ellen Tree, on his now recognized terms of 50*l.* per night. Mr. Webster hearing this, offered him the same sum, with half a benefit, for twenty nights during three successive seasons, which offer he accepted. The Haymarket Theatre thus became, for a time, his London home.

CHAPTER XVIII.

ON Monday, the 8th of June, 1840, the veteran William
Dowton took his farewell benefit at the Opera House, in
the Haymarket. That theatre was selected, as its vast
size could accommodate the looked-for crowds. According to the date on his tombstone, at Norwood Cemetery,
he must then have reached his seventy-seventh year—
the only actor except Macklin who continued to wear
his harness to such an advanced period. But he was
robust and hale as Cornaro himself, who corroborated
his own system by living up to 104. Dowton for
nearly half a century had enjoyed a first-class reputation, but it was found that when extreme old age
came upon him he had saved no money. A powerful body of friends came forward to rescue him from
impending want, by a benefit, with a general subscription. The " Poor Gentleman " was selected for
performance, in which the aged actor appeared as
Sir Robert Bramble. Sheridan Knowles delivered an

address, and Dowton spoke a few valedictory words. With the proceeds, an annuity for a given number of years was purchased, on the amount of which he subsisted in ease and comfort; but to the surprise of every one, by dint of regular habits and an iron constitution, he outlived the calculated time, and there was danger that he might be reduced to penury. He died on the 19th of August, 1849. Many leading unemployed members of the profession volunteered their services on the night of his benefit,—including W. Farren, Bartley, Harley, Cooper, Webster, Miss Ellen Tree, and Mrs. Glover.

Dowton was an actor of strong, correct conception, and sterling powers; hard and testy rather than rich or unctuous, and excellent in passionate old men. To these his own irritable temperament materially contributed. He was by far the best *Sir Anthony Absolute* of his day, and played the sleek hypocritical *Dr. Cantwell* with equal skill and discrimination. An anecdote connected with this part he used to relate himself. During a summer at the Lyceum, the play of the "Hypocrite" formed one of the leading attractions. A lady of fashion drove up to the box-office, and said, "When does Dowton next appear as *Dr. Cantwell*, and what places can I have?" "On Wednesday next, Madam," was the reply, "and you can have Box No. 3. The performance is for Mr. Dowton's benefit." "Oh!" exclaimed the liberal patroness, "I never go to benefits, and shall wait for another opportunity." Dowton, who happened to be standing in the hall, made her a profound bow as she took her departure, and uttered indignantly, "Thank you, Ma'am."

Dowton's *Falstaffs* were sound and judicious, but he lacked the jocund rolling eye, and the rich overflowing humour which should pour out involuntarily, constitu-

tionally, and, as it were, in spite of itself. In 1836, he
ventured to cross the Atlantic, and visit the United
States; but he was too far advanced in life to attract
attention or draw money. He came back almost as
poor as he went; but with a change in his political
opinions, in which he has had more than one companion.
He entered the land of freedom a furious republican,—
he returned from it an ultra tory. He was constitutionally discontented, captious, and fretful, but at the
same time warm-hearted and generous. His oddities
were very amusing to those who were intimate with
him. He would sit for hours in his dressing-room,
arranging and contemplating his wigs, those important
accessories to his stage make-up. One of his peculiar
mannerisms was never to play a part without turning his
wig, a process legitimately belonging to *Lingo*, in the
" Agreeable Surprise." When he acted *Dr. Pangloss*
(which, although not his London part, he constantly
assumed on the Kent circuit, where he was for some
years manager), a bet was made that here he would find
his favourite manœuvre impracticable. He managed it
nevertheless. When *Kenrick*, the faithful old Irish servant, comes in exultingly, in the last scene, to announce
the long-lost *Henry Moreland*, he was instructed to run
against *Dr. Pangloss*, who thus obtained the desired
opportunity of disarranging his head-gear.

Dowton undervalued the elder Kean, whose merit he
could never be induced to acknowledge. When the vase
was presented to that great actor by the committee and
company of Drury Lane, he refused to subscribe, saying,
" You may cup Mr. Kean if you please, but you shan't
bleed me." He said, too, the cup should be given to
Joe Munden, for his performance of *Marall*. Amongst
other eccentricities, he fancied (a delusion common to
comedians) that he could play tragedy, and never rested

until he obtained an opportunity of showing the town that Edmund Kean knew nothing of *Shylock*. But the experiment was, as might have been expected, a total failure. The great point of novelty consisted in having a number of Jews in court, to represent his friends and partisans, during the trial scene; and in their arms he fainted, when told he was, per force, to become a Christian. The audience laughed outright, as a commentary on the actor's conception. Once he exhibited privately to the writer of these memoirs, the last scene of *Sir Giles Overreach*, according to his idea of the author's meaning. It occurred at supper, after a performance at Tunbridge Wells, in one of his own theatres, and a very mirthful tragedy it proved. He had a strange inverted idea, that Massinger intended *Sir Giles* for a comic character. He also fancied that he could play *Lord Ogleby*, when nature with her own hand had daguerreotyped him for *Mr. Sterling*. Such are the vagaries of genius, which are equally mournful and unaccountable.

Charles Kean, still anxious for an original part, having failed in his application to Sir Edward Bulwer, now sought to negotiate with Sheridan Knowles, and wrote to him as follows :—

> "30, Old Bond-street.
> " 15th July, 1840.

" MY DEAR KNOWLES,—

" I am very sorry you should have left London without my seeing you, but I was under the impression that you went into the country on Tuesday and would return in a few days. On the other side I have written a few lines to which I hope you will subscribe, and with which I trust you will be satisfied.

" Sincerely yours,

" CHARLES KEAN."

The accompanying agreement ran thus:—"Upon my approval of a new original play in five acts, written by James Sheridan Knowles, Esq., I will pay to the said James Sheridan Knowles, for the exclusive right of acting it in the United Kingdom of Great Britain and Ireland, and its dependencies, for three years, the sum of 600*l.* (six hundred pounds). On the third night of its being acted, the further sum of 50*l.*; on the sixth night, 50*l.*; on the ninth, fifteenth, twentieth, twenty-fifth, thirtieth, and fortieth, 50*l.* each, making in all, 1,000*l.* (one thousand pounds). In addition I give my consent to the printing of the play after it has been acted six nights, and for Mr. Knowles to derive all the advantages that may accrue therefrom."

This offer Mr. Knowles declined, and there, for the present, the negotiation ended. It has two remarkable features—the large remuneration which dramatic authors look for and receive in modern days, and the novelty of leading actors paying large sums for new plays, with which desirable commodity managers in the olden time were too happy to provide them, at their own expense, and for mutual advantage.

Soon after the conclusion of his Haymarket engagement, which wound up with "Macbeth," on the 7th of August, Charles Kean repaired to Brighton. But before he appeared there, some interest and a considerable difference of opinion had been stirred up in that fashionable suburb of London (as we may in truth now call it), by a misunderstanding which had arisen between Mr. J. Wallack and the managers of the Brighton theatre, leading to the publication of an angry correspondence between them. In this Mr. C. Kean's name was unnecessarily and prejudicially mixed up with a controversy in which he had not the most remote connexion, either directly or by implication. The facts of the case, briefly stated, stood thus:—Very soon after Mr. C. Kean's return from the United States, he had been engaged to represent in Brighton *Hamlet, Richard,* and the range of Shakespearean parts he was in the known habit of performing. This engagement was to commence on the 7th of September, and to run seven nights. According to the usual and reasonable practice in such cases, it was expressly stipulated, that, for the interest of both parties to the contract, those particular characters should not be personated by any one in the interval. Subsequently Mr. Wallack was engaged, and his appearance was to precede that of Charles Kean by a fortnight. No stipulation was made as to what parts Mr. Wallack should perform, the presumption of the manager being that he (Mr. Wallack) would select them from amongst his usual run, and which certainly was not understood by theatrical people to include specially those reserved for Mr. Kean's engagement, but rather the reverse. A London actor when "starring" in the country is usually expected to be most attractive in the line which has won for him his London reputation, and to select the characters which he has made peculiarly his own. The agreement between Mr. Wallack and the Brighton manager was made· in a loose manner. The omitted points ought to have been clearly defined at the time, and then no misunderstanding could have taken place; but for these omissions Mr. Kean, by no possible perversion of reasoning, could be rendered responsible, as he received no intimation of the Wallack engagement until a later period.

When the time for announcement duly arrived, Mr. Wallack gave the manager (Mr. Holmes) to understand, that he intended to commence with *Richard the Third,* and to follow up the first night by playing exactly those parts for which Mr. C. Kean was engaged. This arrangement, of course, would have amounted to a direct violation of the contract with Mr. Kean, and the manager felt himself unable to accede to it. However, Mr. Kean, on being apprised of the difficulty, and requested to forego his claims, refused to do so, but at once offered to relinquish the engagement, if the manager considered it to stand in the way of his interest; and by which means Mr. Wallack might be entitled to play whatever he chose. This the manager declined. Mr. Wallack's engagement was consequently broken off, and in his published comments he complained bitterly of what he denounced as an unjust monopoly, and an unfair attempt to make private property of Shakespeare, to the exclusion of the great body of actors, who had an equal right in the reversionary succession. On general principles, there was reason in the argument; but it could not possibly bear on the individual case,—a previous engagement, based on specific stipulations; and which stipulations Mr. Wallack himself would un-doubtedly have insisted on, had the relative positions been reversed.

Charles Kean, always reluctant to intrude himself on the public in any capacity beyond the direct exercise of his profession, paid no attention to the letters inserted in the local papers from the contending parties, or the comments made on them, tending to foment dis-satisfaction, until his friends impressed on him the necessity of a reply, to set matters right before he appeared. Accordingly, he addressed the subjoined letter to the editor of the *Brighton Herald*, which produced the desired effect in the most conclusive manner :—

> "Old Ship Hotel,
> "31st Aug. 1840.

" Sir,—

"A published correspondence between Mr. Holmes and Mr. Wallack, to which my attention has been

called, imposes on me the duty of submitting to your
readers a brief statement of facts, and thereby enabling
them to judge for themselves whether anything I have
done or written justifies the observations which have
been made upon my conduct.

"*Early in June,* shortly after my return from America,
Mr. Charles Hill called upon me in London, and engaged me to perform seven nights at the Brighton
Theatre, to commence on the 7th of September. It
was *arranged* on that occasion, that I should appear as
early in the season as possible, *for the express purpose of
being the first visitor to personate the characters I am in
the habit of performing ;* as I was naturally anxious that
the attraction of those *particular characters* should not
be diminished by previous representation. On this
point I was the more urgent, as it was to be my first
appearance, for two years, in a town where I had always
been received with so much kindness. The manager
assured me that he should be injuring *his own* interest,
as well as *mine,* by adopting any other course ; and,
had it suited his convenience, I *could* and *would,* for
the reason above specified, have visited Brighton even
earlier than the present period.

"*In the beginning of August,* a letter, written in
answer to one of mine to the Brighton management on
theatrical business, informed me for the first time that
Mr. Charles Hill, who, I believe, had then left this
country for America, had entrusted the control of the
theatre to Mr. Holmes; that an engagement had been
entered into, about the 31st of July, with Mr. Wallack,
to appear on the 17th of August; and that he (Mr.
Wallack) was anxious to perform *Richard, Hamlet,* and
Macbeth.

"Upon receiving this information, I immediately reminded Mr. Holmes of the terms of the understanding
which existed between Mr. Hill and myself, and at the

same time remarked, that I could not consent to any arrangement contrary to those terms; that the manager, however, *was perfectly at liberty to allow Mr. Wallack to perform the characters for which I had stipulated, before the 7th September if he chose; but that I should in such case consider myself released from the agreement with Mr. Hill.*

"This is, in substance, the whole of the intercourse between Mr. Hill, Mr. Holmes, and myself respectively, with reference to my engagement; and shows that, so far from my having '*interfered with the arrangements of others,*' others have sought to interfere with mine; and that I may justly complain of such interference, when, after having formed an engagement early in the season, for the *express purpose,* and *on the condition of being the first in the field*, I find another performer, with an engagement made *long after mine*, endeavouring to anticipate by *only a fortnight*, the *very characters for which I had stipulated.*

"The course Mr. Wallack has thought proper to pursue in involving my name in the controversy between him and Mr. Holmes is to be regretted, and the more so, as the *real* question at issue seems to be one between those two parties alone.

"In conclusion, I beg to assure you that I never in any way, either directly or indirectly, presumed to appropriate to myself any character or characters, and most especially those of Shakespeare, held to be the common property of all actors; but that my engagement was formed solely with the object I have already expressed; and it must be well known to all persons familiar with theatrical matters, that the frequent representation of the same characters in a provincial theatre does not advance the interest either of the manager or of the actor. I disclaim most unreservedly the intention of injuring the prospects of any member of my profession, and as unfeignedly repeat my regret that circumstances should have caused, for the first time in my life, the vindication of my conduct to become the subject of discussion in a public journal.

" I am, Sir, your obedient servant,

" CHARLES KEAN."

The Brighton engagement proved an additional triumph. The correspondent of the *Morning Post* thus communicated the result of the first night :—

"*Brighton, Sept.* 8.—After the recent correspondence in which the name of the popular actor, Mr. Charles Kean, was involved, it was fully expected that his reception on the Brighton boards last night would not have been altogether of so gratifying a character as he has been accustomed to experience in this town. Every part of the house was quite filled, and the boxes included a large sprinkling of fashionable company. " Hamlet " was the play, and on the first appearance of the *Ghost,* the gallery loudly applauded; and the moment Mr. Kean entered upon the scene, a simultaneous burst of welcome proceeded from the pit and boxes, a great portion of the company standing. If there was any displeasure shown in the gallery, which we did not hear, it was completely lost in the cheers from the boxes, which lasted for upwards of a minute. The house then became perfectly silent, and the play proceeded. His *Hamlet* was a beautiful performance; he appeared to have derived fresh vigour from the cordial reception. He was frequently interrupted by loud plaudits from all parts of the house, and when the manager came on to announce the performance for the following evening, there were loud calls for Kean. The actor obeyed the mandate, and bowed his acknowledgments, retiring amidst unbounded applause. He plays *Claude Melnotte* to-night, and repeats *Hamlet* on Saturday."

This Brighton episode, which at one time threatened a storm, having blown over, Charles Kean continued his usual progress through the country, and again visited the leading towns in which he had won much of his early reputation. Everywhere he found his attraction unvarying, and with each succeeding year his fame and fortune steadily advanced together.

On the 17th of May, 1841, his performances at the Haymarket were resumed with " Macbeth." This third engagement, like the two preceding ones, extended far beyond the term specified in the contract, and reached thirty-seven nights. " Macbeth " and " Romeo and Juliet " were the two prevailing attractions, the former being repeated ten, the latter twelve nights. During this season, Charles Kean performed the *Stranger*, for the first time in London, which gave rise to the following epigram in one of the weekly papers :—

" WHICH IS THE STRANGER ?

" On those cocks of the scene,
Macready and Kean,
We thus may decide without danger ;
Throughout all its range,
Though Macready is strange,
Yet Kean, of the two, is the *Stranger*."

In " Romeo and Juliet " the heroine was performed by Miss Ellen Tree ; the *Mercutio* being Mr. J. Wallack. The play was produced under the direction of Charles Kean, affording the first stamp of that rare combination of taste and judgment which he has since carried to such perfection in the Shakespearean revivals at the Princess's Theatre.

On the 1st of July, 1840, " Macbeth " was performed for the benefit and farewell of Samuel Thomas Russell, a very old actor, who had been attached to the London theatres upwards of forty years. On this occasion Kean contributed a donation of 20*l.* Russell was generally known in the profession by the sobriquet of " Jerry Sneak," from his excellence in that one character; just as " Single Speech" Hamilton obtained his distinctive pre-nomen from a solitary display of eloquence in the more exalted theatre of St. Stephen's. But here, as Lord Byron says, " all likeness ends between the pair;" for we never heard that Jerry Sneak Russell was suspected of being Junius, while it is certain that Single Speech Hamilton was included in the list of nominees to the unacknowledged but somewhat dangerous authorship of the far-famed letters.

Charles Kean's third Haymarket engagement termi-nated on the 6th of August. On the 29th of January, 1842, occurred the most auspicious event in his life—the wisest step he had ever taken—and the surest gua-rantee of his future prosperity. He was married at the church of St. Thomas, in Dublin, to Miss Ellen Tree; a mutual attachment of long standing, and in every respect " a well-assorted union." By this, Charles Kean not only secured his domestic happiness, but obtained a large addition to his worldly means, and an invaluable co-operator in his theatrical career. By a rare combi-nation of private and professional excellence, Miss Ellen Tree had already acquired a handsome independence, and had placed herself in the foremost rank of the dis-tinguished females whose names shed lustre on the history of the British drama. In characters requiring great physical power, with the sterner and more com-manding attributes, something might be wanting in which she had been excelled by a few of her predecessors; but in all the softer delineations, in a just discrimination of the tenderer and more womanly passions, in versatility, in natural pathos, or elegant vivacity,—in a clear comprehension of her author's meaning, and in lady-like deportment—she was, and is, without a superior on the modern stage.

Miss E. Tree (now Mrs. C. Kean) is one of four sisters who all evinced a predilection for the drama at very early years. Their father held a situation in the East India House. The mother still lives, happy in "a green old age," in the full possession of her faculties, a remarkable instance of health and longevity. Before Ellen appeared on the boards, the name of Tree had already become celebrated by the performance of the elder sister, Maria, an acting vocalist of superior ability, who will long be remembered, in conjunction with Miss Stephens and Miss Paton, as upholding the charms of pure English song, with combined though varied excellence, at the same theatre (Covent Garden), during several brilliant seasons. Miss Maria Tree, in 1825, married Mr. Bradshaw, a gentleman of fortune, sometime member for Canterbury, and retired from professional life, too soon for the public, although infinitely to her own happiness and advantage.

Miss E. Tree first appeared in public, at Covent Garden, when scarcely seventeen, as *Olivia* in " Twelfth Night," for her sister's benefit. She next acted in Edinburgh and Bath, and after a period of successful practice, obtained an engagement at Drury Lane,—her opening part being *Violante*, in the " Wonder." On this occasion one of her most eminent predecessors, Mrs. Davison, assumed the subordinate duties of *Flora*. To *Violante* succeeded *Letitia Hardy*, *Albina Mandeville*, *Rosalie Somers*, *Charlotte*, in the " Hypocrite," and *Miss Hardcastle*, in all of which she rapidly advanced in public favour, until the production of the " Youthful

Queen," when her admirable performance of *Christina* established her as a permanent London favourite.

In 1829, her services were transferred to Covent Garden, where she appeared in the character of *Lady Townly*. *Françoise de Foix*, in Miss Fanny Kemble's play of " Francis the First " was the first part that gave even herself a notion that she could act tragedy. This induced her to play *Romeo* for her benefit, to Miss Kemble's *Juliet*, which hazardous attempt she achieved with singular success, all the newspapers being unanimous in her praise. In 1832, she made her first visit to Dublin, in which city she was the original representative of *Julia*, in the " Hunchback," when Sheridan Knowles appeared as *Master Walter* in his own play. The period was one of cholera and dreary political agitation, which hung heavily on the fortunes of the theatre ; nevertheless, Ellen Tree, during that short introduction, established a good understanding with her new audience, which increased with every succeeding engagement. During Mr. Bunn's management of both the national theatres, she appeared as *Myrrha*, in " Sardanapalus," which she studied in a few hours when the negotiation (real or fictitious) with Mrs. Mardyn fell through. After this, she represented *Rachel*, the heroine in the successful play of the " Jewess," which ran upwards of a hundred nights. At the close of the Drury Lane season, she went to the Haymarket, where she proved very attractive in *Viola*, in " Twelfth Night, " in a new drama called the " Ransom," and in the youthful hero of Serjeant Talfourd's classical tragedy of " Ion," which ran thirty nights to great houses. Between the years 1836 and 1839, she visited America, and during a lengthened sojourn of two years and nine months, traversed the whole extent of the United States, winning everywhere golden opinions, and bearing away a substantial harvest of enduring metal. Few English performers have been so universally attractive. The sum realized amounted to 12,000*l.*, which speaks for itself. After a short engagement at the Haymarket, on her return from America, she migrated once more to Covent Garden, where she performed the *Countess of Eppenstein*, in Knowles's "Love," for fifty-two consecutive nights. During the year 1840, Leigh Hunt's play of a "Legend of Florence," was produced at Covent Garden. The author and the management were unwilling to offer what appeared such an insignificant part as *Genevra* to an actress of her high standing and attraction; but she saw in it the opportunity which she amply verified, in the overpowering effect of one agonizing burst, "Good God! what have I done?"

If we were to select the two characters in which Mrs. C. Kean appeared to the greatest advantage, before she glided into the more matronly line which she now fills, we should name *Rosalind* and *Viola*. Perhaps the latter was the most faultless performance on the modern stage. It presented one of the sweetest creations of Shakespeare's fancy, embodied as exactly as if the accomplished representative had been foreseen by the imagination of the author. In figure, features, expression, and elegant propriety of costume, in the delicate humour of the lighter points, and the exquisite pathos of the serious passages, the portrait was one in which the most exceptious caviller would have been taxed to discover a defective feature, or suggest an improvement.

Not many years since, we happened to sit in the stalls of the Princess's Theatre, next to an enthusiastic septuagenarian, who proved to be anything but one of Horace's types of old age, represented by the satirist, as—

> "Difficilis, querulus, laudator temporis acti
> Se puero."

He remembered Mrs. Jordan as *Viola*, during the zenith of her reputation. We entered into talk, and he volunteered a comparison. Mrs. Jordan, he said, was, on the whole, inferior to Mrs. C. Kean. She had greater breadth, higher colouring, more exuberant spirits, and a broad-wheeled laugh peculiar to herself, which bore down every thing before it; but all this, he added, would appear coarse and vulgar to modern ideas of refinement. In personal requisites, in elegance and delicacy of manner, in the grace of sentiment and general finish, the picture was incomplete, and much less agreeable than that presented by her successor.

The marriage of Mr. and Mrs. Charles Kean took place on the last day of their Dublin engagement, and on that same evening, by an odd but accidental coincidence, they performed together in the "Honeymoon." For private and professional reasons of their own, the union was not immediately made public. Their first appearance in the acknowledged characters of man and wife occurred at Glasgow, on the 27th of the following February, the combined attraction producing, in five performances, included in one week, the sum of 1,000*l.*

On the 4th of April, 1842, they commenced a joint engagement at the Haymarket, which extended over fifty-two nights, comprised within a period of little more than three months, and ending on the 16th of July. "As You Like It," the "Gamester," and the "Lady of Lyons," were frequently repeated; but the chief novelty consisted in a new play by Sheridan Knowles, called the "Rose of Arragon"—the same for which Charles Kean had offered 1,000*l.* a year or two before, but which the author now placed at the disposal of the Haymarket manager on much less advantageous terms. This play succeeded in representation, and commanded twenty-five consecutive repetitions; but it has vanished entirely from the permanent acting list, and must be looked upon as one of the least agreeable productions of a very superior dramatist.

James Sheridan Knowles has long ceased to write for the stage, and has merged into a theological controversialist, or lay preacher, in the Baptist communion; carrying into his newly selected avocation the same fervid enthusiasm which marked the preceding phases of his chequered career. Under these circumstances, we may speak of him, dramatically considered, as belonging to history. Of his fifteen plays, which will all live in print, six at least are likely to keep possession of the stage as long as the stage lasts in the United Kingdom. These are, "Virginius," "William Tell," the "Hunchback," the "Wife," the "Love Chase," and "Love." After the production of the last, the pen of Knowles moved heavily, and his poetic imagination began to grow torpid. If votes were collected by ballot to decide on the comparative pretensions of all the dramatic writers of the present age, we are inclined to think a large majority would assign the first post of honour to Knowles, and select "Virginius" as the best acting play of modern times. Sharp criticism has pointed out some trifling incongruities in the arrangement of the plot, occasional slips in the diction, and a weakness approaching to anti-climax in the fifth act; but sharp criticism investigates with a microscopic eye, and could detect a flaw in the Pitt diamond, or the Koh-i-noor. The more enlarged and liberal gaze of admiration embraces beauty in the mass, and bestows no thought on an almost imperceptible blemish.

In opposition to the verdict in favour of "Virginius," we shall be told that a subject selected from history, which the adopter finds ready to his hand, draws less upon his genius than one which he must invent. Many authors can write good dialogue who are unable to construct effective plots, or to work up telling situations. The late Douglas Jerrold may be quoted as an example. Beaumont excelled in the one branch, Fletcher in the other. Hence they worked well together, and the conjunction saved time and trouble, while it insured success. For this reason modern French dramatists ordinarily run in couples, and not unfrequently in leashes. So it is with the fashioners of the garments we wear. One passes competition in the cut of a coat, another stands alone in a waistcoat, and a third baffles rivalry in the graceful folds of the nether integuments. But it is most rare to find one pair of shears equally excellent in a complete suit. We once heard an author, of first-rate executive skill, say, "I have no inventive faculty; I cannot imagine a plot. Furnish me with that, and you shall have such a play as you require in a fortnight." The writer alluded to was offered his own price, and would have had no objection to increase his already ample worldly store by a good round sum.

Viewed in the light here stated, such entirely original plays as the "Hunchback," the "Wife," the "Daughter," the "Love Chase," and "Love," are entitled to take rank in a class superior to those selected from historical annals, although embellished with all the charms of poetry, and the full force of distinct, identical character. Yet the great Greek fathers of the drama, Æschylus, Sophocles, and Euripides, invariably drew from the legendary or traditional lore handed down to them through recorded history and mythology. The diction, the imagery, the philosophical reflections, the moral, the consequences, the effect upon human transactions, the happiness resulting from virtue, the misery inseparable from crime;—all these arise, and are em-

bodied as they arise, from that innate power possessed
by the writers of conveying what they feel; but the
power and the feeling are not engendered from imaginary or poetical possibilities;—they are derived from the
study of real events.

Gibbon, in writing of the Emperor Heraclius, has
divided his public life into three distinct epochs—the
opening, the meridian, and the decline. The first and
last, comparatively inferior; the central, effulgent in
greatness. It is so with Knowles in reference to the
order of his plays. The earliest and the latest* are not
those by which his genius can be estimated. The
produce of his mature manhood has elevated him to
his exalted post in the temple of Fame; and by this
posterity will test his comparative excellence. It is
interesting to the curious inquirer as a study, that *all*
the productions of a great writer should be preserved;
but the accompanying reflection, *nemo fuit unquam sic
impar sibi*, presents itself with almost inseparable certainty. Even Homer slumbered sometimes; and there
are passages attributed to Shakespeare which we should
like to feel convinced he had never written.

Knowles has evidently built himself on the dramatists
of the Elizabethan age, with their immediate successors
and followers;—a school which has been pedantically
quoted, and cried up *ad nauseam*, and in imitating
which many have totally failed. He, their most successful imitator, has much of their vigour and intensity,
their nature, their strong sense of the harrowing and
pathetic, their power of condensed expression, and
sometimes more than their flowing poetry. He occasionally copies their conceits, and deviates into their
verbal obscurity; but he never emulates their coarse-

---

* " Leo the Gipsy," " Brian Boroihme," " Caius Gracchus," and
" Alfred," were written before " Virginius."

ness, or heightens a plot by their unnatural and revolting extravagance. Above all, he draws woman as if he loved and reverenced her,—with a delicate and admiring hand, with a fervent and devoted heart. His female portraitures present no Clytemnestras, Messalinas, Medeas, or Lady Macbeths. He reserves the dark, the stormy, and the evil passions for the workings of man's heart, and the process of man's machinations. He contemplates woman in the abstract, as *Jaffier* looks with rapturous affection on *Belvidera* in the individual:—

> " Sure you were made
> To temper man ;—we had been brutes without you.
> Angels were painted fair to look like you ;
> There's in you all that we believe of Heaven—
> Amazing brightness, purity, and truth,
> Eternal joy, and everlasting love."

Knowles's delineations of the softer sex are unexceptionably beautiful. They are finished with a grace and delicacy which Shakespeare only can excel, and entitle him to a laurel wreath, entwined by the fair fingers of the loveliest and the most exalted in the land. We are truly rejoiced at this opportunity of rendering feeble tribute to the first of living dramatists, who combines the truth and energy of the giants of an earlier age, entirely divested of those errors in taste which blacken and deform many of their most resplendent passages.*

On the 21st of June, 1842, poor Frederick Yates died, at the premature age of forty-five. The immediate cause of his decease was the second or third rupture of a blood-vessel, which occurred on the 26th of March, while he was rehearsing a new part on the stage

---

* In 1847, the Whigs offered Knowles a pension of 100*l.* a-year, which, though poor, he indignantly declined. It has since been augmented to 200*l.*, which he now enjoys. It was intended to have made him curator of Shakespeare's birth-place, at Stratford-on-Avon, with a suitable endowment, but both plans failed from want of funds.

of the Dublin Theatre, preparatory to the commencement of an engagement on the following day. He went home to his hotel, and never appeared in public again. He was an actor of very versatile powers, and of indefatigable activity as a manager. After a most successful novitiate in Edinburgh, he made his first bow at Covent Garden as *Iago*, on the 7th of November, 1818, on which occasion Young was the *Othello*, C. Kemble, *Cassio*, and Miss O'Neill, *Desdemona*. During the season he played *Falstaff; Gloster* in "Jane Shore;" *Berthold*, a very striking part in an unsuccessful tragedy by Maturin; *Sylvester Daggerwood*, and *Casca; Flexible*, in imitation of Mathews; *Rob Roy*, *Shylock*, and *Dick* in the "Apprentice." But his *hit* was in "Cozening," an interlude written expressly for him, in which he personated seven different characters. This little piece ran for nearly thirty nights. Yates would have held much higher ground than he ultimately attained if he had confined himself to a more restricted line, and had abstained from imitation, the constant practice of which infected his originality, and infused itself into his natural manner almost without his own consciousness. But it must be admitted that his imitations were almost as good as those of Mathews, his friend and model.

Yates married Miss Brunton, one of the most delightful actresses of her day,* whether in tragedy or comedy, as well as a thoroughly amiable woman, and has left an only son, who has acquired distinction in several fields of literature.

This same year, 1842, witnessed also the short but dazzling career of another scion of the gifted family of Kemble,—Adelaide, the second daughter of Charles Kemble, who flashed with the brightness of a meteor

---

* She came out at Covent Garden as *Letitia Hardy*, on the 12th of September, 1817, and has retired for many years.

across the theatrical horizon, and left a long train of light behind her when she disappeared. Had she continued on the stage, and devoted herself to tragedy alone, independent of her extraordinary vocal powers, she would have carried away the palm from nearly all competitors. She resembled Pasta in style, and her illustrious aunt in appearance, although not on the same majestic scale. Her brief course lasted only from the 20th of November, 1841, to the 23d of December, 1842. No succeeding English singer has rivalled her excellence in the art musical, while acting remains almost a sealed book to the whole race of nightingales.

During the summer of 1843, Charles Kean concluded his three years' contract at the Haymarket. On this occasion he appeared without his wife for twenty nights, Mrs. C. Kean being unable to support him, in consequence of her approaching confinement with their only child, a daughter, born on the 18th of September in that year. During the subsequent winter he entered into another single engagement with Mr. Bunn, at Drury Lane, receiving the same payment as in 1838. In the course of this term, "Richard the Third" was produced in a style of unprecedented magnificence, with historical costumes and appointments. The hostile clique which had so perseveringly attended Charles Kean at the Haymarket, followed him to the changed scene of action. Night after night, penetrating above the loud applauses of the great majority of the house, the two or three dissentient voices made themselves conspicuously audible. Wherever the actor went in London, they dogged his steps, and sought to check his popularity and inward satisfaction, as the slave danced in mockery before the chariot of the Roman conqueror throughout his triumphal progress. The most extraordinary feature of this strange persecution was, that the instigators, whoever

they might be, must have carried it on at the expense
of their pockets—a test of malevolence which the most
determined enemy usually shrinks from, and which
proves the personal animosity in this instance to have
been deeply rooted indeed. Malice will make great
sacrifices, and encounter risk and labour, to attain a
cherished object;—in short, do all but dive into its own
purse. When it goes that length, and pays for indulgence, the exception parallels a black swan in rarity.
Lord Byron, echoing Machiavelli, in verse, says, with
true knowledge of human nature,—

> " Kill a man's family, and he may brook it ;
> But keep your hands out of his breeches-pocket."

CHAPTER XIX.

AMERICA has always been considered an " El Dorado "
by the leading actors of the London stage,—a safe reserve to retreat on should home attraction slumber or
threaten to decline. The truth of the hypothesis has
generally established itself by successful experiment.
The most remarkable instance to the contrary happened
in the case of Madame Vestris and Mr. Charles Mathews,
which infinitely surpassed all previous calculation. Their
want of the expected success could not be traced to any
affectation of squeamish propriety because they bore
different names ; for they were married, and the marriage
publicly announced before they left England. Many
said that the lady would subdue by her exquisite taste
in costume if not by her talent; that she would conquer
with her wardrobe if she failed with her eyes and voice.
They who thought so, forgot that the fashionable dames
of New York are the most showy dressers in the world,
and watch the latest Parisian novelties with restless
anticipation. Some asserted that the clever couple

were received coldly because C. Mathews's father had offended American nationality by an extravagant caricature of their peculiarities. This could hardly be, for their own actors had done the same, although it is true they might tolerate in one " native and to the manner born " what they refused to permit in an impertinent " Britisher." But no matter what might be the cause, the case proved an exception to the standard rule.

Mr. and Mrs. C. Kean (the latter in particular) were desirous of paying another visit to the many kind friends they had formerly made in the great Western Republic. A very tempting offer presenting itself, they laid aside several excellent engagements at home, and in the summer of 1845 once more embarked for the United States. Being at Liverpool for that purpose, they crossed over to Dublin to take a temporary leave of their Irish patrons, and performed two nights, on the 28th and 29th of July, to crowded houses, and sailed from the shores of England on the 2d of August following. Throughout the Union their success was everywhere " prodigious." By the close of the first year they realized and sent safely home a greater profit than had ever before been accomplished on the same prolific ground within the same time. A new play, called " The Wife's Secret," which they imported with them, proved invariably attractive wherever it was performed. This play, a production of sterling merit, combining beauty of language with powerful dramatic incident and situation, was written by Mr. G. Lovell, already well known to the literary and theatrical world by the " Merchant of Bruges," " Love's Sacrifice," the novel of the " Trustee," and many contributions to leading periodicals. The " Wife's Secret " was purchased by Kean, who fully relied-on the talent of his author, for the large sum of 400l., before it was commenced. In the year 1846, Charles Kean ventured on an experiment never before hazarded in America—the production of the two historical tragedies of " King John " and " Richard the Third," on a scale of splendour which no theatre in London or Paris could have surpassed. The scenery, the decorations, the banners, armorial bearings, heraldic blazonry, groupings, weapons of war, costumes, furniture, and all the minor details were so correctly studied that the most scrutinizing reader of Montfauçon or Meyrick would have been puzzled to detect an error. But our brethren of the stars and stripes are utilitarians rather than antiquaries; more inclined to look in advance than to turn over pages of the past, or to pore into ancient chronicles. They appeared not to understand or enjoy with a perfect zest the pomp of feudal royalty, and the solemn display of baronial privileges. The upshot of all was that the expenditure far exceeded the return, and the produce of the second year bore no comparison with that of the first.

In the summer of 1847, Mr. and Mrs. C. Kean left the shores of America (where they had found a second home) with many grateful reminiscences, and once more landed safely in England. Their first act on arriving at home was one of disinterested kindness. Hearing, through a mutual friend, that the lessee of the Dublin Theatre had, during their absence, been less prosperous than his well-wishers desired, or his unremitting exertions might have justified him in expecting, they proceeded at once, after scarcely any interval of repose, to Ireland, and volunteered to perform for his benefit. The attraction of these powerful auxiliaries, added to the personal popularity of the manager, produced a house crowded by all the rank and fashion of the Irish metropolis. The play selected was the " Jealous Wife," in which Mr. and Mrs. C. Kean appeared (for the first time in Europe) as *Mr.* and *Mrs. Oakly.* The Lord-Lieutenant, the Earl of Clarendon, who had very lately entered on his office, was there, with the Countess, and the usual viceregal suite. There were also present Sir Edward Blakeney, the commander of the forces in Ireland; Prince George of Cambridge, commanding the district; the Lord Mayor, with other civic dignitaries; many of the leading judges and barristers, and nearly all the officers of the garrison. A more brilliant assemblage has seldom been collected together within the walls of a theatre. Their Excellencies, the Lord-Lieutenant and his Lady, expressed warm approbation of the performance, and on the following Saturday, the 31st of July, repeated their visit to the theatre, in state, commanding the appearance of Mr. and Mrs. C. Kean in the comedy of the " Wonder." This led to a second house, as numerously attended as the former one. They had thus the satisfaction of rendering a double service to an old and valued friend at a very critical juncture.

After going through a series of engagements, all settled before they had sailed for America, in Birmingham, Manchester, Liverpool, and Dublin, they returned to London, to recommence operations at the Haymarket Theatre, early in January, 1848. They were, as a matter of course, disposed to start with their acknowledged round of Shakespearean characters, but were strongly urged not to do so by more than one judicious friend who had closely watched the shifting temperature of theatrical politics during their absence, and wisely counselled them against this very natural course, which, they said, would assuredly lead to a revival of the old opposition, with added virulence. The advisers had no positive proof to produce, no tangible evidence of premeditated conspiracy, nothing beyond the strong conviction which sometimes impresses itself on the mind, and cannot be shaken by the absence of logical demonstration. They were convinced of the fact, and spoke accordingly. Acting on this suggestion, which entirely accorded with their own feelings, Mr. and Mrs. C. Kean decided on the new play of the " Wife's Secret " for their first appearance, on the 17th of January. The result proved that the selection was judicious. The reception of the returned favourites, and the success of the play, were equally enthusiastic, and no dissent was even faintly attempted. The " Wife's Secret " ran thirty-six nights with undiminished effect; the engagement, originally for thirty nights, was extended to sixty; and on the occasion of their benefit, her Majesty honoured them with her presence, conferring the distinction of a " special patronage." This was the first time during a long service of twenty years that Charles Kean had been fortunate enough to obtain an original part of any importance; but *Sir Walter Amyot* can scarcely be ranked as a first-rate character, being throughout the play subordinate to his wife, the *Lady Eveline.* Up to this period his reputation had been exclusively built on his illustrations of Shakespeare. In this respect his father and himself had been less fortunate than their predecessors. *Rolla*, the *Stranger*, *Penruddock*, and *Octavian* assisted the fame of John Kemble, nearly as much as *Hamlet, Lear, Wolsey*, or *Coriolanus. Virginius, William Tell, Werner, Claude Melnotte*, and *Cardinal Richelieu*, proved more valuable stepping-stones to Macready than *King John, Othello*, or *Macbeth.*

At the close of 1848, Charles Kean was selected, without application on his part, to conduct the " Windsor theatricals "—a series of private performances at the Castle, adopted by the Queen and the Prince Consort, with the double object of promoting the interests of the British drama, while they gratified

their own personal inclinations. The principle proposed
and carried out was, that the performers should be
selected indiscriminately according to their abilities,
and without reference to any particular theatre or individual interest. It was manifest to all, except the
discontented minority who can find good in nothing,
that this was a great step towards the restoration of
fashion to the once crowded but now almost abandoned
temples of dramatic worship. In this her Majesty
inherited the taste of her grandfather, King George III.,
with whom the theatre was ever a favourite relaxation.
When in the comparative retirement of Windsor and
Weymouth, his usual habit was, to command twice
a-week, and to go in private on the other two nights of
performance. The managers made fortunes, and the
actors were exalted. His Majesty and Queen Charlotte
once actually travelled all night from Weymouth to
London to open parliament, that they might not disappoint a favourite comic performer to whom they had
promised their patronage on his benefit night, which had
been unavoidably postponed. It was suggested to the
kind-hearted monarch that he might send the actor
a present, which would compensate for his disappointment. "No, no," replied the King, "I should do that
at any rate; but poor fellow, poor fellow! he will think
much more of our being there than of anything we
might give him."

The compliment of being appointed her Majesty's
"master of the revels" in her own private palace, was
undoubtedly one of the most gratifying nature, both to
the man and the actor; but the difficulties by which it
was accompanied might stand by the labours of
Hercules, and lose nothing in the comparison. A
very general desire was manifested to appear before
royalty, in royalty's select retreat; but it was no easy

matter to reconcile conflicting claims, or bring down expectations, almost invariably preposterous, to a practicable standard. That Charles Kean acquitted himself to the perfect satisfaction of his august employers, may be assumed from the facts that her Majesty presented him with a diamond ring, and accorded him the still more flattering honour of a personal interview.* To satisfy all his brethren of the sock and buskin was a much more arduous undertaking. He worked with unceasing tact, command of temper, and the most perfect impartiality; but he discovered ere long that to roll up-hill the stone of Sisyphus, to draw water in the bucket of the Danaidæ, to carve Mount Athos into a statue, to dance for uninterrupted hours on the tread-mill, to be fitted to the bed of Procrustes, or to lie on the burning couch of Guatimozin, would be gentle recreation compared to the complicated, impracticable, and hopeless task which he had vainly expected to accomplish.

The object and advantages of the Royal Theatricals were well set forth in the following notice, which appeared in the *Times* of Friday, the 26th of January, 1849 :—

"For the last month, the plays acted in the Rubens Room at Windsor Castle, have afforded a fertile topic of conversation to those who take interest in the proceedings of the Court, and those who discuss the fluctuating fortunes of the British drama. The fact that the Sovereign bespoke a series of English theatrical performances as a recreation in her own palace, has at least the charm of novelty to recommend it to the attention of the curious. Fancy has wandered back to the days of Elizabeth and the first James, when such means of amusement were not uncommon; and perhaps,

* On the 21st of February, 1849.

wandering forward, has augured that a new stock of dramatists worthy to compete with those of the Elizabethan era may spring into existence from the effect of the Windsor Theatricals.

" With respect to the performances just concluded, they seem to have been conducted in the very best taste, and to have given unequivocal satisfaction to the distinguished auditors. Mr. Charles Kean, under whose direction the whole has taken place, Mr. Grieve, the head of the decorative department, and the principal performers, have all received the special approbation of royalty; and there is no doubt that an entertainment adequate to the royal wishes has been provided on every occasion.

" The courtly assembly seems to have laid aside that frigidity which is usually the characteristic of private theatricals, and to have applauded with the zeal of a money-paying public, thoroughly pleased with the return for its outlay. It is a fallacy to suppose that a theatrical exhibition can go on briskly without applause. Approbation is the meat, drink, and spirit of the histrionic artist; and his professional life, without this aliment constantly bestowed, is a dreary waste without an oasis.

" With the large public—the public outside the Castle —the question *àpropos* of these theatricals is, whether or not they confer a benefit on the English drama. That the benefit will not be of that immediately palpable nature which would result from half-a-dozen royal visits in state, and the crowds consequent thereupon, must, we think, be conceded by any impartial person. But at the same time we are inclined to decide that an indirect benefit to the English theatres is far from improbable.

" When the highest personage in the land considers

that an English dramatic performance is such an entertainment as to merit the construction of a stage in her own drawing-room, with all the appurtenances of a regular theatre, the opinion that the native drama is unfashionable receives an authoritative rebuke. The plays acted at Windsor Castle are the same that may be seen at the Haymarket and the Lyceum; the actors in the Rubens Room are precisely the same individuals who appear on the public boards; and it would be absurd to say that an entertainment which occupies a high rank at Windsor, loses that rank when it comes to the metropolis.

"The very circumstance that theatricals are now generally talked about, is in itself likely to be of advantage to the English drama. A certain elevated class of the public, by shunning English theatres and skipping English critiques, might soon lose sight of the native drama altogether. But now, the plays and the actors are forced upon the attention of the higher orders from another point. He who studies the proceedings of the Court, has an English theatrical programme thrust into his view; and the same course of reading which tells him that her Majesty took an airing, also informs him that Mr. and Mrs. C. Kean play *Hamlet* and *Ophelia*. The crowded state of the principal theatres would seem to indicate that an awakened interest for theatricals is already taking effect.

" That many private controversies have arisen respecting the formation of the theatrical company at Windsor Castle, we are perfectly aware. Some have considered themselves unjustly excluded; others, although admitted, have thought themselves disadvantageously placed. These controversies, which are almost infinite in number, each involving its own distinct point, are not within our province. That every one of a class should be satisfied when a selection was to be made, was mathematically impossible. The right and wrong of each individual case is a matter of separate discussion, and much more concerns the parties themselves, than the public before the lamps.

"In conclusion, if the royal theatricals at Windsor give an impulse to the drama which proves advantageous to its professors, we hope that the exertions of Mr. Charles Kean may not be entirely forgotten."

The Windsor performances were continued annually at the Castle at the Christmas season, since the first series, interrupted only on three occasions,—in 1850, by the death of the Dowager Queen Adelaide; in 1855, in consequence of the national gloom resulting from the precarious situation of our armies in the Crimea; and in 1858, on the marriage of the Princess Royal, when they were superseded by other arrangements. Mr. C. Kean, in his capacity of Chairman at the dinner of the General Theatrical Fund, on the 21st of May, 1849, when proposing her Majesty's health, spoke as follows with reference to the advantages accruing from the royal patronage; and what he said was unanimously echoed by the assembled company :—*

" The members of the theatrical profession have ever been signalized by their devoted loyalty. You are aware that in the troubled times of Charles I., those times, according to the satiric poet,

> " When hard words, jealousies, and fears
> Set folks together by the ears,"

when political quarrels and puritanic frenzy closed the theatres,—nearly the whole of the actors took up arms in the cause of their royal master. Hart, Robinson, and Mohun, held commissions in the king's service, and

* See published " Proceedings of the Fourth Anniversary Festival of the General Theatrical Fund ; 1849."

were remarkable for their gallant conduct. At a later period, Smith, Griffin, Carlisle, and Wiltshire, served as captains in the wars of William III.; and the two latter fell honourably on the field of battle. I recall these facts with pride and satisfaction on the present occasion. The distinguished company I have now the honour of addressing, are all deeply interested in the prosperity of the Drama. Those amongst us who are not actors, are equally well versed with ourselves in the history of the stage, and as fully impressed as we are with the difficulties that have lately impeded its progress, and somewhat obscured its brilliancy; but a star of light has arisen on the darkened horizon of our prospects, and I hope I am not too sanguine when I hail it as the harbinger of a steady and improving sunshine. I allude to the late series of performances at Windsor Castle, by command of Her Majesty and His Royal Highness Prince Albert. (Loud cheers.) We all owe a deep debt of gratitude for the honour thus conferred upon us, and for the advantages we have thereby gained. By selecting the drama for their hours of private relaxation, by introducing it into the chosen circle of their domestic privacy, by permitting the royal children, in their earliest budding youth, to become familiar with the magic verse of Shakespeare, her Majesty and her royal consort have stamped an importance and impressed a sterling value on the stage, that will be long felt and most thankfully appreciated. Covered by the protecting shield of royal favour, assisted by the powerful influence and commanding prestige of royal taste, and heralded, as I may say, by a patent of precedency, our art and its professors resume their position with increasing hopes and redoubled energy."

On the 30th of March, 1849, the widow of Edmund Kean died at Keydell, near Horndean, in Hampshire,

the country residence of her son, on a small estate he
had purchased in 1844, and where she found a happy
retreat during the closing years of her chequered and
eventful existence.   The history of the elder Mrs. Kean
presents us with a moral lesson of the deepest interest,
a subject for salutary reflection, and a special instance of
the varied dispensations of Providence.   During the
early years of her married life, she struggled with many
privations, and drained the cup of poverty to its bitterest
dregs.   Then came the episode of London success, with
all its unlooked-for luxury and ruinous profusion.   After
that followed the unprovoked desertion of her husband,
the combined evils of broken health and vanished hopes,
with disease, neglect, and destitution, more pungently
felt from an interval of prosperity; until finally raised
again by the filial piety and untiring exertions of her
son, she passed the evening of her days surrounded by
all the comforts of affluence, and all the soothing cares
of the fondest affection.   Her remains lie in the church-
yard of Catherington, a secluded hamlet, not far from
Keydell, where she ended her days.   The following
inscription may be read upon her tomb :—

" NATIVE OF WATERFORD.

IN MEMORY OF MARY,

RELICT OF THE LATE EDMUND KEAN,

WHO DEPARTED THIS LIFE

MARCH 30, 1849,

IN OR ABOUT THE SEVENTIETH YEAR OF HER AGE.

" Flights of angels sing thee to thy rest."

THIS TOMB WAS ERECTED BY HER AFFECTIONATE SON,

CHARLES JOHN KEAN."

On the 21st of May, 1849, Charles Kean presided at
the fourth anniversary dinner of the General Theatrical
Fund (to which we have previously alluded).   It was the
first time he had ever been called on to discharge the
duties of chairman at a public dinner.   The situation

was difficult as well as novel, but he acquitted himself with much ability, and spoke with pathos and effect. The attendance and contributions considerably exceeded those on any of the preceding occasions. He had from the beginning been an annual contributor to this excellent institution, which well deserves the increasing support it appears to receive.

The honour of instituting theatrical funds belongs to Thomas Hull, for several years stage manager at Covent Garden, until declining strength compelled him to resign the duties of that troublesome and thankless office to Mr. Lewis. He was highly respectable both as an author and actor; in the former character more particularly, and ranks with the patriarchs of the stage, having played up to 1808, being then in his seventy-eighth year. But he has a higher claim on the consideration of all who feel an interest in the dramatic art, as being the founder of the Covent Garden Fund for the support of decayed actors, the oldest establishment of the kind in the kingdom, which has given comfort to many who during their best years contributed to the solace and amusement of others, and has cheered the desolateness of old age with the certainty of an adequate subsistence. Too much honour cannot be paid to those who have been the means of carrying into effect such permanent benevolence. The case of Mrs. Hamilton, in 1762, who had filled a position of importance at Covent Garden, but then reduced to such distress as to depend entirely on the contributions of her professional fraternity, alarmed the whole body of actors. Hull was the first who conceived and brought to bear a rational project for a substantial remedy against this evil to which all were exposed. To promote the common end, he addressed the performers of Covent Garden in a printed circular, in which, after showing the necessity of some mode of provision, he stated several reasonable propositions as the foundation of his plan. Sixpence in the pound was named as a weekly subscription out of the respective salaries. His address produced an immediate effect; a collection was set forward at once, under the joint efforts of himself and Mattocks, who became also a strenuous promoter of the scheme. They were most liberally assisted by the patronage of Beard and Rich, the then proprietors of Covent Garden. Gibson, an actor of that theatre, was, at his death, a large contributor, dividing his accumulated savings of 8000*l.* between the fund and the poor of Liverpool, where he was buried, and had for many years managed a summer theatre. Cumberland and Mrs. Donaldson were likewise liberal benefactors. During the first six years, or thereabouts, the fund received considerable augmentation by the profits of annual benefits; but under the elder Colman's management, these benefits were stopped, and never afterwards regularly resumed. To them succeeded dinners, at which the chair was generally filled by a member of the royal family, or a nobleman of the highest rank. At these charitable festivities, the collections frequently exceeded 1,000*l.* The fund grew rapidly, and in 1776, received the sanction of an Act of Parliament, the subscribers being thereby declared a body corporate.

The Covent Garden Fund was first proposed while Garrick was travelling on the Continent, with the double object of recruiting his health, and of stimulating by absence, his somewhat ebbing attraction. The " Box Book fever," as it is technically called, was supposed to be his principal complaint. It is a well-known fact, attested by the books, that, before his departure, he played his most popular parts to receipts falling under

20*l.* On one occasion, although supported by Mr. Cibber, to less than 5*l.* This may appear incredible, but it is nevertheless true. Those " palmy days " of the drama were not all to be marked by a white stone.

On Garrick's return home, he felt exceedingly angry and mortified that a movement of such importance as the establishment of a fund should have been carried on without the least communication with him, who, as the head of his profession, and as manager and joint patentee of Drury Lane, might reasonably have expected to have been consulted. But out of evil came good, and two charitable institutions were created instead of one. Garrick, naturally benevolent, was easily pacified by the excuses which were made to appease him, and with his partner Lacy, in 1766, very heartily concurred to set on foot a similar fund at Drury Lane. They were unanimously seconded by their company, with the exception of Mr. and Mrs. Yates,* who were not ashamed to assign the selfish, short-sighted reason for non-cooperation, that they should never want its assistance ! The Drury Lane managers contributed a large sum at the first onset, and gave an annual benefit for the new fund while the patent remained in their hands. On these occasions, Garrick rendered essential service by acting himself. In January, 1776, he paid the expenses of an Act of Parliament, for the legal estab-

* Mrs. Yates was the immediate predecessor of Mrs. Siddons, and by some ardent admirers supposed to exceed her in certain characters. Yates, her husband, stood high as a comedian ; but he had a defective memory, for which he fell under the lash of Churchill. He lived up to ninety, and may be included in the list of eccentrics who have jested when dying. The day before his decease, he complained to a friend that he had been extremely ill-used by the managers of Drury Lane, who denied him an *order!* " That was unkind indeed to an old servant," rejoined the friend. " Yes," replied the dying comedian, " particularly when my admission could have kept no *living* soul out of the house ; for I only requested an order to be *buried* under the centre of the stage, and they were hard-hearted enough to refuse me."

lishment (as at the rival house), and it has been computed, that by various donations and bequests, as well as by performing annually capital parts, he personally gained to this institution near 4,500*l.* The proceeds of his last appearance, on the 10th of June, 1776, were handed over to it without deduction. But the funds of Drury Lane and Covent Garden are subject to many restrictions, and hemmed in by difficulties, arising from the misfortunes which have fallen on what were once the two great national theatres. No one could be a member or a claimant unless he or she had served a given number of seasons in companies which no longer existed. The stock increases, but those who alone can demand its relief are rapidly verging to extinction. These and other considerations have led to the establishment of a "General Theatrical Fund," open to every member of the profession throughout the empire, who chooses to become a subscriber, and fulfils the regulations of this noble institution, which sprang into existence in 1839. Her most gracious Majesty is the Patroness, and annually contributes 100*l.*

The theatrical funds reflect great and lasting credit on the actors with whom they originated. Every true lover of the drama must say of such laudable undertakings (and of similar ones in the provincial theatres), may they flourish in perpetuity, and may the shadows of their founders increase. Formerly, the managers of the funds sought for a name of high rank and aristocratic influence to fill the chair at their anniversary dinners. With the latest institution of the three, the gift of oratory has been held in higher estimation. They judged that their cause would be better advanced by a *rex convivii* who could plead while he presided, and could touch the feelings while he aimed at the pockets of the company. With this object they have sought for such presidents as Charles Dickens, Sir E.

Lytton Bulwer, Macready, Charles Kean, Webster, Buckstone, and Phelps.

On the fourth annual meeting, Charles Kean detailed the purposes and condition of the fund, at full length, as we find in the following published report of the proceedings on that day :—

" GENTLEMEN,—In the order of toasts as I am instructed to propose them, I now arrive at that which brings immediately before us the object of the present meeting. The cause entrusted to my feeble advocacy is one so interesting in itself, so all-important to the numerous parties whose welfare it embraces, appealing so exclusively to the kindliest feelings of our nature, and at the same time so dependent on the power or weakness of its intercessor, that I shrink embarrassed, under the consciousness of my own inability. (Cheers.) I feel myself unequal to the task of carrying up this noble argument to its full vindication, and regret that it has not devolved on one (and such could easily have been found) more experienced in the duties of a chairman,—on one less accustomed to repeat exclusively the thoughts of others,—on one more gifted with the grace of speech, and endowed with that captivating eloquence which enchains the reason, wins the heart, and controls the sympathies. (Loud cheers.) I stand before you as the advocate of Christian charity, of simple, pure benevolence ; as counsel for the old, the indigent, and helpless members of our profession. Your own generous feelings will supply my deficiencies, and plead for my clients more gracefully and effectually than any effort of mine, even though I were inspired for the occasion, as I would I were, with a power of utterance—

> " Great and commanding as the breath of kings,
> Sweet as the poet's numbers, and prevailing
> As soft persuasion."

(Cheers.)

" At the three annual festivals which have preceded this, the origin, nature, and object of this institution have been amply detailed. Its peculiar and most valuable feature of universal association— (cheers)—unrestricted by age or special service in any particular establishment, has been already explained by the gifted gentlemen who presided on those occasions. (Loud cheers.) In the absence of Mr. Buckstone (the honorary treasurer), who is unavoidably detained at the Haymarket Theatre, the present condition and prospects of the fund will be laid before you by your zealous secretary, Mr. Cullenford. (Cheers.) I will not intrude on his province further than by remarking, which I do with earnest satisfaction, that his statement will show you the progress is steady, and the prospect cheering. But there are still two or three leading points, not connected with these details, to which I will venture to call your attention for a few passing moments ; and, if I can put forth a single plea in aid of those already pressed upon your notice, or, if I can excite an additional throb of sympathy in a single bosom, the time will not be wholly consumed in vain, and you will pardon the tediousness I inflict on you, for the motive by which it has been occasioned. (Cheers.)

" The advantages of a national drama, its influence on the civilisation, the morals, the manners, the habits, and, I may say, the happiness of men, is so generally felt and admitted, save by those whose minds are clouded by the mists of prejudice—and with such we deal not —(cheers)—that I may be allowed to look upon and name it as a proved fact and admitted principle. Looking, therefore, to the means of upholding and invigorating this valuable institution, I hail the establishment of a General Theatrical Fund, open alike to the members of every theatre, and the professors of every branch of this most complicated art, as a valuable auxiliary, a steady prop, a solid buttress of support; giving to and deriving from the parent edifice an increase of strength and power, elevating both art and artist in the scale of respectability, and affording to the latter a haven of refuge when age and infirmities admonish him that—

> " Time steals on, and higher duties crave
> Some space between the theatre and grave."

" The present position of the two great houses of Covent Garden and Drury Lane—those splendid structures so long and fondly designated as the legitimate temples of Shakespeare and the British Drama, so associated with all that is grand, and classical, and ennobling in the art, so inseparably connected with the brightest names that shed lustre on its annals; the strange uses to which they are perverted;* the long and apparently interminable eclipse by which they are obscured—these circumstances engender feelings of regret in all, and despondency in many. (Cheers.) In the regret I cordially participate, but I am not amongst the despondent. (Loud cheers.) The prospects of the drama may be darkened by a passing cloud, but I cannot feel that they are extinguished, even though the great houses should never again resume their ancient ascendency. (Cheers.) The tide of fashion, ever varying in its capricious course, may run for a season too strongly in favour of the exotic ballet, the gorgeous spectacle, or the imported opera; but Shakespeare still maintains his hold on the hearts of his countrymen, and will stand pre-eminent on his time-honoured pedestal as long as truth and nature hold their sway, and men can feel the power of language and the grace of action. (Enthusiastic cheers.) I hope, and think, that good days are in store for us, and, as the

* The one, at that time, was an Italian Opera House; the other, an arena for equestrian exercises.

number of actors will increase with the increasing prosperity of the stage, so will the necessity and advantage of
a well established and liberally endowed general theatrical fund impress itself forcibly on all convictions.   I
trust we shall make a giant's stride to-day in advance of
our object. (Cheers.) The report of our proceedings,
the augmentation of the invested property, the amount
of our collection here, will give an impulse to opinion
without, draw to us the support of strangers, and the
favour of the general public.   I trust, by steady perseverance, to see this comparatively private effort expand
into a national institution.   (Cheers.)

" In the long struggle of professional life, and more
particularly in the actor's life, distinction and independence are achieved only by the fortunate few, while the
laborious but 'deserving many toil on in the ranks, earning with difficulty a subsistence for the present, and
utterly unable to lay by any provision for the future.
(Cheers.)   Let it not ·be said that the disciples of
Thespis are universally thoughtless and improvident.
There are many who have never had the opportunity of
laying in store. Amongst the intellectual avocations, ours
has attached to it some melancholy peculiarities.   Brilliant and captivating as the actor's triumphs may appear, they are as perishing as the applause by which
they are accompanied.   The poet, the painter, and the
sculptor leave behind them lasting memorials of their
creative genius, in the living page, the glowing canvas,
and the enduring marble. The actor's brightest achievement dies with himself, or survives but in the fading
records of imperfect tradition.   (Loud cheers.)   By
ceaseless study and long experience only can he hope to
master the difficulties of his art; and before his mental
faculties have attained their full meridian, his physical
powers are on the decline, and warn him that he can no

longer execute his own conceptions. He must leave the field to younger candidates, and retire into solitude and oblivion; too often with but little to console him in the remembrance of the past, no comfort in the privations of the present, and scarcely a ray of hope from the darkness of the future. (Cheers.) A great moralist, Dr. Johnson, tells us, and truly, that " Youth is the season of enjoyment; the utmost that age can look for is ease." Aye, gentlemen—but let us contemplate age without ease —age with its natural accompaniments of disease and pain, and decaying faculties; age without the affectionate hand to smoothe the pillow or the consoling voice to assuage the anguish; age, bowed down by penury and indigence, with cultivated mind, polished manners, and habits of refinement, linked to squalid beggary, racked by the agonizing doubt that the scanty pittance of to-day may cease to be forthcoming to-morrow—(hear, hear) —aye, that even the dismantled garret may not yet be exchanged for the still more loathsome poor-house. (Cheers.) This, though a harrowing picture, is no creation of the fancy, but a stern reality, too often exemplified in the fate of the superannuated actor, whose only refuge from such complicated misery is a nameless grave.

" Let us endeavour to reverse the gloomy picture. Be it our task to step in between our aged brethren and their prostrate helplessness; to restore hope to the despairing heart; to substitute contentment for repining, and competence for destitution. (Cheers.) To effect this, we must press forward the growth of this fund with active zeal and untiring energy. Let us set an example of liberality in our own contributions to foster and enkindle liberality in others. (Cheers.) In such a cause the smallest offering has its full weight and value. Individual efforts, though weak in themselves, produce collective strength, and as the union of labour speedily raises a stately edifice, so the combination of many small sums soon amasses a mighty capital. This institution may yet be considered in its infancy, and already there are five annuitants dependent on its resources and secured from want. Like the disbanded soldier on his pension, they rest from toil in humble but honourable retirement. (Loud cheers.) There are many more hands extended to us in supplication, many other voices sounding plaintively in our ears. They have powerful claims and we are bound to entertain them. Whatever may be the faults and professional jealousies of actors, (and from what profession or what pursuit in life are jealousies excluded?)—(hear, hear)—they are ever found ready to assist their poorer brethren. (Cheers.) Those who are now dependent, while they had means themselves, and the appeal was made, gave cheerfully. In their own hour of need let us remember this, and cheerfully requite them. (Cheers.) We cannot, it is true, bring back the manly vigour or restore the faded loveliness; we cannot check the unsparing scythe of time, call up again the form that delighted the eye, the voice that charmed the ear, or the thrilling energy that commanded the applause—(cheers);—but we *can* make glad the spirits that are now depressed in sorrow; we can repay them something for the many hours of recreation that soften the corroding cares of life; we can give peace and calm repose where there is doubt, and gloom, and poverty; we can cause the flush of joy once again to mantle on the pale cheek from which it appeared to be for ever banished. Above all, let us remember that in thus establishing an asylum for the worn out members of the stage, we advance the importance of the stage itself—(cheers);—and while we advocate the purest doctrine of Christian charity, we give new strength and value to the noble science we study to illustrate, and which the poet of Hope thus beautifully eulogises in reference to one of its most stately ornaments :

> ' His* was the spell o'er hearts
>   Which only Acting lends ;
> The youngest of the sister arts,
>   Where all their beauty blends.
>
> For ill can Poetry express
>   Full many a tone of thought sublime ;
> And Painting, mute and motionless,
>   Steals but a glance from time.
>
> But by the mighty Actor brought,
>   Illusion's perfect triumphs come ;
> Verse ceases to be airy thought,
>   And Sculpture to be dumb !' "

During the seasons of 1848-9, and 1849-50, Charles Kean departed from the plan he had hitherto adopted in his London engagements of making occasional visits at stated intervals only, and accepted a permanent situation with Mr. Webster at the Haymarket Theatre. In this determination he was principally influenced by family considerations; the declining health of his mother, which made him unwilling to leave her for any lengthened period, and a desire to superintend the early education of his daughter and only child, then in her sixth and seventh years. At the commencement of 1849, "Othello" was brought forward, when Charles Kean personated the *Moor* and *Iago,* alternately with James Wallack; Creswick being *Cassio,* Wigan, *Roderigo,* Mrs. C. Kean, *Emilia,* and Miss Laura Addison, *Desdemona.* On the 20th of June, during the same season, Mr. Westland Marston's " Strathmore " was performed: a play abounding in poetic beauty and worked up at the close with intense interest and effect; in our humble opinion, by far the best acting drama which the talented writer has yet produced. The London attraction of " Strathmore," was somewhat weakened by the lateness of the season and the extreme heat of the weather. In

^x John Kemble.

Dublin and Cork it met with deserved success. Mr. and Mrs. C. Kean were again, in this instance, fortunate in original parts of great power and passion, in which they carried out to full reality the author's conception, and added materially to their own established fame. In March, 1850, they concluded their engagements at the Haymarket. On the occasion of their last benefit, the Queen a second time honoured them with her presence and special patronage. The play selected was "Much Ado about Nothing;" they appeared as *Benedick* and *Beatrice*, characters in which they had won much reputation throughout the season.

On the 12th of July, 1850, the veteran mother of the stage, Mrs. Glover, took her farewell benefit at Drury Lane, under the patronage of her Majesty. The bill consisted of the "Rivals," with the farces of "Delicate Ground" and "Friend Wraggles," supported in all the principal parts by volunteer members of the leading theatres. William Farren and Madame Vestris were prominent in the list. The time-worn actress had been confined to her bed for a fortnight previous to the appointed time, and considerable apprehensions existed that she would be unable to present herself on this the closing, as also the most interesting scene in her long professional life. But strong determination can sometimes obtain a momentary victory over physical weakness, and so it proved on the present memorable occasion. She repaired to the theatre, went through the part of *Mrs. Malaprop*, with debility visibly increasing at every moment, but was unable to utter the few words of farewell which had been announced to the public. When the curtain rose again, after the conclusion of the comedy, Mrs. Glover was discovered seated in a chair surrounded by her professional brethren and sisters. She bowed to the crowded audience in silent but expressive acknowledgment, and was carried from the theatre to the bed from whence she rose no more in life.   On Tuesday, the 16th of July, her death was announced, and within one short week from her last appearance in public, a grave in the churchyard of St. George's, Bloomsbury, covered her remains.   It was a sudden close to a long career.

In early life, Mrs. Glover was eminent for personal beauty, both in face and figure; but as the latter expanded into rotundity with advancing time, she relinquished the juvenile heroines before her personal attributes unfitted her to represent them.   She had not the idle vanity of wishing to retain *Juliet* for forty years, but subsided in due course into the *Nurse,* with the *Mrs. Heidelbergs, Candours,* and *Malaprops.*   Histrionic ladies in general fall into a great mistake, from a natural disinclination to adopt the old women, until they are actually old.   There is no line on the stage that requires more vigour than the simulation of the passions and humours of age.

Mrs. Glover, when she died, was in her seventy second year, having been born at Newry, in Ireland, on the 8th of January, 1779.   She had been fifty-three years a London actress.   Her first appearance at Covent Garden took place on the 12th of October, 1797.   She was then Miss Julia Betterton, and scarcely in the first bloom of womanhood.   Her selected trial part was *Elwina,* in Hannah More's long-interred tragedy of " Percy;" of which Hazlitt says, on its second exhumation twenty-eight years later, " we never can forgive Hannah More for making us feel that Miss O'Neill could be tedious."

The authoress of this same " Percy" composed two other tragedies, "Fatal Falsehood," and the " Inflexible Captive."   In her youth she was an enthusiastic admirer of Garrick, and a constant visitor at his house.   As she progressed in life she became serious and thoughtful, and her early opinions changed.   She convinced herself that the stage was an irreligious business in its very essence, and wrote an essay to that effect, which she prefixed to a republication of her tragedies. She was sincere, no doubt, according to her convictions; but to have been consistent, and to have obtained weight for her arguments, she should have put forth the essay alone, and withdrawn the tragedies. A little of the vanity of authorship prevailed, and she was thus driven to maintain that a play might be a lawful recreation in the closet, but a very criminal indulgence when acted; a refinement of casuistry scarcely intelligible, and which amounts to saying that things are not to be applied to the purposes for which they are intended. If anything, no matter what, is good in itself, that which sets forth its qualities in the strongest light is *best*. If it be bad, away with it altogether, as equally unfit to *see* or *read*. All professed writers against the stage endeavour to set up general rules, founded, however, on exceptive cases. But if we test these rules by general application,—and there is no other way of proving their value fairly,— we shall find that, from the beginning to the end, from Stephen Gosson, Prynne, and Collier, down to Hannah More, Styles, Best of Sheffield, and Close of Carlisle, inclusive, they are based on fallacy.

A Roman satirist says, " Totus mundus exerceat histrionem." * Everybody follows the trade of acting; or, as Shakespeare more beautifully amplifies the thought,—

" All the world 's a stage.
And all the men and women, merely players."

This sentence, forming, perhaps, the truest and most comprehensive apology for the theatre, suggests the following paraphrase :—

" Oh, Inconsistency, all mankind are thy disciples !"

---

* Tit. Petron. Arb. Satyræ, p. 521.—Ed. 1669. These words were affixed as a motto to the Globe Theatre in Shakespeare's time.

When Miss Betterton adopted the stage as her profession, she found in the Covent Garden company, acting with her from night to night, as models to study from, Mrs. Crawford, Mrs. Abington, Mrs. Litchfield, Mrs. Davenport, Mrs. Gibbs, Mrs. Mattocks, and Mrs. Martyr. Where, in the present day, could a young beginner look for such a galaxy of talent, on which to found an incipient style? In a school like that, if there was ability, excellence was sure to be achieved. When the rising actress had scarcely entered on her twentieth year, the control of a tyrannical father compelled her to a distasteful marriage, and she became Mrs. Glover, under which name, for half a century, she won and maintained her high position in the estimation of the public. For many years she had to struggle with domestic difficulties, arising from the extravagance and persecution of a neglectful husband, the maintenance of a numerous family, and the support of a parent who had not discharged his duties as faithfully as she performed hers by supporting him in aged destitution.

Assuredly, Mrs. Glover has left no duplicate behind her; no, not even the shadow of a double, amongst her still-living contemporaries. That any of her most renowned predecessors, including Miss Pope and Mrs. Mattocks, excelled her, we may reasonably doubt. Her acting, in her peculiar line, was perfection. The most prominent features were, a nice discrimination of character, a rich vein of comic humour, more in the domestic than in the refined or romantic cast, joined to a constitutional buoyancy and energy which suffered no diminution under the inroads of time.

END OF VOL. I.

R. CLAY, PRINTER, BREAD STREET HILL.